MARIE-MADELEINE
WWII WOMEN SPIES

KIT SERGEANT

ALSO BY KIT SERGEANT

Historical Fiction: The Women Spies Series

355: The Women of Washington's Spy Ring

Underground: Traitors and Spies in the Civil War

L'Agent Double: Spies and Martyrs in the Great War

The Women Spies in WWII Series

The Spark of Resistance

The Flames of Resistance

The Embers of Resistance

The WWII Women Spies Series

Marie-Madeleine

Nancy Wake (Coming soon!)

Virginia Hall (Coming soon!)

Be sure to join my mailing list at www.kitsergeant.com to be the first to know when my newest Women Spies book is available!

***

Contemporary Women's Fiction:

Thrown for a Curve

What It Is

Copyright © 2023 by Kit Sergeant

All rights reserved.

No part of this book may be reproduced in any form or by any electronic or mechanical means, including information storage and retrieval systems, without written permission from the author, except for the use of brief quotations in a book review.

Although this book is based on real events and features historical figures, it is a work of fiction.

This book is dedicated to all of the women who lived during the Second World War and whose talents and sacrifices are known or unknown, but especially to the real-life Marie-Madeleine Fourcade

And to my Aunt Jody, one of the strongest women I know

GLOSSARY OF TERMS

Abwehr: German Military Intelligence

Ausweis: German for an identification document

Boches: a derogatory term for Germans

Doodlebug: German V-1 flying bomb named for the sound it made when in air

Feldwebel: a German military rank, approximately equivalent to a sergeant

Gestapo: Nazi Secret Police

Gibbet: an Alliance term for the combined cooperation of the Gestapo and Abwehr

Gonio: slang term for German detection vans

Luftwaffe: the aerial branch of the German armed forces

Lysander: a British bomber plane, typically used for reconnaissance and agent pick-ups

MI6: British Secret Intelligence Service

QS-5: Radio operator code for being received loud and clear

Sked: slang for the schedule kept by wireless operators when contacting Britain

Wehrmacht: the German armed forces

CHARACTER LIST

Below is a record of the real-life people featured in the novel, in order of appearance. They are listed by their code name (or name used in the novel), their legal name and age at the start of the novel (June 1940), and, when possible, their pre-war occupation.

Part I: The Alliance

Navarre (46)
AKA: Georges Loustaunau-Lacau
French army officer and Marie-Madeleine's former boss at *L'Ordre National*

Édouard Meric (38)
Marie-Madeleine's estranged husband

Noble (early 20s)
AKA: Maurice Coustenoble
Formerly of the Air Force reserves

Henri Schaerrer (23)

CHARACTER LIST

Former naval engineer

Gabriel Rivière (38)
Ran a fruit and vegetable shop in Marseille as a cover for his Alliance activities

Léon Faye (41)
AKA: Eagle
Former Air Force pilot

Jean Boutron (35)
A naval officer who was pulled from the water at Mers-el-Kébir
Alliance role: head of operations in Bordeaux and courier who went to and from Spain

Gavarni: first name and age unknown
Former air force officer
Alliance courier based in Pau

Jacques Bridou (28)
Marie-Madeleine's brother
Olympic bobsled team member and journalist during the Spanish Civil War

Marie-Claude Paupière
Clairvoyant in Paris who lived in Marie-Madeleine's brother's apartment

Lucien Vallet (25)
Former army officer
Alliance role: wireless operator

Antoine Hugon (50)
A garage owner from Brittany who received the Iron Cross during WWI

Bishop
AKA Marc Mesnard
Alliance role: treasurer

Part II: Noah's Ark

Ernest Siegrist (44)
AKA Elephant
Former member of Interallié
Alliance role: security chief and head of the forgery department

Georges-Picot (46)
Marie-Madeleine's brother-in-law, married to her sister, Yvonne

Colonel Kauffman (45)
AKA Cricket
One of Léon Faye's Air Force colleagues
Alliance role: originally head of the Dordogne region

Jack Tar (22)
AKA Lucien Poulard
One of Léon Faye's Air Force colleagues who became his adjutant

Monique Bontinck (18)
AKA: Ermine
Fiancée of Alliance member, Edmond Poulain (25)

Beaver
AKA Émile Hédin
Former policeman who owns a bar in Marseille that doubles as an Alliance safehouse

Mandrill (21)
AKA: Philippe Koenigswerther
Member of the Free French who was parachuted into the wrong area and then joined Alliance

CHARACTER LIST

Saluki (27)
AKA Maurice MacMahon, the Duke of Magenta
Associate of Léon Faye before joining Alliance

Mahout (23)
AKA Pierre Dallas
Pilot recruited by Jack Tar
Worked with the aviation team for Lysander landings

Magpie (25)
AKA: Ferdinand Rodriguez-Redington
Alliance role: wireless operator

Part III: The Worst Year

Petrel (25)
AKA Georges Lamarque
Mathematician, recruited by Léon Faye into Alliance

Swift (47)
AKA Paul Bernard
Former army officer who received the Croix de Guerre during WWI,
he was a colleague of Navarre

Bumpkin (19)
Jean-Philippe Sneyers
Student, worked with Colonel Kauffman's section

Lanky (27)
Jean-Paul Lien
Associate of Bumpkin's

Part IV: London

Sir Claude Dansey (63)
Assistant chief of MI6

Kenneth Cohen (40)
MI6 contact

Jean Sainteny (33)
AKA Dragon and Jean Roger
Insurance consulting

Flying Fish
AKA Raymond Pezet
Alliance agent

Part V: The Beginning of the End

Grand Duke (23)
AKA Helen des Isnards
Alliance role: head of southeast France

Dr. Pierre Noal
AKA Grouse
Head of Alliance agents in the northern zone

PART I
THE ALLIANCE

CHAPTER 1

JUNE 1940

The Nazis were coming. "We must keep going," Marie-Madeleine said to no one, for she was alone in her Citroën. Alone in the car and alone in the world. Even the French government had abandoned her, and all the people of Paris, when they fled the city in the middle of the night.

Sweat dripped down Marie-Madeleine's back. She was baking inside the car—it was June after all—but she refused to roll down the windows, wanting to keep out the dust and stench of desperation.

The never-ending line of cars, wagons, taxis, and push-carts paid no heed to Marie-Madeleine's sense of urgency, and her foot began to ache from pressing the brake so hard. Frustrated, she looked out the window. The evacuees on foot were moving faster than the wheeled-vehicles, even as mothers burdened by bags and babes called to their exhausted, lagging children to hurry up.

A woman beside the car pulled a wailing infant off her breast. The woman's wild eyes met Marie-Madeleine's before she opened her mouth. Though Marie-Madeleine couldn't hear her over the car engine, she could read her lips: *No milk.*

At the blaring of a car horn, Marie-Madeleine gingerly touched her foot to the gas pedal, longing to stomp on it and drive out of the ceaseless swarm.

A cloud of smoke appeared, choking the walkers and surrounding the cars in blackness. *The Boches must have set the fuel dumps on fire,* Marie-Madeleine decided. In a way, it was a relief not to have to stare at the line of vehicles ahead of her, or the poor woman and her baby.

She silently thanked Navarre for suggesting she send her own children away a few weeks ago. Christian, who had just turned ten, and Beatrice, who was eight, were safely tucked away with Marie-Madeleine's mother on Noirmoutier, an island in the Bay of Biscay that was only accessible from the mainland during low tide.

When Marie-Madeleine had asked her mother to take the children away in the case of a German invasion, she could practically read the superciliousness on her face. By all accounts, and Marie-Madeleine's own recollections, Mathilde Bridou had once been a free spirit, but since her husband died when Marie-Madeleine was eight, she had turned quite the opposite. She now approved of very little of Marie-Madeleine's life—from her working for Navarre to owning her own car—but it was her daughter's decision to raise her two children alone that irked her the most. Though she had never been fond of Marie-Madeleine's husband Édouard, she had been downright vehement in her disapproval of the couple's separation.

At the tender age of seventeen, Marie-Madeleine had given up her dream of becoming a concert pianist to follow Édouard to Morocco, and Christian was born barely a year later. After Beatrice arrived, Marie-Madeleine began to chafe at Édouard's expectations for what he considered a "proper" wife and mother. He had hated the social events and dinners that Marie-Madeleine often attended, and he was insanely jealous of the attention the other officers showered on his young wife.

They'd been separated since 1933, when Marie-Madeleine had taken the children with her to Paris. While Marie-Madeleine loved Christian and Beatrice desperately, she was determined to challenge the restrictive conventions of society and live life on her own terms in a way that her mother would never understand. When Navarre had offered Marie-Madeleine a job helping him form a network to collect information on Nazi activities, she jumped at the chance. Even then, he had been certain that war was on the horizon and that France was not in a position to win.

As the smoke cloud thickened into a dense fog, Marie-Madeleine abandoned her thoughts to concentrate on driving. The last thing she wanted to do was hit one of the miserable souls outside her window.

The parade of vehicles began to dwindle after she'd passed Orléans, even despite the fact that the smoke was finally clearing. Judging by the number of deserted cars on the side of the road, many people presumably ran out of gas. Once again, Marie-Madeleine had Navarre to thank for procuring extra petrol cans, which rolled around in the trunk of the car every time she came to a sudden stop.

It was Navarre's house in Oloron-Sainte-Marie to which she was headed. The last time she had seen him, he had narrowly escaped execution for accusing the French military of treason through gross incompetence. His case was brought before the Parisian magistrate on the same day Hitler began his western offensive. The magistrate, of course, had no choice but to acknowledge that Navarre had been right and he was released with a stern warning and a new assignment.

"They're sending me to the Maginot Line," he'd told her when she met him at the Palais de Justice. "I'm going to see what I can do in the ranks, but at this point, I think it's hopeless. We should prepare for the possibility that the Germans will seize Paris."

At the time, the notion had seemed so absurd that Marie-Madeleine found it hard to believe. "Navarre—"

He thrust a crumpled piece of paper into her hand. "This is the address of my place in the Pyrenees, where I've sent my wife and children. If the French troops are demobilized as I predict, that's where I'll be headed. Get your family to safety and then, once those Boches come marching through, meet me in Oloron-Sainte-Marie."

It had not been Marie-Madeleine's intention to desert her children, or her mother for that matter, but she had been left running the newspaper practically single-handedly after Hitler invaded Poland and Navarre was mobilized. Although France and Britain had declared war in September 1939, there were no real battles, and the paper's title, *L'Ordre National,* had become laughable in the circumstances of the 'phony war.'

Still, Marie-Madeleine was determined to keep publishing—focusing now on the shortages of essentials, like coal, cigarettes, and coffee—even after the news came that German forces had breached the Maginot Line and entered France. Despite her uncertainty about how to hold on once the French government made it clear that Paris would not be defended, she remained convinced that the paper—and by extension, herself—stood for something meaningful amid all the chaos and destruction.

At the start of June, the Luftwaffe carried out its first aerial attack on Paris, aiming for key locations that were considered vital assets for the French war effort, such as the Citroën automobile factory. When Marie-Madeleine had purchased her own Citroën a few years earlier, she had been excited by the freedom it had provided her, the ability to come and go as she pleased. The irony was not lost on her now—it was the bombing, combined with Navarre's summons, that ultimately persuaded her to flee the city in her beloved car.

Even with the now-open road, she knew it would take days to travel the several hundred kilometers that still lay ahead. Clearing her head of reverie, she pressed the accelerator pedal, giving the car as much gas as she dared.

She squinted her eyes against the sun as she heard a faint buzzing sound. Soon a few planes came into view. As one of them dipped low, Marie-Madeleine could see the swastika painted on the side. *Nazis.*

They were moving in the opposite direction as she—toward Paris. As she watched, one of the planes, its engines screaming as it dove close to the ground, released a black, round object. Her hands tightened around the steering wheel as she realized the object was a bomb.

The piercing shriek of the plane flying over the car was so intense that it made her ears throb with pain. She bore down on the accelerator, but the car was already going at top speed. *This is it. This is how I die. A bomb from the sky, dropped by cowards.*

After what seemed like an eternity, she heard a muffled boom, the car rattling with the impact. The bomb must have landed somewhere behind her.

Once the planes were a safe distance away, her foot reflexively stomped on the brake. She exited the car to watch in horror as the planes discharged more black ovals of doom, turning the distant landscape into a fiery inferno.

She clenched her fists, feeling a sudden swell of anger. The hordes of people clogging the roads leading away from Paris would be easy targets. How dare those Boches come into her country like that and slaughter her people? She heard the faint buzzing once again, like a swarm of mosquitoes, and realized that she was no safer than the crowds on the roads.

Glancing about, she figured she was somewhere in the Loire Valley. A summer spent with Aurore Sand, the grand-daughter of the great female novelist George Sand, suddenly sprang to Marie-Madeleine's mind. Aurore lived around here, in the rural town of Berry.

She was able to get directions from a frightened young woman at a petrol station, but when Marie-Madeleine arrived at Aurore's house, she found it was filled to the brim with friends and family who were also fleeing Paris.

"Here," Aurore said, dangling keys in Marie-Madeleine's face. "Make yourself at home at the Château de Nohant, Grandmother's house. God bless her soul—I could only imagine how outraged she'd be at the current situation if she were still alive."

At any other time, Marie-Madeleine would have been ecstatic to be staying at the famed novelist's estate, but now she was exhausted. She did manage to locate a bedroom which, based on the piano occupying half the space, she assumed had once belonged to one of Sand's many lovers, Frédéric Chopin.

Marie-Madeleine collapsed onto the bed and immediately fell into a deep, dreamless sleep.

. . .

When she awoke a few hours later, the quietness was disconcerting and she couldn't resist sitting at the piano. She laid out her hands and began to play, letting her fingers pick the tune, which marched along with her still-pounding heart. After a moment, she recognized that she was playing Chopin's own *Étude Revolutionnaire*, which she knew he had written after an unsuccessful uprising by his Polish countrymen against their Russian oppressors.

As she landed on the last chord, the thought that she couldn't let France fall rang through Marie-Madeleine's head, followed by a feeling of overwhelming helplessness. What could she, a lone woman, do against the most formidable army the world had ever seen?

The prospect of meeting up with Navarre was starting to feel implausible. Perhaps she should switch directions and find a way to get to Noirmoutier to see her children.

What would she do then? Live out the duration of the war in hiding, at the whim of her mother's demands? That would mean turning her back on Navarre.

Surely Navarre, who had made himself a name by rebelling against the crooked political powers driving his country towards disaster, would have a plan. Besides, she had been blindly following Navarre's orders for years to help transform France for the better. Now was not the time to start questioning him.

She decided to get back on the road, figuring the planes would have trouble spotting good targets in the dark.

She drove for what seemed like forever. At one point, her stomach flipped when she glimpsed something out of the corner of her eye, but it was only a stray piece of blonde hair that had freed itself from her hastily-done chignon.

When the sun reached its highest point, she pulled her car off the road and parked it beside a tree. She locked the door behind her, deciding it was too hot to try to sleep in the car, and headed for a copse of trees. She fell asleep in the cool shade and woke up an hour later to continue her journey.

She stopped again in some small village, which consisted of one café-bar and one hotel. She estimated she was only a day—perhaps even just a few hours—ahead of the throng of refugees that was sure to descend upon the village square as if they were insects, eating all the bar's food and overcrowding the hotel.

She told the proprietor of the bar as much after she'd ordered a sandwich and coffee.

"Why would they still be fleeing Paris?" the bar owner asked, giving her the once-over with a customary expression of appreciation, which she, as usual, disregarded. "Philippe Pétain was just declared prime minister and has signaled his intention for an armistice."

Marie-Madeleine, who had been stirring her coffee, dropped her spoon. "What do you mean, armistice?"

The man sitting next to her, who had obviously had quite a few beers already, lifted his glass unsteadily. "Cheers to Marshal Pétain."

"Why?" she asked. "He's a coward who has just betrayed his country."

The man set his glass down, spilling half of its contents on the bar top. "He's a hero. He proudly served France in the first Great War and has now managed to avoid being drawn into a second one."

She stood and threw a couple of francs down on the table. It was clear that the people in this bar, much like Marshal Pétain, had lost their minds. Obviously they had never read *Mein Kampf,* Adolf Hitler's frenetic, raving piece of antisemitic garbage. Was this what France had become—a nation willing to roll over and let Hitler and his men stomp their jackboots through the countryside?

Dusk was falling as Marie-Madeleine left the bar, and she inhaled the cooler, crisp air, feeling invigorated by the stillness outside. Her mind was still reeling from her conversation, but as she walked back to the hotel, her anger dissipated somewhat. Until she heard a fife playing.

She looked up to see *them*—a troop of Boches marching across the bridge toward her. A handful of locals who had been crossing the bridge paused to stare down at the water instead of watching the troop's progress.

For her part, Marie-Madeleine stood frozen to the sidewalk. The troop was like a flock of birds attuned to each other's movements, parading along the curved roads as if they anticipated every little twist and turn.

She steeled herself as they approached, resolving to give them false directions if they asked, but they clearly had no need. They passed her without making any eye contact.

Marie-Madeleine, having never seen anything like that, couldn't help but watch them march away. The bastards! How dare they look so fresh like that, after traveling all that way. *We'll be killed off like rats.*

She went straight to the hotel and cancelled her reservation, deciding instead to take her chances driving. She had to make it to Navarre's as soon as possible.

CHAPTER 2

JULY 1940

Oloron-Sainte-Marie was a picturesque town nestled at the feet of the Pyrenees. Navarre's *maison de campagne* was located a couple of streets west of the town square, which was populated with beret shops and cafés.

His wife, Linette, answered the door. The two women had met each other a few times, but were no more than casual acquaintances. Linette had always been the quintessential devoted wife and mother, and, though Navarre's wife had never said anything to her directly, Marie-Madeleine had the sense that Linette didn't approve of any woman working with her husband.

"I have no news on Navarre's whereabouts," Linette said after greeting her.

As she stepped inside the hall, Marie-Madeleine noted how well-kept the house was. "Do you know anyone who might have information about him, or the latest on what's happening with the armistice? I've been on the road for several days and have been out of touch."

"I don't know anything about the armistice, but the Spanish consul might." Linette gave her directions to the hotel he was staying at, a stone's throw away from the majestic Sainte-Marie Cathedral.

As Marie-Madeleine entered the warm, earthy-hued hotel lobby, she was welcomed by the aging Spanish diplomat. "I'm looking for Navarre," she said by way of greeting, wondering if she should have referred to her boss as Commandant Loustaunau-Lacau instead. To safeguard his anonymity from the French government—whom he often attacked in the press—Navarre wrote under a pseudonym. He'd chosen it in honor of Henri de Navarre, the late 16th century king of France, who managed to escape multiple assassination attempts before he was murdered. The name stuck, and Marie-Madeleine rarely used his real name.

"Ah, the local hero," the consul replied. "Or rebel, some might say. I don't know where he is. Were you supposed to meet him?"

"Yes." Given how adamant Navarre had been about their rendezvous, Marie-Madeleine decided to reserve a room and summoned the clerk.

Room key in hand, Marie-Madeleine turned to see the consul sitting in a worn leather armchair. She settled into the chair across from him. "Can you tell me more about this so-called armistice that Marshall Pétain agreed to?"

The consul scratched his graying beard. "From what I've heard, according to the terms, German troops are going to occupy Paris and most of the northern regions, including the Atlantic coast and Alsace. Less than half of France will be known as the 'Free Zone'."

"Free? Can any part of France be considered free anymore?" Marie-Madeleine murmured. Her resentment boiled to the surface: there was not one cell in her body that wanted to step aside and let the Boches rule her country. "We must do something," she declared.

"Like what? Warn the British that Hitler is coming for them too?" the consul asked. "You shouldn't worry your pretty little head about this anymore—their fate will be the same as France's."

Accustomed to men attempting to diminish her because of her looks, Marie-Madeleine was about to retort when the consul pulled at his collar and spoke again. "Since Navarre is not here, I take it you do not have a companion for dinner tonight?"

"No," she replied, caught off-guard. "I was just planning on eating a sandwich in my room."

"Nonsense. The restaurant here is known for its hearty soups made from local vegetables, and, of course, its cheeses and pastries. You will join me in the dining room tonight," he finished, leaving no room for refusal.

Back in her room, Marie-Madeleine wrote a quick note to her mother, informing her of her whereabouts and the address of the hotel in case she wanted to try writing back, although who knew if there was any mail being delivered. She ended the note by asking about her mother's health and how the children were doing.

As she dressed for dinner, Marie-Madeleine reflected on what the consul had told her. Regardless of Phillipe Pétain's actions, she still refused to concede France's defeat. Though her wardrobe choices were limited, she managed to show her patriotism by pairing her calf-length red silk dress with a white scarf and sapphire earrings.

The other guest of the consul's, who ironically was named Philippe, seemed to echo Marie-Madeleine's sentiments, with his red-and-blue striped tie and the tricolored flag pinned to the breast of his tweed suit.

"Did you hear General de Gaulle's speech over the BBC?" Phillipe asked during their pastry course. "He proclaimed that the 'Flame of French resistance should not be extinguished,' and requested that Frenchmen gather in great forces to help overcome the enemy."

Marie-Madeleine felt her spirits lift ever so slightly. "Do you think many people were listening?"

The consul grunted. "I doubt it. Most of the radios have been confiscated by the Boches. Not that it matters…" He waved his arms around the nearly empty dining room. "Who would risk their life to join some cowardly general they've never heard of?"

"I've heard of him." Marie-Madeleine set her fork down and wiped her mouth with the crisp linen napkin. "I've even met him." Charles de Gaulle had been a guest at one of her sister's parties a few years prior, when he had gotten into an argument with Navarre over whether France could defend itself from a possible invasion.

In fact, that was also the night she'd first met Navarre.

Another grunt emerged from the consul. "Your so-called general was broadcasting from England. He fled the country, like everyone of any intelligence and means."

"Yes, he is in England," Philippe acknowledged. "But the point was that he gave hope to millions of Frenchmen who had lost theirs. The armistice doesn't have to be the last straw. If America—"

"They will never join the battle," the consul said firmly. "Trust me, I've worked in foreign relations for decades. No one will be coming to our aid. The French are still haunted by the memories of past wars, and they are unwilling to fight again. In fact, most of the people I've talked to believe they can survive just fine under Hitler's jackboot."

"You are wrong. And you should make no mistake about this..." Phillipe pointedly tapped a finger on the wooden table. "This is a world war, and freedom is what we will be fighting for."

"Fighting?" the consul sneered. "I suppose you want to fight side-by-side with the British. Do you know what they did to our ships at Mers-el-Kébir?"

"No," Marie-Madeleine replied softly.

He turned to her, anger etched over the lines on his face. "In the beginning of July, the Royal Navy had attacked the French fleet stationed at Mers-el-Kébir, the French naval base in Algeria, supposedly to prevent the Germans from getting their hands on them. Over a thousand French servicemen were killed, compared to only a handful of British crewmen."

Marie-Madeleine pushed her plate away, contemplating his words. The conflict with Britain, France's steadfast ally in the Great War and now the last defender of the free world, was almost too incredible to comprehend. But perhaps it was less incredible than the thought of France surrendering to the Nazis.

After the waiter had taken away her plate, she broke the silence by stating, "Surely there must be some people in France who are willing to fight for freedom."

"Bah." The consul got up from the table, clearly finished with his meal and the conversation.

After he left, Marie-Madeleine asked Philippe what he had in mind for them to strike back at the Boches.

"I don't know yet," he replied. "But we have to do something."

. . .

A few days later, the consul greeted Marie-Madeleine with the simple words, "Navarre has returned."

She set down the weak tea she'd been drinking and left the chateau to head straight for Navarre's house.

After greeting Marie-Madeleine, Linette led her into the living room, where an old man was lying on the couch. Upon seeing them, he tried to rise.

"Don't," Linette said, but he got heavily to his feet anyway, leaning unsteadily on a cane.

Marie-Madeleine drew in a deep breath when she realized the old man was Navarre. He must have lost nearly forty pounds off his already trim frame, and she could tell by the way he was hunched over that he was in great pain.

"You really should sit down," Marie-Madeleine said, offering Navarre her hand as Linette retreated into the kitchen.

His blue-eyed gaze was as piercing as ever as he obeyed. "You made it."

"Yes. My children are on Noirmoutier, as you suggested. I left Paris after the first bombing, and now I've just been waiting for you." That last part came out sharper than she meant it to.

He leaned back against the couch, gasping audibly. "We're both lucky I managed to escape. It wasn't easy, considering I still have a couple of bullets in my neck."

This time Marie-Madeleine's tone was gentler. "You were at the Maginot line."

"Yes." He shook his head. "And just as I warned Pétain, it didn't keep the Germans from invading. The Luftwaffe flew right over it."

"And now they are here."

"Yes," Navarre repeated before falling silent.

"Well, what are we going to do about it?" She finally asked. "Your old nemesis de Gaulle is calling for troops to rise up against the Nazis."

"Is that so? I heard the coward ran off to England. Is he expecting forty million Frenchmen to follow him and carry out his bidding from across the Channel?"

She shrugged. "I don't know."

"We must resist from within France. As soon as I can walk more than ten steps, I'm going to Vichy."

"Vichy is nothing but a phony capital," she sneered.

"But it is still a capital, and it is where the foreign embassies have taken refuge. If you want information, you have to go straight to the source. Pétain is my former boss and I want to get the real story of why he is now in league with Hitler."

Ever since she'd known him, Navarre had only accepted secrets if he unearthed them himself. "I suppose you are right." She got up from her chair. "Will you be ready in a few days' time?"

"I'm hoping for less than that. We have to get there as soon as possible." Navarre shifted his position with another grunt of pain. "I take it you are planning on coming with me?"

"Of course I am."

"Then let's try for tomorrow."

CHAPTER 3

AUGUST 1940

The atmosphere in the spa town of Vichy was not quite what Marie-Madeleine had predicted. Instead of lamenting over Pétain's capitulation to Hitler, the townspeople, in their fashionable clothes, gave the impression of being in a celebratory mood. This time the long lines consisted of people waiting for tables at the best restaurants or gathered outside the luxurious Hôtel du Parc, trying to get a glimpse of Marshal Pétain, who had requisitioned the hotel for government use.

Which, of course, made Marie-Madeleine despise Vichy even more. It seemed to her that the villagers had nothing else to do besides gossip and bicker with each other in an attempt to gain favors from those at the top. She referred to Pétain and his worshippers as the 'Aristocracy of Defeat' and wanted nothing to do with any of them.

Navarre, however, insisted they play the game and made an appointment to meet with Pétain.

"I don't suppose Pétain has any speck of remorse," Marie-Madeleine stated when Navarre had returned from his meeting.

"No." Navarre looked thoughtful. "It was almost as if he views the collapse of France as nothing worse than a badly cooked meal."

"I figured as much."

"Still, I got him to agree to make me a delegate of the *Légion Française des Combattants*, an organization of military veterans that the government will be funding."

Marie-Madeleine couldn't hide her irritation. "What good will that do us?"

He sat down in the desk chair and rubbed the back of his neck. "Don't you see? We'll be able to do what we did before the Occupation —traverse the countryside gathering intelligence and making contacts."

"I don't think it will be all that easy to get around in my Citroën now, what with the shortage of petrol and the debris from the Luftwaffe bombings blocking the roads."

"We will use trains. I can get us both an *Ausweis* to go to and from the demarcation line. We'll contact all our old sources and recruit fresh ones to set up patrols all throughout France. We'll be like crusaders of freedom." Navarre nodded to himself. "That's what we'll call our organization: Crusade." After a moment, he added, "But, I of course, in my new position, must remain above suspicion if I'm going to do business with these Vichy hypocrites. It will be up to you to organize the underground side."

"You want me to be in charge of an underground network and command seasoned old war-horses like yourself to get back at the Nazis? Other than being employed by you, I have no experience in these sorts of clandestine things."

"But that's exactly why I'm asking you—I need someone I can depend on. And you are making too much light of your experience— you worked for me for years, and quite adeptly, I might add."

"Okay then, perhaps you've neglected to recognize the obvious: the fact that I'm a woman."

"Which is another point in your favor—the Germans are suspicious of anyone they believe is trying to undermine them. But who would ever suspect a woman?"

She stood and went over to the window overlooking the main street. Below her, groups of men in grayish-green uniforms were roaming around, popping in and out of shops to get their hands on the last silk stockings or leather goods that could be found in Vichy. Most of the French people on the streets greeted them cordially. Already rumors had been spreading of German reprisals against citizens who had refused to welcome the invaders with open arms: dissidents who cut Wehrmacht communication lines in Rouen had been executed, and a man was shot in Bordeaux for shaking his fist at a military band.

Woman or not, if she were caught, the punishment for organizing a network to defy the Nazis was sure to be swift and brutal. And what about her children? Surely they needed their mother now more than ever.

When she turned back to Navarre, he was bent over his desk, furiously scribbling on a piece of paper. From that angle, the scar on the back of neck was obvious, its jagged edges peeking out from the collar of his shirt, a battle wound earned whilst trying to keep the Germans out of France. She thought of the other conflicts Navarre had been in, the ones she knew he'd taken on unassisted, mindless of what impact they might have on his distinguished career in government. He had lived his whole life without ever questioning the consequences of his actions, and now he was asking her to do the same.

She cleared her throat. "You don't think someone else might be better suited?"

"No. I've been betrayed too many times already. If it's not you, I will have to do it myself."

She resisted the urge to glance at the scar again. Throughout the years she'd known him, Navarre had always been fearless—sometimes downright reckless—but after his meeting with Pétain, he seemed even more determined than ever. This was the opportunity she'd been waiting for. What other choice did she have than to comply? "Well, then, I accept. I will try not to let you down."

"Thank you, Marie-Madeleine. And I don't think you will ever let me down." He set his pen on the desk and handed her the sheet of paper. "These are my objectives, which will become your orders. Memorize them and then burn this. I told you before the invasion that Hitler's power is neither unlimited nor indestructible." Navarre held up his clenched fist. "And we are going to gnaw it away."

CHAPTER 4

SEPTEMBER 1940

According to the terms of the armistice, the Unoccupied Zone was only allowed an army of one hundred thousand men, and therefore, thousands of Frenchmen had been decommissioned. Navarre had somehow persuaded Pétain not only to fund his league of now-demobilized veterans, but also to pay for their lodging at the Hôtel des Sports. The Marshal was under the impression that Navarre's legion would provide former servicemen with shelter, meals, and medical care to help them acclimatize to life as civilians.

The Hôtel des Sports was not nearly as extravagant as some of the other local lodgings, but it suited their purposes fine. During the day, Navarre and Marie-Madeleine would strike up conversations with some of the men in the lobby. At night, they traded notes, and chose who would be best to recruit for their new venture.

The induction itself took place in a secluded conference room on the second floor. As Navarre said, the hotel was a house of glass, and they needed to keep their selected recruits out of sight.

Their first pick was a rather unassuming young man with slicked-back hair full of pomade and a neatly trimmed mustache, who, Marie-Madeleine decided, looked more like a clerk than a soldier.

He had been sitting in a threadbare armchair but stood when he saw her approach. "Well, what do you say? I didn't come here to twiddle my thumbs."

She was taken aback by his directness. "Who are you, anyway?" Navarre had never told her his name.

"I'm Maurice Coustenoble, although most people call me Noble. Formerly of the Air Force reserves. And now…" he adjusted the collar of his leather jacket. "Unemployed."

"Indeed." She took the lounge chair across from him.

He seemed reluctant to sit again but did so anyway. "When they shot me down in Bordeaux, I set fire to my plane and swore I'd fight any way I could until they got me into another bird."

"I don't know about fighting, but there are other ways to agitate the Germans."

He shrugged off his jacket. "Whenever Navarre says the word, I'm prepared to take up arms."

"Take up arms? We're not ready for that yet. There aren't enough of us—the French people are still paralyzed by fear of the invaders. We have to wait for England or America to intervene. Some people are saying this will be a decade-long war."

Noble's determined look faded into one of anguish. "Ten years? I can't handle being occupied for ten more months."

Marie-Madeleine decided not to dash the young man's hopes any more. "Hold off on attacking the Nazis for now. What we need you to do is start recruiting other people around Vichy who are sympathetic to our cause and who can act as conductors of information. People who travel regularly for work, like truck drivers and railway men. Oh, and see if you can dig up a wireless operator."

"What for?"

"To handle radio communication, of course. We are planning to get in touch with London and provide them with the intelligence we gather."

His eyes sparkled with glee—possessing a radio in Occupied France was a transgression almost akin to brandishing a firearm. "Now you're talking. But how will you get your hands on a transmitting set? The Germans confiscated all the local ones."

She shot him a furtive smile. "Perhaps via Spain, or perhaps by parachute."

"In that case," Noble rose. "I will also look out for drop zones." He wiggled back into his jacket. "Imagine—parachutes coming down like daisies!"

"Monsieur Noble?" Marie-Madeleine raised her eyebrows. "You do know this job is very dangerous, don't you? If you have any doubts that you can handle it, say so now."

He stopped fiddling with his coat and gave her a thoughtful look. She wondered if he resented having to take instructions from a woman and would back out, rendering her first attempt at recruitment a failure.

"I'm ready," was his simple reply.

Little by little, Marie-Madeleine managed to recruit new members for Crusade, drawing from all walks of life and military backgrounds, with one notable exception.

"We need naval men," Navarre told Marie-Madeleine one night.

"I don't think we'll be able to convince any of them to help us. Not after what Churchill did to their subs at Mers-el-Kébir."

As usual, Navarre didn't take no for an answer. "See what you can do."

Marie-Madeleine didn't necessarily blame the French Navy for looking upon the British as murderers. She was therefore surprised a few days later when a young man named Henri Schaerrer informed her that he was a former naval engineer.

"You worked for the *Marine Nationale?*" she repeated, dumbfounded. He didn't look a day older than eighteen, and, in fact, he reminded her a bit of her own son, Christian.

"Yes, madame. I was on a destroyer at Dunkirk, when it, quite frankly, was destroyed by a German torpedo. I nearly drowned, but I was saved by a Brit." Schaerrer gave her a sheepish smile. "So I can't hold everything against them."

"Do you think you can get other naval men to help us?"

The sheepish smile turned into a disarming grin, one that lit up his whole face. "I can try. One of my former officers, Commandant Boutron, would probably be willing to join."

She made a mark on her dog-eared map. "Seems like you'll have to make a trip to Marseille, given that it's the only port in the Free Zone."

He nodded. "How will I contact you?"

"We're hoping to secure transmitters soon, but for now you'll have to recruit couriers who can travel back and forth from here to Marseille."

"If we're picking up intelligence on U-boat movements, that information will only be valuable for a few hours, a day at most."

"I know."

He stood up and, unexpectedly, saluted. "Thank you, madame, for giving me this opportunity. You can trust that, if I'm arrested, I would rather be shot than say a word about your organization."

"You do know what we're asking you is incredibly dangerous."

His face paled, making his freckles stand out even more. Marie-Madeleine suppressed the urge to cry. Somewhere this Schaerrer had a mother who was probably worried about him just the way she worried about her own children. What dent could this eager young man possibly make in the most indomitable war machine in history? Was she just sending him to certain death?

But at the same time, what alternative was there? As if hearing her thoughts, Schaerrer replied, "I'm willing to accept any risk, no matter how great."

"Thank you," Marie-Madeleine told him, deciding that it was worth a few lives, however precious, to save France. "And good luck."

CHAPTER 5

OCTOBER 1940

A few weeks after Schaerrer arrived in Marseille, he sent word that he wanted someone to inspect his operations.

"You go," Navarre told Marie-Madeleine. "I've heard that Pétain is planning on meeting with Hitler face-to-face and I want to see what the results are. Hopefully Pétain doesn't give in any more than he already has."

"Hopefully," she repeated, but privately she had lost all faith in Pétain and the Vichy government.

"And be careful on the train," Navarre warned her. "This is supposed to be the Free Zone, but the Nazis are everywhere."

The fall had turned frigid in Vichy and she looked forward to the warm breezes of the Mediterranean. Not to mention that Marseille was technically her hometown—she'd been born there, although as soon as her mother gave birth, she returned with the new baby to Shanghai, where Marie-Madeleine's father worked as an executive for a French shipping line. Marie-Madeleine, her older sister Yvonne, and younger brother Jacques grew up amidst the lively, vibrant cityscape of Shanghai, but moved to Paris after the death of their father.

As she stared out the train window, Marie-Madeleine found herself agonizing over the future of the fledgling Crusade. Her personal funds were almost exhausted, and Navarre's had run out weeks ago. If they couldn't find more money soon, would she have to tell all the new recruits to quit just when they were getting started?

Somehow she dozed off and was still only half-awake when she walked into the café at the train station. She had paused to readjust her purse strap when she heard someone bark out, "Good God, it's a woman."

Schaerrer, who was sitting with an unfamiliar man, blushed so hard his freckles nearly disappeared.

She took a seat in the empty chair at their table as she addressed the stocky man with the loud voice, "Did Schaerrer not have the chance to tell you that one of his new leaders is female?"

"I'm sorry, madame, I just didn't realize…" He raked his fingers through his rust-colored hair and then stuck his hand out to Marie-Madeleine. "I'm Gabriel Rivière. Sorry about that, outburst." His grin was infectious, and she forgave him instantly, even before he added, "Schaerrer told me about your operation, and I have to say I'm quite excited."

"No one knows more about maritime traffic than Rivière," Schaerrer stated.

"Except maybe the Germans," Rivière retorted.

Marie-Madeleine swiveled her head around, looking for potential eavesdroppers. No one was in earshot, but Rivière took the cue anyway and lowered his voice. "I despise the Boches as much as anybody and am ready to join with you today. In fact, I know many others who will help us. Hardly anyone in Marseille is a fan of the new government, nor of the Occupiers."

"I appreciate your passion. But we're starting off the Marseille sector slowly… we're going to need to find a headquarters—"

"I've already thought of that," Rivière interjected, as though he'd been part of the network forever, and hadn't just officially joined a few minutes ago. "On my way here, I passed a vegetable shop for sale. In the back is a huge storage warehouse." His voice dropped once again. "My wife can run the books. We can actually sell vegetables, and it would be a great cover for our more... underground activities."

Slightly taken aback, Marie-Madeleine agreed that it sounded like an excellent cover. She pulled out her checkbook, knowing that the sum she'd have to front for the purchase of the shop would either wipe out or make a serious dent in the 40,000 francs left in her bank account. "Can you make the arrangements? We are trying to recruit communication specialists, but in the meantime, we will have to keep in touch in person."

"Communication specialists? I know of a radio operator who would be willing to help us. Lucien Vallet's his name."

She sat back in the chair, priding herself on her recruits: first Noble, then Schaerrer, and now Rivière was proving to be a worthy find. Of course, Schaerrer was the one who brought him on board in the first place, but still, Navarre was certain to be impressed with the burly man. "Okay, you work on both of those and we'll meet again in a few days. Hopefully by then we'll be able to secure a transmitting set."

"You got it, chief," Rivière replied.

Schaerrer offered to escort her to her hotel. "I'm sorry, madame," he told her once they'd left the station. "I didn't see the need to warn him about... you know."

"Me being a woman." She patted the young man's shoulder. "Somehow I don't think it would have dampened Rivière's enthusiasm in any way."

* * *

A few days after Marie-Madeleine returned from Marseille, she found herself on yet another train, staring down at a female Nazi auxiliary's dark roots as the woman dug through her pockets. With her gray uniform and shrewd look, she reminded Marie-Madeleine of a rat.

"What is your purpose for crossing the demarcation line?" the rat barked as Marie-Madeleine handed her the *Ausweis* Navarre had obtained.

"I am going to Paris on a business trip, to arrange for the sale of rice to the Spaniards."

While the rat jotted this down in her notebook, Marie-Madeleine glanced at Noble, who stood off to the side, the scowl obvious on his face. Next to him, Navarre pretended to read a German newspaper, watching the rat out of the corner of his eye.

"You will come with me," the rat yapped in a high voice. She led her to an adjacent compartment, which was empty save for yet another uniformed rat, who searched Marie-Madeleine's luggage before commanding her to take off her clothes.

Marie-Madeleine's pulse quickened, but she made no move to undress. "What is this all about?"

The rat digging through the suitcase paused, a pair of Marie-Madeleine's panties hanging off her baton. "Just do what we say!"

Marie-Madeleine peered at the other woman, hoping to discern some trace of compassion, to no avail. Like a true rat, her eyes were steely and emotionless, void of humanity.

Ten minutes later, Marie-Madeleine rejoined Navarre and Noble.

"Not bad," Navarre told her admirably. "You were immediately suspected of being a spy."

"Is that a good thing?" Marie-Madeleine barked, pulling her jacket belt tighter around her waist.

"There must be something fishy somewhere," Noble remarked. "Was Madame's name on their list?" He turned to Navarre. "Are you sure your friend who got us the passes is on the up-and-up?"

"Of course," Navarre replied before burying his nose back into the newspaper.

The incident with the Nazi rats left Marie-Madeleine feeling distinctly uneasy. She pulled his newspaper back down. "We should split up when we get to Paris, especially if Noble is right and I'm on their list. I don't want to take any chances."

"Fine. You go to the *L'Ordre National* office while Noble and I head to our respective safehouses."

. . .

It had been Navarre's idea to travel to Paris in order to extend Crusade's reach into the Occupied Zone. Despite being still officially listed as an escaped POW, he decided to go on the journey with Noble, who had been assigned to scout out places from which to transmit, and Marie-Madeleine, who was charged with recruiting what friends she had left in Paris.

It was a warm, pleasant day for late fall, yet the city was devoid of its usual liveliness and the air was heavy with silence. Even the people sitting at the decidedly less crowded cafés appeared uncharacteristically reserved.

As Marie-Madeleine walked the streets, the unsettling stillness was occasionally disturbed by the honking of a Citroën or soldiers calling out to each other in German. Like a distorted version of the city she used to love, this new Paris seemed both familiar and alien at the same time, which only amplified the unease she'd been experiencing since encountering the Nazi rats on the train.

She hadn't been to the *L'Ordre National* office since the spring, when rumors regarding a potential invasion had abounded and opinions were divided over the French army's ability to repel the Germans. Although Navarre had repeatedly warned all the top military officials that the Nazis were planning to come through the Maginot line, they refused to listen, insisting that if they did decide to invade, they would follow a path similar to World War I's: through central Belgium. Of course, Navarre had been right, and here the Germans were, roaming Paris in their jackboots and grayish-green uniforms.

The building's concierge, Lily, gasped upon seeing Marie-Madeleine enter the lobby. "I never thought you would return. The Boches, as soon as they got to Paris, came here and turned the entire office upside down."

"What were they looking for?" Marie-Madeleine asked, her unease rapidly giving way to anger.

Lily shook her head. "I don't know, but they kept asking about you and Navarre."

Marie-Madeleine looked around the empty lobby. "Like you, the Boches probably doubt I'd ever come back. I'll take the keys."

"Don't worry, madame," Lily said as she handed them over. "I would never say anything to them."

Marie-Madeleine's next stop was her brother's old apartment on the rue Jean-Jacques-Rousseau. He had rented it out to a woman with bright red rouged cheeks who went by the name of Madame Paupière. Despite having only met the woman, an aspiring fortune teller, a few times, Marie-Madeleine had a hunch that she wouldn't mind storing equipment and taking messages for Crusade. Although Marie-Madeleine herself was no psychic, her intuition proved correct when Madame Paupière readily agreed to help.

Though many of Marie-Madeleine's friends and relatives had scattered after the Germans had marched in, a handful had stubbornly chosen to remain. One of them, an engineer in the Renault factory, volunteered to move all of Marie-Madeleine's possessions from her apartment to the *L'Ordre National* office, and another offered up the maid's room in his house on Avenue Foch for transmitting once Crusade was able to secure radios. The Paris sector was starting to come together.

Navarre's efforts, however, proved to be far less fruitful than hers. The city's occupation authorities rejected his proposal to set up a Paris branch of the Lègion and his own relatives didn't seem thrilled to see him.

"The arrogance," he stormed when he met her at their old office. "Can you believe my own flesh and blood is collaborating with the Boches? They're even helping with so-called 'reconstruction work.'"

"It's like making a deal with the Devil," Marie-Madeleine replied.

"Exactly." He shook his head. "I guess it's their way of coping with defeat."

"Clearly we must stay away from your ranks for our Paris recruits, Navarre." She shot him a triumphant smile. "I've managed to make some headway on my own."

"I can tell you're relishing the situation, though I do agree with you. I'll go back to Vichy to see how things are getting along. I advise you not to linger too long in Paris."

* * *

Marie-Madeleine knew Navarre was right, but there were more arrangements to make and people to see. She spent a lonely holiday in the deserted office building, reminiscing with the ghosts of Christmases past, when she had held her children close as they sang carols together and she could witness the delight in their faces as they opened their presents.

Despite the lingering emptiness in her heart, Marie-Madeleine recognized the necessity of her work—the only way to ensure there would ever be another Happy Christmas was to liberate France.

CHAPTER 6

JANUARY 1941

When Marie-Madeleine returned to Vichy, Navarre had bad news: he'd lost his post in the *Légion Française des Combattants*. Though she consoled him the best she could, she was secretly pleased—she'd never liked Navarre's association with Pétain or his cronies.

At the same time, it meant the loss of their lodgings at the Hôtel des Sports. Navarre had taken a much smaller office at another hotel, which, when Marie-Madeleine met him there for the first time, seemed even more cramped by the stack of papers on his desk. "Laval's been arrested," he announced by way of greeting.

Up until then, Pierre Laval had been serving as Pétain's deputy, though many Frenchmen called him an agent of Germany, especially after the recent news that he had relinquished the majority of France's copper mines and gold reserves to the Nazis.

Marie-Madeleine crossed her arms over her chest. "I suppose the Germans are going to demand Laval's release."

"And then strengthen their grip on the Free Zone." Navarre sighed. "We must continue our efforts. But we're going to have to get money from somewhere—and we need transmitters. Your men in Marseille are doing a great job gathering intelligence, but the information they provide is only good for a couple of hours. We have to find a way to get it to the British, and fast."

"Can we send someone to London?"

"Maybe, although I'm not sure who. It's not like they can just get on a plane or cross the Channel by ship. They'll have to go through Morocco and then Gibraltar. It might take months, and besides, it's an exceedingly dangerous trip."

Deep in thought, she was startled when Schaerrer entered the room, accompanied by a man whose confident posture made his athletic frame seem even taller.

"Ah, I'm glad you're both here," Schaerrer said, nodding at the man. "This is Commandant Léon Faye of the Air Force. The only way I could stop him from having a show-down with Pétain was to persuade him to join Crusade. He's like quick-silver and completely fearless."

"Oh?" Marie-Madeleine asked. For some reason she felt disdainful toward this cavalier newcomer. "So you've brought us another man who thinks he can convince Pétain to quit capitulating. As if Navarre wasn't enough."

"I assure you I would have indeed turned Pétain's head, if only they would have let me into his office." Faye's voice was a deep baritone. "But now I have a better idea—a plot for inciting the army in North Africa to revolt."

Marie-Madeleine's sharp breath was overpowered by Navarre's enthusiastic cheer. "Plot you say?" he asked, leaning forward in his chair. "How far along have you gotten?"

She held out her arm, afraid Navarre would fall out of his chair. "Now wait a minute—"

Faye interrupted her. "The Air Force groups in Tunisia have all agreed. The Algiers Air Force is easy—I've got the telegrams ordering hostilities. The Navy is also going well, but the Army needs some convincing."

"I can help," Navarre said.

Marie-Madeleine tapped her foot impatiently. Although Faye and Navarre were off and running with their plans, she worried that Navarre would be getting himself into trouble. In the past few months, she'd met many men who were steadfast in their determination to strike back at the Germans, but the boldness of this Faye's scheme astounded her nonetheless.

She turned to Schaerrer. "I'm sorry," he told her, nodding at the two men, who were now consulting a map of Africa. "I didn't expect this to happen, I just thought he'd make a good addition to Crusade."

"With those two heads together, it seems all hell will break loose now."

"Sorry," Schaerrer repeated before replacing his hat. "But I've got to get going. I'm meeting up with Noble in a few minutes."

After he left, Marie-Madeleine tried once again to sway Navarre. "Don't you think we should limit the network to gathering intelligence at this stage in the game? Like you were saying, what we really need right now are transmitters... and money."

Faye fixed his probing gaze on her. His eyes were the same grayish-green color of his sworn enemy's uniforms, a fact she was sure he would deride. Not that she would ever tell him. "And how do you expect to get that?"

"As Marie-Madeleine suggested, perhaps we send a delegate to London," Navarre answered. "I have contacts there."

"De Gaulle?" Faye asked.

Navarre sneered. "I suppose we should approach him too, but I don't necessarily see us being a part of the so-called 'Free French' unit he is trying to run from across the Channel. We'd have to work in parallel—the decisions will need to be made as soon as possible, which means from the ground here in France."

"I can be your London delegate." Faye folded up the map. "By the time you are all feeling sorry for yourselves, I shall be in a position to save you."

Marie-Madeleine harrumphed. "You and your plots are the danger. My job isn't the least bit risky."

His left eyebrow rose. "No? You're never worried about a Boche searching your person on the street? And you are able to travel to and from the Occupied Zone with no problems?"

She thought of the gray rats who always seemed to be waiting for her when she crossed the demarcation line but didn't reply.

Faye clearly took her silence as an admission to the contrary. "I thought not. The people who usually work for Resistance are the type who can go unnoticed, but something tells me, with your looks, you've never blended in a day in your life. Don't worry, we can work on that when I get back from London."

Marie-Madeleine, too astounded by his cheekiness to think of a rebuttal, merely harrumphed again.

Navarre's head had been bouncing back and forth between them during the exchange. He now nodded at her. "Get Faye his code, Marie-Madeleine, and pass on any information you want to deliver to London directly. He's now an official member of Crusade."

Faye followed Marie-Madeleine into her room down the hall, which had been doubling as her office. He looked surprised when she took out the pad of paper where she kept the list of Crusade members' code names.

"You probably shouldn't store all that information in one place," Faye told her.

She rolled her eyes—this man never seemed to cease criticizing. "I know. But we have nearly one hundred members now, and this is the only way I can keep track of them." She grabbed her pen. "You'll be ROK 41."

"ROK. Rock, I like that. Is there any rhyme or reason to the lettering?"

"No," she said simply. She wrote Faye and then the code name in her ledger.

He took a step closer to her. "Seeing as we're going to be working together, you might as well call me Léon."

For some reason, her hand trembled, causing a blot of ink to spill on the page.

"I can make a copy of that when I get back," Léon nodded at the ledger, apparently forgetting that a minute ago he told her not to have it written in one place. He watched as she wiped at the blot with a tissue. "You're married," he said finally.

"What?"

He picked up her now ink-stained left hand and touched her wedding ring. "I can't seem to picture you with a husband."

She snatched her hand away from him. "We're estranged. We haven't been together for over eight years, since shortly after my second child was born."

"You must have married young then."

"I did," she acknowledged, a touch of regret in her voice. "He was an army captain, I met him when he was at Saint-Cyr, the military academy." Marie-Madeleine had been drawn to Édouard not only because he was handsome, but because he was about to be posted to Morocco and she could feel her sense of adventure calling to her. She'd loved France, but her fondest childhood memories were of Shanghai.

"I'm familiar with Saint-Cyr," Léon replied. "Your boss, Navarre attended it, at the same time as his nemesis, Charles de Gaulle."

She welcomed the change of subject brought about by the obvious bitterness in his voice. "I take it you did not attend Saint-Cyr."

"No. I left high school to fight in the Great War. I was at Verdun and received a Croix de Guerre. Afterward, I decided to become a pilot. Eventually the *École de Guerre* invited me to apply. I had only just graduated when this current war began."

"Impressive." She did the math in her head: that put him at around forty or so, several years older than her and similar in age to her husband, Édouard.

"Let me guess, your marriage fell apart because your husband wanted you to stay home to cook, clean, and take care of the children."

"Indeed." She reached into a desk drawer and pulled out a few pages of coded intelligence.

"And where are the children now?"

"They are safe," Marie-Madeleine replied coldly, handing him the papers.

Léon must have sensed that the window into her life had closed. He stuffed the papers into the false bottom of his briefcase. "I assume we are finished here."

She sat behind the desk and folded her hands. "Yes. Normally I would set you up with lockboxes and cash but I don't suppose that's necessary."

"No. Hopefully I will bring Crusade back the money and transmitters you need."

"Good luck," Marie-Madeleine told him with forced cheer.

He opened the door. "I don't need luck."

CHAPTER 7

MARCH 1941

*C*rusade had greatly expanded its reach by March, extending from Vichy and Marseille to other regions of the Free Zone and even to some parts of the Occupied Zone. Rivière, operating out of his vegetable stand, was a force to be reckoned with in Marseille, and—as Schaerrer was now traveling all over the countryside—Navarre had appointed a new head of operations in Bordeaux, Jean Boutron, who was laboring tirelessly.

Despite working sixteen-hour days, Marie-Madeleine was too plagued with concerns about Crusade's future to sleep properly. One night in mid-March, during yet another restless night, she found herself agonizing over finding funds to keep the network afloat. She was therefore alert when the door to her hotel room opened. She reached over to the nightstand, searching for something to use as a weapon, but the frame outlined in the light of the hallway was unmistakably Navarre.

"Léon Faye is back," he whispered.

She threw a robe on and followed him down the hallway to his suite. Léon, looking exhausted, was slumped into a chair in the living room/ office area.

"Look at this," Navarre said, practically shoving a letter at her. She quickly scanned it. General de Gaulle had a reply to Navarre's request that they work together. It ended with the sentence, 'Whoever is not with me is against me,' and bore the signature 'Charles.'

She folded the letter back up. "What about the money and the transmitters?"

"Keep your shirt on." Léon's eyes traveled over Marie-Madeleine's nightgown, which she pulled tighter around her. "The British seemed open to negotiation. Of course, they want to meet with Navarre in person before agreeing to anything."

Her gaze shifted to Navarre. "Are you off to London now?"

"They said they can send someone in to rendezvous in a neutral country," Léon replied. He too turned to address Navarre. "Intelligence is London's top priority at the moment, and your previous efforts have been well regarded by them. Your reconciliation with de Gaulle can wait." He stood up and reached into his pocket. "In the meantime, to convince us of their good faith, London has given us several thousand francs."

A few nights later, the shrill ringing of the phone awoke Marie-Madeleine from a nightmare-ridden slumber. She'd been dreaming that the British had outright rejected Crusade's pleas.

"Yes?" she croaked into the phone.

"It's me." Even through her sleep-racked brain, Navarre's voice was distinct.

"Where are you?"

"In Pau."

"Pau?" Marie-Madeleine repeated, recalling that Navarre's old war buddy, Colonel Bernis, was running a sector out of the charming resort town. "Why?"

"One of our contacts warned me that Darlan was planning my arrest. Now that the old Admiral has replaced Laval as Pétain's deputy, he's making waves against resistors. How soon can you get here?"

"Are you saying we're permanently moving headquarters?"

"Yes. Do you have a problem with that?"

"Of course not." In fact, Marie-Madeleine was only too happy to be leaving the collaborator-infested Vichy.

Navarre began dictating a list of things he needed from his office as she grabbed a pad of paper.

When she unlocked the door to Navarre's suite, she was surprised to see two people sitting on the couch: Schaerrer and a blonde.

"What are you doing here with her?" Marie-Madeleine asked, her mouth hanging open.

The blonde sat up, laughing. 'Her' voice was deep and familiar.

"Is that you, Noble?" In addition to bleaching his back hair, he had shaved off his mustache.

Schaerrer grinned as he stood up. "Did you really think I would bring a woman to Navarre's apartment?"

"For one moment, yes," Marie-Madeleine admitted. "Why the disguise, Noble?"

His mood darkened. "I was betrayed."

"By whom?"

"It was Red," Schaerrer said, naming one of the more recent recruits in Vichy. Marie-Madeleine knew that Noble had been friendly with the young man.

"Yes," Noble confessed sheepishly. "I fell out with him regarding his handling of information, and he in turn revealed my name to the police. I believe they're after me now."

Schaerrer shook his head. "I knew Red was no good. He had connections to Geissler."

"Geissler?" Marie-Madeleine repeated, sitting down. Geissler was a Vichy Gestapo agent.

"Red is known to exaggerate. I think he made up that meeting with Geissler just to show off," Noble insisted. "His real motive is money: he needs it now especially since he's run off with the fiancée of one of the boys."

"Made up or not, you still should have told me. Crusade comes before anything else, even friendships." Marie-Madeleine stood up to walk the length of the room. "If Red's true motive is only money, he'll sell the information off in pieces, which gives us time to clear out of Vichy."

Schaerrer gave Noble a dirty look before asking, "Where are we going?"

"Pau. Navarre's there now. I can drive you both there in my Citroën, but what about all of Navarre's things?" She gestured around the room.

"Lucien Vallet's here from Marseille," Noble said as Schaerrer started stuffing papers into a bag. "He can bring it on the train." After a moment, Noble added, "I'm sorry."

She touched his shoulder. "I know. It's hard to judge others' trustworthiness when you are always on alert for your own safety."

He stood up, causing her to drop her hand. "It's not like there's a manual to fall back on." Suddenly, his dark eyes crinkled.

"What's so funny?"

"I never noticed how short you really are. You always seem like such a large presence, in command of the room as soon as you walk in." He patted her on the head. "From now on, I shall call you 'little one'."

Schaerrer paused his packing. "That's pretty rich, coming from someone who almost got arrested."

"All right," Marie-Madeleine said, drawing herself to full height. "You have your orders… Let's get moving."

CHAPTER 8

MARCH 1941

Like his namesake King Henry IV, whose castle still stood in the center of the city, Navarre had been born and raised in Pau, a once-famous vacation destination for the European elite. To Marie-Madeleine, the idyllic city was even more enticing due to its secluded location in the foothills of the Pyrenees, which allowed couriers to cross the Spanish frontier. It was also close enough to the demarcation line that agents could easily travel in and out of the Occupied Zone.

Navarre had set up shop in the Pension Welcome, a quiet and comfortable boarding house run by two hospitable spinsters. His hometown hero status had won the two sisters over, and they turned a blind eye to the unusual comings and goings of his visitors with their bulky suitcases.

Marie-Madeleine informed Navarre about Noble and Red as soon as they got there. Despite the close call, and the ever-present threat of his own arrest, Navarre didn't seem overly concerned. "We shall carry on," he told her over breakfast. In his canvas shoes and red felt beret, he looked like a true local.

She then filled him in on the latest updates from Paris. "The White

Russians apparently think Hitler is going to launch an attack against Stalin. Can you believe it?"

"It isn't our job to think, just to pass things on. The British can be the sole judges of what intelligence is reliable."

"And have you figured out how to pass this intelligence on to the British?"

"Not yet. That's the snag, isn't it?" Navarre asked rhetorically. "We have a grand hiding place for a transmitter right here at the Pension Welcome, only no transmitter to hide. As of now, we are dependent on Gavarni's car and petrol to pick up and drop off reports."

"Who is Gavarni?"

"A local boy. Brave, but a bit careless." Navarre pointed his fork at her. "You'll have to teach him to stop sending uncoded postcards over the demarcation line."

Marie-Madeleine shuddered involuntarily. She was about to ask for more information about the Pau sector when Schaerrer walked into the dining room.

"Ah, just the man I wanted to see," Navarre said. "You're going back to the Occupied Zone. I need to know how many U-boats are at the mouth of the Gironde estuary and time is of the essence."

With a nonchalant air, Schaerrer clicked his heels and left, his confidence suggesting that he was prepared for whatever challenges lay ahead.

Navarre turned back to Marie-Madeleine. "As de Gaulle was unwilling to consider my proposal, Léon Faye has arranged a meeting with British Intelligence in Lisbon."

"And you're going to use Schaerrer's reports so you don't show up empty-handed?"

He gave her a wry smile. "I'm not a beggar."

"And what shall I do in your absence, oh esteemed leader?"

"You will go to Périgueux, in the Dordogne. I want to set up a drop zone in the west-central area, and it should suit perfectly. Take Noble with you, he can report back on the results. Then go and see your family."

She had to admit that his offer was tempting. Her mother had recently written that she and Beatrice had returned to the family villa in the Côte d'Azur and Christian was back at boarding school. Still… "You don't want me to stick around here and supervise?" she asked Navarre.

"No. Colonel Bernis has Pau under control. And I always say not to put all your eggs in one basket."

"What if you are caught, Navarre? Everything we've worked for will be in ruins."

"No." He laid his fork down and wiped his mouth. "You would simply carry on."

The road from Pau to Périgueux was quite scenic, Marie-Madeleine noted as she drove in her Citroën. She chatted mindlessly to Noble, who seemed to still be sizing her up. Navarre had instructed him to follow her directives, but Noble couldn't resist the urge to call out, "Watch out for that car, little one!" every five minutes.

The daylight quickly gave way to a dense fog that crept in from the hills, shrouding the landscape in an eerie darkness, the ominous clouds indicating that a fierce storm was imminent. Indeed, the pitter-patter of rain soon escalated to a deafening roar. As Marie-Madeleine tapped her foot on the brake, the left rear tire blew out, causing the car to spin out of control. They came to a halt perilously close to a ditch just as the storm unleashed its full force.

"That was close," Noble said, his voice wobbly. "I'll help you change out the tire."

For some reason, Marie-Madeleine felt the need to prove herself to the young man. "I can do it."

"I know you can, but two pairs of hands are better than one."

Marie-Madeleine was grateful for his assistance, as the repair proved to be an arduous undertaking with her rusty tools, one that took over thirty minutes to complete. When they finally got back on the road, they were caked in mud and shivering from the cold.

Noble let out a harsh cough. "I have to admit, up until now, I thought you were sort of high and mighty, a real wet."

"Oh, I'm wet all right." They laughed together, Noble's chuckle interrupted by more hoarse coughing.

MARIE-MADELEINE

. . .

The sector in Périgueux, a beautiful province known for its truffles, was headed by a man by the name of Lagrotte. As they discussed crossing points to Bordeaux, Lagrotte mentioned that he used one that was also utilized by the Free French.

Thinking of what Navarre would say about the rival organization, Marie-Madeleine told him to find a different route.

"But this one is perfectly fine for our purposes. It's relatively free of obstruction—and patrols, for that matter." Lagrotte's words were laced with cynicism.

Marie-Madeleine was put off by his aloof demeanor, but Navarre had hired him and she placed trust in the young man's extensive knowledge of the area. "According to your reports, Lagrotte, the Germans are exporting massive amounts of goods."

"Yes, they are depleting France of supplies: military equipment and the like."

Marie-Madeleine's thoughts went to White Russians. "We need to know what the Germans are up to. Send your couriers back to Paris right away to gather more information."

"What about the dropping zone?" Noble asked, his mind clearly on the white daisies flowering from the sky.

"I'll leave you to that," Marie-Madeleine told Noble, confident that he was far more trustworthy than the aloof Lagrotte.

On her way to the Côte d'Azur, Marie-Madeleine picked up her son from boarding school for Spring Holiday, deciding it was time to share with him the secret of what she had been doing. He was not quite twelve yet, still a boy at heart, perhaps too young for such a secret. But more than anything, she wanted to convey that the reason for her extended absences was not because she was deliberately abandoning him or Beatrice.

As she pulled away from the school, she told him, "Please understand that if I don't write as often as you like, it's because I have a duty to my people: they depend on me. I can't put myself in any unnecessary danger."

She took her eyes off the road to see Christian's eyes sparkle. "So you are fighting the Germans."

"In my own way, yes."

Christian turned serious. "How much danger are you already in?"

"No more than the danger all Frenchmen are in during this time of war."

"But what if the Nazis catch you?"

"There are very few Nazis in the Free Zone." The lie came easily—he didn't need to know everything. "And I take so many precautions, it's almost like a game."

This seemed to cheer him up again.

As Marie-Madeleine followed a winding route, surveying the area for possible landing spots, Christian watched the passing landscape. She stopped briefly in Toulouse, where she intended to set up a provisional hub that would link the Atlantic and the Mediterranean. Thanks to a local agent, she was able to rent a furnished room for Noble under a false name.

Christian trailed his mother around the town without saying a word as she conducted her business. She finally broke the silence. "I'm giving you a funny sort of holiday, aren't I?"

"Don't worry, Maman. It's like being at the circus, except that we seem to be the clowns."

Both of them brightened as they reached the coast. Just beyond Cannes, she turned onto a narrow, gravelly trail that wound its way to the family compound. She parked in front of the villa, its white-stucco walls and terracotta-tiled roof set against a backdrop of magnolia trees in magnificent bloom. She was about to turn the car off when Christian said, "Maman, not here."

"What do you mean?"

He pointed toward the back of the lot, where the farmhouse was. "Grandmère moved there."

Confused, Marie-Madeleine kept driving until she reached the wooden farmhouse, with its small windows to keep out the Mediterranean sun.

Beatrice ran into her arms as soon as she walked inside and Marie-Madeleine picked her daughter up before kissing her mother and brother Jacques hello. After exchanging polite pleasantries with the housekeeper, Sylvia, Marie-Madeleine asked her mother why they'd left the villa.

"Oh, I rented it out," she replied loftily. "We're less conspicuous back here anyway."

Marie-Madeleine shot her mother a curious look. She hadn't been fully truthful about what she'd been up to since the Occupation, but, as always, her mother seemed to be one step ahead of her.

After putting the children to bed, Marie-Madeleine sat her mother and brother down at the kitchen table and shared what she could about Crusade.

"I figured you were up to something along those lines," her mother stated when Marie-Madeleine had finished.

As Marie-Madeleine opened her mouth to ask why, her mother continued, "Why else would a mother go so long without seeing her children?" She patted Marie-Madeleine's hand in a rare loving gesture. "I'm proud of you for standing up for what's right. We need to defeat these Nazis so France can be France again."

Stunned, Marie-Madeleine didn't have a reply. She'd spent years trying to get her mother's approval, but it wasn't until she put her own life in danger—and by extension, her family's lives—that she apparently earned it. "Thank you," she finally replied.

"You're welcome." Her mother gave her hand another pat before she stood up and declared she was going to bed.

"I want to help in any way I can," Jacques said after she had left.

Tears stung Marie-Madeleine's eyes as turned to look at her younger brother, who had recently returned to the Côte d'Azur after sustaining a leg injury in the Battle of France. She was well aware that Jacques shared her love for risk and adventure—he had been on the Olympic bobsled team and had won a bronze medal in Berlin in 1936 before going on to work as a journalist during the Spanish Civil War. He was no doubt feeling restless waiting for his injured leg to heal.

"The best way for you to help is to stay here and assist Maman with the children, but rest assured, if I need you, I will contact you."

He nodded. "Please do."

"In the meantime," she thought of the papers she'd been carrying in the trunk of the Citroën, including the letter General de Gaulle had written to Navarre. If anyone asked her to open the trunk… "Jacques, I do have a favor."

At dawn the following morning, Marie-Madeleine and a limping Jacques went out to the pigsty in the back of the property. She carried one of her mother's beaten-up suitcases, into which she had stuffed the compromising papers from her car.

Together, under the blooming cherry tree, they dug a wide hole and then tossed the suitcase in before filling the hole back up.

Marie-Madeleine spent the next few days in a peaceful bliss, playing hide-and-seek in the fragrant gardens with her children during the day, and, in the afternoons, taking long walks together to appreciate the breathtaking views of the glittering Mediterranean. She hadn't realized until then how dearly she'd missed the sound of her children's laughter and their playful antics and, knowing she'd soon have to return to her work, tried to soak up every moment.

Her mind was still not completely at ease, however. One morning, as she lay in the shade of a flowering cherry tree, she reflected on what she had explained to Christian. His question had been similar to the one she had asked Navarre: *What if you are caught?* How would Christian feel—and little Beatrice for that matter—if they were told they simply had to carry on without a mother?

. . .

She was still brooding half an hour later when heavy boots came crashing through the garden and startled as a shrill voice called out, "There you are!"

"Schaerrer, what are you doing here?"

"Looking for you, of course. Navarre's returned from the Lisbon meeting."

She slowly got to her feet. "And? How did it go?"

"Quite well, I think. We have a transmitter!"

"Finally!" She threw her arms around Schaerrer and they danced for a few moments before she held him at arm's length. "Do you see? The real war is just beginning."

"Indeed. We have to get back as soon as possible. There's a train leaving—"

"With all those crowds of miserable travelers? Not to mention the gray rats…" She dangled her car keys in front of his face. "I'm driving."

As Marie-Madeleine said hasty, but still tear-filled good-byes to her family, her daughter clung to her legs. "Don't go, Maman."

Christian winked at Marie-Madeleine as he took his sister's hand. "It's okay, Beatrice, Maman has to leave now, but she'll be back soon enough."

She pinched his cheek before giving Beatrice one last kiss. "Be good for Grandmère and Uncle Jacques."

Marie-Madeleine was silent as they drove toward Pau, her heart aching over leaving her children again. The sun sank into the horizon, nearly blinding her. As she adjusted the visor, she noticed Schaerrer was staring straight into the rays.

"How can you look at the sun like that, Schaerrer?"

"It's a habit I learned as a sailor, madame. The sea teaches a lot of things landsmen don't usually know about."

"Do you long to be a sailor again?"

"No. Only actions count now. And results," he added in a gloomy voice.

She reached over to pat his hand. "Think of all we can accomplish now that we have the support of the British. In fact, I'm thinking we change the direction of Crusade."

"Will Navarre agree to that?"

"He will in time. I'll start by making Noble my adjutant."

"That's a swell idea. Noble's a hard worker and he's earned the respect of the rest of the crew."

"And I'll suggest that Navarre put you in charge of the patrols in the Occupied Zone."

"Me?" For a moment, he brightened, but then sank back into his glumness. "I can't be in charge of Frenchmen—I'm not French."

She knew that Schaerrer's father was Swiss by birth and that he'd grown up in the Dutch Indies. "Nonsense. You have more French spirit than a million of my countrymen combined. It's an honor to command the Occupied Zone and a testament to your abilities. You cannot refuse just because you don't think you deserve it."

He nodded. "All right. But first I have to make a complete list of all the U-boats in Gironde."

When they arrived at the Pension Welcome, Lucien Vallet, the wireless operator, came out to help them with their bags.

"I hear you've got your 'piano' at last," she told the burly man.

"Yep." He thumped his chest with pride. "I've already made four transmissions on KVL and the British received me QS-5. I'm finally doing something for the war."

"KVL? QS-5?" Schaerrer heaved his bag over his shoulder. "What is this, new coding?"

"KVL is our call sign, and QS-5 means they're receiving me loud and clear," Lucien replied loftily. He led them into the living room, which was filled with people and smoke. Navarre sat at the desk, chain-smoking the cigarettes he'd brought back from Lisbon, while Noble and another man listened to Colonel Bernis dictating orders.

"Who is that?" Marie-Madeleine asked Lucien, pointing to the tall, unfamiliar man.

"Gavarni, a local recruit."

"Ah." She recalled that Navarre had mentioned Gavarni's somewhat questionable mode of communication with the Occupied Zone.

"Lucien," Navarre checked his watch. "What do you say we show Marie-Madeleine the new headquarters? It's just about time for your sked anyway."

She quickly deduced that *sked* was slang for 'schedule.' "You've moved again, Navarre?" she asked. "Haven't you just returned from Lisbon?"

"We had to. The ladies running the Pension Welcome were starting to question what all the wires for his aerial were for, not to mention I'm sure they could hear Lucien tapping away late at night." Navarre stood up, gathering his papers. "We can still meet up here, but it's better for Lucien to transmit from the Villa Etchebaster. We can house many of our boys there too—I've already convinced some of the locals that the *Légion Française des Combattants* is housing escaped prisoners of war."

One by one, the members of Crusade headed toward the Villa Etchebaster, a sizeable ranch house on the edge of town. It was surrounded by a walled garden containing an untamed wilderness of plants.

When Marie-Madeleine arrived, she found, despite the late hour, there was a flurry of activity. Lucien got busy setting up his aerial while Gavarni built a secret compartment behind a mirror in the bathroom to store codebooks. The rest of the men were milling about, assigning bedrooms and chores.

"Chores?" Gavarni repeated disdainfully. "Who's got time for that? We should hire a housekeeper."

"Who will know all of our secrets," Marie-Madeleine stated.

"I know someone who will suit our purposes—her name is Josette," Noble interjected. There was something in his voice that made Marie-Madeleine peer at him curiously, but he didn't meet her eyes.

Navarre put his hand on her arm. "Let's leave these boys to work things out for themselves. I want to fill you in on what happened in

Portugal." He led her into the drawing room, where the walls were already covered with maps.

"How did you manage to get into Portugal?" she asked, sitting down on a worn leather couch.

"The *École de Guerre* has links everywhere, rather like the Masons."

For some reason, the mention of the military academy reminded Marie-Madeleine of her conversation with another graduate. "Was Léon there?"

"Léon Faye? He's been in Algeria these past few weeks." Navarre waved his hand. "Anyway, my contact with British Intelligence was Kenneth Cohen. We talked for two days straight. He's well aware that France, with its three seas, is Hitler's launch point for attacking their country and was adamant that London should be kept abreast of everything that happens here."

"And he wants us to supply them with that information."

"Yes, though I made sure he understood that we are not spies, but soldiers fighting with the best weapons we can access at this point: confidential information. Cohen agreed and offered us the resources we've been asking for: money and…" He gestured toward the living room, where they could hear Lucien tapping on the Morse key. "Radios."

"So now we are part of British Intelligence," Marie-Madeleine's tone was awed.

"Indeed—MI6 to be exact, but I'll remain the head of the network, free to make my own decisions. We've even given the network a new name—from now on we'll be called Alliance instead of Crusade."

She digested this new information. "Since we're restructuring…" She filled him in on the new vision she'd discussed with Schaerrer in the car.

"Sounds excellent. I agree with you on the merits of both Noble and Schaerrer, and Cohen stressed multiple times that MI6's top objective for Alliance is to gather as much intelligence as possible about the movements of the Boches' U-boats, especially in the Occupied Zone. With his naval background, Schaerrer will be invaluable for that."

Her eyes widened as something else occurred to her. "What about General de Gaulle?"

Navarre shrugged. "We'll help the Free French when we can, without going out of our way, of course. But England is fighting this war, and getting them the information they need is our first priority. Your workload is going to increase tenfold now, Marie-Madeleine." He reached into his briefcase to pull out a novel and then handed it to her.

She turned it over. It was an English translation of *The Lady of the Camellias* by Alexandre Dumas. "Did you buy me a book?"

"It's your new code," Navarre explained. "The British have come up with alternative methods so that, if you're caught, the Germans won't be able to find codes on your person. The pre-arranged key will be made up of the book's page number, paragraph, and word. So, for example, page 30, paragraph 4, word 20 would read 30-4-20. It will change all the time, so it can't be broken." Once again he reached into his briefcase. "And here are their questionnaires."

Flipping through them, she noted that they were mostly concerned with German movements: the troops, planes, and, of course, U-boats.

"And here's a copy of the network's call signs."

She scanned this one too, which was similar to the one she'd shown Faye, with the exception of two new names: N 1, which clearly stood for Navarre and another one which prompted her to ask, "Who is POZ 55?"

"You are."

"You told Cohen about me?"

Navarre cleared his throat. "I informed him that I have the most intrepid chief of staff, but I didn't give him any names." The meaning of his unspoken words was clear: *I didn't tell them you were a woman.* "We were also given five million francs."

She opened and shut her mouth before saying, "That's far too much money."

"No, it's not—it's enough to get us started." He stood up. "By the way, I also mentioned Faye's proposal for North Africa. Cohen's going to meet with Churchill about it."

"I still don't think that's a good idea. Why don't we deal with France first?"

"Cohen says Churchill is haunted by the problem in the Mediterranean. I think we could help him out by speeding things up in Algiers."

"Navarre—"

"In the meantime, why don't you head to Paris with the new questionnaires? Take Noble and Schaerrer with you." He tossed an envelope full of money at her. "And find a good use for this."

CHAPTER 9

APRIL 1941

Once again, Marie-Madeleine encountered the Nazi rats as the train entered the Occupied Zone. This time they dragged her into the bathroom at the end of the carriage before forcing her to take off her jacket and skirt so they could search the pockets.

"What about the questionnaires?" Noble hissed when they arrived at the station.

Instead of responding, Marie-Madeleine reached into the double lining of her hat and pulled out several crumpled sheets of paper.

Noble raised his eyebrows. "You are lucky they didn't find those on you."

"The rats will never outsmart me." She handed the papers to Schaerrer. "London is asking for information on the U-boats at the port near Bordeaux. They are suspected to possess some sort of new sonar device."

"It's not a problem." Schaerrer took off his shoe and inserted the papers inside. "I will simply get a crew member of the U-boat drunk, steal his uniform, and go aboard."

"You? With that face?" Schaerrer's boyish good looks and easy charm didn't give off the slightest hint of German vibe.

"My face will be all right. Everyone looks the same in the dark anyway."

"No." She reached for the young man's hand, suddenly feeling motherly. "Promise me you won't do anything foolish."

"Let's just drop it for now," Noble said. "We've all got to get going."

Marie-Madeleine experienced a pang of sadness as she watched Noble and Schaerrer disappear into the crowd of travelers. She reflected on the people she'd been working with for the last few months—united by the shadows of war, they now felt like long-lost friends. Her heart filled with a deep desire that nothing terrible would ever befall 'her boys,' especially Schaerrer, Noble, and Navarre.

Marie-Madeleine had always thought that there was no place better than Paris in the springtime, and this year proved no different. Walking toward her former office building, she noticed that the towering plane and chestnut trees, which were dotted with the occasional blooming magnolia, were beginning to form their bright green leaves.

Though the alluring scent of flowers filled the air, an eerie silence still clung to the streets, broken mostly by the flapping of the red and black swastika flags that flew over the public buildings.

As soon as she entered the lobby, the concierge, Lily, rushed over. "Madame," she said breathlessly. "Two men were here just yesterday asking about you. I said I had no idea of your whereabouts, but they told me to contact them when you arrive. I have no intention of doing so, of course, but I don't think you should stay here anymore."

Marie-Madeleine frowned. "You are right, Lily. Tell them if they come back that I came to Paris to attend the funeral of an uncle, but left again straight after."

Lily went behind the desk and returned with a set of keys. "Maybe you'd want to take one last peek before you leave forever?"

Marie-Madeleine accepted the keys and then climbed the stairs with shaking legs. Throughout all of her adventures thus far, she had yet to experience real fear. All of a sudden, she was on edge and half-expected to see Wehrmacht officers waiting for her when she opened the door.

The office, however, was empty.

I've gotten too comfortable during my time in the Free Zone, Marie-Madeleine scolded herself. *I can't be so naïve anymore.*

As she turned around, a rush of nostalgia overtook her. The furniture from her old apartment, and her former life, was now stacked in the otherwise austere room where they had once run *L'Ordre National.*

Her heeled shoes echoed on the wood floors as she walked toward her desk, piled high with papers, piano music, and mementos from the Far East where she had spent her childhood. She picked up a picture of herself and Édouard on their wedding day, gazing upon it with the detachment of a stranger. Her hand froze as she heard the sound of hundreds of boots marching on the street below. She convinced herself it was just a drill.

Regaining her composure, she tossed the photo back onto the pile. The only purpose her past served now was to draw the enemy's attention. Still, it was clearly time to vacate the office and leave all the memories of her pre-war life behind.

She had just finished packing the essentials when someone knocked on the door. *Naïve isn't even the word.* She was sure the Gestapo had come for her and looked for a place to hide. She knew it would be near impossible to escape off the balcony…

"Little one, open the door. It's me."

She found Noble standing in the hallway with another, unfamiliar man.

"This is Armand Bonnet," Noble informed her. "He's my main contact here."

Marie-Madeleine invited them in. Noble proudly displayed the British Intelligence questionnaires, which had all been filled out, revealing plans for airfields and positions of the German troops in Paris and its vicinity.

"Your patrol is proving to be quite competent," she remarked to Bonnet.

He grunted. "Yes, but we are still in dire need of a radio set."

"Well, we only have the one at the moment, but hopefully that will change soon. Send more couriers to Pau, and we can transmit your information to London. Do you have anyone in Brittany? We're concerned that the Wehrmacht is sending units there."

"I do," Bonnet replied. "Antoine Hugon, a garage owner, will know if anything is afoot. He's already informed us about nests of U-boats gathering near the coast. Of course," Bonnet stepped closer to her. "We're going to need money."

She pulled out the envelope. "How much do you think?"

"At least a few thousand francs."

From behind Bonnet, she could see Noble shaking his head no.

"A few thousand is too excessive," she told Bonnet. "How about four hundred?"

"If that's all you can spare," Bonnet replied, his eyes on the bulging envelope.

After Bonnet left, Noble stated that he was suspicious of the man.

Marie-Madeleine didn't hide her surprise. "He was so good with the questionnaires."

"Yes, but I know he didn't have a penny to his name when he joined the network, yet now he's gone and bought an expensive watch."

She wrinkled her nose, glad she'd offered Bonnet less money. Taking advantage of the situation during such a time did not sit comfortably with her. If what Noble said was true, Bonnet was no better than the black marketeers and the people who stole food from the starving.

Marie-Madeleine moved to Avenue Foch, to the maid's room lent to the network by one of her recruits. Her daily routine consisted of organizing letter boxes, teaching coding to the Paris agents, and verifying intelligence. At night she pulled out her pad of paper and planned for the new wave of Alliance that she'd envisioned, having gained a firsthand understanding of the key components necessary for an effective surveillance organization. It started with the source: an individual responsible for collecting intelligence who would then pass it on, either directly or via a letter box, to the courier—a local agent responsible for gathering and sending information—and, ideally, a radio operator to transmit the intel. She could envisage setting this protocol up all around France. That way, if one sector should fall... she could hear Navarre's advice playing in her head: *Don't put all your eggs in one basket.*

The next afternoon, Marie-Madeleine was strolling with Noble near the Place de la Concorde when they passed by Maxim's, the most expensive restaurant in all of Paris. She had often gone there before the war to dine and, of course, to see and be seen. She'd heard that the owner had been ousted and that the red-plush chairs were now filled by Germans.

Without saying anything, she and Noble both paused to gaze through the glass windows at the elite of the Germany military in their fine uniforms, escorting the prettiest of the gray rats. While Marie-Madeleine couldn't imagine they were being served the same delicacies as before the war—truffles, caviar, foie gras—the scent of whatever they were eating wafted through the doorway, causing her stomach to rumble.

Standing there on the street, looking in on the crème de la crème of the Wehrmacht, she was suddenly seized by a feeling of hopelessness. Could their feeble resistance serve any real purpose against the most formidable military power the world had ever seen? And was it justifiable to enlist her boys—who crisscrossed France on empty stomachs, wearing tattered raincoats instead of uniforms—in a quest that might result in their deaths?

The light shifted and Marie-Madeleine's reflection replaced the Nazis in the glass, revealing her sunken cheeks and the bags under her eyes. The war had taken its toll on many things, and Marie-Madeleine supposed her appearance was no exception. She reached up to touch the roots of her poorly dyed hair, but Noble took her hand in his. "We should go. It won't be carelessness or rashness that will be our undoing. All in all, it's better to have done the best we could."

"Thank you, Noble," she said simply as they resumed walking down the street.

CHAPTER 10

MAY 1941

"Things are humming along in Bordeaux," Schaerrer told Marie-Madeleine as he pulled her toward the third-class train car. Noble was a few steps behind and got into another car, accompanied by his new courier. Not wanting to draw attention to themselves, Marie-Madeleine and Schaerrer also separated into different compartments.

She sat next to a mother, who readily handed over her wailing infant when Marie-Madeleine offered to hold her. The baby stopped crying as Marie-Madeleine started rocking her. When her little blue eyes widened to peer at the stranger, Marie-Madeleine couldn't help thinking she looked a little like Beatrice.

Despite Marie-Madeleine's hopes, the baby in her arms did not keep the relentless gray rats from searching her. Right when they passed the demarcation line, the witch on duty put her bony fingers on Marie-Madeleine's shoulder. She gave the baby back to her mother before the rat led her away and repeated the humiliating examination procedure.

. . .

After she got off at the Pau station, she once again joined Noble and Schaerrer, complaining how she was tired of being interrogated every time she rode a train.

"Let me see your pass," Noble said.

She handed him the *Ausweis* Navarre had given her. Noble turned it over. "Aha, here's your problem." He pointed to a sequence of letters and numbers next to her name. "I heard someone talking about it in my compartment: the numbers vary based on how suspicious you are." He gave it back to her. "Your coding is a hair's breadth away from getting you shot on the spot!"

"I guess Navarre's contact wasn't so great after all." Marie-Madeleine ripped the pass into shreds, which she then tossed into the wind.

Navarre was seated at the dining room table of the Villa Etchebaster, sporting a white Stetson as if he were an American cowboy, and stylish leather boots.

"What are you wearing?" Marie-Madeleine asked as she sat across from him.

He lit a cigarette. "You got here just in time—I am about to set sail for Algeria."

"Why Algeria?" She folded her arms over her chest. "Does this have to do with Léon Faye's plot? I told you it's a ridiculous idea."

Navarre blew out a ring of smoke. "It's not that ridiculous. Faye's well-crafted plan is already in motion and Army intelligence officials in Marseille have secured new papers for me." He adjusted his Stetson. "I'll be posing as Monsieur Lambdin, a wine merchant wishing to purchase a supply of vintage Algerian rosé."

"Please tell me you didn't summon me back from Paris to tell me about this preposterous ploy. I really don't want to hear it."

"The time is ripe for a revolt in the African Army."

"No. You are needed here, in France. If you'd seen what is going on in the Occupied Zone, you'd agree with me. There are enough Nazis there to make mincemeat out of all of us French natives, and the Brits as well." She thought about telling him about the *Ausweis,* but decided it wasn't the time. "Forget your revolt—it is too premature."

"In war, nothing is premature. The greater the possibility of defeat, the greater the effort that must be made."

She sighed, recalling that trying to argue with Navarre once he set his mind to something was always a pointless endeavor. He was going to go to Algeria no matter what, leaving her to run Alliance. "What is it that you want me to do now?"

Lucien Vallet, the radio operator, suddenly burst into the room. "Everything's going fine," he announced. "I've received confirmation that Churchill is tremendously interested in the whole venture."

Navarre shot her a glance, glee practically erasing the lines on his face. "Marie-Madeleine, take Vallet here with his radio—"

"KVL," Lucien cut in.

"Right. You two go to Marseille. That way you will avoid any, ah, repercussions there might be from Algeria. You can catch up with Rivière at the vegetable shop. Noble will stay here, in Pau."

It definitely felt safer in Marseille than in Paris. It was as if the policemen didn't notice the Resistance activity going on under their noses, or, if they did, they pretended not to. Marie-Madeleine spent her days coding and decoding all of Lucien's transmissions to and from London, using work as a distraction while she awaited updates from Algeria.

When she heard the somber news of the sinking of the *Hood* by the *Bismarck,* and the subsequent death of over a thousand British sailors, she was compelled to express POZ 55's sincere condolences in a message to the War Office, which Lucien transmitted.

The reply was gracious and straightforward: *Thanks for your friendship STOP We shall avenge them together END.*

Marie-Madeleine was starting to grasp the transformative power of radio communication. Even through the abridged dialogue and codes, it served as a lifeline, allowing people in different parts of the world to share a bit of humanity amidst the brutality of war. She made a solemn promise to stay connected to the Allies no matter what.

Her reverie was shattered when Rivière barged into the office. "You'll have to clear out at once, for two reasons..." Rivière's voice was hollow. "In the first place, some imbecile in this building has been going about town, talking about suspicious sounds coming from this room."

"It must have been my Morse key," Vallet declared. "Even though I run the faucet when I'm transmitting, I can't seem to disguise the noise."

Marie-Madeleine's heart, which had started pounding as soon as Rivière burst into the room, accelerated even more. "What is the second reason?"

"The Deuxième Bureau has just informed me that Navarre and the others have all been arrested in Algiers and that there isn't a chance in hell they'll be released."

Marie-Madeleine threw the pen she'd been holding across the room, cursing. "I knew the whole idea was doomed from the start. Damn that Léon! He and Navarre are an explosive mixture."

"What are we going to do?" Lucien asked, his eyes wide with fright.

"Carry on, of course," Marie-Madeleine snapped back, but then immediately felt bad. It wasn't Lucien she was mad at. It was Navarre, for not listening to her when she advised against the Algeria plot. And she was even angrier at Léon Faye for coming up with it in the first place.

Lucien's voice took on a whiny tone, like a child who knew he was annoying his parent but had no choice. "Alone?"

"Yes." She pointed to his transmitter. "Inform London of the new information. I'm going off to Pau to let Noble know of the change in command."

The rest of the boys at the Villa Etchebaster didn't seem to notice Navarre's absence. As it was, most of their contact had been with Marie-Madeleine—to them, Navarre had always been the enigmatic face of the network while she was the one managing the day-to-day operations.

Feeling somewhat assured by their nonchalant reactions to the shift in leadership, she made the decision to transfer Alliance's headquarters. It had been Navarre's idea to relocate to Pau, but Marie-Madeleine's affinity for Marseille was rooted in her childhood, and now more than anything, she needed comfort and familiarity.

Noble immediately accepted the proposal to relocate, and volunteered to oversee the move while Marie-Madeleine went back to find housing for them all.

As the stations rolled past the train window, Marie-Madeleine reflected on what British Intelligence would think when they learned that Navarre had been arrested. Would that be sufficient cause for them to abandon Alliance? And what about Navarre? Did his family know of his arrest?

She adjusted her wide-brimmed hat to further cover her face. It was hot in the car, and the book in her hand wasn't the distraction she'd hoped it would be. Too occupied with worrying, she hadn't eaten much in the past two days and her mouth was dry from thirst.

The man who'd been sitting across from her kicked her foot with his own. Marie-Madeleine pushed her hat back, raking her eyes over his checked trousers and disheveled coat, ready to shout at him for his impertinence. On his head he wore a white Stetson, which he tipped back in order to meet her gaze. The brilliant blue eyes staring back at her were familiar.

Navarre.

She kept her expression as neutral as his. Not a muscle in either of their faces moved. Marie-Madeleine closed her book as he pulled a packet of cigarettes out of his pocket and got up.

She found him in the corridor. "What are you doing here?" she whispered.

"A police commissioner helped me escape. The boys told me you were on this train."

"You were betrayed?"

"Yes."

"Was it Léon Faye?"

"No."

She wondered why she felt relieved at Navarre's denial. "Where is Léon now?"

Navarre shrugged. "I heard he was let go, but it's unlikely he will remain free for long. There are bound to be repercussions. Pity—it was a good scheme. I expect we'll take it up again someday."

Marie-Madeleine gripped a handrail as the train gave a sudden jolt. Before she could admonish him, Navarre continued, "You'll have to get a new identity. Your name appeared in the documents seized in Algiers."

That didn't faze her—as usual, she wasn't concerned about her own safety. Navarre's, however, was a different story. "Where will you be going?" she asked.

"Back to Pau, of course. They'll never believe I'd have the gall to return."

"I thought it would be better to move Alliance's headquarters to Marseille."

"No, I prefer Pau. Our so-called government would never dare to arrest me there."

She tightened her grip on the handrail. "You probably shouldn't stay in France at all. Perhaps we can find a way to get you to London."

"No. I've still got fight in me. Let's see this thing through."

Though she still had misgivings, the conviction in Navarre's voice was as unwavering as always. Marie-Madeleine reached out to pull his Stetson back over his face. "Just promise me you'll lie low for a while."

CHAPTER 11

JUNE 1941

Noble was still in Pau, supervising the relocation to Marseille. He looked surprised to see Navarre and hear of the change in plans but said nothing.

At first, Navarre wanted to move into his old room at the Villa Etchebaster, but Marie-Madeleine reminded him of his previous warning not to put all the eggs in one basket.

Schaerrer, back temporarily from Bordeaux, found Navarre a room in a flat overlooking Pau's Promenade des Pyrenees. At Marie-Madeleine's request, Navarre was only allowed to venture out to the headquarters at Villa Etchebaster, where she had released most of the staff. Only the housekeeper, Josette, knew that the supposed retired schoolteacher who arrived at the villa on his bicycle in the cover of darkness was actually the hometown hero and Resistance outlaw, Georges Loustaunau-Lacau.

Clearly unabated by his arrest, Navarre kept up his steady stream of outlandish ideas: he somehow even established a contact within the Abwehr itself.

The members of Alliance now exceeded a hundred. Partly due to the network's growth, and partly, Marie-Madeleine mused, due to Hitler's invasion of Russia in June—the White Russians had been right after all—British Intelligence decided to provide the network with both more money and more transmitters. They sent both in via Jean Boutron, the courier who went to and from Spain and to whom Vichy had just assigned a new post at the French Embassy in Madrid. Navarre had been overjoyed when he'd heard the news—Boutron could now move freely between a neutral country and France with diplomatic mail bags and, of course, Alliance's clandestine messages and equipment.

The only downside to this spectacular operation, in Marie-Madeleine's view, was lending Boutron her cherished Citroën, which was now fitted with diplomatic plates and acted as a transport linking France and the free world.

But the little Citroën couldn't transport everything the British wanted to send in. The RAF proposed to use the dropping zones Noble had scouted, and their first operation was scheduled for the upcoming full moon. Navarre had sent Noble to the Alps on courier duty, but he promised Noble he would be back in time for the drop since he had been so eager to participate.

The remarkably smooth progress of events made Marie-Madeleine uneasy, and she was consumed by the thought that something was bound to falter. She therefore was not overly surprised when a courier arrived from Paris bringing word that one of their boys had been arrested.

The usually ebullient Schaerrer took the news the hardest. He was set to depart the next day on his latest mission to Bordeaux, where he would be responsible for assessing the U-boat situation. Recalling his audacious plan to steal a German uniform, Marie-Madeleine reassured him that he did not have to board the U-boats unless the circumstances were completely ideal.

"No one's irreplaceable," he said nervously as he packed up his things.

She watched him, that familiar motherly feeling washing over her. "Schaerrer…"

He walked over and wrapped his arms around her. Instead of allaying her fears and insisting he'd be fine, which is what she'd been hoping for, he whispered, "It's for France."

"Remember what I told you—you are more French than anyone I know."

Just then, the courier came into the room. "It's time to go. Our escorts at the demarcation line are ready."

Schaerrer gave Marie-Madeleine one last squeeze before following the courier. As she watched them leave the villa and head off into the darkness, she had the thought that Schaerrer had been wrong. To her, he was indeed irreplaceable.

A few days later, Noble returned from his trip to the Alps earlier than expected, looking more drained than she'd ever seen him. "Navarre is going to be arrested. Again."

"How do you know?"

He waved his hand. "Call it intuition."

She decided not to tell him she'd also been feeling something similar. "Noble, you have no right to keep your sources secret from me."

"My sources?" He rolled his eyes. "I have no sources." He grabbed her arm. "But trust me, little one, when I say his arrest is a certainty. Léon Faye has been transferred to a jail in Clermont-Ferrand to await trial for the conspiracy, and I don't imagine that Vichy is content to let Navarre walk the streets clear of charges. He has to vacate Pau, now. Tomorrow will be too late."

Realizing she had never seen Noble so distraught, she rose from her chair and went into the map room, where Navarre was barking orders at a few of his men. "Noble's here."

Navarre looked startled. "Already?"

"Yes."

He crushed his cigarette into the ashtray. "I take it there's been no news of Schaerrer."

She shook her head.

"Any need to worry?"

"I'm worried about *you*."

"Why?"

She knew that Navarre would never abandon Pau on the strength of Noble's intuition. Nor hers. "The police," she lied. "While Noble was traveling, he got wind that they know you are in Pau. You'll be arrested in a matter of hours if you don't leave straightway."

Navarre, clearly in no hurry, lit another cigarette.

She glanced at Noble, who was standing in the doorway. "Navarre—"

He exhaled, forming a cloud of smoke. "I'm not sure how much your information is worth, but I suppose I have been a bit too brash lately. I'll leave Pau tomorrow."

Noble stepped into the room. "Why not now? We can help you make a quick getaway."

"Impossible." He stabbed out his cigarette with more force than necessary. "I'm expecting my family to meet me at the cathedral tomorrow morning. I must see my wife and daughter one last time. After that I'll place myself in your capable hands."

"Navarre," Marie-Madeleine said as he went back to his maps. "We all miss our families. But they are the only lead the police have. They will certainly be followed here. And you don't want to put them in any more danger than they already are, do you?"

"I know a shortcut from the train station. They'll be fine," he said firmly. Once again, Marie-Madeleine knew it was useless to argue.

Navarre spent the night at Villa Etchebaster. In the morning, Marie-Madeleine and Noble waited for him by the front door.

He adjusted his Stetson as he approached them.

"We're going with you," Noble told him.

"No need. Especially not with those toys. We don't shoot Frenchmen," Navarre declared, nodding at Noble's bulging pocket.

"What if they attack you?" Marie-Madeleine demanded.

"They won't. I know what they're like. Tell Josette to set the table for noon." Navarre slipped past them and exited, slamming the door behind him.

"What now?" Noble asked Marie-Madeleine.

"We must go to his flat and get rid of anything compromising."

. . .

They promptly departed on their bikes. When they arrived, they tore through the flat, burning stacks of papers and out-of-date documents. Before they left to return to the villa, Noble hid the codebook under the carpet in the front room.

They pedaled slowly back, Marie-Madeleine's head pounding from a sense of foreboding combined with lack of sleep.

Josette stood waiting at the garden gate, and Marie-Madeleine could tell from the expression on the housekeeper's face that her worst fear had come true.

Noble clearly came to the same conclusion. "Was it the Gestapo?"

"No. It was French policemen. They called Navarre a German spy."

Marie-Madeleine threw her bike against the fence. "Did they shoot Navarre?"

"No madame," Josette replied.

"What about his family?"

The maid's eyebrows furrowed. "They weren't with him."

"They probably knew better than to get on that train," Noble said bitterly. "If only he would have listened to us."

"Where is Navarre now?" Marie-Madeleine asked Josette.

After the woman shrugged, Marie-Madeleine—overwhelmed with a sudden outrage directed at Pétain, at Vichy, and her foolish, spiteful countrymen—burst into tears. Noble wrapped his strong arms around her and steered her toward the house. "That's enough, now, little one: a soldier doesn't cry."

Her shoulders felt heavy from both the weight of his arms, and the weight of her new responsibility. Navarre had been betrayed by his own countrymen. Until that moment, she'd thought she'd been fighting for France, but what good was it if men of authority were willing to capitulate to the Nazis? "I can't do it, Noble. I can't take over Alliance."

"Come eat. If the boys don't see you at lunch, they'll think they've been left without a leader."

Unlike Marie-Madeleine, the boys' appetites did not seem to suffer from hearing the news of Navarre's arrest. She managed to slip the immense Lucien Vallet a large portion of her fish without Noble seeing. He shot her a grateful smile, which for some reason, lifted her spirits. As she gazed around the table, at which sat some of the most fervent and patriotic men France had to offer, she realized that she couldn't just give up. Alliance would have to go on, without Navarre.

"What time will you be transmitting to London again, Lucien?" Marie-Madeleine asked.

He answered through a mouthful of fish. "An hour from now, madame."

She set her fork down, knowing she had little time to code her message.

She went into her bedroom and quickly scrawled: *N1 arrested this morning again STOP Network intact everything continuing STOP Best postpone parachuting next moon STOP Regards POZ 55*

The response from British Intelligence was typically succinct and sympathetic, ending with *Who is taking over?*

Marie-Madeleine wondered if she should inform them that the new leader was actually a woman—she'd always assumed the Brits thought POZ 55 was a man.

In the end, fearing that they might dismiss her based on gender, she kept her reply as concise as theirs. *I am as planned STOP POZ 55.*

CHAPTER 12

JULY 1941

Marie-Madeleine thought about moving once more to Marseille, as she'd originally planned, but she grew weary every time she pictured packing up all the equipment, again. She decided to stay at the Villa Etchebaster to be close to Lucien's transmitter.

One morning she was awakened by Gavarni, the local courier. "I've been looking everywhere for you," he said as he went to the window and pulled down the shade. "The Pension Welcome has been raided."

"Raided?" She sat up in bed, not caring that she was in her night clothes. "Do you suppose it's safe to stay here?"

"I should think so. The townspeople are still accepting Navarre's story that the villa is housing POWs."

She watched as his mustache twitched nervously. "Then what are you afraid of?"

"Me? I'm not afraid of anything. I've observed your work for weeks and I have complete faith in your abilities. However, there are others…"

"Who think it is absurd to take orders from a woman?"

"You have to admit, you are very…" he paused, searching for the right word. "Young."

She accepted that. "Nonetheless, we must find a way to survive and keep Alliance running."

After Navarre's arrest, Noble had gone to Bordeaux to try to locate Schaerrer. The three men she counted on most were all unavailable so she asked Gavarni if he would be willing to be her chief of staff. Despite Navarre's warning that Gavarni's delivery methods were suspect, she knew the other boys respected Gavarni, whose leadership qualities came naturally. Besides, he was a former air force officer, like Léon Faye and Noble.

"I'd be honored, madame."

Once again, Marie-Madeleine considered fleeing Pau, but knew it would take at least a week to relocate. At any rate, she knew she had to return to the Pension Welcome to erase any potential links to her, regardless of the risk. She waited until night fell and then stole away down the darkened Pau streets.

One of the spinster owners was sitting in the living room, working on her needlework in the dim light of a lamp.

Marie-Madeleine said a quick hello and then got straight to the point. "The Commandant has been arrested."

The old woman set down her sewing. "Sweet Jesus. Is it possible?"

"Unfortunately, yes. He was betrayed by the French police."

It was obvious from the expression on the woman's face that she was aware of the implications of Marie-Madeleine's statement. "Is there something I can do to help?"

"Yes. If the police come here looking for me, you must tell them I left for the Riviera on the first train out."

The woman nodded. "Do you want me to find a carriage to take you to the station?"

"No thank you. I have arranged for transportation through a friend."

The woman brought Marie-Madeleine a cup of tea as she packed up and promised she had nothing to fear.

. . .

According to plan, Lucien Vallet arrived at the Pension Welcome just before sunrise and grabbed Marie-Madeleine's suitcases. The old woman waved goodbye with her handkerchief, watching as the two set out in the direction of the train station.

After they were out of sight, Marie-Madeleine and Lucien doubled back toward the Villa Etchebaster, using a side street and keeping close to the buildings.

Josette had left the gate to the villa unlocked, and the two stole in. Marie-Madeleine found an empty bed and collapsed—nearly 48 hours had elapsed since she'd last slept.

But her much-needed nap was once again disrupted by Gavarni intruding into her room. "Thank God you're here. The police have been at the Welcome since dawn."

"As far as they're concerned, I'm on my way to the Riviera." She shut her eyes and rolled over. "Now, if you'll excuse me, I need some sleep."

He walked over to stand next to her, causing her eyes to fly open. "Madame, I changed my mind about you staying here. We have to find somewhere else—the police suspect this place is connected with Navarre."

Knowing he was right, Marie-Madeleine climbed out of bed.

CHAPTER 13

AUGUST 1941

*G*avarni found Marie-Madeleine a modest room at the Hôtel du Lycée, in the center of Pau. The owners were kind and didn't ask questions, not even when they delivered all her meals to the room where she had become a veritable recluse. She never went out by day—and very seldom at night—figuring it was the only way to save the network.

The boys' confidence never faltered, however, and they tripled their efforts after Navarre's arrest, especially since MI6 had increased its demands for intelligence, mostly concerning the whereabouts of German U-boats. There had been no news of Schaerrer, so Marie-Madeleine distracted herself from worrying by coding the information her agents gathered, some of it slated to be delivered by Lucien over the radio, and some of it to be transported to London via Boutron and her Citroën through Spain. Every morning, Gavarni would pay a visit to her to go over how to answer the endless questionnaires London supplied.

One morning she was surprised to welcome Antoine Hugon, a garage owner from Brittany, into her room. Hugon had received the Iron Cross from Germany for saving a soldier's life during the first Great War, which he now wore prominently on his lapel.

"Helps with my disguise," he told Marie-Madeleine when he caught her staring at it. She was taken aback as Hugon's weathered hands undid the buttons on his jacket, which he quickly shrugged off.

She went back to her work, thinking he must be hot, but then he took off his tie.

"Monsieur Hugon, I don't think—" He held up his hand before removing his shirt.

"What is that?" she asked, pointing to the large paper wrapped around his distended torso.

"You'll have to excuse my impertinence." He carefully detached the paper and set it on the table in front of her. "But I thought the Brits might be anxious to take a gander at this."

Marie-Madeleine studied it as Hugon dressed. It was an incredibly detailed, scaled drawing of the submarine base at Saint-Nazaire. "I believe you are right—British Intelligence will indeed be pleased with this. I'll have Boutron deliver it to them as soon as possible via his routes through Spain."

As predicted, MI6 was enthused about the submarine base intelligence, which only increased their thirst for more. Through Lucien, London announced they were sending in a new, specially designed transmitter, along with a radio operator to teach them how to use it. Once the newcomer had finished imparting his instruction, he was to be dispatched to Normandy to set up his own sector.

The thought of heading the reception party for the incoming Brit pleased Noble, who wanted to play "God Save the King" while the parachutist dropped from the sky.

"You can't do that," Marie-Madeleine admonished him. "What, are you going to hire a violinist? Not to mention the Boches will surely hear."

"Well, we can't receive him like a sack of peanuts! He'll be the first real Tommy to work with Alliance."

Marie-Madeleine decided to ignore this statement. "Did you get his papers?"

"Yes." Noble retrieved them out of his briefcase. "And for Josette, too, his pretend wife."

Lucien accompanied Marie-Madeleine to the Villa Etchebaster to meet the new arrival. As she entered the villa, she heard someone playing, "God Save the King," on the piano, which was quickly followed by an emphatic rendition of the Marseillaise.

Marie-Madeleine stopped abruptly in the drawing room, confronted by the most ridiculous-looking man she'd seen in a long time. He was dressed in striped pants and a short jacket complete with a polka-dot cravat and a shirt with a cutaway collar. A pince-nez was balanced on his bulbous nose, above a meticulously trimmed goatee. It was as if the British had based this man's outfit on a caricature of a typical Frenchman.

"This can't be the work of British Intelligence," Noble whispered in her ear. "He looks as if he's going to a village wedding."

The parachutist blinked his wide eyes as he removed his bowler hat.

Marie-Madeleine decided to welcome him in English.

"Don't bother, madame," he said in French with a heavy cockney accent. "I've spent most of my life here in France." He stuck out his hand. "You can call me Bla."

She shook his hand for the briefest second before dropping it and glancing around the room. Lucien was already fiddling with the new radio, which was smaller than his original.

Noble had unpacked the latest treasures and Marie-Madeleine went over to inspect the unfamiliar, silky paper for messages, invisible ink, crystals for the transmitters and, of course, more questionnaires.

Tucked among the chocolate and cigarettes was a small envelope addressed to POZ 55. She picked it up and ran her fingers over the embossed seal of the royal coat of arms. Inside was a polite letter containing instructions for Lucien Vallet, her faithful wireless operator, to be relocated to oversee the growth of the network's radio operation in Paris.

"Little one," Noble hissed as she replaced the letter in the envelope.

"What should we do about him?" He nodded at Bla, who stood staring back at her, his hands thrust into the pockets of his absurd trousers.

"Take forty-eight hours rest," she instructed Bla directly. "And then find some new clothes, and for heaven's sake, shave off that ridiculous beard."

"Yes, madame."

Losing Lucien Vallet—who had always seemed larger than life to Marie-Madeleine—to the Paris sector was difficult, but an even more devastating scenario unfolded a few days later when Noble came back from another scouting trip. "Schaerrer's been captured."

Marie-Madeleine's heart sank. "What happened?"

"The Gestapo got a hold of him outside of Bordeaux, carrying incriminating documents regarding the positioning of U-boats."

She felt tears come to her eyes. "He succeeded in his mission, but at what cost?"

Noble's voice was also wobbly. "I suppose that remains to be seen. Right now he is in Fresnes Prison under a false name. Clearly he's not given anything up, otherwise the Gestapo would be roaming all over Pau, looking for us."

She closed her eyes, picturing the courageous young man undergoing torture for refusing to divulge any information about the network. She forced herself to take comfort in the fact that he would be exemplifying the same bravery he had displayed during his time in his naval service, and, of course, while he worked for Alliance.

CHAPTER 14

OCTOBER 1941

One horribly gray day in October, Noble entered Marie-Madeleine's little hotel with more bad news from the Occupied Zone: Admiral Darlan, Pétain's new deputy, was tightening the rope against the Resistance. In the wake of Germany's invasion of the Soviet Union, the French Communist Party had started outright attacking the occupying soldiers. The goal of the FCP was the same as Alliance's—to strengthen the Resistance and hamper the Nazi war machine. The reprisals were swift and brutal: in Brittany, fifty Frenchmen were executed by firing squad for killing one regional commander of the German occupation forces.

To make matters worse, Noble had just been notified that Navarre was sentenced to two years' prison time, and Faye, four months, for the failed Algeria plot. Presumably Navarre received a harsher sentence because of his escape attempts.

Marie-Madeleine anticipated that Navarre's imprisonment would cause considerable anxiety among his former cronies, but she hadn't expected such a rapid response, as quite a few had already communicated that Alliance could not expect their continued support.

Even though it was already dark enough outside, Noble closed the blackout drapes before taking a seat in the wooden chair next to

Marie-Madeleine's desk. "We must eliminate Admiral Darlan. I've discussed it with some of the other boys, and we all agree that Darlan is to blame for the outcome of Navarre's trial."

She sighed. "I'm not sure anybody but Navarre is to blame. Except for maybe Léon Faye."

"There is a way we can win back Navarre's men," Noble told her.

"Oh? What do you propose?"

"I can kill Darlan myself. Just give me the order."

"Noble, I could never order that. Look what the Germans have been doing as a result of the FCP's actions. Fifty Frenchman for every Boche—we can't afford that toll."

He looked at her as if he thought she'd gone mad instead of the other way around. "The fact is," he said slowly, as if she didn't understand, "Some of the boys want to avenge the sentences of Navarre and Faye. If you don't act, they'll view it as a sign of weakness."

"And what about you?" she asked gently, fearing the answer.

"I have more confidence in you than in anyone."

"Then trust me when I tell you that your life is worth more than a thousand Darlans."

"But our colleagues will think us—"

"They can think what they like." Her voice had regained its typical firmness. "Go to bed. I'll take care of the rest."

After he'd left, she pulled out a piece of paper and set it on the desk, intending to write to Navarre's associate, the one she believed was most responsible for the fallout, but she found she was at a loss for words.

She put her pen down, wishing she could ask Navarre for advice, but unless he escaped or was released—an increasingly unlikely scenario—he would be inaccessible until the war was over. She had to rely solely on her own judgment.

In the end she requested that Navarre's old cronies limit their efforts to resisting the invading Germans and made no mention of Admiral Darlan or anyone else in the Vichy government.

. . .

MARIE-MADELEINE

Despite all the turmoil, Alliance continued to grow in both strength and numbers. There were now six transmitters throughout the country sending information to British Intelligence. The largest shipment the network had ever received was scheduled to arrive in mid-October, a development Marie-Madeleine deemed as undeniable evidence of the critical role the network was playing in the Allies' effort.

The second parachute drop was due to take place in a farm field belonging to a couple who were part of Lagrotte's patrol. British Intelligence had started passing on coded missives—especially regarding the arrival of planes—to the Resistance over the BBC's *Radio Londres* station during their *messages personnels*, but no one in Pau had a radio. A sense of anxious, unsettling tension permeated the nights around the full moon as the reception committee had to spend the entire evening in the increasingly frigid, rainy weather awaiting a plane that didn't come. Noble's hacking cough grew worse and Marie-Madeleine vowed she would force him to take a long rest after the parachuting operation was complete.

Finally Noble arrived triumphantly at her little room. After she'd let him in, he walked past her, muddying the carpet with his filthy boots. He set something down on the desk and Marie-Madeleine went over to inspect it. It was a small, navy-blue trunk, with locks that gleamed even in the dim light. The case could have very well come from London's most expensive shop.

"What's in there?" she asked.

"Francs. Lots and lots of francs." Noble's voice, even in his glee, sounded hoarse and he clearly hadn't shaved in several days.

She unsnapped the locks and peered inside. There must have been thousands of banknotes, possibly even a million.

"It wasn't easy getting that thing here, I'll tell you that. I nearly fell asleep on the train with it between my legs." He shook his head. "Ersatz coffee doesn't really do the trick when you've been up for a week straight. But luckily a pretty girl came along and talked my ear off."

"Oh?"

"Yes. Can you believe that she was telling me all her troubles would be solved if only she were to meet a rich man?" He chuckled. "Lucky for you she didn't know what was in the case, and that I didn't run off with it—and her—full stop."

"Lucky nothing—you would never do such a thing."

"No. Not while we still have so much to do."

She clicked the case shut. "What about the transmitters?"

"There are six new ones. I stored them for safekeeping at my house until we figure out where to send them."

"Okay good." She shoved him toward the door. "Now off you go—and get some rest, please."

A few minutes after Noble left, Jean Boutron came in with his diplomatic bag. He blinked at the money she'd been counting. "It seems like we're getting help from all directions." He lifted the Pétain seal on his bag and then dumped more francs onto the bed. "Here's my contribution."

She sighed, looking at the piles of cash. "So much for not putting all our eggs in one basket. This has become a giant omelette."

The next day, she set about distributing the several million francs. Gavarni, who was making arrangements for the departure of a few agents into the Occupied Zone, would receive a quarter of the money, and Bishop, Alliance's quick-witted treasurer, would take another third to allocate it among the various branches in the Free Zone. While she was in the midst of dispensing cigarettes and chocolate among the dispatches, Noble arrived.

"Thank goodness," she told him. "Do you mind helping me put the finishing touches to everything? I should have been in Marseille by now. The hustle and bustle here is overwhelming, and I don't feel as safe anymore."

"I know what you mean."

The tone of his voice made Marie-Madeleine look up from her work.

"The parachute operation went off without a hitch, and..." He coughed before nodding at the dispatches. "All the goods are about to be distributed, but I have this funny feeling in the pit of my stomach."

"Me too," she acknowledged quietly.

"Well, in that case," He coughed again as he stood. "I'm going to make arrangements just to be safe, like hiding the transmitters."

After he left, she went to the window and watched as he turned the corner, the sound of his dry cough still echoing in her ears.

Early the next morning, Tringa, the radio operator who'd replaced Lucien Vallet, arrived at the Hôtel du Lycée. "Noble's driving me crazy," he said after greeting her. "He spent the whole night sifting through papers, deciding which ones to keep and which ones to burn. Here…" Tringa dumped a sizeable pile on her desk. "He told me to give you the ones he marked as important. He also wants me to move my transmitter as soon as my morning sked is over."

"I guess it's better to be safe than sorry." After a moment, she asked, "Did Noble get any sleep at all?"

"No. He left at dawn to meet Gavarni."

She handed Tringa the latest stack of messages. "Go and get these off quickly and then do what he said. If you happen to see Noble, tell him to stop by here before he crosses the demarcation line."

She waited for hours but nobody came. Marie-Madeleine couldn't sleep that night—she just stayed up late coding transmissions, trying to keep her mind from thinking that the worst had happened. For countless weeks, Schaerrer and Noble had been her trusted lieutenants, her sixth and seventh senses in the wilderness of France. They had helped her to do her duty, no questions asked and no objections raised. What if they had both disappeared forever?

Tringa returned to her room two days later, his face pale. "They've all been arrested," he panted.

Marie-Madeleine sank into a chair, her blood feeling as though it had turned to ice. "How?"

"The French Police raided Villa Etchebaster. They got everyone there, and then cast their net wide. They swept up the men at the villa, and some of the other agents who were on the way to Paris, including Gavarni."

She cursed aloud. "And Noble?"

"Him too." Tringa nodded at her suitcase in the corner. "You'd better start packing—I heard the police are searching for you, now."

She stuffed what papers she could into a case before Tringa ushered her into a waiting car. As they drove down the hill, a black car passed, heading toward the house. Marie-Madeleine drew in a breath as she realized it was the police. She had left in the nick of time tonight, but what about the next time?

The car took Marie-Madeleine to Tarbes, which was about thirty miles from Pau. She stayed at the house of a married couple with whom Tringa was acquainted. There, she took stock of her next move. Almost all the people she trusted the most had been arrested. There remained only Jean Boutron, the French ambassador to Madrid. She immediately sent Tringa to locate Boutron, hoping he hadn't made the return trip to Madrid yet.

Clearly he hadn't, for he came to Tarbes the following day.

"You have to get out of France as soon as possible," Boutron said when Marie-Madeleine had finished filling him in on the arrests of Navarre and her Pau agents..

"I'm not leaving France. There has to be somewhere I can go." She thought longingly of her family on the Côte d'Azur, but knew she'd only be putting them in more danger if she went there.

"You have to come to Madrid with me," Boutron stated finally.

"How? I can't just cross the border."

He stared at her for a few seconds, as if sizing her up. "I think I know a way to smuggle you."

"What should I do about the papers?"

"Papers?" he repeated.

"I brought some records of Alliance: lists of code names and copies of transmissions."

He furrowed his eyebrows. "Where are they now?"

She pointed down, toward the lower level. "I'm keeping them under a coal bin." Her hosts hadn't objected to her using their cellar as a temporary storage area.

"It's not the greatest place to store them, but you definitely can't bring them over the border. We'll come back for them later."

CHAPTER 15

NOVEMBER 1941

The pain was unbearable. Marie-Madeleine shifted her body as best she could, but the spasms shooting up her legs would not abate. She'd been bundled up in a mail sack for nearly nine hours. It had been Boutron's brilliant idea to put her in one of his diplomatic bags and then load it into the back seat of her Citroën, which was now on a train heading toward the Spanish frontier.

She was freezing: she had to wear minimal clothing to fit into the bag, and, of course, the railcars storing the automobiles were not heated. To make matters worse, one of the tires that had been piled up on the seat to disguise the lumpy bag had slumped onto Marie-Madeleine's already stiff neck.

Finally she felt the train jolt to a stop. After a minute, she could hear the sound of several boots approaching. A beam of light shone through the burlap and she crossed her icy fingers, hoping they wouldn't find the shape of the bag suspicious.

"These are diplomatic bags, you see," Boutron's normally booming voice was muffled. "They contain top secret information that I must deliver to Madrid immediately. It's for the Marshal…"

The voices drifted away and it was silent again. *Please get me out of here,* Marie-Madeleine begged silently. Every minute in her personal hellhole felt like an eternity.

A blast of cold air rushed in as the car door was opened. She wanted to call out to Boutron but her mouth was too dry. Someone lifted the tire away and then she felt the pressure of a hand touching the bag. The hand traveled over her head, patting it, and then down her arm, evidently moving past her elbow, but she had lost feeling in the lower part of her arm.

Clearly this wasn't Boutron. Although by this point no one could doubt there was a person in the sack, she held her breath anyway.

"Okay, old chap? It's me, Lelay." The hand thumped her head roughly. "Schoofs? Answer me, old pal. Imagine burying you in that! Boutron had told me you were in the boot, which could only have been slightly more comfortable than this."

Marie-Madeleine's thoughts stumbled in her low oxygen stupor. Lelay must be the customs officer, who was friends with both Boutron and Schoofs, the British Intelligence agent who was currently stuffed into the trunk. Boutron had apparently neglected to tell him that there were two stowaways in the car, not just one.

"Speak to me, Schoofs. Did you faint?"

"Shut up!" Schoofs called from the trunk.

The effect of his words was immediate: the hand was snatched away as though it had been bitten by a snake. "I'll make sure to speed you through customs, whoever you are," Lelay whispered.

There was another stomping noise, and then Lelay asked louder, "How many have you got in that car?"

Marie-Madeleine could just make out the sound of Boutron's voice through the ringing in her ears. "I haven't got time to go into all that."

He started the engine and a few moments later she smelled the sharp stench of a cigarette as the car drove off the train ramp. She mustered all the strength she had to call through the bag, "Jean can you let me out? I'm terribly thirsty."

She heard him curse as the car braked hard. "I forgot you've been in there all this time." She thought he might have said something else, but she felt as though she were sinking into quicksand, her body being pulled under against her will. *I can't breathe…*

When she awoke, she was lying next to a stream, Schoofs and Boutron peering anxiously down at her. Someone had thrown a coat over her nearly naked frame.

Boutron shined a light into her eyes. "Thank God. You were out cold and we couldn't feel a pulse—I was afraid you were done for." He straightened up. "What she needs now is some brandy and then it's off we go."

CHAPTER 16

DECEMBER 1941

Once they had safely reached Madrid, Boutron sent a message to MI6 saying as much. A female relative of Schoof's, who was a prominent fashion designer, provided Marie-Madeleine with a new suit and cork-soled shoes, as her wooden French ones had been rendered unwearable. After months of wearing threadbare clothes and subsisting on corn cobs and boiled turnips, she felt she had entered paradise, with real coffee, ham, and tea.

The day after her arrival, Boutron informed Marie-Madeleine that the Brits were requesting she travel to London.

"No," she replied. "Out of the question. I need to be back in France by the first of January, at the latest."

He raised his eyebrows and opened his mouth as if to argue, but the determined expression on her face probably convinced him otherwise. "I'll see what I can do."

The next morning, Boutron triumphantly announced at breakfast, "The plans have been changed. MI6 now knows that you are a woman. They are sending in a representative to have a meeting here."

Marie-Madeleine didn't know how to feel: relieved that she definitely didn't have to travel to London, or worried that the jig was up now that MI6 found out 'POZ 55' was female.

She took her coffee to the window to look at the Madrid landscape stretching beneath her. The city had been significantly damaged in the Spanish Civil War a few years prior. Even from a distance she could see that the once-magnificent edifices were riddled with holes from Luftwaffe bombings, and weeds had sprung from spots where the buildings had been completely obliterated. Nazi flags flew from any pole that was still intact. Although Spain had officially proclaimed itself neutral, the sympathies of the fascist government clearly aligned with the Third Reich, which had aided them during the preceding civil conflict.

From her perch above the city, Marie-Madeleine, in her fine new clothes, felt like a princess whose castle had become a jail cell. She was haunted by the thought of her friends being tortured. At this point, it seemed that anyone who got close to her ended up in prison. Perhaps she should just give it all up, go back to the Côte d'Azur and wait out the war, her children in her arms. That way she wouldn't be responsible for anyone else's misfortune.

It had all become too dangerous anyway. Not that she ever worried about her own safety, but Pau had been a close call—she had left only moments before the police came looking for her. Her breath grew heavy, fogging the window, as a realization washed over her: she would never give in. *I'm still here, for now anyway. And I have to fight while I can.*

MI6's representative in Spain was tall, with blonde hair and a youthful, but serious face. "I'm Major Richards," he said, reaching out to shake Marie-Madeleine's hand.

"Thank you for meeting me here. I don't need any more travel adventures at this time."

"Ah, yes." He took a seat at the dining room table. "When we finally realized that POZ 55 was not the mustachioed army officer we had pictured, I was ordered to come to Madrid." He tapped his finger on the table. "You had us all going for a while there."

"You sound disappointed." She sat across from him. Though she was fully clothed, she suddenly felt exposed, even more so than when she emerged from the mail sack wearing practically nothing. "I didn't exactly conceal the fact that I am a woman. The reason I wasn't upfront about it was because I was afraid you wouldn't take me seriously and I didn't want my boys, who risk their lives for the cause every minute of the day, to be abandoned. I felt like I had to prove myself before you found out the truth."

Richards waved his hand, as if to brush her words aside. "Rest assured, we appreciate courage more than anyone."

She held her breath, wondering if he was about to fire her.

"You are still willing to volunteer, right?" To her surprise, his voice sounded anxious and she found her spirit returning. After all, this was war, and volunteers were needed regardless of their gender.

"Yes." She leaned forward. "But Major Richards, you should know that after the November drop, there was a terrible tragedy in Pau."

"Oh?"

She filled him in on the whole disaster, from Schaerrer to Noble. It was a difficult conversation, not only due to the subject matter, but also because she had to translate her boys' code names into their real identities for Richards' sake.

Throughout her story, Richards stayed rather quiet, only offering a few 'ohs,' and 'really's' here and there. She wasn't sure if it was his unflappable British manner, or if something else was going on. Finally she stated, "You know more."

"We do indeed."

Richards' so-far inscrutable voice had dropped and she could tell it was bad news. "What is it?"

"Paris." He took a sip of water. "We've heard the French police have turned your agents over to the Abwehr. They've been put in Fresnes Prison and, we assume, have been treated rather poorly by the Germans."

She looked down at the tabletop, feeling small and helpless—once again it had been her fellow French who had betrayed them. Noble, her closest confidant and Lucien Vallet, her faithful wireless operator, had been part of the compromised Paris branch. After a moment of silence for her fallen friends, she looked into Richards' blue eyes. "How do you know this if everyone has been arrested?"

"Not everyone. Gavarni is still free."

"No. Gavarni was in the Villa Etchebaster roundup."

"After his arrest, we got a transmission from him letting us know that he had been taken to Vichy. Gavarni met with Commandant Rollin, the head of the Surveillance du Territoire, France's intelligence agency."

"I know what the Surveillance du Territoire is," Marie-Madeleine snapped.

Richards had the courtesy to look embarrassed. "Of course you do. Anyway, Gavarni told Rollin that you indeed had left for London and that, in the wake of the arrests and the absence of a leader, Alliance had officially collapsed. Since he no longer needed the money he'd been allotted, he offered it to the Vichy government."

"Now wait a minute…"

Once again Richards held up his hand. "On the condition that the arrested Alliance agents all be released."

Boutron had entered the room and obviously heard the last bit. "Gavarni, that traitorous bastard. I never liked that skunk—now I know I had good reason not to."

Marie-Madeleine was just as shocked that Gavarni could offer up such a large sum, and that Richards could deliver the news so calmly. "So is Gavarni roaming around Vichy in a police car, squandering our money on Pétain and all his hangers-on?"

"Possibly. But at great risk to himself. Gavarni insists that giving them the money will prove that Alliance is no longer functioning."

"To hell with his risks," Boutron roared. "He gambled and lost. Let him fraternize with Vichy but tell him to keep quiet. You intelligence people calculate everything in terms of risk." He slammed his hand down on the table. "We run one long risk and its consequences are permanent. Do you hear me, Major Richards? The risk we take is permanent."

"All right, Boutron." Having at last come to a decision, Marie-Madeleine tried to make her voice as soothing as possible. "If Gavarni were really a traitor this whole time, then we both would have been arrested weeks ago. At this point, we can only grant him the benefit of the doubt." She turned to address Richards. "Give Vichy the two million francs with the contingency that they release all Alliance prisoners in their possession."

Richards slid a piece of paper across to her. "You will write a message to Gabriel Rivière using your terms, so he will know it came from you."

She did as bid.

Richards picked up the paper. "I will code this and send it to London for transmission to Rivière." With that, he left the room.

Boutron sighed audibly. "Even if all of the agents are indeed released, they are now compromised and can never be associated with Alliance again."

"I am aware—our eighteen months of hard work have now gone down the drain."

"Not down the drain. Think of all we've accomplished."

Marie-Madeleine clasped her shaking hands together, thinking of Navarre's words, "You will simply carry on." Despite MI6 knowing in detail what had happened to Alliance, they were still backing her as its leader. At least for now.

After a while, she told Boutron, "You are right. This was only the first wave, and now it's come to its conclusion. We must rebuild the network."

CHAPTER 17

DECEMBER 1941

For the remainder of her time in Madrid, Marie-Madeleine met with Richards every day to work out how to best streamline the communication between the network and MI6.

"Your new network needs to last, Poz," Richards told her as she was getting ready to depart. "U-boat hunting is still our top priority—our troop transfers and convoys must be protected. Although," he continued thoughtfully, "the priorities for intelligence may very well shift to the air at any moment."

"I understand." She shook Richards' hand with sincerity, knowing that they had formed a real friendship, grounded in mutual respect.

With the addition of the new transmitters Richards had provided, she was even more cramped than before in her mailbag prison, but Marie-Madeleine was so thankful to be returning to France that she refused to give in to the pain.

They arrived in Marseille on December 31st. She had brought back treats for her remaining agents and decided to host a small New Year's Eve party in the apartment above Rivière's vegetable shop.

They clinked glasses after Marie-Madeleine informed her boys that the network would go on.

After the toast Rivière cornered her. "I just want you to know that I have complete faith in you."

"Thank you." Marie-Madeleine took another sip, swallowing hard before she asked, "And Gavarni?"

Rivière glanced around the room and then stated in a low voice, "I hear he's still in Vichy, spending money on himself."

"What about the others? The money was supposed to set them free."

Rivière's face fell. "They are still in prison. But they haven't breathed a word about us, despite being tortured. I heard Noble was made to kneel for hours while the Germans threw lit matches on his naked skin."

Marie-Madeleine felt tears well up. "Do you think it was Gavarni who betrayed the network?"

Rivière shook his head. "As much as I despise what he is doing now, I don't think Gavarni is a snitch. Vichy knew what they knew, but it wasn't Gavarni's fault."

His last words were nearly drowned out by a chorus of cheers from the rest of the boys. The clock had struck midnight.

Boutron held up his empty glass. "It's a new year, madame. Time to get cracking."

She clinked his glass. "Indeed it is. And our first priority is to free Noble." She nodded at Rivière. "Send word at once that I need to see Gavarni."

"You got it, chief."

PART II
NOAH'S ARK

CHAPTER 18

JANUARY 1942

Since no one wanted Gavarni to find out where Marie-Madeleine was staying, the meeting took place in the back room of the vegetable store. Rivière acted as bodyguard, leaning against one of the asparagus bins near the front.

As she waited for Gavarni, she reminded herself to reserve judgment until she got the whole story. Her mind drifted back to the period following Navarre's second arrest, when Gavarni had insisted he was merely voicing other people's misgivings about her taking over as leader, as he himself had complete faith in her. She speculated now that he had been lying and that it was his own doubts he'd been expressing.

Gavarni appeared to have changed: there was a hardness in his eyes that hadn't been there previously and his mannerisms seemed callous. He didn't even stomp his muddy boots outside before he walked through the back door. "I carried out the orders you sent from Madrid," was his greeting. His voice broke on the words "you sent," and Marie-Madeleine wondered if he were here to deny her as leader.

"I know."

"It was Lagrotte, one of the couriers, who betrayed the network. He fell in love with a policeman's daughter, and, to please his potential new father-in-law, he talked. He gave up names, hideouts, even where we keep the transmission sets. They seized the ones Noble was hiding."

She drew in a deep breath, recalling how she'd met the cynical Lagrotte in Périgueux, but didn't reply.

"I suddenly realized," Gavarni continued, "in the wake of such a disaster, I needed to knock loudly in high places. While I was in prison, I asked to speak to Commandant Rollin, head of the Surveillance du Territoire. I offered him the full two million francs we had in my possession. When our boys are finally let out, the Deuxième Bureau will provide them with new papers."

"And when will that be?"

Gavarni shrugged as he pulled out a cigarette. "Your British friends will probably have to put up more money."

"Haven't they given Vichy enough?"

His face was like a mask as he looked her up and down. "I see you are wearing new clothes."

Marie-Madeleine felt the need to exert her own authority. "You didn't answer my question."

"Don't you see?" he exclaimed. "We have to have money, so much more money." He grabbed her arms and, in his furor, his next words were nearly incoherent. "We'll be under the protection of Vichy as we fool the British, accumulating masses of cash, some of which we will give to Rollin. We'll pocket the rest of it, for the network of course."

Marie-Madeleine wondered where Rivière was. She pushed Gavarni off of her and knocked over a chair, hoping to get her bodyguard's attention.

It worked. "Did you need me, chief?" Rivière asked as he stormed in.

"Yes. Please make sure our friend Gavarni here doesn't miss his train back to Vichy."

Gavarni ducked under Rivière's arm, which had reached out to guide him to the door. "But it's you, madame, who hasn't given *me* an answer."

Rivière cracked his knuckles.

She righted the chair as she thought of a response, one that would firmly close the door on Gavarni's participation in the network. "You can tell Commandant Rollin that we've agreed to the dissolution of Alliance. When he has released everyone, then we can have another meeting."

"Not before?"

"No. If you want to go forward with your plan, I mustn't compromise myself."

This seemed to placate him. "Right. Thank you, madame. I was sure you'd agree." He allowed Rivière to seize his arm and drag him toward the door.

"By the way," Marie-Madeleine asked. "Why did you give up the whole two million francs to Vichy? You probably could have offered less and kept the rest for yourself."

This inquiry fell on deaf ears, however; Gavarni said nothing else as he was dragged out of the store.

She was no closer to freeing Noble, but at least she'd gotten rid of Gavarni, if only for the moment. She had a feeling that Vichy would not accept that Alliance was truly done and would someday resume looking for her.

She pushed that thought of her mind, for she had more pressing matters at that point. Like finding a new chief of staff, for instance.

CHAPTER 19

JANUARY 1942

A few days after the encounter with Gavarni, Marie-Madeleine trudged to the vegetable shop for a long day of meeting with agents and couriers. She was so engrossed in thinking about the future of the network, she nearly collided with someone sitting on the steps outside.

It was Léon Faye.

Whenever she'd thought about him in the weeks following Navarre's arrest, it was mostly with resentment, considering that it had been his idea to stir up trouble in Algeria in the first place. Now, however, she found that her heartbeat sped up when she made contact with those grayish-green eyes.

Other than some new strands of gray in his wavy hair, he didn't seem much changed by his prison stint. He even sported a new suit coat, which, she noted as he stood up, fit his athletic frame remarkably well.

"Is this the soonest you could get here?" Marie-Madeleine asked as she started up the stairs.

"I know. It was very bad of me." His stance was wide, making it difficult for her to squeeze by without touching him. "But I had to let loose a little bit, considering I'd been holed up in jail for four months. I don't think I'm suited to prison."

She unlocked the door to the back room. "Who is?"

"Right." He gave her a disarming grin, which disappeared as quickly as it had come. "I was lucky to get out so soon, while poor Navarre is still languishing. I promised him I'd check up on what remained of the network. I'm sorry it took me so long, but you aren't easy to find."

"By design of course." She took a breath to slow her heart, which was still beating abnormally fast. "What are your plans now that you have found…" She'd almost said, "me," but stopped herself. "Us?"

"First, to get you somewhere safe. I have good friends in Algeria who have agreed to shelter you."

She practically threw her purse down on the desk, feeling suddenly angry. "And the network?"

His pilot eyes, so used to scanning the infinite sky, seemed to penetrate her soul. "The network doesn't exist anymore."

"Who told you that?"

"Navarre."

"And what if *I* told you that the network is still carrying on?"

Even he couldn't hide the surprise in his face. "Is that so? Tell me about it."

Her fury at him dissipated, replaced by a sense of vindication. "I can do better than that…" She gestured toward one of the chairs behind the desk. "Take a seat and you'll see for yourself." She then called for Rivière.

"Yes, chief?" he asked as he eyed Léon wearily.

"This is Commandant Faye. He's a friend of Navarre's. He'll be observing my meetings today."

"Ah." Rivière nodded and then turned his gaze to her. "Ernest Siegrist is here. He was a member of the network Interallié before it collapsed and is looking for a new network."

"Interallié?" Marie-Madeleine repeated.

"So he was part of The Cat's lair," Léon stated. "Are you sure he's legit? I heard there were other traitors besides The Cat in Interallié."

Rivière set a decoded transmission down on the desk. "According to London, Siegrist is reliable. He wants to continue the fight by joining us."

"Show him in," Marie-Madeleine told him.

Siegrist was a great bear of a man, even more burly than Vallet, and tall, with large, pendulous ears.

"I'm a former policeman," Siegrist said after he introduced himself. "I obviously changed careers when they asked me to arrest Frenchmen for daring to resist the Occupiers."

"Since London has already confirmed you, we are in need of a security man," Marie-Madeleine informed him. "And..." She thought of the gray rats and her discarded *Ausweis*. "Someone to help us forge papers."

He flashed her a broad grin.

"I imagine you don't mind hard work and moving around? You'll be attached to my headquarters."

"And what about my family? Siegrist asked anxiously. "I have a wife and two small daughters. After the fall of Interallié, I am always fearful of putting them in danger."

She avoided glancing at Léon, though she could feel his eyes on her. "Perhaps I'm not the most knowledgeable person to advise you about spouses, but I do know they are an excellent way of getting caught. If you were a soldier, you'd never consider taking your wife to the front line. We'll take care of your family, of course, but don't forget that your safety will be their best reward."

Siegrist looked down, his big ears quivering. "Thank you. If I hadn't stumbled upon your organization, I'd be working as a docker in the Old Port until the end of the war."

After Siegrist left, Rivière brought in Denise Centore, a courier who was there to complain about the new ink from London. She displayed a piece of light brown parcel paper on which was written, clear as day, a description of the Boulogne sector's anti-aircraft sites.

Frowning, Marie-Madeleine picked up the paper.

"It seems that the writing becomes visible due to body heat when it's stored on someone's person," Denise said.

Marie-Madeleine instructed Rivière to draft a message to London informing them of the flawed 'new brew' they'd sent them. "It's a miracle the postman didn't notice."

Léon studied the offending paper. "Is this what you use to convey intelligence?"

"Normally it's far more encrypted," Denise explained. "We send innocuous-looking parcels into the Occupied Zone. The intel is encoded in invisible ink, which is only supposed to be revealed by special potions only our agents have access to."

"There's a better way," Léon replied. "Coded interzonal cards. I'll get started on implementing these right away."

"Now hold on," Marie-Madeleine interjected. "Other than this small setback, our way has been working just fine."

Léon raised his eyebrows but didn't say anything else as Denise took her leave.

One by one, Rivière brought the visitors in to give their reports. In the mid-afternoon, Léon asked, "When do we get a break? I'm starving."

Marie-Madeleine shrugged. "We don't really have set hours."

"Well, come on then." Léon stood. "I'm declaring it's time for lunch."

She wrinkled her nose, resenting the way he seemed to be taking charge.

"Don't look at me like that," he said. "I'm only trying to get you to eat. You've become awfully thin."

Suddenly self-conscious, Marie-Madeleine smoothed her skirt over her admittedly slender thighs.

"What do you say we go to one of the black-market bars on Canebière?" he asked.

"No. There's too many people who might recognize you... or me, for that matter."

"Well, then." He put his overcoat on. "It's off to my hotel. We can speak more openly there anyway. Not to mention that I have a few goodies in my cupboard."

After a moment's hesitation, Marie-Madeleine let him escort her to his room at the Hôtel Terminus. As she sipped a glass of wine, she became more candid, sharing details about the raid in Pau and her meetings with Richards in Madrid.

Over a bite of *foie gras*, which he had managed to procure from one of his contacts, Léon asked, "What is your main worry?"

Without pausing to think, she blurted out, "I need a new chief of staff to reassemble the existing sectors and create additional ones."

"Chief of staff? How about someone like me?"

She'd been hoping he'd volunteer, but she didn't want to give in too easily. "Isn't your job in North Africa?"

He shrugged. "I could do both at the same time. At the very least, let me assist you in getting things back together here. Ever since you told me that the network is still intact, my head has been spinning with ideas. Besides, I can always go to Africa after I help you sort everything out." He looked at her earnestly. "I'm at your disposal, and so are all of my friends: a whole squadron of my former air force colleagues."

There it was: the inroad for her to ask what was really on her mind. "These friends of yours: would they be willing to take orders from a woman?"

His face widened into a grin before he answered her unasked question. *"I'm* prepared to, and I'm sure they will be too, especially when they realize what a capable woman you are."

The compliment was unexpected and Marie-Madeleine decided not to acknowledge it. "Consider the job yours then. I'll get back to you tomorrow with some ideas." She glanced out the window. It was getting dark. She hadn't realized how much time had gone by. "I have to get back to the shop."

Léon stood. "I'll come with you."

The once busy streets of Marseille were eerily silent, amplifying the click of Marie-Madeleine's heels. In the distance, a train sounded, and she felt resentment bubble in her stomach as she pictured more Germans disembarking in their padded trench coats.

Rivière was sitting at the desk in the back room, going over his ledgers, when they returned. He set his pen down and announced,

MARIE-MADELEINE

"The fellow who is storing your papers at Tarbes is refusing to give them to anyone but you."

"Why?" Marie-Madeleine removed her scarf.

Rivière shrugged. "Apparently he told Boutron, 'She gave them to me to look after, so she has to retrieve them herself.'"

"Are the papers compromising?" Léon asked.

"Only for me," Marie-Madeleine said with a sigh. "The real names of the agents are in code, but everything's in my handwriting. I've got to get them back—they are records of the information we've sent and questionnaires for the Occupied Zone. I have no other copies."

Léon cracked a knuckle. "Well, I guess our first order of business is to go to Tarbes and show this bonehead what's what."

Rivière gave Marie-Madeleine an inquiring glance, as if to ask, 'Why is this guy butting in?'

"Never mind him," she told Rivière.

"Well, in that case…" Instead of relaxing, Rivière seemed suddenly agitated. He got off his chair, almost knocking it over, and came over to Marie-Madeleine. He put his hands on her shoulders, causing Léon to say, "Now wait a minute…"

Rivière ignored him. "Chief, there's something I have to tell you. I wanted to tell you alone, but…" he shot a pointed look at Léon.

Rivière's strange behavior was starting to make her feel uneasy. "What is it?"

He released his hands. "Henri Schaerrer has been killed."

Her voice dropped to a whisper. "No."

Léon deposited Rivière's abandoned chair behind her. As she sank into it, recalling Schaerrer's impish, freckled face, she demanded, "How do you know?"

"From his uncle." Rivière pulled something out of his pocket. "The German chaplain sent him a letter that Schaerrer himself wrote." He handed it to Marie-Madeleine.

She bent over the desk, squinting to read the letter in the dim light. The envelope was postmarked from Fresnes Prison. Schaerrer had written the words, "I'm glad that I have preserved my honor," which she knew meant that he had refused to give up any information about

Alliance. "He signed it with his real name." She tried to recover her composure as she refolded the letter.

"Somehow they found it out," Rivière stated.

"But how?" Marie-Madeleine asked. "He was arrested long before the rest of our boys, and none of them would have any cause to identify with a spy who had been caught red-handed. There was no reason to reveal his real name to the Abwehr."

"We don't know how they knew," Rivière said.

She shifted her gaze to Léon, who was running his finger over the prison emblem on the envelope. "I've seen many comrades disappear." His face looked pale. "And I know only too well that men like Schaerrer are few and far between."

"We will avenge him," Rivière said.

"No," Marie-Madeleine told him with a timbre of sorrow. "Schaerrer wouldn't like that word. We shall carry on, and somehow we'll have to replace him. I know that's what he would have wanted."

Rivière checked his watch. "It's almost time for the last trolley."

The two men silently escorted her to the terminus. Marie-Madeleine longed to be alone to reflect on Schaerrer, but to her dismay, a crowd of people was waiting. She managed to find standing room in the end car.

She was the final stop, and with each passing station, the crowd grew thinner until she was the only one in the car. Finally alone, she now felt afraid. Schaerrer was the first real casualty in this escalating conflict, though she knew he wouldn't be the last.

But, what a loss. She had feared hearing about Schaerrer's death ever since she first learned of his arrest, yet still the news somehow caught her off-guard. It wasn't only that Schaerrer was the first of her agents to die. It was the man himself—the exuberant Schaerrer, who had been there from the beginning, and had done so much for the network, was indeed irreplaceable, and she didn't know how Alliance, or herself, could ever be the same.

As she exited the train station, a Citroën passed by, its lights turned off. She refused to slow her pace, but a chill ran down her spine as she caught sight of the passenger leaning out of the window, his hat low over his face. It was most likely a Gestapo agent, but since the car sped up and disappeared, he must have decided that a lone woman walking down the street with tears rolling down her face was not worth his time.

When she reached her flat, she went to the window and opened it. She could see the shoreline and beyond it, the infinite black ocean. Somewhere out there was Algeria. Perhaps she should take Léon up on his offer to relocate there for safety. Maybe everyone in the network should pack up and leave France. She wasn't sure if she could take any more deaths.

For a long time she lay awake, staring at the pockmarked ceiling until she finally fell into a sleep filled with nightmares.

CHAPTER 20

JANUARY 1942

The morning after learning of Schaerrer's death, Marie-Madeleine was awakened by a banging on the door. Still sleepy, she rolled out of bed, noting that the sun was already high in the sky and the ocean was a gentle blue. She'd slept in for once.

She crept cautiously toward the door, wondering if she was in any danger. But someone called out, "Chief? Are you in there? Open the door."

It was Bishop, Alliance's jovial treasurer. "Oh thank goodness," he said as he strolled into the flat, seeming overly cheery, even for him. "You had us all going when you didn't show up at the shop first thing."

"You do know about Schaerrer, don't you?" she asked.

His expression grew somber. "Of course. But in war, one must never talk about those who have disappeared. We all know our turn might come." His eyes traveled briefly over her nightgown but then went to the window, his face reddening slightly. "You should get dressed. I'm here to escort you."

. . .

When she arrived at the vegetable shop, she found it filled to the brim with her agents and couriers. Léon stood in the corner, talking to Rivière, but he paused to nod at her.

She climbed onto the desk to address the room. Rivière gave a loud whistle, and they all turned to her expectantly. "I have offered Léon Faye here the post of chief of staff until the conflict in North Africa can resume. If you all agree, I will inform London of the changes."

A few members of the crowd murmured softly and she caught the name, Navarre. She knew what they were thinking: that if she were putting Léon into such an elevated position, it must mean Navarre was never coming back.

She cleared her throat. "It was Navarre himself who asked Léon to come to our rescue."

"Indeed," Léon cut in. "And my first act will be to arrange his release from prison."

"Excellent," Rivière exclaimed. He shook Léon's hand. "Welcome aboard." He turned to Marie-Madeleine. "Believe it or not, I have good news: the boys from Pau have been released and have returned to Villa Etchebaster."

"And Noble?"

"He is there too."

Relief washed over her. This was the best news she could have hoped for after Schaerrer. "I'll leave for Pau in the morning."

"I'll come with you," Léon offered. "We can also pay a visit to Tarbes to retrieve your papers."

Rivière's eyebrow raised ever so slightly but he didn't say anything else.

Noble was waiting for them at the gate to Villa Etchebaster. "You shouldn't have come," he said in a gruff voice. "It was difficult enough concealing your name in the interrogations. Now you've put yourself in the tiger's jaws."

Marie-Madeleine, shocked by the cold behavior of her first lieutenant, didn't reply.

Tringa, the radio operator, appeared from behind the walled garden and made his way toward them, dragging his feet in his ragged slippers.

"Welcome, boss," he said to Marie-Madeleine before his gaze landed on Léon.

"This is Léon Faye. He is replacing Gavarni as my chief of staff."

"Gavarni," Noble repeated. "I hope to never hear his name again." He finally stepped away from the gate, allowing Marie-Madeleine and Léon to enter the garden.

"We promised the Deuxième Bureau that we'd obey Gavarni," Tringa said as the four of them walked toward the house.

"They gave you your false papers, correct?" Marie-Madeleine asked.

"Yes." Noble replied tersely.

"But did they give you any other instructions? Any cash?"

"No, nothing like that," Tringa stopped walking. "Boss, if you don't mind me asking: what's to become of us now?"

She smiled. "I am in desperate need of a radio operator in Marseille." She turned hesitantly to Noble. "And I'd really like my first lieutenant back, if you are willing."

His mustache twitched. "You'd take me back? You still have confidence in me?"

"Of course," she said warmly, realizing that his aloofness stemmed from him fearing that he'd let her down. She put an arm around his shoulder. "More than ever, in fact, seeing as how you both refused to give anything up in prison." She lowered her voice. "I heard what they did to you."

"I'm sorry," Noble said. "I feel like such a fool having gotten caught like that. I promise it will never happen again."

Léon asked Tringa to show him the transmission room while she and Noble went to Navarre's former office, which was still in disarray from when it had been searched.

"How's your cough?" she asked Noble. "I was told you were spitting blood in prison. Perhaps you should rest a bit before resuming your duties."

"Rest? You know perfectly well that I shall never voluntarily take a rest. At any rate, I've had plenty of involuntary rest these past months. I'm ready to work like hell again, especially after what happened to Schaerrer."

"You heard."

"News gets around in prison, just like anywhere else." Noble straightened a pile of papers on the desk. "And speaking of which, I'd watch Tringa if I were you. The boy is soft as butter."

"But you know I have an iron hand."

Léon reappeared. "Are you ready to go? We shouldn't stay too long here—it might be dangerous."

Noble's eyes narrowed as he looked from her to Léon. As she went to hug him, Noble whispered in her ear, "I hope it's still *you* at the helm of Alliance."

She broke the embrace, nodding at him emphatically. "I'll see you in Marseille as soon as you get this business with the Deuxième Bureau figured out."

After Pau, she and Léon headed for Tarbes to call on the couple who had sheltered her that fateful time after the raid.

The husband—Marie-Madeleine recalled his name was Mathéo—answered the door.

"We've come about her papers," Léon said, gesturing toward Marie-Madeleine.

"I'm not sure what you are talking about." Mathéo moved so that his body was blocking the entrance to the hallway.

Léon held up his clenched fist. "Her papers. The ones she left in the coal cellar."

"Oh, right, those papers. We thought they might be important and so we gave them to a friend for safekeeping."

"What friend?" Marie-Madeleine demanded.

"He's a Jewish friend. We put them in a strongbox at his villa."

"Where is this friend of yours?" Léon raised his hand a little higher and Mathéo backed up, still holding onto the door handle.

"He's out of town at the moment." Mathéo's eyes shifted from Marie-Madeleine to Léon, landing on his tightened fist. "But don't you worry, he'll return soon. We'll let you know the second he does so you can retrieve the papers."

"Now wait a minute," Léon stepped closer to Mathéo, but he slammed the door in their faces.

Léon reached out to knock again, but Marie-Madeleine put her hand on his arm to stop him. "There's no use."

"The whole story sounds fishy."

"I know." Marie-Madeleine's fingers tingled from where she had made contact with Léon's body. "Let's just get the train back to Marseille."

CHAPTER 21

FEBRUARY 1942

A few days after Marie-Madeleine and Léon returned from their trip, she was walking down a street in Marseille when her brother-in-law, Georges, came running up to her.

She started to greet him, but he grasped her shoulders to shake her instead.

"Who is ASO 43?" Spit flew out of his mouth. "Who is PLU 122?"

ASO 43 was Jean Boutron's code name, and PLU 122 was Bishop, the treasurer. As if a bolt of lightning struck her, Marie-Madeleine instantaneously grasped that the Tarbes files had fallen into the wrong hands. She knew Georges had remained an ardent supporter of Pétain and had ties to the new government and the Surveillance du Territoire. Someone had undoubtedly told him about the files. "Does Vichy have my papers?"

"Yes, they've got them. They've been hunting you for months and they know everything, including that you traveled to Madrid in a way that makes the Marshal look foolish." Georges finally dropped his hands. "Have you gone mad?"

Marie-Madeleine's mind was on her agents. "What about ASO 43 and PLU 122?"

"They are expected to be snatched up at any moment."

"No."

"Indeed." He grabbed her arm and pulled her down the street. "For once, you pig-headed creature, you are going to do what I say."

"Where are you taking me?"

"Vichy."

She planted her feet firmly on the sidewalk. "You are handing me over to the police?"

"It's better to turn yourself in than wait for them to arrest you in Marseille."

"Those papers aren't really incriminating. They are just a log of transmissions and some names."

"They are agent code names for a Resistance network, and they are in your handwriting!" He yanked her forward. "The police now know that Gavarni is just a minor character and that you are not. They hoped to trace you through your friends who were freed from the Pau prison, but they seem to have already disappeared. After inquiring around the area, they found some people in Tarbes who, for some reason, were holding onto papers of yours."

"I knew it." A horrid feeling of guilt washed over her. If Boutron and Bishop were arrested, it would be her fault. The guilt turned to anger at Georges, who, after all these years, was so willing to deliver her to the enemy. "Well, I suppose you're making their job that much easier," she hissed at him. "If you take me to Vichy, they are sure to lock me up."

"No, they won't. I've made arrangements—Commandant Rollin is a friend of mine and I've managed to convince him that you are incapable of the deceit they are accusing you of. He's promised a 48-hour truce if you go to his office and explain yourself."

"But how do we know he will keep his promise?"

"I will ensure that he does. I'm giving you my word of honor: if things go wrong, I'll help you get away."

She stopped again. Georges's word counted for a lot, but not even he could stand up to the French police. There was only one man she trusted to aid her in a situation like this. "I need two hours to arrange things before I leave."

"Marie-Madeleine—"

"Two hours. After that, you can put the rope around my neck." She held out her hand. "It's time for you to take *my* word."

He sighed heavily as he shook her hand. "Two hours."

Marie-Madeleine went straight to the vegetable shop. Luckily Rivière was in the back room, bent over his books. She sent someone to fetch Léon at once. While she waited, she paced nervously up and down the room as Rivière eyed her warily. He didn't ask questions, however, knowing she'd explain in her own time.

"What is it?" Léon asked breathlessly when he arrived.

"Sit down," she told him. She gulped a glass of water before telling them what had transpired on the street that morning.

When she was finished, Léon cursed. "We've got to get you out of town."

"No. Boutron is due to return from Madrid at any hour, carrying intelligence from London that was too large to transmit. We have to warn him."

"We can do that without you," Léon insisted.

"The only way to save the network is for me to submit to the interrogation. They already know about Boutron and Bishop. It's only a matter of days before they get to the rest of you. Somehow I have to throw them off the trail."

Léon looked at Rivière. "Alert both Boutron and Bishop and then send a message to London. They too should be informed about what is happening."

CHAPTER 22

FEBRUARY 1942

Marie-Madeleine shifted uncomfortably next to Georges on the train to Vichy. A deep sense of remorse had settled over her like a thick, black fog. They had just reformed the network after the November disasters. And now, thanks to her own negligence, it was about to be obliterated again.

Like she'd been doing the past few hours, she mentally went over what she could remember about the records. She was almost positive that they contained only code names and symbols, but how long would it take the police to connect them to her boys?

She shut her eyes, thinking about her agents being hunted. Instead of seeing people, she saw animals—all different kinds, from an ant to a lion—fleeing from the police across a wide, green plain. In the next instant, they were trapped in cages, away from any human contact.

She opened her eyes to see Georges beside her, snoring softly. With his tall frame, he could be a giraffe. She realized that, rather than using numbers for code names, she could use animals. The new wave of recruits she'd find as soon as she got out of this mess would represent a veritable jungle. Or better yet, Noah's Ark. And just as the animals aboard the ark had been rescued from a certain fate, the members of Alliance would survive and prosper.

Noble, with his fierce loyalty, would be Tiger. The forger Siegrist, the burly one from the Cat's lair with his prominent ears, would be Elephant. Rivière would be Wolf. One by one, she mentally assigned the Alliance members to their representative animal code names. Léon's airmen recruits would be birds, and the radio operators, fledglings. The agents who watched over the ports would be fish.

And what about her? She closed her eyes once more. Right now she felt like a hedgehog, curled up in defense, its spiky quills erect.

As the train stopped, she caught sight of Léon, who had insisted on following her to Vichy. He stood up from the cramped seat and stretched his body out in the aisle, revealing his lean, muscular form, before meeting her gaze. His piercing eyes and commanding presence were reminiscent of a watchful bird of prey gliding effortlessly above the mountaintops. In a flash, Léon's new code name came to her: Eagle.

Commandant Rollin was a short, stocky man with graying hair. "So you want to kill the admiral," he growled by way of greeting.

"What are you talking about?" she snapped.

The desk in his office was cluttered with stacks of papers that looked as if they might topple over at any moment. Georges took a seat in the more comfortable-looking chair, but Marie-Madeleine refused to sit down.

Rollin handed her the top piece of paper from the highest pile. It was obviously a photostat taken from one of the notebooks she'd stored at Tarbes. It had been enlarged, the words, "Darlan must die," magnified as if by a microscope. It was Noble's handwriting and Marie-Madeleine recalled how it had been his idea to murder Admiral Darlan.

She laughed loudly, trying to exude more confidence than she felt. Georges rudely pushed the chair at her so she had no choice but to sit.

"You want to kill the admiral," Rollin repeated. "And here you are, laughing your head off, while the Admiral is too terrified to sleep at night. Do you care to explain yourself?"

"You've already enlarged the copy," she said, pointing. "Surely you can see that is not in the same penmanship as the rest." She picked up another photostat from the stack. "This is my handwriting: you can see there are more swirls on the letters. And," she waved her hand over the other copies, "these are all in the same script."

"We know," Rollin admitted. "And trust me, we've called in experts. But whose writing is it?"

Marie-Madeleine set her purse on the floor, stalling for time. She mustn't admit it was Noble's. Finally the reasoning came to her—the fortune teller, Madame Paupière, who'd been living in her brother's apartment in Paris, had once mentioned Darlan's name to her. "It was a clairvoyant's. They were predicting the death of Darlan, but, as you can see, it didn't come true."

"A clairvoyant?" The doubt was obvious in Rollin's voice.

"She lives in the Occupied Zone. In Paris, to be precise." Marie-Madeleine crossed her fingers at her side, hoping he wouldn't ask for a name.

"Paris," Georges repeated. He and Rollin exchanged a glance.

Rollin scratched his nose. "You know perfectly well we don't like to deal with the police in the Occupied Zone."

Actually, that was news to Marie-Madeleine, which she stored in her mental vault, wondering if she could exploit it someday.

He picked up the paper. "Our experts seemed to think this was a man's handwriting."

"Well, she is a clairvoyant. Maybe it was a spirit that dictated this to her. A male one."

"But why would she send this to you?"

"She sends me all the prophecies that have to do with government officials. I usually throw them right into the trash, but I kept this one for some reason. You never know…" She shrugged for good measure.

"You see," Georges leaned forward to address Rollin. "Clairvoyants and prophecies. I told you it would be nothing to make a fuss over."

Rollin picked up his phone and dialed. After a brief pause, he barked into the receiver, "Tell the Admiral he shouldn't be concerned about the death threat. I will explain it all to him later, but there is no need to worry." He hung up the phone. "For the moment, anyway." He dug into his desk drawer to pull out a pack of cigarettes, which he offered to her and Georges.

Her brother-in-law accepted one eagerly, but she waved the pack away.

Rollin lit his cigarette. "Someday when we have more time, I'd like to hear more about this clairvoyant of yours."

He'd forgotten to ask for her name. Marie-Madeleine breathed a sigh of relief, not caring that it was laced with tar smoke.

"But now we must talk about the pending arrest of ASO 43. It's Jean Boutron, isn't it?"

Marie-Madeleine's relief quickly disappeared. "No. ASO 43 is indeed a Frenchman living in Spain, but it is not Boutron."

Rollin flicked his cigarette into the ashtray. "So you do know Boutron, then."

"Of course. He used to sail with my father." The lies were coming even easier now.

He stared at her for a long time. She steeled herself to keep her expression neutral. "Then who is ASO 43?" he asked finally.

She shook her head. "I'm not here to reveal names. I came here to see if there was a way that we could work together—we've been in dire need of true patriots in Vichy."

"Did you think we were *not* patriots? We are far greater patriots than anyone. You people, with your incoherent networks, are a nuisance. I long to get rid of the Germans as much as you do, but believe me, Britain won't help us."

Marie-Madeleine threw up her hands. "Well, no, they can't help us now. Your police have seized all of our transmitters."

Rollin picked up another paper. "What did you go to Madrid for? I don't think it was for the bull fights."

Marie-Madeleine started to deny that she traveled to Spain, but Rollin waved her off. "We'll continue this tomorrow." He checked his watch before nodding to himself. "I have to interrogate your friend Mesnard. He is at least helpful."

Mesnard was Bishop. So they had indeed found out the real identity of PLU 122. Rollin continued to peer at Marie-Madeleine curiously, though she refused to give any sign that she recognized the name.

"Don't worry," he said finally. "The Admiral is going to dispatch Mesnard to Algeria where he won't pose a threat to anyone. But…" his voice turned harder. "Your friend the vegetable dealer is going to have a funny sort of awakening tomorrow morning."

Feeling numb, Marie-Madeleine rose from her chair. Poor Rivière would be picked up like one of his vegetables, but instead of testing for ripeness, they would put the squeeze on him in order to extort the network.

Léon was waiting for her in the hotel lobby. After Marie-Madeleine told him what had transpired, he sprinted to the phone to alert Rivière, directing him to dispose of all the papers in the vegetable shop, conceal the remaining transmitters, and tell everyone to lay low.

The next morning, Marie-Madeleine sat as stiff as a stone in Rollin's office as he made cracks about the "vegetable dealer who will soon be cooked."

When she didn't reply, he switched tactics. "Now your friend Boutron, when he was questioned, gave up everything. So who is lying, you or him?"

The remark failed to hit its target—she knew Boutron would never talk. "Bring us face to face and you'll see for yourself."

Rollin strolled to the coat rack and put his hat on, once again surprising her with his unpredictable behavior.

"Are we going to see Boutron now?"

"No." He shrugged on his coat. "You're coming to my house in the country to have lunch with my wife and me."

"What are you talking about?"

"My wife is dying to meet you." He turned to Georges, who had been uncharacteristically silent during the past exchange. "I know you advised me that your sister-in-law was stubborn, but my gosh, she's worse than a mule."

Marie-Madeleine really couldn't figure Rollin out, but decided his proposal was preferable to sitting in that hard chair, undergoing interrogation.

Rollin's wife, Odelie, had large, brown eyes and a faded prettiness. After pumping Marie-Madeleine's hand several times, she told her she appreciated the sacrifices Marie-Madeleine and her friends were making. "And my husband better leave you all in peace, or else…" Odelie gave Rollin a stern look.

He sheepishly pulled at his collar. "We don't aim to defeat your organization, we are simply trying to put you in a position to serve France."

Marie-Madeleine folded her arms across her chest. "You claim that you are arresting us in order to help us?"

He shrugged. "I had no choice: my colleagues were aware of your operations—you weren't exactly discreet about it." He motioned for Marie-Madeleine to follow him along the garden path while Odelie and Georges made small talk by the gate.

"Your police in Pau set a trap for Navarre," Marie-Madeleine stated bitterly.

Rollin's mouth turned down and for a moment she thought he actually looked ashamed. "That also was Navarre's own doing."

"And now Navarre is gone."

"But you are here, Marie-Madeleine. And I'm going to protect you the best I can."

"You are going to protect me?"

"I'm going to try. I, too, feel as if I'm dancing with the noose."

"What do you mean?"

"My police force is not the only one in Vichy—Darlan has a unit of his own. If they captured you, there's nothing I could do to ensure your safety."

Feeling more mule than hedgehog at that moment, Marie-Madeleine didn't want to submit to Rollin. "I won't accept a thing from you while my friends are still in prison. Free Lucien Vallet now."

"Trust me, I've been working on it. But when they are released, tell them to join the Deuxième Bureau if they want to carry on the fight. The bureau urgently needs men with their level of expertise."

She waved her hand dismissively. "They can have Gavarni. He has conned us completely."

It was Rollin's turn to act contemptuous. "Rubbish. You must receive handsome sums from the British—the eighty thousand francs he gave us couldn't have been a drop in the bucket."

Marie-Madeleine tried to hide her shock. Gavarni had only given them a fraction of the money he'd had in his possession.

As she was trying to figure out what Gavarni could have done with the rest of the two million francs, Georges joined them, asking Rollin if he had told her yet.

"Told me what?" Marie-Madeleine demanded.

Georges put both of his hands on her shoulders. "You've already contributed more than your share. Now it's time to focus on your children." He paused, as if expecting a thank you, but after she didn't reply, he continued, "I'll accompany you to the Côte d'Azur tomorrow." The firmness in his voice left no room for argument.

She knew her work was not yet finished, but a few weeks of staying under the radar couldn't hurt. Besides, she was desperate to see Christian and Beatrice again. "Fine."

When they returned to Rollin's office, an officer stopped in to say that Boutron and Rivière were in separate interrogation rooms.

"May I see them?" Marie-Madeleine asked Rollin. Once again he astonished her by nodding.

She went to Boutron's room first. The look on his weathered face was so forlorn that it nearly brought tears to her eyes. She sat next to him and patted his hand. "Why didn't you deny everything?"

"The Vichy police probably saved my life." His voice was hushed. "As I left Madrid, I noticed I was being followed by men in civilian clothes."

"Abwehr agents."

Boutron nodded. "They were waiting for their opportunity to capture me, so I figured it would be less dangerous to surrender here."

Now it was his turn to touch her hand. "Don't worry, everything is all right in regard to Madrid. I didn't say anything about your adventure in the mail bag."

"Rollin is going to try to send you to Switzerland, but we will rescue you. Bishop is being sent to Algeria." She decided to omit Georges's demand that she go back to the Côte d'Azur.

Boutron buried his head in the crook of his arm. "All our hard work…"

"Is going to continue. Be patient: you'll be back on the job in no time. And so will Bishop." *And so will I.*

Boutron didn't reply, and in the silence, someone could be heard shouting. Marie-Madeleine drew in a shaky breath when she realized it was Rivière.

She moved closer to the wall and was able to catch snippets of what he was saying. "I only knew Madame… through Mesnard. She lent me a little money… vegetable business."

The responding voice was too low for her to discern.

"Resistance? Heavens no." There was something about Vichy and Gavarni, and then Rivière fell silent.

She was so focused on trying to hear that the sound of the door being thrown open startled her and she jumped in her chair.

It was Rollin. He looked from the sullen Boutron to Marie-Madeleine. "Do you mind coming with me, madame? We have some further things to discuss."

She laid a hand on Boutron's shoulder as she left the room.

As soon as Rollin shut the door to his office, he asked her what identity she'd like to adopt.

"What about Rivière?"

"We're done with him. Predictably, he had nothing to say. Apparently not even our pressure was enough to cook the vegetable man properly. He'll be returning to Marseille tonight."

Marie-Madeleine nodded with approval. "Since you offered to protect me, I'm quite happy with my own identity, thank you."

Rollin gestured for her to sit down. "I don't think you understand—I've been bombarded with phone calls about you from Darlan's parallel police department. Remember what I said would happen if they arrested you. At the very least, you need a genuine ID card with a false name."

She sighed. "Fine."

He called in one of his officers and she dictated to him, "Claire de Bacqueville, born in Shanghai…" The name had been Marie-Madeleine's maternal grandmother's.

After the officer left, Rollin walked Marie-Madeleine to the front door of the station. "Keep me informed on how you are getting along."

"And you will send the order to free the people remaining in prison?"

"It might take a little longer for Vallet, but you have my word."

She turned to shake his hand. "Thank you."

He tipped his cap toward her as she left.

Outside, the sun was shining and Marie-Madeleine felt warm. To a certain extent, Rollin had earned her trust, and, for now at least, the network was secure.

As she walked down the sidewalk away from the station, she crossed paths with a man strolling in the opposite direction. He looked familiar, though as she got closer, he pulled his coat collar up and readjusted his hat to cover his face.

"Gavarni!" She refrained from shoving him as he tried to pass her.

He took his hat off, looking sheepish. "Madame. I've been searching everywhere for you. Things have worsened since I last saw you: Rivière, Bishop, and Boutron have all been arrested."

"Yes, I know. I just came from Commandant Rollin's office. It seems I've followed in your footsteps."

Gavarni's face, already pale, took on a sickly green hue. "You've talked to Rollin?"

"Indeed. He told me how much money you'd offered. I'm not sure what you did with the rest of it, but at this point it doesn't matter." She continued on her way, her heels clicking on the sidewalk.

"What about the network?" he called after her.

"It's still on, but you're out," she said without stopping.

CHAPTER 23

MARCH 1942

True to his word, Georges accompanied her to the Côte d'Azur, though he didn't stay long. His parting advice was to watch herself around Léon Faye.

"Léon?" she asked, confused.

"Yes. I saw Faye wandering around Vichy, chasing after you. You don't do your reputation any favors, gallivanting about the countryside with another man. You are still married, you know." Georges had not known Édouard well, but clearly he still had old-fashioned values, war or no war.

"You don't have to worry about Léon."

He grunted instead of replying.

Spring in Nice was the perfect blend of warmth and cool breezes, which made the palm trees lining the cobalt Mediterranean appear as if they were dancing. Marie-Madeleine enjoyed an idyllic few days frolicking with her children in the garden, the sweet scent of blooming flowers filling the air.

Not everything went as smoothly as planned, however. Despite Commandant Rollin's best efforts, he was unable to release Lucien

Vallet and the other agents still languishing in Fresnes Prison outside of Paris. Noble wanted to organize an escape, but after exploring the outside of the expansive building, with its towering gray walls, he decided only an armored tank could charge such a fortress.

There were other ways to communicate with their boys inside, however. Their families managed to convince the guards to let them deliver care packages to the prisoners. They contained clean underwear, food, and the occasional chocolate, courtesy of British Intelligence. The prisoners sent their soiled laundry back, along with a few tiny scraps of paper on which were scribbled messages.

Only Marie-Madeleine and MI6 knew Lucien's code so Noble traveled to Nice. He arrived as she was relaxing in the garden one day and handed her Lucien's latest messages.

She quickly translated them and then set her pencil down with a sigh. "They all end in the word, 'hungry'."

"It means the Gestapo are hungry for intel." Noble picked up the pencil and then put it down again. "The others say they were also interrogated."

"Were they beaten?"

"Yes." After a moment he added, "I think the Germans know more about our network than we know ourselves."

"But how is that possible? Are the boys giving up that much detail?"

"No, I don't think so. I think it's Bla."

"Bla? The radio operator?" Marie-Madeleine hadn't heard the name of the strange fellow who'd parachuted into France for months.

"He's been approaching the families of our imprisoned men, trying to get information for some reason." He reached out to stroke a rose petal. "Are you going to be able to communicate with London from here?"

Nice was beautiful, a pleasant resting spot, but Marie-Madeleine had been chafing to get back to work. "Yes. I've been thinking that we need to decentralize the network, anyway, and give the local sectors more autonomy. Not to mention, I've thought of new code names." She went on to tell him her idea of the animal names.

"So we're about to spring back as a menagerie."

"Indeed. You will be henceforth known as 'Tiger.'"

He fluffed his normally well-groomed mustache so that he looked more tiger-like. "If I understand this new layout correctly, there will be a lot more traveling."

"Indeed," she repeated.

"Well, no matter how much you bristle, Hedgehog, you'll always be 'little one' to me." He gave a soft growl. "So now I'm off to Marseille to report to Léon… Eagle, and then back to Paris." He picked the rose from its stem and handed it to Marie-Madeleine. "Don't worry about the Occupied Zone, little one. I'm on Bla's trail and we'll soon figure out what his game is."

Though Marie-Madeleine herself was impatient to leave the Côte d'Azur, the evening after Noble left, Beatrice fell to the ground while playing and cried out in pain.

Marie-Madeleine wasted no time in taking her to see the best surgeon in the area, who worked at a clinic in Toulouse.

Dr. Charry confirmed that Beatrice had a congenital hip displacement and would need surgery. Marie-Madeleine convinced him to schedule it as soon as possible.

Luckily, the surgery went fine and Marie-Madeleine was allowed to stay in Beatrice's oversized room as she convalesced.

Duty, and London were calling, but Marie-Madeleine could never leave her daughter in so much pain. She did, however, have the idea to set up an office in the hospital room, and, while Beatrice was sleeping, she set about redesigning the entire organization. First, she created a list of the sectors from strongest to weakest, and plotted ways to exploit the most robust ones and shore up the weaker units with fresh recruits. She also developed a plan to establish new sections in Bordeaux, Brest, and Strasbourg.

She usually hid the maps and organizational charts behind the many dressers in Beatrice's hospital room before the doctors or nurses came in, though one day she didn't have time to conceal what she'd been working on. Dr. Charry looked curiously at the piles of paperwork on either side of her chair. "Are you writing a book?"

Grateful for the excuse, Marie-Madeleine cheerily replied that she was. "I'm still in the research stage."

His eyes zoned in on a hand drawn map of the Alsace region. "Is there anything I can do to help?"

"As a matter of fact, yes. I was hoping, now that Beatrice is well enough, we could receive more visitors."

"Visitors? Will they be coming from different parts of the country?"

"Yes," she admitted, knowing Dr. Charry had caught on. He was a surgeon, after all.

"I see." Dr. Charry shut the door and walked closer to her. "I'd like to be of service to you, as well."

"You've already done so much for my daughter."

His voice was low as he insisted, "But I want to help France."

She stood up and put a hand on his shoulder. "I understand. But the work you do as a surgeon is even more important to the citizens of France than our work."

He gave her a solemn nod. "Thank you, madame."

CHAPTER 24

JUNE 1942

After eight weeks in the hospital, Beatrice was finally released. It broke Marie-Madeleine's heart to have to leave her so soon after she'd gotten better, but she had to get back to Marseille.

"Maman, please don't go."

"You know I have to, *mon amour*." She held her little girl tightly, burying her face in her soft hair and inhaling her scent, trying to etch every detail of her into memory.

When Christian joined them, the trio huddled together in a tight embrace, the tears falling fast and warm down Marie-Madeleine's cheeks as she promised to find a way back to them as soon as she could.

Her heart again feeling like it was being ripped apart by leaving her family, Marie-Madeleine forced herself to return to Marseille. Her first stop was Léon's house on the Corniche, a stunning roadway that ran parallel to the coastline, offering spectacular views of the ocean below.

She took a seat in the surprisingly well-decorated living room across from Léon as a servant entered, carrying a tray of coffee.

"This is Mastiff," Léon told her. "He runs our mess. You look like you could definitely use something to warm you up."

Marie-Madeleine took a sip of real coffee before setting the cup on the lacquer table. "It's nice to have familiar comforts, but what about intelligence?"

He got up from the couch. "I have your mail for you."

She followed him to the desk on which was piled messages from London and information from the sectors. She flipped through them, noting the new developments in her head. Clearly Léon had been handling the day-to-day operations with his usual efficiency. Despite the ongoing efforts to rebuild the Paris sector, the network had successfully established sectors in nearly every other region and now included more than a thousand members.

She held up the most recent questionnaire. "I take it this has been answered?"

Léon nodded. "Rivière and his crew are remarkably thorough when it comes to monitoring the Boches' shipping endeavors in and out of Marseille, giving the RAF substantial targets in terms of trains and truck convoys."

She set the mail down. "By the way, what's the reaction to the new code names?"

"They've caught on famously: people are using nothing else now, Hedgehog."

She gave him a shy smile.

"And of course, I am a big fan of mine." He puffed out his chest. "What part of my magnificent persona made you settle on Eagle?"

She didn't want to flatter him too much. "It was more how far, and how quickly, you've traveled for the network than any particular personality trait."

For some reason, this seemed to deflate him. "Right. Well, Noble's due to arrive any minute. Why don't you try to nab some sleep and I'll let you know when he arrives?"

But Noble burst into her bedroom a few minutes later without any announcement, shouting, "Bla's the traitor!"

"How do you know?" she asked sleepily, sitting up.

"He's had the whole network in Normandy arrested." He tossed another message from Lucien on the bed. "I'm sure Vallet will confirm our suspicions."

Léon, who'd followed him into the room, peered over Marie-Madeleine's shoulder as she decoded the message. When she'd finished, she read it aloud:

Last interrogation made me certain treachery Bla STOP I've been handed the trans set which had been delivered to him after my arrest STOP Pray for us regards hunger END

She carefully set the message on the bedside table. "I guess the Boches don't realize their prisoners can still communicate with the outside world. Luckily Lucien recognized the transmission set and put two and two together."

"I propose that Noble heads to Paris right now to fix that bastard," Léon said.

Something told her that MI6 wouldn't accept the fact that the first man they'd parachuted into Occupied France was a traitor. "No, hold on. We should gather more evidence."

"Evidence?" Noble repeated. He pointed to Vallet's message. "What more evidence do you need?"

"Not for us. For London."

A few days later a message from MI6 came in, stating that it seemed Bla indeed was working for the Gestapo, and that they were issuing execution orders for him.

Noble was dumbfounded. "Can't British Intelligence kill off their own men? Finding Bla now that he's been exposed is like looking for a needle in a haystack."

Léon rubbed his forehead. "He knows everything about everyone. Me, you, Marie-Madeleine…"

"And Bouvet," Marie-Madeleine cut in. Bouvet was the lawyer who'd been providing Bla with money to run his operations.

Noble picked up his bag. "I'll head to Paris now to warn the lawyer."

. . .

Two days later, Marie-Madeleine found out that sixteen of her agents, including Bouvet, had been arrested and were joining Vallet and the others in Fresnes Prison. Her message to Major Richards was simple: *The damage is done.*

His reply suggested that she reestablish contact with Bla with the intention of 'taking him out.'

Bishop, who'd returned from Algeria courtesy of Commandant Rollin, offered to do the job. The task seemed a bit sinister for the always chipper Bishop, but he was resolute in his willingness to do it. He traveled to Lyons and waited for over three hours, but Bla never showed up. Two Abwehr agents waited on a bench across from Bishop and attempted to seize him as he was leaving. He managed to outrun them, but the call was close enough to worry Marie-Madeleine.

CHAPTER 25

AUGUST 1942

After Bishop's failure to take out Bla, Léon sent information with Bla's description to all of Alliance. Occasional sightings of him in Pau and Toulouse would surface, but nothing concrete. The revived network picked up steam, and by the late summer of 1942, the Bla affair had nearly been forgotten.

Since returning from Madrid, Marie-Madeleine had taken to heart Richards' advice about ensuring that the restored network would last. The treacheries of Red and Bla prompted her to thoroughly verify the legitimacy of any new recruit, although she made an exception to Léon's suggestions, such as Colonel Kauffman, a kindly old man who was nearly deaf, and Jack Tar, who, as a pilot, had once reported to Léon and was now his adjutant.

While Rivière continued to head the local sector out of the vegetable shop, the official national Alliance headquarters was established at Léon's flat on the Corniche. In addition to forging a wide variety of documents for the new recruits, Ernest Siegrist, the policeman from the Cat's Lair, was in charge of safety for the entire complex, which now housed twelve letter boxes, transmitter sites, and hiding spots, and a new drop box located at a bar on rue Saint Charles. Beaver, another one of Léon's contacts, owned the bar. Like

Siegrist, he was a former policeman, and looked the part with his barrel-shaped body and enormous hands.

Léon's latest invention, the Corniche code, was developed for communicating with the Occupied Zone. Each agent was given a unique keyword to embed a secret message in the text of an innocuous interzonal card. Over time, this became the standard method and significantly reduced the need for agents to travel back and forth across the demarcation line.

Of course, sometimes personal communication was still necessary. Noble's news from Paris regarding the agents still in Fresnes Prison was bleak. As soon as he arrived in Marseille, he handed Marie-Madeleine a message from one of their men, Edmond Poulain, which had been tucked away in the hem of a soiled piece of cloth.

I shall certainly be condemned to death and I have only one request: save the girl I love. Please don't let anything happen to her STOP I entrust her to you STOP

Farewell

Unable to form any words, Marie-Madeleine looked at Noble.

"His fiancée is here," he replied to her unasked question. "I thought it better to bring her straight away. She's a bit reckless—she climbed up the trees to try to catch a glimpse of our friends in their cells and shouted at them to cheer up. One day she even managed to get into Fresnes to see them through the peepholes."

Marie-Madeleine's lips formed a tiny smile. "By all means, send her in."

The girl entered the room, her spine straight and her cork-soled shoes barely making a sound on the tile floor. She tossed her long blonde hair aside as she addressed Marie-Madeleine. "Look, madame, I only agreed to accompany Tiger here so that I can offer my services. Please don't ask me to go into hiding."

The girl, with her airy cotton skirt and unyielding attitude, reminded Marie-Madeleine of herself. "What is your name?"

"Monique Bontinck."

"Your code name will be Ermine. Welcome to Alliance."

. . .

Monique's skills as an agent became quickly evident, and Marie-Madeleine appointed her as her personal courier.

Determined to match the strength of her friends still behind bars, Monique volunteered for any mission, no matter the risk. When Marie-Madeleine questioned her about the potential danger, Monique shrugged it off.

"Hedgehog, I have to do it. The boys are exhausted and are in need of rest."

A few days after she started working for Alliance, Monique arrived with a rather cherubic young man. "He came from London," she announced.

"London?" Marie-Madeleine inspected him more closely. He didn't look much older than eighteen, though his posture exuded a confidence well beyond his years. "Are you with MI6?"

"No. The Free French."

Léon looked up from his work. "You are in with de Gaulle?"

"Yes. I trained in England and was supposed to meet up with a Free French Resistance group, but when I landed by parachute, it seems…" He blushed as he looked down. "I got lost."

"He's been in hiding at Dr. Zimmern's house," Monique added.

Marie-Madeleine was aware that Dr. Zimmern was a Jewish man taking refuge in Marseille who, despite the danger to his family and himself, had also offered his cottage for use as a safehouse.

"Monique mentioned that you might be able to help me find some work." The young man's air of indifference seemed too contrived to be genuine, making it clear that he wanted to be seen as someone he was not.

"We do not know anyone with the Free French," Léon told him.

"Then maybe you can employ me—I'm a radio operator, but I've also been trained to gather naval intelligence. My destination, where I should have been months ago, is on the Atlantic coast."

Léon glanced at Marie-Madeleine with raised eyebrows. She knew what he was thinking: Schaerrer's death left them without a reliable means of obtaining intel on the movements of German submarines.

. . .

Although Marie-Madeleine had initially been unsure about accepting an agent who wasn't meant for Alliance, British Intelligence soon authenticated his account and expressed their satisfaction in discovering him after he'd been presumed lost. With his golden hair and wide blue eyes, the young man looked like a Little Lord Fauntleroy, but he chose the rather incongruous code name of Mandrill, stating that he 'loved the little monkeys with the blue, red, and white faces.'

Now fully convinced of his abilities, Marie-Madeleine dispatched him to Sarlat to be installed by Colonel Kauffman as the leader of the Bordeaux sector.

To accommodate all the new agents arriving in and leaving Marseille, Marie-Madeleine found a large villa named La Pinède, which was only a short tram ride away from the center of the city. Situated on a hill and surrounded by gardens, it was the perfect place to run the network. She turned the drawing room on the first floor into a general office from which Ernest Siegrist ran his forgery studio and the dining room was converted into a radio transmission hub for Tringa. Léon was given an office/bedroom of his own on the second floor, next to the room Marie-Madeleine shared with Monique.

One night, with only a faint light from a lamp to guide her, Marie-Madeleine worked to decipher a transmission from London. Disbelieving what she herself had just written, she picked up the message to peer at it:

Richards to POZ strictly confidential STOP Have learned heroic escape of General Giraud STOP Repeat Giraud STOP Believed to have fled to Lyons STOP Would be most happy if you would agree to contact him to discover his intentions STOP Would he serve again STOP If so where END

She immediately got up and went to Léon's room. Her first instinct was to barge right in, but she paused in front of the door before deciding to knock gently.

He was, predictably, seated at his own desk. His eyebrows raised when he caught sight of the expression on her face. "What is it?"

She shoved the message under his nose. He whistled softly after reading it.

"What kind of service do they want Giraud to do?" she asked. Giraud was a military commander who had been captured by the Germans in 1940. He'd managed to escape to Switzerland, but had recently returned to France and was currently making his opposition to the armistice well known. "I assume it's political?"

"Most likely, yes,"

"You know I don't want to get involved in any politics. Besides, it's the final outcome that matters." She sat on Léon's bed. "Do you think that Churchill wants to set up a rival to de Gaulle?" Mandrill had told her about the feud between de Gaulle's Free French organization and MI6.

"Could be." There was a quizzical glint in Léon's eyes, but his tone was resolute. "It isn't our job to think, just to act. Though if the Allies are requesting Giraud, I'd assume it would be for the North African landing. The African Army is neither Gaullist nor pro-British. They need a French general, and Giraud is well known over there." He nodded to himself. "Can you imagine? The entire world would take notice if the Allies gained a foothold in North Africa."

"Who are we going to get to contact Giraud?"

Léon didn't even stop to think. "Saluki will do it. He's coming to Marseille tomorrow anyway."

Saluki was the Duke of Magenta, a flamboyant young pilot who also happened to boast the most distinguished lineage of any Alliance member. His family, who had a long history of serving France, had been given their title by Louis XV in 1750. His grandfather had been a celebrated war hero and the first president of France's Third Republic, while his great-grandfather had fought alongside the Marquis de Lafayette in the American Revolutionary War. Having encountered the Duke on several occasions prior to the war, Marie-Madeleine was as equally charmed by his wife. A true picture of elegance and nobility, the Duchess demonstrated her mettle by joining the network with her husband.

. . .

Saluki had little trouble arranging a meeting with Giraud, but convincing the anti-British general to correspond with MI6 proved to be a challenge. Giraud ended up offering to become chief of the European Resistance, provided that the British supplied him with enough money and weaponry.

"The chief of the European Resistance!" Marie-Madeleine exclaimed when Léon broke the news to her. "First of all, there is no such organization at that level. And second of all, does he think my job being a minor network leader is easy? The man sounds irrational."

"I know." Léon reached out, as if to put a consoling hand on her arm, but thought better of it and shoved his hands in his pockets. "However, MI6's idea is not irrational. It's just going to take some more convincing."

"What are you saying?"

He squared his shoulders. "I'm done with retail and am now in the wholesale business. We're beyond the Army's Intelligence Service—we're the Intelligence Service's Army."

She opened her mouth to retort, but Léon wasn't finished yet. "Send me to England. I can shed some light on the best approach to take when dealing with Giraud."

Her heart sank unexpectedly. "You want to leave now? We're finally getting somewhere with rebuilding the network."

The quizzical look was back again, for only an instance, before Léon's wide grin wiped it away. "It will take a few weeks to organize my departure. Don't forget, we're still waiting for MI6's 'expert' to teach our boys how to help land Lysanders."

"Maybe this whole Giraud thing will have fizzled out by then."

"Maybe." Léon didn't sound convinced.

CHAPTER 26

SEPTEMBER 1942

With the arrival of the September moon came Arthur Crowley, MI6's expert, who was there to instruct them on the intricate and high-stakes procedures essential for properly receiving Lysanders. By implementing his strategies, Alliance was hoping to avoid relying on parachutes for supplies, not to mention the travel could go both ways: agents would be able to exit France when needed, instead of solely entering from England.

In fact, Crowley's landing more than demonstrated these new advantages when one of the parachutes failed to deploy. Examining the obliterated container, Marie-Madeleine was thankful that the defective chute hadn't been attached to a person.

Crowley was greeted warmly and got right to work leading the so-called reception committee, called the Avia team, which so far was comprised of only one other man, code-named Mahout.

As the balmy summer gave way to a crisp autumn, and the September moon by which Léon was to leave approached, Marie-Madeleine was seized by a growing apprehension. It didn't help one day when, as she was returning from one of her sector inspections, Léon met her at the train station and immediately grabbed her suitcase from her.

"What's going on?" she asked as his free hand clutched her arm.

"Come on," he said, leading her toward a car that was waiting with its engine running.

As the car sped away, she demanded to know what was going on.

"They're after you again," Léon said through gritted teeth. "This time it's the Boches—they've been scouring Paris to track you down and paying visits to some of your relatives."

She sat up, recalling that Jacques had moved back into his apartment in the city a few months ago. "My brother?"

"He's the one who warned us. The Gestapo told him you were another Mata Hari and that you now have a price on your head."

She opened her mouth to say something, but Léon continued, "I know you don't care about your own safety, but I've arranged for Jacques to stay at La Pinède, in my room while I'm gone." He gave her a wry smile. "I'll feel better knowing he's there, looking out for you."

She decided to ignore the faint suggestion of sentiment in his voice. "Has Marseille heated up?"

"Yes. The Boches are disguising themselves as French policemen and are driving around in vans the boys call *gonios*. They are equipped with direction-finding instruments."

Marie-Madeleine gasped. "If they hone into a transmission signal…"

"They can find our hideouts and nab every one of us."

"How long does it take?"

"Our guess is twenty minutes, so I've told all the radio operators to keep their transmissions under 15, and to change frequency as often as possible. And…" His grayish-green eyes focused on hers. "I want you to lay low for a while."

"Not on your life. I certainly don't consider myself another Mata Hari."

"No," he agreed. "To me, you're like Minerva."

Marie-Madeleine accepted the compliment with a shy smile. If Léon wanted to compare her to the Roman goddess of wisdom and war, who was she to object?

He patted her leg in an attempt to bring her back to reality, the heat of his palm radiating through her skirt. "I'll be leaving for London soon, so please be extra careful. If anything happens to you, I won't be able to go."

"Is that so?" She assumed he meant because he'd have to take over the network in the event of her capture, but a part of her wanted him to tell her there was another reason.

Once again his face clouded with an emotion that Marie-Madeleine couldn't interpret, but before he could reply, the car stopped. They had arrived at La Pinède.

Alliance's first official Lysander landing took place in late September. Léon left on this plane, and the next evening, a BBC *message personnel* let Marie-Madeleine know that he was by then safely strolling the streets of London.

She shut the radio off and turned to Monique, who gave her a knowing smile. "He'll be back in a month."

"I'm not worried about him," Marie-Madeleine snapped back.

Monique clearly thought it wise to change the subject. "Come, let's look at the new goods that London sent us."

Denise Centore, the courier who had once complained about the faulty ink, was in the living room, fingering the sheets of paper that had been parachuted in. "It's like silk," she murmured, the flimsy tissue fluttering like a butterfly in her hand. "The gray rats could run their hands all over me and never feel a thing!"

"And here is the latest model." Monique picked up another paper and brought a lighter close to its edge, igniting it in an instant.

"I like to roll my papers into little balls and store them in the false bottom of my handbag," Marie-Madeleine said, still bitter over the loss of her Tarbes records. "They are impossible to find."

As Marie-Madeleine was getting ready for bed, her brother, Jacques came in. He'd spent the day forging documents with Ernest Siegrist.

"Everything go okay with Léon?" Jacques asked.

"Yes. He's probably dining on fish and chips as we speak."

Jacques put on his most posh British accent "Right. Well then, goodnight." At the doorway he turned and paused. "Are you going to be able to sleep?"

She gave him a wide, fake smile. "Of course. Why would you ask?"

He returned the grin. "No reason."

Marie-Madeleine had a hunch that Léon's negotiations regarding Giraud would stir things up, and she wanted to create a branch in Avignon as a safety net in case they needed to flee Marseille for any unforeseen circumstance. Noble had arranged for one of his contacts, Hubert Fourcade, to travel from Paris to meet her in Avignon.

Noble had vouched for Fourcade, but Marie-Madeleine found herself at a loss as to how she could ask the rather unassuming man with kindly brown eyes to take command of a brand-new headquarters.

Fourcade spoke first. "Noble has told me a lot about you, and I have to say, your refusal to simply stand by in the present situation is truly admirable." He rubbed a hand over his neatly-trimmed mustache. "Let me come straight to the point—I can't bear this Hitlerite France anymore. Your dedication has inspired me to seek revenge myself, by fighting."

"Fighting?" she repeated, picturing her as-yet unbuilt Avignon sector already crumbling.

His eyebrows raised. "I heard you have routes for men to get to England."

"They're not exactly my routes." She reigned in her disappointment. "My expertise actually lies more in intelligence gathering."

His warm brown eyes brightened. "I wish I could help you, but I'm not quite cut out for that line of work. My calling is for a different type of battle, and I couldn't forgive myself if I ignored it."

Her disappointment resurfaced—the kind of determination he'd shown was precisely what she looked for in a potential agent. "You really want to go to England?"

"Yes. I want to join up with de Gaulle. All Frenchmen my age should be with him. I regret I couldn't do it sooner, but I was finishing my military service in Marrakesh when the war broke out. My comrades and I were forced to stay on the sidelines as France fell."

"If that's the case, then I can help you."

"I'm not the only one involved in this," he clarified. "I've made a commitment to assist a number of my friends."

"That makes things more difficult. The Lysanders can only take one passenger at a time." As his face fell, Marie-Madeleine continued, "I do have a number of assembly points for getting to Spain."

He stared at her in disbelief, as if she possessed some magical ability to convert pumpkins into submarines. "I feel petty," he said abruptly. "Here you are, risking your life for the cause, and I'm preoccupied with my own concerns."

"It's not a problem."

"I appreciate your offer, but I can't risk endangering your work. I'll find another way out. Incidentally..." He boldly took her hand in his. "Is there anything I can do for you before I leave France?"

"No, but thank you anyway." She released his hand and stood up. "I should get back to Marseille immediately."

"Nonsense. I've borrowed a car to get here, and I'm taking you to lunch at *Le Prieure*."

As she indulged in carrot soup in the restaurant's garden, Marie-Madeleine found temporary relief from her all-consuming fixation on Alliance. Hubert—she couldn't help calling Fourcade by his first name now—told her about the men he'd worked under who were now in with de Gaulle, and they bonded over their mutual deep love for France.

The time flew by. As Hubert was escorting her to the station to catch the last train, he squeezed her hand. "If you were thinking that I could become part of the network..."

"Hubert, you must follow your conscience," she interjected. "I know what it's like if you don't. Join de Gaulle, and good luck to you."

He reached out, as if to brush a stray hair away from her face, but thought better of it. "Wherever I am, Marie-Madeleine, you can always count on me. I'm sure we shall meet again."

The train whistled, and she bade him a final farewell before she boarded the carriage.

As the train pulled away, she glanced out of the window to see Hubert still standing on the platform, lost in thought. She had a feeling that he was right and that someday their paths would indeed cross again.

CHAPTER 27

OCTOBER 1942

The October landing was officially called Operation Vesta. Jean Boutron, who'd been given the code name Bull in honor of his Madrid operations, was slated to depart for Britain on the same plane on which Léon was due to return. Eager to repay Boutron for helping her with her mailbag escapade, Marie-Madeleine had arranged for his release from a guarded boarding house in Switzerland. A doctor, who doubled as an Alliance agent, injected him with a substance that mimicked symptoms of a urinary disease, necessitating his transfer to a hospital, where the nurses were able to facilitate Boutron's escape. He was now staying at an inn not far from the landing ground, keeping a low profile until it was time to go.

Although she had meticulously reviewed the details of Operation Vesta with Mahout a dozen times, she spent the next few nights fluctuating between hopefulness and overwhelming anxiety. The Avia team was supposed to remain on high alert for any police activity in the area, but they were burdened by the need to maintain constant radio surveillance and the multiple bags of mail they had to haul back and forth to the landing ground. What if they were captured?

And then there was the possibility that the Lysander wouldn't arrive. Even after its departure, it could still turn around and head back to England. There was also the risk that the plane and its occupants would be obliterated by anti-aircraft fire.

The first eve of the full moon presented inclement weather conditions, yet Mahout phoned Marie-Madeleine to say that Operation Vesta was still on. She slept more soundly that night than she had in weeks.

Mahout called the next day to say that the Avia team had waited all evening in vain—the plane never arrived.

She spent a bleak day filled with dread, keeping an eye out for the liaison agent who would deliver the message that would confirm Léon's demise.

Indeed, her forehead broke out into a sweat when Rivière walked into La Pinède, his eyes bulging. "Fox has been arrested."

She tried to slow her breathing, to no avail. "What happened?"

"It was Canary who betrayed him."

She sat down in a chair, trying to gather her spinning thoughts. "Canary?" He was the son of an established Boulogne agent and seemed well vetted. Parrot, their chief radio operator, had been the one to bring Canary to Marseille. Recalling Léon's warning, she asked Rivière, "Do you think the police will stop with Fox's arrest or will they continue to close in on us?"

"I'm afraid that Laval's return to power has eroded Commandant Rollin's influence." He put a plump hand on Marie-Madeleine's shoulder. "But of course, thanks to your brother-in-law, Rollin burned all the relevant paperwork on the Gavarni affair. And Fox surely covered up all his tracks. We have nothing to worry about, besides cutting out Canary."

For the next few minutes, they bent their heads together over the dining room table, plotting out any threat to Parrot and his radio headquarters, which now must be relocated.

Suddenly Rivière smacked his forehead. "With all this commotion, I totally forgot... the Avia crew had news of Léon."

She squeezed his forearm before quickly retracting her hand, embarrassed at her own reaction. "What happened to the plane?"

"The foul weather forced it to turn back to England. Apparently on the way back, a German fighter tailed them."

Marie-Madeleine's voice was barely a whisper. "And?"

"The fighter never fired at them, though he was well within range. Maybe he thought the plane was German. They're back in London, but the forecast doesn't look good. At this point, they'll probably have to wait for the next moon."

"Another month?" Despite Rivière's assurances, Marie-Madeleine could not shake her sense of foreboding. Rollin's remarks about the parallel police repeated in her brain. If she were to be called in for questioning again, she would not be let off easily.

As Rivière left, the thought occurred to her that the network was like a hot ember perched on a stack of kindling, where any small misstep would be like a gust of wind, turning it all into a raging inferno.

Would they be able to hold out until Léon's return?

She was still ruminating over all of this when her brother walked into her bedroom. "Hey, sis." He must have sensed from her facial expression that something was bothering her. "What's wrong? It's not Georges again, is it?"

"No. It's Léon."

"Ah, I should have known." Jacques sat down on the bed.

"What's that supposed to mean?"

He raised his eyebrows, clearly thinking of a suitable reply. Finally he said, "It's this fearless leader stuff—"

She was about to counter him when he held up his hand. "Look, I know you are incredibly brave, you always have been, but even the most dauntless person can crumble under the type of pressure you're facing. And who could blame you if you need someone to help shoulder the burden?"

"You are talking about Léon."

"I am indeed."

Was that the real reason she was so upset about the delay in Léon's arrival? Because she needed him to 'help shoulder the burden?'

"Is there anything I can do to help?" Jacques asked, a hush in his usually thunderous voice.

"Yes." She'd been haunted by the possibility that both her and Léon would be captured, or at least incapacitated. In order to ensure the network's survival, it would be necessary to keep track of all of the sectors and transmitters, including the call signs, frequencies of the radios, and transmitting schedules, to pass on to whoever took over. Jacques had neat, meticulous handwriting and could be trusted with sensitive information. Obviously Léon would never approve of such a list, but he wasn't here now to argue over it anyway.

After she explained what she wanted him to do, Jacques nodded. "I will do what you ask if you promise me one thing."

"What's that?"

"Sleep well, for once. I hear you tossing and turning all night."

She gave him a small smile. "I'll try my best."

CHAPTER 28

OCTOBER 1942

The weather improved slightly in the waning moon and Marie-Madeleine requested that Mahout and Crowley go to the landing ground just in case.

"It's still raining," Mahout insisted. "No one is going to fly a plane in conditions like this."

"What if Léon—the Lysander arrives—and no one is there on the ground?"

Grumbling, Mahout finally gave in.

The next morning, Mahout returned to La Pinède with two very large and rather muddy suitcases, which he laid at her feet. "Operation Vesta was fifty percent successful."

"What does that mean? Is Léon—"

"He's here, but Bull didn't leave. I didn't actually think the landing was possible, so I never fetched him from the inn." He glanced at her sheepishly. "Are you upset with me?"

Her face had flushed with relief at Léon's return. "No. There will be other moons." She tried to keep her voice casual. "Where is Léon now?"

"He took a separate trolley car, to lessen the risk in case the Gestapo were watching."

A few hours later, Léon burst through the door, announcing, "Minerva, I've got what you wanted."

Marie-Madeleine had been sitting in the living room, keeping an eye on the door, but even so, was still thrown off as Léon picked up Mahout's discarded suitcases and set them on the coffee table. She swallowed hard. "Is that so?"

He flicked open the locks with ease and then pulled out a couple of envelopes. "They gave us oodles of francs and promised the same amount every month, in addition to as much equipment as we request to be parachuted in."

He peered at her as she came over to stand next to him, speechless. After a moment, he asked if she was displeased.

"Of course not," she snapped back. "Direct contact is always the superior form of communication: it worked for Navarre in Lisbon, me in Madrid, and now you in London."

In the silence that followed her tongue seemed to stop working, and she struggled to find something else to say. Finally she picked up the new questionnaires. "They're doing them as microphotos now. What a remarkable advance."

As Léon started sorting through the first case, he cast a surreptitious glance at her. "Is something wrong?"

"Not necessarily." She filled him in on Fox's arrest and Rivière's suspicions about Canary, though in truth, that was not at all what was bothering her. During his absence she had found herself missing him, and not just because the network needed his presence in France. What she most feared was that *she* needed him. She had always trusted him more than anyone, including Navarre, but now there was an unfamiliar emotion, one she refused to act on for several reasons. For one, they were the leaders of a network who needed them, and two, she was still married.

Just as another spell of awkwardness settled over the pair, Saluki, the Duke of Magenta, arrived. "I hope you got something for General Giraud," he told Léon by way of greeting. He held up a bottle of burgundy and Léon nodded.

"Giraud's ambition to become the head of the Resistance in Europe caught the British off guard," Léon said as the three of them sat down at the dining room table.

"I had a feeling it would," Marie-Madeleine stated, thankful for the distraction. "What did they expect?"

"That he would go to London, naturally. When I arrived, neither Churchill nor de Gaulle were around. Churchill was in Moscow and de Gaulle was somewhere between Cairo and Beirut."

She couldn't keep her mouth from dropping open. "You asked British Intelligence about their whereabouts?"

"Of course. I immediately got the impression that the Giraud problem would not be solved without their presence, especially if the British weren't willing to give Giraud something for his efforts."

"Too bad. Our army comrades will be shattered," Saluki remarked before taking a drink of his wine.

Léon nodded. "I explained this to them, repeatedly—so many times that they discussed it with Churchill after he returned. Kenneth Cohen, with whom I spent a lot of my time, told me that the prime minister was indeed interested in the Giraud affair."

"So Giraud can count on the Allies' full support?" Saluki asked.

"Yes. You can tell Giraud as much, but in return, you'll need to ask him to provide a memorandum for his vision as far as the Resistance goes."

"I guess that means your theory about the Allies needing him to back a landing in North Africa was wrong," Marie-Madeleine commented, secretly wondering why the British had agreed to indulge Giraud's unrealistic visions of grandeur.

"Not so wrong," Léon said under his breath. He turned to Saluki. "Your wine is, as always, excellent." He took a long swig and she decided not to pursue the matter.

Saluki raised his glass. "Let's drink to your return." After they had said their cheers, Saluki asked Léon what London was like.

For the next half hour, Léon recounted his experience, painting a picture of an unoccupied country where daily life existed without the constant threat of the Gestapo's noose. He also talked about a 'sensational' radio operator he'd met, code-named Magpie, who was due to arrive to work with Alliance by the next moon. Léon then gave Saluki a considerable sum of money and the Duke departed for his mission to meet up with Giraud.

After he left, she and Léon sat in silence, avoiding each other's gaze. Finally she asked, "Why were you so cagey about the landing in North Africa?"

"Because they told me to say absolutely nothing about it to anyone except you. Churchill is using his powers of persuasion to convince the Americans to make a landing. All the evidence goes to suggest that, in order for Europe to be liberated, we will need to conquer the enemy on two fronts, one of them being in the south. My impression is that an agreement has been reached on the North African site."

"So what you are really saying is that your long-standing obsession is finally becoming a reality."

He shot her a lopsided grin. "One of my obsessions, at any rate."

"I hate to burst your bubble, but according to Noble, the latest word is that Pétain sent Hitler a telegram proposing that 'France should contribute towards the safeguarding of Europe.' Meaning, if the Allies attempt a landing, the French will be commanded to fire upon them."

"Frenchmen working side by side with the Nazis to defeat the Allies? That would be reprehensible." Léon's face twisted in revulsion. "Have you radioed London to let them know?"

"No. I was too ashamed."

As if by instinct, he reached out to put his hand over hers. His was warm and surprisingly soft, and Marie-Madeleine resisted the urge to snatch her arm away.

He rubbed his thumb over her wrist, sending a jolt of electricity down her spine, as he stated, "I missed working with you."

Marie-Madeleine hadn't realized how badly she'd been wanting to hear him say those words, but they came out so casually that she decided to ignore them. Clearly he missed the action of being in

France, not actually her. She got up from the table. "You must be exhausted."

"You know I don't sleep." He raised his eyebrows, leaving Marie-Madeleine to wonder if he was extending an invitation.

"Goodnight Léon."

"Goodnight Minerva."

CHAPTER 29

OCTOBER 1942

A few mornings after he returned from London, Léon had been out running inspections in the city when he barreled into Marie-Madeleine's office. "Bla is in Marseille."

She stood up, her hands shaking. "How do you know?"

"Crowley. They'd trained in the same radio operator school in London and bumped into each other again at the Marseille station. Bla told him he'd been attached to a network run by a woman but it had been smashed and he had only just escaped arrest. Now he's been wandering about France without a penny and no transmitter, trying to join another organization. Because of all the notices we sent out, Crowley recognized at once that he was the traitor radio operator and arranged to rendezvous with him at a bar on the Rue de Paradis."

"I'll go meet him."

"No. Bla knows you already, but he's never met me."

"Good luck," she called as he turned to leave.

He tipped his hat and gave her his signature lopsided grin.

. . .

While Monique sat coding Tringa's latest transmission, Marie-Madeleine paced the room anxiously, feeling that the impending violence in the middle of Marseille was sure to end badly.

Finally, as the sun fell, Léon arrived back at La Pinède declaring, "I need a drink."

Monique fetched him one. Léon took a gulp and then relayed what had transpired.

Léon had pretended to be a policeman and asked for Bla's identity papers. He handed them over easily since he'd probably already made a deal with the Marseille police. Léon then led him to his house on the Corniche, telling him that the chief wanted to meet with Bla. Once they'd gotten him inside, Léon roared, "We've got you at last," before punching Bla in the face.

"Has he confessed?" Marie-Madeleine asked.

Léon frowned. "No. He refuses to admit anything, claiming that his name is not even Bla, though he's insisting we phone a Gestapo number." He set his drink down. "I was hoping to keep you out of it, Minerva, but I think you're the only one who can get him to talk. He's never met the rest of us."

"I'll come straight away."

"I want to go too," Monique declared. "He's the one who betrayed us in Paris, and now my poor Edmond…" She wiped a tear from her face.

Marie-Madeleine handed her a tissue as Léon fiddled with his coat. "Well, let's get going then," he told them.

There was no mistaking the look of sheer panic that appeared on Bla's clean-shaven face when he caught sight of Marie-Madeleine entering the small bedroom. He coughed into his hands to cover up his shock. "Ah, madame, you are just who I was looking to find in Marseille."

Léon stood behind him and cracked his knuckles. "Should we begin the interrogation?"

"Yes," Marie-Madeleine answered. "But no one is to lay a hand on him." She nodded at Rivière, who had been pointing a gun at the prisoner. "You can wait in the hall with Monique." Rivière gave the gun to

Léon and then left the room with Beaver, who'd been lurking in the corner.

She turned to Bla, who was wearing nondescript trousers and a brown shirt, while a red beret lay on the ground beside him. "Tell me the real reason you are in Marseille," she snapped as she walked toward him.

His eyes, unburdened by his pince-nez, which Léon said had broken when he punched him, widened. "I told you, madame. I was looking for you."

"In order to hand her over to the Abwehr," Léon added bitterly.

Bla tried to look surprised. "I would never."

"Cut it, Bla," Léon said. "We know you are working for the Germans."

He shook his head. "No."

Marie-Madeleine switched tactics. "When was the last time you were in Normandy?"

"Not for months."

"Well, that's strange. MI6 told us that your radio set had been transmitting fine from there for several weeks."

He looked confused. "I've mostly been in Paris."

"We know." Léon lit a cigarette. "Causing the downfall of many of our best agents there."

Bla eyed Léon's cigarette eagerly. "Can I have one of those?"

Léon looked at Marie-Madeleine. "Only if you start telling us the truth," she stated. "It had to be you transmitting, since London would know your fist. Did you send messages from Paris?"

"Yes," Bla said quietly.

Léon handed him a cigarette but didn't light it. "Were you in the offices of the Abwehr while you were transmitting?"

When Bla didn't say anything, Léon lit a match and waved it under the cigarette. "Were you?" he prompted.

"Yes!" Bla shouted. "My radio set is still there. I sent London genuine information, though most of it was out of date or irrelevant. Once in a while, the Germans would give me false reports to send, to keep them running around in circles, you see. The Abwehr call their radio games *Funkspiel*. If you hadn't caught me, we would have continued to infiltrate the Free Zone…"

"And are you here now in Marseille to find Hedgehog so the Abwehr can arrest her?"

Bla nodded.

Léon finally lit the man's cigarette. "You should go back to La Pinède, Minerva. What happens next should not be your concern."

Hearing of Bla's treachery was no shock to her, but she had to admit she was rather taken with the way Léon was defending her honor. "What are you going to do?"

Bla's gaze shifted back and forth between them as he smoked.

Léon took Marie-Madeleine's arm and led her out of the room. In the hallway, he retrieved a packet of pills from his pocket. "MI6 gave me these to take in case I'm interrogated by the Gestapo. They're poison, cyanide to be exact, and they're supposed to work quickly."

She didn't exactly relish the death of a man under her watch, but a quick glance at Monique, who was sitting in the hallway, her eyes red, convinced her of the necessity of Bla's murder. "They'll cause no pain?"

"None," Léon assured her.

Marie-Madeleine had another one of her sleepless nights and rose early. Oblivious to the Bla drama, the network still carried on, and she found a slew of new messages and couriers waiting to report to her in the morning.

Rivière came into the office shortly after eight am. He had dark circles under his eyes and his mouth was held in a tense line.

"Is it done?" she asked.

Rivière threw his clearly exhausted form into a chair. "After you'd left, Eagle informed me that we weren't going to waste any more time with the bastard and to give him some soup. Eagle put a pill into Bla's bowl and then we ate together so Bla wouldn't think anything of it. Bla was, well, so blasé, that I was afraid we'd mixed up the bowls. I myself started to develop a stomach ache, but it was only nerves, I guess. Still, nothing happened."

"Léon told me it would go quickly."

"Me too. Finally Bla got up from the table, holding his stomach and claiming an old rugby injury. We advised him to lie down and thought that would be the end of it."

"It wasn't?"

"No. He laid down and just kept talking, not about anything important, just his days growing up in France, and then occasionally he'd tell a dirty joke. Once he even got up to show us some dance moves!"

Marie-Madeleine began to twirl a stray piece of hair.

"So finally Eagle decides to give him more, this time in a cup of tea. When I gave it to him, Bla pulled a face—I'm assuming the stuff tastes bitter—and then asked, 'Was this an order from London?'"

"What did you say?"

"I told him yes. He took another sip and then said, 'It can't be much fun for an officer to do this sort of thing.'"

"It's not."

"No indeed, especially because nothing happened this time either."

"Nothing?" Marie-Madeleine stood up. "Is he still alive then?"

"Yes. It went on all night, but he's definitely alive."

She grabbed her purse. "Then we should go back."

Bla was lying on the couch in the living room of the Corniche, talking incessantly in a posh English accent while Léon sat in the dining room, staring off into space.

"You probably shouldn't have mixed that stuff into hot water," Marie-Madeleine admonished him.

Léon focused his red-rimmed eyes on her. Like Rivière, the circles under his eyes were like black holes. "London assured me they would work no matter what. But I guess it's a lesson learned if we ever want to use the pills on ourselves."

"Stop joking around. You should flush the rest of that pack down the toilet. And…" She threw her arm toward the living room. "What are we going to do with him now?"

"I think I might know," Rivière piped up. "There are some

Marseille gangsters I've interacted with from time to time. They told me that when they need to rid themselves of someone, they bring him down to the river and put him in a boat…"

"What happens then?"

Rivière raised one eyebrow. "The boat goes out to sea, I guess. And stays there until its passenger dehydrates or the sharks get him."

"And if he's rescued?"

"I think it would be better to take care of him before you place him in the boat," Léon declared.

"What if he starts kicking and fighting?" Marie-Madeleine asked. Both Léon and Rivière shrugged, so she went into the living room. "Bla?"

"Yes, madame?" He tried to sit up, which was clearly an effort.

"Don't get up." She couldn't help the motherly instinct that suddenly came over her. "Are you in much pain?"

He shook his head. "No, madame, but I would like a cold drink."

She asked Beaver, who was acting as his guard, to fetch him some brandy with ice. "And bring two glasses."

Bla watched, a smug smile on his face, as she poured. She took a long sip before she told him, "A royal submarine will be cruising offshore tonight. We're going to send you out to meet it on a fishing boat. They'll take you back to England so MI6 can deal with you." She masked the lie with another gulp of brandy. "I know your word is not worth much, but please promise me you will behave properly during this latest adventure."

"Yes, madame. And thank you for treating me with dignity." His voice was still grandiose as he said, "Whatever you've decided, I accept my fate."

Marie-Madeleine spent the night at La Pinède, staring out at the gardens, wishing she had a view of the ocean. For once, the villa was empty of the usual crowd. Even Tringa had gone to the Corniche flat for a good night's sleep, and his receiver was quiet.

As dawn broke, she saw Léon's tall form striding up the gravel. He must have taken the first tramcar out.

He walked in and flopped down on the couch but didn't say anything.

After a few minutes, she asked, "Did something go wrong, again?"

"Yes."

She sighed. "I suppose I never thought it would be smooth: what with gangsters and fishing boats."

Léon buried his head in the crook of his arm, murmuring, "I couldn't do it."

She had never seen Léon so vulnerable. Confused, she asked, "Couldn't do what?"

"It, okay? *It*. It's too horrible to even think about." He dropped his arm. "The evening was otherwise beautiful: the sea was literally glowing with phosphorescence and there were no clouds. It would have been a marvelous night for a landing, but not so much for killing someone. Bla never flinched, though he must have known what was up. And then, just when I'd made my mind up to send him unconscious, a shooting star lit up the sky. Rivière said that the time had long passed for them to bring the boat around and then asked what next. I told Rivière we were going back. *All* of us."

She gingerly sat on the edge of the couch near his feet. "Listen, Léon, we're all going mad. This war is horrible, and we're both working too hard. We've thrown our own lives into the ring, and the lives of our loved ones as well. The business is despicable but we haven't the right to let it drop. You're clearly exhausted, and so are the rest of the boys. To their worn-out minds, and even to yours, this traitor might seem like a kindhearted person, whereas he is, in fact, the enemy. A German spy, to be precise."

Léon sat up a little and stared back at her, his handsome features contorted with anguish.

"It's my fault too," she continued. "I gave into my own feminine impulses and treated him like a man yesterday."

"What do you have in mind?"

Struck by inspiration, her voice grew louder. "We're going to put him on trial. That way it will no longer seem like an execution. It's our duty to do so."

"Good idea."

She patted his legs, but he made no move. "You know what I was thinking all last night?" he asked loftily. "That instead of Bla, I wish it was *you* sitting next to me."

"You want to kill me?" She meant the question to be a joke, but it sounded flat even to her.

"Of course not." He sat up completely this time, moving his legs to the floor.

"You should get some sleep while you can."

"In there?" he asked, nodding toward her bedroom.

"I suppose you could. I was going to run errands anyway."

"I was hoping you would be sleeping too."

Again, a bewildered feeling washed over her. She put her hand on her hip in an attempt to hide how his words made her heartbeat accelerate. "What's gotten into you?"

"Nothing." He fluffed the pillow and lay back on the couch. "I'm just tired from being up all night, I guess."

"Sleep well, Léon."

Already snoring, he didn't reply.

A couple hours later, Marie-Madeleine took a seat at the round table in the Corniche office. Wanting to set the scene, she had ordered Bla to be placed in handcuffs. Léon sat across from him, Rivière next to him, and a few more of the boys were seated at the table or scattered around the room.

Bla looked pale and unsteady.

Léon rose and read the lengthy indictment that Marie-Madeleine had spent the morning preparing, ironically, to keep her mind off the very person who was reciting it.

When he finished, she asked Bla if he wanted to add anything.

"No." Though his voice was hushed, it was laced with defiance. He shook his head as if to free his thoughts. "Everything he just said is true. I worked for the Germans. I've betrayed you. I've gambled and lost."

"Then we condemn you to death," Léon stated.

"What right do you have?" Bla asked.

"Because most of us at this table are French officers who have rejected the armistice. By virtue of the fact that we are on the battlefield. And, let's not forget this…" He took from his pocket the order of execution that London had sent.

Blinking hard to read it without his glasses, Bla then raised his chin high, refusing to respond.

Léon put a hand on the small of Marie-Madeleine's back. "Minerva, you may go now. Rivière and I will handle this."

"Will you need anything else?" she asked Bla gently. "Perhaps a priest?"

"No, madame. I don't need anything from you."

"Well, then," she got up from the table. "I guess this is goodbye."

Knowing she would have a difficult time falling asleep, Marie-Madeleine took a sleeping pill that night.

She woke up to someone pounding on the door. It was Monique. "Hurry up, madame. You're going to miss your train. Rivière is waiting for you."

Rivière was accompanying her to Toulouse to oversee Operation Mercury, a Lysander landing that would take Jacques to London. After the Bla affair, he'd decided he'd had enough of his sister's 'underground intrigues' and was seeking to join de Gaulle's Free French. "Now that Léon's back, my presence is no longer needed," Jacques had told her when he had proposed the idea. He was to leave on the same plane that was scheduled to deliver Magpie, the 'sensational' radio operator from London.

Marie-Madeleine shook her weary head, trying to shake herself alert. "Where's Léon?"

"He had an appointment in Beaver's bar, but he asked me to give you this." Monique handed Marie-Madeleine a slip of paper, which read, "I'm going to fetch the Giraud memorandum. Don't stay away too long." The unfamiliar feeling she'd been doing her best to keep at bay escaped, spreading a warm sensation through her chest. She took a cold shower to try to get rid of it.

. . .

Rivière met her on the train. As the conductor collected tickets, Marie-Madeleine thanked Rivière for his help with the Bla situation. "It wasn't too difficult, the deed?"

"No, chief. It was necessary. You needn't worry anymore, he—"

She held up her hand to cut him off. "No details needed."

"I know, Léon told me to spare you, but there's something I need to tell you… Bla had a message for you. He said to tell you that it must be terrible for a lady like that to have to do all the things she's obligated to, and he wanted his last act to be one of help to her…"

He paused talking as the conductor made his way back down the aisle, announcing the stop. A crowd of ladies got up, plunking their suitcases on the arms of the seats as they left. Rivière leaned over to whisper in Marie-Madeleine's ear, "Bla said that you have to leave Marseille, because the Germans plan to invade the Free Zone on November 11th."

CHAPTER 30

OCTOBER 1942

Operation Mercury, the Lysander landing that would exchange Jacques for the radio operator Magpie, was slated to take place at the end of October. When Marie-Madeleine and Rivière arrived at a local inn, Jacques informed her that Crowley was already at the landing ground in Ussel, but Mahout was nowhere to be found.

Marie-Madeleine checked her watch. Mahout was supposed to escort Jacques on the train to Ussel, although they would travel in separate cars, of course. "What do you mean, he's not here?" It was already past four, and the last train out was in an hour.

The three of them froze as someone knocked on the door. Rivière shot Marie-Madeleine a searching look and she nodded.

He opened the door to find Mahout standing there. "Sorry I'm late, madame." Mahout walked into the room, his shoulders slumped and his eyes heavy with fatigue.

Marie-Madeleine had no choice but to forgive him for his tardiness. Mahout's main duty was to head the Asia reception committee for Lysander landings, but on moonless nights, he doubled as a courier. For weeks he had been perpetually on the move, snatching some sleep on trains or in waiting rooms, ferrying documents that would get him shot on the spot if the Gestapo caught a glimpse of them.

Jacques picked up his case and the mailbag meant for London. "We should get going."

She wrapped her arms around her brother's neck. "Be safe."

"I will." With that, he nodded at Mahout and the two of them left.

They were back the next morning, along with Crowley.

"What are you doing here?" Marie-Madeleine asked Jacques as the three of them entered the room. "You're supposed to be in London."

Mahout cleared his throat. "I'm the one to blame for that, madame. I fell asleep on the train and missed the Ussel stop."

She turned to Crowley. "And the landing?"

"Still happened. The torches were with Mahout, but I made do by lighting fallen leaves in the correct pattern and then signaled the plane with my pocket flashlight. Magpie and another passenger arrived and then the Lysander took off, right before Mahout and Jacques came tearing through the bushes like a couple of Olympic sprinters."

Jacques, who had actually been an Olympian, barely managed a smile.

Crowley dumped a sack on the table. "Here's the London mail."

"I'm so sorry," Mahout offered. "I won't let it happen again."

She sighed. "Magpie and another passenger you say? I guess the good news is that more than one person can fit on the Lysander."

Mahout scratched his head. "We could probably squeeze three men on there if need be." Clearly he was attempting to make up for his egregious mistake.

"That should work for the next moon—I've been meaning to send Parrot back in the wake of Canary's betrayal. And Jean Boutron as well. That makes three already, so I hope we can get through the next month without any more mishaps." She focused her gaze on Mahout as she said that last part.

He mumbled an agreement. "I ought to get back to work."

"Mahout?" Marie-Madeleine called as he opened the door to leave.

"Yes?"

"Make sure to get some rest."

"Yes madame."

Crowley also bid them farewell, leaving brother and sister alone.

She'd never seen Jacques look so weary. Clearly the trials from the night before had been too much even for an Olympian.

"Everything should be ready to go for the November moon," she told him.

"I hope so."

She began packing up her things. "I'll let you rest for a few hours, and then we'll go back to La Pinède together."

"Right."

"Jacques," she said as something occurred to her. "What's Magpie like?"

"He seemed grand, and, unlike Bla, spoke French fluently, without an accent."

"Well, at least that's something." With that, she left the room so her brother could get some much-needed sleep.

CHAPTER 31

OCTOBER 1942

When Marie-Madeleine returned to La Pinède after the half-successful Operation Mercury, she found Léon in his office, fervently poring over a document.

She stood behind him, resisting the urge to put a hand on his broad shoulder. "Bla told Rivière that the Germans are preparing to invade the Free Zone."

He set down his pen. "Do you think he was being truthful?"

"Why would a person on the brink of death lie?"

Léon rubbed at his five o'clock shadow. "How could a low-level spy—and a terrible one at that—be privy to the confidential movements of the Third Reich?"

"He mentioned that he'd been instructed to go to Algiers at the end of the month. Besides, the bigger the operation, the greater the chance of a leak. The invasion of the Free Zone would require a massive amount of planning, though I can't imagine that even Pétain would allow the Nazis to violate the terms of the armistice so openly."

Léon harrumphed. "They've been violating the armistice since it was forged. What difference does a few more regions make?" He got up to pace around the office. "If the Germans really are coming, then we must do something about it."

She peered at the document he'd been studying. "What is this?"

"It's Giraud's memorandum. Saluki dropped it off this afternoon."

She picked up the stack of papers and scanned them—they seemed more like a tactical delusion than a memorandum. "He's asking the Allies to supply loads of equipment."

Léon nodded. "He's looking to reinstate France's army in order to fight the Occupation."

"Well, if the Germans do seize the Unoccupied Zone, Giraud will have to recruit a pretty large army." She set the papers down. "At any rate, this sounds well beyond the scope of Alliance."

Léon ignored that last sentence. "If Hitler does intend on invading, it won't do for London to send stuff *in*, we'll have to get it out of the so-called Free Zone. No more landings, no more drops… it's enough to make you mad." He nodded at Giraud's papers. "Nevertheless, you should code those for transmitting."

She picked up a pen and sighed. "Do you think I could summarize them? It's a lot to write."

Léon continued his pacing, grumbling until Marie-Madeleine told him to go do it somewhere else. His mere presence in the room was always a distraction, and his distress over the invasion only added to her consternation.

The next afternoon, Léon came into Marie-Madeleine's office. "I've just talked to Beaufre, who advised me that the Allies are planning to land in North Africa any day now. Given the unreliable methods of communication with the Americans, Beaufre wants us to coordinate the operation."

Marie-Madeleine sat back in her chair. "Operation? What are you talking about?"

"General Giraud's departure to take command in Algiers."

Her mouth opened and shut several times before she asked, "What about the General's memorandum?"

Léon waved his hand. "Dead in the water. The Americans are clearly interested in recruiting an anti-Gaullist, pro-Vichy French general for their purposes and Giraud fits the bill perfectly."

"Anti-Gaullist? I told you I don't want to get involved in any politics." It seemed the Americans had sided with the British over de Gaulle. "Besides," she told Léon, "Alliance is an intelligence organization—we have no business meddling in affairs of the military."

"That's true, but think what a coup this would be for us!"

Although Marie-Madeleine still had her misgivings, she couldn't help admitting that Léon's enthusiasm was contagious. "So what do they want from us?"

"They want us to make arrangements for General Giraud to depart for Algeria, where he will take command of the army. I asked them to call it, 'Operation Minerva.'"

She started to chuckle at the name but frowned as something occurred to her. "The moon's already on the wane, so Giraud's departure will have to wait for a few weeks."

"We don't need a full moon for submarines." Léon snapped his fingers. "Oh, and I almost forgot: Giraud's demanding the submarines and crew be American. No Brits—like most people in Algeria, he's still bitter about the British attack on the navy ships at Mers-el-Kébir."

"Giraud seems to think that I'm running a transportation company at his personal disposal."

Léon clapped her on the back as if she were one of his Air Force comrades. "You can do it, Minerva, I have complete confidence in you." He put his coat on.

"Where are you going?" She tried to act nonchalant, though every time he called her 'Minerva,' she felt her cheeks get hot.

He adopted a serious expression. "If the invasion of North Africa is truly imminent, then I have to alert my Air Force buddies. If you need me, I'll be in Poitiers. Jack Tar should definitely get wind of this."

She pointed her pen at him. "Don't get any ideas—you are still my second-in-command of Alliance."

"Oh, I know. I'm not planning on leaving the network... yet. You work on Operation Minerva, and I'll take care of the rest."

The operation turned out to be more complicated than even Marie-Madeleine had feared. There were two possible ports to depart from:

Le Lavandou, where one of their agents, Bee, had a villa; and Cros-de-Cagnes, where a 'friendly' hotel could shelter the General for a night or two.

Ecstatic at the progress of the Giraud affair, Saluki helped Marie-Madeleine thoroughly hash out the security considerations of the proposed sites. She decided to inform the British about both of them, though she stressed her preference for Le Lavandou because the Germans seemed to be less vigilant there than in the Nice area.

The worst part was that each small detail had to be written down, coded, and then transmitted to London by Tringa. Some of the longer messages reached up to sixty-five letter groups; too large to send in a single transmission. Léon had cautioned Tringa to keep his session as short as possible, especially since the presence of the *gonios* had been reported in Marseille. If they glommed on to his frequency, they could trace it to the house it was being sent from, endangering the lives of everyone at La Pinède.

The evening Tringa was supposed to confirm the Le Lavandou landing, she heard his call sign come over the radio. This would usually be followed by the sounds of his furious tapping on the Morse key, but that night, it was only Tringa cursing loudly.

She raced into the room. "What's wrong?"

"I've burned out my frequency," Tringa responded.

"Use another."

"I can't. The 6897 is the only one that's working right now."

Marie-Madeleine understood that frequencies only functioned sometimes: mysterious forces within the universe would occasionally render some of them unusable, a phenomenon that seemed to occur more often in the fall. "We have no other alternative. Try everything you've got."

He turned the dial and tapped his Morse code again. After a moment, he repeated the process, cursing some more. Finally he looked up. "That's all I've got: London won't be listening for the night signals."

She picked up a pen. "Give me three different frequencies close to 6897. I'll find someone to transmit them to London as soon as possible."

After he did as he was bid, Marie-Madeleine gave Monique the new frequencies, along with the messages needing to be sent to London to be brought to Colonel Kauffman's wireless operator out of the Dordogne. Even then, she knew it would be at least twenty-four hours before MI6 learned about Tringa's radio issues.

Léon returned from Poitiers a day earlier than expected. "The landing's going ahead," he announced when he walked in.

Marie-Madeleine peered at him over the message she was reading. "Is it really?"

"I believe so, though Vichy is aware that large Allied convoys are moving from west to east. They probably figure they're aiming for Malta."

She twiddled her thumbs for a minute, wondering how best to break the news to Léon. She decided to just come out with it. "What would happen if the Americans can't provide the submarine?"

"No submarine?" His face turned a peculiar shade of purple. "Haven't you got all the details for the operation all worked out?"

"No. Tringa's unable to get a signal out."

Léon crumpled onto the sofa like an eagle who'd damaged his wings.

The phone rang. It was Monique, letting Marie-Madeleine know that Colonel Kauffman had sent out the messages.

"Cheer up," she told Léon after she'd hung up the receiver. She walked over to the couch and held out her hand. Clearly puzzled, he took hold of it, allowing her to lead him into the dining room, where a dazed-looking Tringa was sitting in front of his still-silent transmitter.

"Put your earphones on," she commanded Tringa. "I have a feeling London's going to be calling *us*."

Léon and Marie-Madeleine pulled up chairs and sat around the transmitter expectantly. After the normal sked time came and went, Léon checked his watch and said he had work to do.

"Just wait," Marie-Madeleine replied. He got up and retrieved paperwork from his office. She considered doing the same thing, especially after another ten minutes went by.

To quell her impatience, she folded her idle hands in her lap, but Léon was sitting close enough to her that she bumped his elbow. He shot her a knowing smile but Marie-Madeleine, feeling her face grow warm again, averted her gaze.

Just then Tringa straightened and placed his hands over his earphones. His eyes grew wide as he whispered, "W.C.S… W.C.S… they're calling!"

"Then answer, dammit, answer!" Léon shouted.

Tringa tapped out his call sign on the Morse key, letting them know he was prepared to receive them, and then grabbed his pencil and started writing furiously. Marie-Madeleine got the grid ready and then anxiously waited for Tringa to finish.

Léon stood over her shoulder as she decoded. "The submarine is coming," he announced as soon as she'd written the words. "The landing is imminent!"

"Very imminent." She looked over the details she had deciphered. The sub would be in the vicinity of their chosen landing spot on November 4th. It would deliver Giraud to a seaplane which would then bring him to Gibraltar. "Do you think they are pushing the operation to an earlier date because they know the Germans are about to invade the Free Zone?"

Léon looked thoughtful. "Is it too much to hope that Hitler will be so distracted from the North African invasion that he'll give up France completely?"

She frowned. "I do indeed think that's too much to hope for."

Just then, the front door swung open and Saluki bounded into the room. "The General's delighted about going to Gibraltar, where he's certain to meet Eisenhower, but now he is requesting a second submarine."

Marie-Madeleine threw her hands up in exasperation.

"Maybe you really can start that transportation company now," Léon told her in consolation.

Tringa, finished with his work for now, got up from the table and

Saluki took his seat. "Giraud wants several of his generals to accompany him, necessitating the second sub," Saluki stated.

"Where are they coming from?" Marie-Madeleine demanded.

"They'll be streaming into Marseille soon. I've arranged for them to use Beaver's bar as a rendezvous," Saluki replied.

"And you're positive they will come?"

Léon gave Marie-Madeleine a funny look. "What do you mean by that? You think they won't?"

"Oh I'm sure they'll be fawning all over Giraud, once he's won, but not before." She turned to Saluki. "I will ask for that submarine, but to ensure that the Allies are not going to all this trouble for nothing, I'm going to have replacements ready, just in case." This might be the perfect opportunity to send Jacques—and Parrot and Jean Boutron for that matter—to London.

Saluki nodded. "I'll let them know, but, for what it's worth, I think you're wrong about the generals."

"That's a bet I'd be willing to take."

Léon stood up. "Well, considering that the first sub is on its way, I guess I better head to Le Lavandou." He paused and put a hand on her shoulder. "Minerva, you should think about leaving Marseille for a few days. If the police catch wind of Giraud's escape plan, they might be on the lookout for anyone they suspect of aiding him."

"I'll be all right." She shrugged off his arm to gesture toward her office. "I've been so occupied with this Giraud situation that I've fallen behind in the rest of my work."

"Take it with you to Toulouse. It will just be for a couple of days," he added when she didn't say anything.

She started to protest again, but he cut her off with one simple word. "Please."

"Fine," she agreed.

CHAPTER 32

NOVEMBER 1942

Giraud's rescue plan went off with only a few mishaps: namely that the submarine was a day late in picking him up and that Giraud himself fell into the ocean while trying to board. Fortunately, he was easily pulled back inside and the sub went on its way. Giraud never even appeared to notice the accents of the crew, who were mostly British after all.

In the early hours of November 6th, Marie-Madeleine left Toulouse for Marseille, making a quick stop at Beaver's bar to check that it was safe to return to La Pinède. Saluki had told her that Giraud's generals would be congregating at the bar before leaving for Le Lavandou to catch the second submarine.

None of them seemed to be around, however, even though the sub was scheduled to leave the next night. London was firm that no more transports would be available after that date, and for good reason, Marie-Madeleine assumed, as they would be needed for the North Africa landing.

She informed Beaver of her plan for Jacques, Parrot, and Jean Boutron to replace the generals and then left for the villa, which was surprisingly quiet. She resumed her work, occasionally pausing to wonder when Léon would return.

In the mid-afternoon, the phone rang and Marie-Madeleine answered it.

It was Bee, the woman who had hosted Giraud in Le Lavandou. "I'm sorry, madame, but it seems I have come down with the flu. I won't be able to host the holiday party after all."

Marie-Madeleine's voice cracked as she thanked her.

Although Bee had hung up, Marie-Madeleine was still holding the receiver in her shaking hand when Léon walked in.

"What now?" he asked.

"That was Bee—Le Lavandou is out for the second sub's landing point."

"Did she give a reason?"

"No. I can only imagine the Germans figured out something had been up and are prowling around."

He nodded. "We have to let MI6 know as soon as possible."

Together they went into the dining room, where Tringa was coding a message.

"Notify London of the need to divert the sub to Cro-de-Cagnes instead of Le Lavandou," she told him.

"Got it," Tringa scribbled something on a piece of paper and then pocketed it. "I'll send it out on my next sked." He looked up, noting the concern on her face. "Don't worry, madame. The sub will be alerted in time."

Early in the next morning, the villa stirred with its customary harried activity. Léon returned from Beaver's bar, slamming the front door. "You were right after all. The generals still haven't shown up."

"Then I guess it will be our men going aboard," Marie-Madeleine replied.

He nodded. "Jacques is coming by later to say goodbye." He hung his coat on a hook. "And worse than the generals, Beaver overheard talk in the bar that the Boches are close to homing in on a radio signal around town."

She rubbed at her eyes. "We've been transmitting too much lately. We should move soon."

Ernest Siegrist, who had been working on his forgeries, set his pen down. "I have some contacts in the police department. Do you want me to find out what they know?"

"Yes," both Léon and Marie-Madeleine replied at the same time.

Siegrist heaved his heavy body out of his chair, donned his hat and coat, and left.

"Madame?" Tringa stood in the doorway of the dining room, looking unkempt, his clothes wrinkled and his wiry hair sticking straight up. "I stayed up all night calling, but I never got through." He held out a limp wrist. "I tried so much that I sprained my hand, but no one answered. I could only hear a distant whistling."

"The sub!" Marie-Madeleine exclaimed. "It's still on its way to Le Lavandou?"

Tringa hung his head. "As far as we know, yes."

"Have you got a sked now?" Léon asked.

Tringa looked at his watch. "Not for another couple of hours."

"Try anyway," Marie-Madeleine told him, conscious that the submarine would be entering dangerous waters if it wasn't instructed to change course. "London has been listening constantly the past few days. I'm sure someone will pick up if you call."

Tringa retrieved the tattered message from his pocket and sat down at the dining room table, his Morse key in front of him, and started clicking away, his rhythm slowed by his sore hand.

"I'll be in my office," Léon said gruffly. "Let me know if you get through."

Marie-Madeleine went to the window to stare out at the gardens of La Pinède, her fingers grasping the threadbare drape. The rustling of the fig trees outside seemed to echo Tringa's tapping.

Faster, she silently chastised him as a few yellow and orange leaves cascaded to the ground below. *You have to work as fast as possible if we are going to save that submarine.*

To her relief, his tapping finally stopped and she knew he was receiving a message from London.

Her relief, however, was short lived, as a moment later, the front door burst open and a uniformed man barged in. "Police!"

Marie-Madeleine rushed to the other window, which overlooked the street. More uniformed men were pouring out from dark-colored vans sloppily parked on the hill. They were surrounded.

Tringa picked up his message and tried setting it on fire with his lighter, but a policeman grabbed him from behind. Marie-Madeleine turned her focus to another man in a black raincoat, who had opened a desk drawer and was tossing papers into his bag.

The turmoil of the past two years boiled into a rage inside her. Screaming the words, "Dirty Boche," she flung herself at the man. She scratched his face and nearly knocked his glasses off before he threw her to the side and picked up a chair. He brandished it defensively, as if he were an animal trainer trying to guard himself from a lion's wrath.

Indeed, in her fury, she felt like a caged animal clawing to escape its enclosure. Who would have thought that Hedgehog, who was usually so calm, could ever become so maniacal? In a flash, she recalled that her current purse, a dilapidated cloth bag, was full of incriminating notes.

She dashed upstairs, stomping her feet down the hallway in the hopes that Léon would hear and take cover in his bedroom. She slammed the door to her room and picked up the purse, digging through it to find one of her wadded-up messages. Casting her eyes around the room, she realized she had no other choice and stuffed it into her mouth. She'd succeeded in doing the same to a few more notes before the man she'd attacked charged into the room.

"Spit those out!" He held up his hand as if to slap her.

The little balls of paper had bloated with saliva, filling her mouth, but she still managed to choke out, "No, you vile Boche!"

The man, his face still bleeding, blinked behind his spectacles. "I'm no Boche."

Her mouth dropped open involuntarily.

"Keep chewing," he commanded in a low voice. "In fact, keep trying to attack me."

She swallowed a mouthful of paper. "Who are you?"

"I'm a fellow countryman."

"You're still a swine." Her pitch rose as another policeman walked into the room. "You are in the Unoccupied Zone, and therefore have no right to arrest us."

Her attacker waved at the other man to leave before stating, "I am forced by Vichy to escort the Germans on their raids. I know who you are..." In a quieter tone, he continued, "and I want to help."

Keeping her eyes on the man, she gulped down the remainder of the paper. She wanted to believe him, but if she'd learned anything in the last few months, it was that she couldn't trust anyone new. Besides, his accent held a trace of German.

She tried to move past him, but he grabbed her arm. Once again trying to alert Léon, she shouted, "Get off me, Boche!"

"I told you, I'm no Boche," he said through gritted teeth. He let go of her arm. "I'm Inspector Boubil of the Surveillance du Territoire. My fellow policeman and I—not the Germans—are tasked with taking you and your comrades into custody." Again his voice dropped. "And that includes any incriminating material we find in our search."

She sighed, knowing she had no choice but to take a chance on this man. "There is a trunk of papers underneath the bed."

Boubil reached out to retrieve the trunk and, without opening it, stashed it in the wardrobe beneath a pile of moth-eaten coats.

"Inspector, look at this." Another man stood in the doorway, gripping something in his fat hands. To Marie-Madeleine's agitation, she recognized it as the chart Jacques had made, outlining the locations, call signs, and transmission skeds for all of the network's transmitters. Without thinking, she grabbed the paper from him.

"Give me that," Boubil said. He tucked it into his coat pocket before nodding at the man. "Good work. See if there is anything more."

As the man left, Boubil opened his mouth to say something, but then Tringa shouted, "QS-5, QS-5!"

Marie-Madeleine entered the living room to see the first man slap Tringa, declaring, "This man is mad."

She sighed to herself. QS-5 meant that London had received Tringa's transmission and the submarine was safely heading for Cros-de-Cagnes.

She shut her eyes and then opened them wide. Her brother,

Jacques, was now standing in the doorway, holding a suitcase and dressed in traveling clothes.

These policemen are rubbish. She knew the filthy suitcase in Jacques's hands was the one they had buried over a year ago in the back of their mother's house in the Côte d'Azur. It was filled with early records of Crusade, including a letter from Charles de Gaulle from 1940. Jacques was probably intending to bring it aboard the submarine and hand-deliver it to British Intelligence.

"I thought the papers would be ruined if they stayed in the pigsty much longer," Jacques declared, his voice trembling.

"Your timing stinks as bad as that suitcase," Marie-Madeleine told him.

Boubil took the case from him and stuffed it into a corner, throwing a quilt on top of it. "Did you take my comrades and me for furniture movers?"

"No," Jacques stammered. "Someone outside said the Gestapo was here, but I didn't believe…"

"It's true." Marie-Madeleine felt like the air had left her lungs. "We're being arrested."

Another man appeared. This one was considerably younger than the rest, with fair hair. "I am Xavier Piani, the Superintendent of the Surveillance du Territoire. We'll take it from here."

"We're with the Abwehr," one of the other men grunted.

"I am aware, but under the terms of the Vichy agreement, German agents are obligated to leave prisoners, and all of their documents, in the possession of the French police."

The Abwehr agent looked unconvinced. "You do realize these people in here are members of the Resistance group Alliance, which we have been tracking for months."

"Yes," Piani replied. "And as I said, we'll take it from here."

The Abwehr men, grumbling, reluctantly left.

Marie-Madeleine hoped Piani and Boubil would let them go free, but to her dismay, Piani said he would be taking her, Jacques, and Tringa to the police headquarters in Marseille, along with "the other members we picked up."

Her heart leapt into her throat when Piani led them downstairs and she spotted Léon waiting with another policeman in the courtyard.

"The sleazy dogs," he hissed to Marie-Madeleine. "We're caught for now, but you can be sure I'll take care of everything."

"I've already started," she declared, trying to sound more confident than she felt. She nodded at Boubil. "He's not so tough. I feel somewhat hopeful."

Léon turned to Jacques. "Looks like you missed the boat again, old sport."

"Forget your Lysanders and submarines—next time I cross the Pyrenees on my own accord," Jacques replied. "I've grown weary of all this cloak and dagger stuff, anyway."

As they passed through the gate, Marie-Madeleine caught sight of Ernest Siegrist, who was watching the procession, hiding behind a tree in the park. He locked eyes with her and gave her a slight nod, indicating he would let the others know of their capture.

When they arrived at the police headquarters, a large stone building, they were given a decent meal before being taken into separate interrogation rooms.

The policeman in charge of Marie-Madeleine seemed rather unassuming, with a receding chin and wide eyes. He offered her the only other chair and asked for her name.

"Bacqueville," she replied, using the alias printed on the papers Commandant Rollin had provided her.

"I'm not asking you my name, but yours."

Marie-Madeleine blinked a few times. "But that is my name: Claire de Bacqueville."

He looked even more confused as Marie-Madeleine whipped out her false identity card. "You see?" she said, pointing to the name.

"But my name is also Bacqueville!"

"Then I suppose we're cousins." Bacqueville had been Marie-Madeleine's grandmother's name. She decided this was a stroke of pure luck and launched into the family history. "And the marquis was said to have invented a flying machine, with which he flew across the Seine in 1742."

He nodded, his eyes bulging even wider than normal. "I've heard that. And about the aunts exiled in Russia."

They spent the next hour exchanging Bacqueville legends. Her cousin seemed disappointed when Piani came to fetch her.

"Did you find out any new information?" Piani asked.

Her cousin blinked rapidly, clearly having forgotten his mission. "No, sir."

"It is no matter." Piani held out Marie-Madeleine's coat. It was a fine American one that she'd been lugging around since the start of the war.

He helped her into the car waiting outside the police station. To her dismay, it was empty save for the driver. "Where are the others?" she asked Piani.

"Still in their interrogations," he said cryptically.

She wondered why they were being so seemingly thorough with the Alliance men when they'd let her off so lightly.

She thought for a moment they'd decided to release her, but then the van pulled up beside the imposing L'Évêché prison.

The inside of the prison was predictably austere, lined by rows of cells on either side. The guard pulling Marie-Madeleine along paused in front of a woman clerk, who asked Marie-Madeleine to remove her jewelry: her sapphire earrings and diamond wedding ring. The woman then dropped them into an envelope and sealed it. "And your coat."

Marie-Madeleine wrapped the belt tighter around her waist. "If you don't mind, I'd like to keep it with me."

She looked doubtful. "Don't complain to me if it walks out by itself."

"How could it do that?" Marie-Madeleine attempted to be playful. "It hasn't any feet."

"Feet? Oh there will be hundreds of feet—you'll see them once you're in the cell," the woman replied.

Marie-Madeleine found out what she meant after the door of her cell had slammed shut, sounding like a bolt of thunder. Several cockroaches and a few rats emerged from the corners of the dark, dank cell, lit only by the lone electric bulb dangling from the ceiling.

Once again, she pulled her coat tighter around her, forcing herself to think about the submarine rescue operation that should be happening shortly, thanks to Tringa's successful transmission. *If Boutron and Parrot arrive safely at Gibraltar, it would all have been worth it.* She squeezed her eyes shut as a large rodent scurried across the room. *All worth it,* she repeated, lying back on the filthy bed, doing her best not to picture her brother undergoing his own interrogation. If only he too were on that sub!

A tiny smile came to her face as she wondered how long it would take the police to find out that Léon was completely imperturbable. She herself couldn't read him most of the time, and she'd worked closely with him for almost two years.

Turning her thoughts away from Léon, she forced herself to get some sleep, figuring she needed to muster all the strength she could for the next day.

CHAPTER 33

NOVEMBER 1942

Marie-Madeleine was awakened at dawn by a guard. Like many of her captors, he too seemed more friendly than the situation would warrant, prompting her to ask why he wore such a large grin.

"The Allies have landed in North Africa."

"That is marvelous news." She couldn't help embracing him. When she broke from him, she asked him what day it was.

"November 8th, 1942."

"My birthday," she murmured. "What a wonderful present."

The guard pulled at his collar. "If that's the case, I should inform you that I've been instructed to bring you back to police headquarters."

She picked up her coat. "Show me the way."

The French police were also celebrating the news and let Marie-Madeleine help herself to the large spread of crackers and cheese that was in one corner of the station.

She nearly choked on her cracker as Léon was led into the room. He ran his hand through his thick dark hair as he headed straight for her. He had obviously given up his jacket, and his athletic build was quite visible through his shirtsleeves. Even in prison, he still managed to look regal, like a true eagle. "Happy birthday," he said as he picked up a cube of cheese.

"I suppose you've heard the latest development."

"Yes." His eyebrows raised above his grayish-green eyes. "It's what we've been waiting for."

She munched on the cracker. "But yet we are still here."

Piani strolled over. "Faye. I've just got word that they are requesting your presence in Vichy."

"Vichy?" Marie-Madeleine repeated. "Why?"

Piani shrugged. "I imagine the government is in a state of turmoil over the invasion." He gave them a little bow before walking away.

"Don't go," she blurted out, causing Léon's eyebrows to rise even higher.

"Why not?" he asked. "We all know that the Boches' annexation of the Free Zone is inevitable. Maybe now Vichy will acknowledge the need to actually fight instead of running away with their tails between their legs."

Marie-Madeleine was insistent. "Don't you remember what happened last time you attempted to influence the tide of the war yourself?"

"I have to at least try to persuade Vichy to do the right thing and mount an opposition to the invasion. As the former deputy chief of the air force, I consider it my duty."

She reminded him again of his allegiance to Alliance. "Not to mention that you and I both know everyone in Vichy is corrupt to their cores."

"Minerva," he reached out as if to touch her shoulder but picked up a cracker instead, which he turned over in his hand instead of eating. "I'll agree to travel to Vichy on the condition that the rest of you are released."

Her lips turned up for the briefest second. "I still don't think you should go. Besides, I'm personally going to do everything I can to escape, so I have no need for these men's promises."

Piani returned with a short, stocky man, whom he introduced as Superintendent Cottoni before he left again.

Cottoni shook both of their hands warmly. "I'm honored to meet the leaders of Alliance." In a lower voice, he added, "The network I've been working with for the past few months."

"You are with Alliance?" Marie-Madeleine asked, her voice also a whisper.

"Code name Alpaca." Cottoni leaned in toward Léon. "I must inform you that the Germans are in a fit of rage over your arrest and will stop at nothing to get their hands on you. How about instead of taking you to Vichy, I drive you to the Swiss border?"

"Yes," Marie-Madeleine said firmly as Léon shook his head. She resisted the urge to shake him. "Léon, please listen to Cottoni."

"As persuasive as you can be, you know I will be sticking to my guns on this. After the armistice, I promised myself that I would urge France to fight, and I'm going to damn well try." Léon searched her face, as if looking for some sort of validation. "If you don't hear from me in 48 hours, go your own way. We'll meet in Ussel."

She frowned as he walked away.

"I'll take care of him the best I can," Cottoni told her before he too strolled off.

Marie-Madeleine watched as the two men left the police station, clad in long trench coats, their hats sunk low over their faces. She knew Léon would always go to great lengths to maintain his dignity—not to mention try to preserve France's—but that didn't make his leaving any less distressing.

To distract herself, Marie-Madeleine walked over to Inspector Boubil's desk. "I have bad news," he said, refusing to look her in the eyes. "The Abwehr is requesting that we turn over all the Alliance papers we have in our possession, which includes the diagram we found."

"No," she replied firmly. "That would mean we are handing over the locations of all of our radio sets—not to mention our call signs—to the enemy, which would result in the end of Alliance, forever."

"I have no choice," Boubil insisted.

She sank into a chair, breathing heavily. After a moment, she looked up. "What if we make a copy of the diagram with false information?"

Boubil scratched his head. "I suppose that might work, if it looked exactly like the original."

She pulled a piece of paper off his desk and started writing a list of things she would need from the villa, including the colored inks and square paper Jacques had used to make the first diagram.

Boubil watched over their shoulders as she and Jacques worked on the counterfeit diagram, changing the radio frequencies by random numbers and forging call signs. It took the rest of the afternoon, but Marie-Madeleine was thankful for the distraction—it kept her from thinking about Léon.

At long last, the task was completed. Boubil raised up both diagrams. "I can't tell which is which."

Marie-Madeleine pointed. "That's the forgery."

"Well, then." He took a lighter out of his pocket and held it under the original. "I guess there is no longer any need for this one."

Feeling relieved, she watched it burn.

That night in her cell at L'Évêché, the blazing light from the lone bulb made her eyes ache and hearing the relentless rush of water through the pipes felt like torture. She was utterly alone in the world—more so now than when Navarre had been arrested and left her to deal with the entire network. In the past few weeks, she had become even more reliant on Léon. But now he too, had abandoned her.

CHAPTER 34

NOVEMBER 1942

The next morning when Marie-Madeleine returned to the police station, she found the main room nearly empty save for a couple of clerks.

"Where are Boubil and Piani?" she asked one of them, who shrugged in return.

She walked into the small kitchen in order to wash up. The kitchen reeked of fire, overwhelming even her own prison stink. She went over to the pile of ash in the corner and poked through it to find pieces of leather and two metal buckles. It was clear that someone had set fire to Jacques's pigsty suitcase.

Inspector Boubil entered the kitchen, his shoulders slumped.

Marie-Madeleine could sense that he had more bad news. "Is it about Vichy?" she asked, her heart pounding.

"Yes. Marshal Pétain refused to leave for Algiers or even lift a finger to prepare for the imminent German occupation of the Free Zone."

"And Léon Faye?"

"He was put in jail."

She buried her face in her hands.

"And Vichy has also requested that we send you and the other agents to a prison in Castres, an intermediary point before you end up in Fresnes Prison in Paris."

"You are handing us over." He avoided meeting her gaze, but Marie-Madeleine could tell these newest orders were going against his will.

"You will be safer in Castres than Marseille, where the arrival of German troops is imminent." His voice was filled with dismay, and she could only assume that he knew as well as she did that Castres would be a temporary stop before they were all extradited to Germany.

She trudged from the kitchen into the main office, where Jacques and Tringa were waiting expectantly. She could feel each of them searching her face, hope in their eyes. They didn't know yet that their fate had been sealed.

She managed a slight smile as Piani entered the station. He unwound the scarf wrapped around his neck before pulling Marie-Madeleine aside. "I have it on good word that there are other Alliance agents poised to attack your transport van. I was able to convince the commandant that we won't need a full police escort, just a few of my own men." He nodded at Boubil who had come up behind her. "We will ensure that this attack is successful. We've both come to the conclusion that we can no longer work for a collaborationist government and are committing ourselves to the Allies."

This time her smile was genuine. "And, in turn, I will ensure that you escape safely to London."

He jerked his head to address Boubil. "You should be sure to say your goodbyes to your family. I know this lady's word is good, and so you might not see your loved ones until the war is over."

After the two of them walked out, Marie-Madeleine went into the bathroom to try to clean the blue suit she'd been wearing for the past few days as best she could. It seemed like they would be safe. Léon, however, was another story altogether, but now wasn't the time to figure out what to do about him.

Jacques was waiting in a chair when she returned to the big room. He stood up and grasped her hands. "Marie-Madeleine, what about your jewelry? Where are your earrings and your wedding ring?"

"I gave them to a prison clerk."

Piani, who was overseeing the burning of the rest of the papers, paused. "We can arrange to pick them up on our way out of town."

"Nonsense," she replied. "Freedom is worth all the jewelry in the world."

But Jacques commanded Piani to have the driver go to the prison as soon as possible.

As they prepared to leave, Marie-Madeleine shook the hands of all the policemen who had helped them. While Jacques and Tringa grabbed the revolvers and Sten guns that the policemen had so kindly left unguarded, her supposed cousin, Bacqueville, whispered that he would be leaving that evening to join the Alliance division in Nice.

Boubil handed Marie-Madeleine a cream-colored envelope. "Your jewelry, madame. And you mustn't forget this." He put another envelope in her hands.

Peeking inside, Marie-Madeleine saw hundreds of francs, and knew it was the envelope of money that had been hidden in the desk drawer at the villa. "Thank you. Your kindness will not be forgotten."

The countryside on the road to Avignon was familiar, though the trees were now covered with frost. At the rendezvous point, they found Rivière waiting with a host of other Alliance agents in a black lorry.

"Let's go," Rivière commanded. "We can't wait around here—the Boches are marching toward us."

"So they are invading the Free Zone," Marie-Madeleine murmured.

After they'd all boarded the van, Piani and Boubil included, they continued on to Avignon.

She froze as she spotted a grayish-green, open-topped car approaching from the other direction. As it came closer, she saw a Wehrmacht officer in the passenger's seat. Jacques stiffened beside her, his finger on the trigger of his Sten gun.

She put her hand on his arm. "Don't."

"You know there will be a slew of troops to follow. They are breaking the terms of the armistice."

"I know, but as tempting as it is, killing them would really be pushing our luck." She dropped her hand as Jacques relaxed his trigger finger. "Our duty lies elsewhere, for now."

She couldn't help turning in her seat, watching as the German car continued its journey.

CHAPTER 35

NOVEMBER 1942

Marie-Madeleine was now a fugitive. Rivière drove them to Châteaurenard, where an elderly couple offered up their guest room. There she and the other exiled Alliance agents waited for Ernest Siegrist to provide them with different identity papers. Once again, the network had been broken, and Marie-Madeleine was eager to patch up the holes.

As soon as she had her new papers, proclaiming that Marie-Madeleine was a fruit dealer from North Africa, she set out for Ussel to fulfill her promise to help Piani and Boubil reach London. Tringa had informed M16 about her arrest, and the reply had urged her to get on a flight to England during the next moon.

She arranged for the Lysander landing, conveniently leaving out the actual passenger manifest, which included the two French policemen and Jacques, but not herself. She was sure M16 wouldn't be exactly pleased with her little ruse, but she also knew they would eventually get over it, especially when they found out what the policemen had done for Alliance.

Mahout sent word that the second submarine had left Cros-de-Cagnes as planned, with Boutron and Parrot on board. The news from Algiers, however, was puzzling. The Allies had successfully invaded North Africa and had captured Casablanca, but apparently Giraud played no part in the coup, for he never reached North Africa. Somehow, convinced that only a native Frenchman could lead the assault on French territories, he had mistakenly believed that he would be the Supreme Commander, even ruling over the Americans' Eisenhower.

Yet Giraud was no longer her concern. She had learned her lesson the hard way—by altering the objectives of Alliance to save a ship in distress, she had nearly gone down with it.

In the wake of the arrests, Monique, who had luckily been running errands in town that fateful day, had packed up the remains of La Pinède and met up with Marie-Madeleine in Ussel. Rivière had arranged for their lodging at a milk farm owned by a man named Lemaire.

As Monique and Marie-Madeleine entered the spacious living area, she saw an unfamiliar fair-haired man sitting at a wooden table, a transmitter in front of him.

"Marie-Madeleine, have you had the pleasure of meeting Pie yet?" Monique asked, strolling over to the man.

"Pie?"

"Magpie." The man stood up and reached out his hand. "I wouldn't want to confuse the animal names with desserts, although I guess 'Turtle' might work for both." His blue eyes sparkled with the joke and Marie-Madeleine had to agree with Léon's assessment of the illustrious Magpie.

"Your reputation precedes you," Marie-Madeleine told him as she shook his hand.

"I don't know about that." He gestured toward the desk. "I've just been trying to hold down the fort with the arrests and all."

"And he's been doing a great job," Monique added. "I've been helping him code."

"I appreciate that. Do you have a sked tonight?" Monique asked Magpie.

"Yes." He checked his watch. "In about an hour. Do you have

anything you'd like to pass on?"

"Not exactly." By now British Intelligence would have received Boubil and Piani and were probably wondering why the leader of Alliance herself hadn't arrived.

Magpie settled back down in his chair. "Have you met the owner of the house yet?"

"No."

Magpie and Monique exchanged glances. "Well, let's just say he's a little… ornery," Monique said. She brought a chair over to Magpie's table and picked up a pencil. Since it appeared that the two of them had things well in hand, Marie-Madeleine took a seat in a sturdy armchair situated next to the fireplace. She had actually dozed off when the door banged open.

She stood up, her heart racing. A craggy-faced man in stained denim overalls entered the room.

"You must be Monsieur Lemaire," Marie-Madeleine said.

"Yes, and you are?" His tone held a hint of suspicion, as if she were there to rob him.

"She's the head of Alliance," Monique informed him.

"Her? A woman?" Now he seemed even more suspicious. "I thought the leader would be male."

"I assure you, monsieur, I am most decidedly female."

Lemair's eyes raked over her frame. "I can see that. But I'm not convinced you are the leader of this so-called network. Have you any proof?"

All of her identity papers were, of course, written in a false name, not that any of them proclaimed her as being in charge of Alliance. She hoped his suspicion wouldn't result in the three of them being kicked out of his farmhouse.

Inspiration striking, she pointed to his radio in the corner, only half-hidden by a blanket. "I take it you listen to the BBC?"

"That's illegal."

Marie-Madeleine harrumphed. "What if I told you I can get them to make an announcement on the *messages personnels*?" She nodded at Magpie. "We'll call you 'The Mayor', a play on your last name."

"You got it…" Magpie gave her a little salute before adding pointedly, *"boss."* He picked up another pencil. "I'll pass on the message to London."

Monsieur Lemaire fussed in the kitchen, occasionally pausing to stare at her. Marie-Madeleine had offered to help him prepare dinner, but he refused, saying if she were really the head of the network, she must have work to do.

She probably did, but the messages Magpie had piled up were all queries on the whereabouts of Léon, which she, of course, could not answer. She sat back down in her chair as Magpie's transmission started.

When he and Monique had finished decoding, Magpie handed Marie-Madeleine a slip of paper. "I let them know you were here, and they asked me to hand this to you directly."

It was from Richards.

POZ, good trick with the policemen STOP We understand the reasoning by it especially as they explained their role in your escape STOP Of course we are still anxious for your presence in London STOP Please make arrangements for next moon STOP

"I didn't get out of jail just to dash off to London," Marie-Madeleine said aloud, crumbling the message in her hands.

When she looked up, Lemaire was standing at the entrance to the little kitchen, his arms folded across his chest. "Dinner is ready."

They sat down to a simple but satisfying meal of buckwheat pancakes and, of course, fresh milk.

Afterward, Lemaire went straight to the radio and flicked it on, leaving the others to clean up. Apparently he now had no qualms about letting the Alliance head do housework.

When the broadcast announced it was time for the *messages personnels,* Lemaire turned the volume up.

"He can't possibly think we got the message to them that quickly, can he?" Magpie asked quietly.

Marie-Madeleine shrugged before going into the living room, wiping down a plate with a wet towel.

"Frenchmen speak to Frenchmen," the radio called. "And here are your personal messages. The eel has been caught, repeat, the eel has been caught." The announcer went on with more nonsensical ramblings, to which Marie-Madeleine was only half-listening. *Magpie's right—there's no way...*

Suddenly the announcer declared, "We thank the Mayor and are counting on him. Repeat, we thank the Mayor and are counting on him."

"Did you hear that?" Lemaire practically jumped out of his chair.

Marie-Madeleine went to hug the chuckling Magpie and then Monique.

"Well, I'll be damned—the British really can move quickly when they want to!" Magpie said through his laughter.

After that, Monsieur Lemaire turned into the consummate host, giving up his own bedroom to Marie-Madeleine and Monique. It had its own fireplace, and the large bed was covered with an eiderdown spread and soft sheets, which to her, especially after L'Évêché prison, felt like a piece of paradise.

CHAPTER 36

NOVEMBER 1942

The next morning, Marie-Madeleine actually slept in. When she awoke, she noted that Monique's side of the bed was empty.

She rubbed sleep out of her eyes as she heard a pounding on the front door. She threw on her dress, wondering if there would ever come a time when her heart didn't race at the sound of someone at the door.

She assumed Monsieur Lemaire was out, so she answered it herself.

Léon strolled into the farmhouse as if he owned the place. "Why do you look so surprised? I said I'd meet you in Ussel."

"You were arrested," she managed to choke out.

"I escaped."

"How?"

He sank into a chair in the living room. "It's a long story. Let's just say I made a friend and we succeeded in sawing through the bars in the bathroom windows and then lowered ourselves down from the fourth floor via a rope. How did you get away from the French police?"

"Something rather similar." Léon didn't need to know their liberation was due to the patriotism of the policemen, and not necessarily through her own cunning.

"What about the network?"

She sat across from him. "It's still running, no thanks to you."

For once, Léon looked surprised. "What do you mean?"

An anger Marie-Madeleine didn't know she'd been harboring boiled to the surface. "I told you not to go through with your plan. Just like I told Navarre—"

"Hey." Léon grabbed her hand. "It's okay."

She hated showing any sign of weakness, especially in front of Léon. "I could run Alliance alone, if I had to. I've done it before."

"I know. But I'm here now, and I will help make sure the network operates as smoothly as it can."

Just then, Bishop entered the farmhouse. "Madame, I was hoping to find you here." He nodded at Léon. "Looks like you were able to escape."

Léon shot Marie-Madeleine a grin before answering, "Indeed."

Marie-Madeleine eyed the pack Bishop had slung over his shoulder. "Do you have news of the southern zone?" It had been weeks since she'd heard any updates regarding the other sectors, and she wasn't going to let an exchange of pleasantries make her wait any longer.

"Yes, but I only bring bad news. We're afraid of a revolt. Spaniel gave Cockroach the bag with two million francs and the mail to put in his safe, but Cockroach won't give any of it back. Tringa is joining them and urging the rest of the radio operators to desert us."

"Why would Tringa leave Alliance?" Léon asked.

Bishop sighed. "I've been meaning to talk to you about it—all these secret armies that keep springing up are trying to pinch our London-trained radio operators. They're offering them as much as 10,000 francs a month."

"How can they even afford that?" Léon exploded.

"It doesn't matter." She put her head in her hands. "Now all that garbage with Giraud makes sense: I could never figure out why Tringa was having such trouble contacting London."

"The dirty traitor," Léon declared. "If he wants to leave to try to get rich quickly, then let him go—we have no place for men like that. Plus, we have bigger birds to fry than radio operators." He got up to pace the room as he shot off his instructions. "Bishop, get hold of the men who volunteered to go to the Occupied Zone. That's where the real action will take place from now on since the south of France is becoming less relevant. And if that crook Tringa makes one false move, he'd better watch out."

Bishop looked expectantly at Marie-Madeleine, who nodded.

He then took a deep breath. "Before I go, I have one more thing to tell you." His gaze focused on Léon. "Sir, you ought to sit down for this."

Bishop brought another chair in from the kitchen, and lowered himself into it with a heavy sigh, as if he was weighed down by the news.

Marie-Madeleine grabbed the arms of her chair, bracing for the worst. "What is it?"

"They've been shot. Lucien Vallet, Antoine Hugon, Edmond Poulain, and all the others who were in Fresnes Prison." Bishop stared straight through them, his eyes distant and haunted, as if he were seeing his friends killed right before him.

Tears pricked Marie-Madeleine's eyes. Léon reached out and grasped her hand so hard it felt like her bones might break.

After a moment, Bishop blinked rapidly, bringing himself back to reality. He retrieved a soiled envelope from his bag. "Lucien's final message," he said sadly, handing the envelope to her. "I believe it was meant for you."

With shaking hands, she withdrew the letter.

My hour has come and I am forced to leave you, Mother, darling. I have had courage and hope to the end. I thank you, Mother, for the last time, for everything you have done for me and ask forgiveness for all the worry that I may have caused you. I await the decisive hour with courage and peace in my heart. I think of you and our dear family and I think I have done my duty to my country and my comrades. You will never need to blush on my account. That is a great comfort to me. Be courageous, all of you. Farewell everyone. Farewell Mother!

Marie-Madeleine refolded the now tear-stained letter and put it back in the envelope. "Lucien didn't give up any information," she said aloud.

No one said anything for a few minutes. Despite her overwhelming grief, she fought to keep her composure. She wanted Léon to reach for her again, but she could tell he was also struggling to control his emotions, and seeing the unflappable Air Force man so disturbed upset her even more.

Finally, Bishop rose and placed a hand on Marie-Madeleine's shoulder before leaving the farmhouse.

"I have to break the news to Monique that her fiancé is dead," Marie-Madeleine told Léon, her voice heavy.

"No. She'll find out soon enough." He came over and kneeled in front of her, forcing her to look at him. "Minerva, you should know that the sacrifices we've made are worth it."

"How can you say that? First Schaerrer, and then Lucien… and Hugon…" her lips curved into the suggestion of a smile, recalling how the latter had stripped down to his bare chest in her room when he'd brought her the map of the submarine base. The almost-smile faded as she thought about Lucien, the immense former officer whose warmth and wit rendered him as gentle as a teddy bear.

Léon took her hand. "It *is* worth it. And the best revenge you can get is to destroy the demons who killed your comrades."

"They were more than just comrades. They were my friends."

"I know…" After a moment he added, "they were mine too."

She burst into tears. He let her cry for what seemed like an eternity without saying anything, offering silent support as his thumb caressed her hand. His touch alone was a soothing balm to her wounded heart.

But was Léon right? Had it really all been worth it? Doubt began to creep into Marie-Madeleine's mind and she rose, carefully maneuvering past Léon to walk to the window. *There had been so many close calls lately, and too many betrayals: first with Canary, then Bla, and now even Tringa.* And what would prevent other radio operators from deserting them? Ten thousand francs was an exorbitant amount of money. *Magpie…* She shook her head. She'd only met the man last night, but something told her Magpie would never willingly leave Alliance.

Outside it was beginning to snow, and her thoughts wandered to Beatrice and Christian. The holidays were coming, but she couldn't risk leading the police to her mother's doorstep. They would have to spend yet another Christmas without their mother.

She turned to see Léon still kneeling in front of her vacant seat, looking crestfallen. "I'm glad you're back," she said softly.

His tone matched hers. "Me too."

CHAPTER 37

DECEMBER 1942

Once Marie-Madeleine was firmly settled in Ussel, she and Léon were inundated with six weeks' worth of reports flooding in from all over France. As they meticulously combed through the descriptions of troop movements, cargo lists, and intelligence maps, Marie-Madeleine was filled with a sense of pride. A year prior, there had been a hundred agents, and now there were nearly a thousand members of Alliance, preparing to put an end to the Nazis' reign of terror.

However, the imaginary safe havens of the Unoccupied Zone were no more. The latest report was that the subtle yet insidious Abwehr intelligence agency and the Gestapo, which relied on intimidation and brute force to achieve similar objectives, had joined forces to systematically conquer every slice of France with brutal efficiency. Léon nicknamed this terrifying partnership 'Gibbet.'

One morning she arose even earlier than usual to dig through the messages that Magpie had dropped off at Monsieur Lemaire's. She barely heard Léon enter an hour later. Not wanting to impose, he'd been staying at a local inn.

He cleared his throat. "Someone ought to tell MI6 in person what's developed now that France is totally occupied."

She felt his eyes on her as she sat up straight and rotated her shoulders to relieve the ache that came from being slumped over her desk for hours. "Well, I don't think it should be me." MI6 was still trying to convince Marie-Madeleine to come to London, but she had no desire to accept the invitation.

"I'll go," Léon volunteered.

Once again, Marie-Madeleine wanted to refuse his offer, but she knew there would be no suitable reason for him not to go. The only danger would be in the Lysander pick-up and travel; once he was in London, there would be no threat of harm. Her reasons for wanting him to stay were purely selfish. "I'll make the arrangements."

The plane never came. Mahout blamed it on the horrible December weather.

Forced to wait for the next moon to leave, Léon was afraid that their presence in Ussel, so near the landing field, was becoming a hazard. Once again, they packed up and moved, this time to an isolated château that stood on the fringes of Sarlat in the Dordogne.

Sarlat had been in existence since the Middle Ages, which was obvious from its jumble of stone houses connected by narrow alleyways. Marie-Madeleine was sure the town would have been charming in the pre-Occupation summertime, covered in flowers, but now, in the gray winter, it just seemed gloomy.

The same could be said for the château, which struck her as melancholy and dusty, with an eerie stillness disturbed only by the frigid draughts that ran through it. She felt frozen solid as soon as she stepped foot inside the enormous, stone-floored entry hall.

"You'll thaw out in no time," were the welcoming words of Colonel Kauffman, the head of the Dordogne region. He ushered them into the kitchen, where an ancient stove was giving off a comforting glow and a veritable feast of ham, truffles, and wine lay on the massive countertop. "From my farm," Kauffman said in response to Marie-Madeleine's questioning look.

"If the boys arrive on time, we'll all be able to greet the New Year properly," Léon stated from the corner of the kitchen, his mouth clearly watering. He poured three glasses of wine. Kauffman took his with him as he went to make sure the rooms were ready.

"Cheers." Léon held out his glass.

"Cheers," she replied, steadily meeting his grayish-green eyes. She heard someone cough from behind her. "Noble!" she cried, barely suppressing her shock at his emaciated frame.

"Little one," he managed to gasp through another fit of coughing. "I'm glad that submarine business didn't finish you off. You're definitely a survivor."

She wished she could say the same for him, but the sight of the bright red blood on the handkerchief he pulled away from his face frightened her. "Noble. You look…" she wanted to say 'terrible,' but gestured to the ham instead. "Like you could use this."

His face lit up at seeing someone behind Marie-Madeleine. "Little one, have you met Jack Tar yet?"

"No." She extended her hand to the man with fiery orange hair and liquid brown eyes. She knew he had once served under Léon in the Air Force, though he looked impossibly young.

"How did you manage to get across the line, Jack?" Noble asked.

"The line?" Léon repeated. "I wouldn't think there would be a demarcation line now that the Free Zone has been abolished."

"Oh there is," Noble told him. "And it's well guarded." He pointed to his jacket, which was torn, a small hole the size of a bullet in the shoulder.

"You were shot at?" Marie-Madeleine asked incredulously.

"Yes, but I managed to swallow the papers I was carrying."

Jack Tar set his suitcase down. "Well, it was much less trouble for me. I was arrested."

Léon nearly dropped his wineglass. "Arrested? You should have abandoned that suitcase then."

"Probably, but I don't think, I just act. It's the number one rule when you're caught in an unexpected situation."

Léon and Marie-Madeleine exchanged an amused glance at Jack Tar's remark.

"Besides, I couldn't just abandon all of our friends' reports," he went on. "I sat on the case when I got to the train station. And the

Nazi officer who interrogated me wasn't the usual obnoxious, cruel type. When he asked why I was crossing the line illegally, I explained that I was a student on my way to visit the Eyzies caves. He seemed to like that and told me that it was usually terrorists who slipped across the frontier, carrying weapons and documents that could lead to the death of thousands of Germans."

"If only he knew what was in that suitcase," Marie-Madeleine murmured.

"Right." Jack Tar accepted a glass of wine. "In the end, he ended up giving me an *Ausweis*. For both ways!"

Noble chuckled as he heated up milk on the stove. The castle's Sleeping Beauty atmosphere dissipated as more people filled the immense kitchen. Monique, who, along with Magpie, had arrived earlier in the day, scrambled eggs to go with the truffles and put the thick ham on plates.

They sat down to a festive banquet accompanied by more fine wine that Colonel Kauffman had found in the cellar. The only one who didn't seem to partake in the celebration was Noble, who sipped on his warmed milk.

In an attempt to cheer him, Marie-Madeleine remarked, "It's a miracle that the east sector didn't fall into complete catastrophe, especially after the business with Bla."

"Our people are grappling with some obstacles, but the radios are still transmitting," he replied. "If you don't mind, I would like to leave tomorrow for the forbidden zone. I still have some loose ends to tie up."

"Leave?" she asked. "So soon? You just got here. And we both know that you could use a rest."

"I tell you, little one, it isn't lack of work that will be our undoing."

That was the second time Noble had mentioned this mysterious 'undoing.' Someday she resolved to ask him what his prediction would be for the undoing. But not tonight. It was New Year's Eve, and she felt like celebrating all that they had accomplished this year. "You can go in the morning. But make sure you say goodbye. And try to see a doctor about your lungs." The heartfelt glance they shared felt like an emotional farewell.

Tears welled up in her eyes as she looked around the table encircled by her agents, both the familiar and the fresh-faced, rejoicing together and welcoming a new year filled with hope. *Maybe this will be the year the Allies finally conquer the Nazis.* With the help of Alliance, of course.

CHAPTER 38

DECEMBER 1942

After the midnight revelry, the members of Alliance had scattered among the château's many bedrooms, but Marie-Madeleine found it impossible to sleep in her icy first-floor room. Throwing the sheets back, she crept toward the desk and turned on the lamp. She had just started coding a transmission when someone knocked on the door.

She felt her heartbeat speed up, knowing an unexpected, late-night visitor could possibly mean the Gestapo.

Taking a deep breath, she opened the door to find Léon standing there, still dressed in his clothes from earlier. "I saw your light was on," he said as he strolled into the room.

"You couldn't sleep either?"

"No. My room is right above Noble's and I can hear his coughing."

"I'm worried about him."

Léon sat on the bed. "I know you are."

Her heart was still racing, but now it was for a different reason. An uneasy silence settled between them, the air palpable with something, but what it was, Marie-Madeleine didn't know.

He opened his mouth as if to say something but thought better of it. After a moment, he stood and a part of her was disappointed that he was leaving.

But instead of moving toward the door, he approached her. "There's something I've been wanting to do for a very long time." He leaned in closer, his breath smelling like cherries from the wine.

"What is it?"

Time seemed to slow down as their lips met, and then a swell of longing washed over her. She hadn't been aware of how badly she'd wanted to kiss him until she realized how much she didn't want it to end.

He broke away from her to gaze into her eyes. "Was that okay?"

For a moment she thought he wanted her to grade him on his kissing ability. When she figured out he was asking for permission to do it again, she nodded.

This time she let her hands travel up and down his muscular arms before pulling him gently toward the bed.

"Minerva, I don't know if we should—"

She repeated Jack Tar's earlier remark: "Don't think, just act. It's the number one rule when you're caught in an unexpected situation."

Léon grinned at her. "Was this unexpected?"

"A bit, yes."

"Not for me. I've been wanting to kiss you ever since I met you. I just didn't know—"

"Shh." She put her finger over his mouth for a brief second before reaching for his belt buckle.

After they'd made love, Léon exhibiting the same intensity with which he tackled everything else, he fell asleep in her bed. As she snuggled next to him, she placed a hand on his chest to feel his steady heartbeat. That night was the first in a long time when her sleep wasn't plagued by nightmares.

"Breakfast!" Someone was banging on the door. Marie-Madeleine, noting that the other side of her bed was empty, sprang up.

"Breakfast!" Magpie shouted again. She opened the door before he could bang again. "Or lunch, actually," he said, dropping his hand.

"Lunch?"

"It's nearly noon, boss."

"Right."

After she'd put on a robe, Magpie accompanied her into the dining room, where Léon was already seated, digging into the leftovers from the previous night.

"Where are the others?" she asked, rather shyly.

"They're gone." Léon's voice held a hint of gloom. "They said they didn't want to wake you."

"But I told Noble to make sure he said goodbye—"

Léon got up to pull out a chair for her. "You know him—his duty will always come first."

She sank into the proffered chair, feeling a sharp pain penetrate her core, afraid she'd never see Noble again.

Léon watched Magpie walk into the kitchen. After he was safely out of ear shot, Léon ventured, "About last night…"

"What about it?" She didn't mean the words to come out as sharp as they sounded.

His lips curled into an easy grin. "I just wanted to say that I thoroughly enjoyed myself and would like a repeat if possible. Although…" his voice dropped even lower. "I suppose this time we should take the proper precautions."

"Yes." Her face grew red at the realization that they hadn't done so last night. "I suppose we should."

He raised his glass of orange juice at her. "Tonight then?"

She couldn't help but laugh as she clinked his glass. "It's a date."

PART III
THE WORST YEAR

CHAPTER 39

JANUARY 1943

The first night of the new year, Léon again paid Marie-Madeleine a midnight visit. Somehow his presence transformed her dark and dreary bedroom into a warm, cozy sanctuary.

After they made love again, she and Léon stayed up talking. He regaled her with tales of his childhood and what it was like growing up with six siblings, while she in turn shared stories of Christian and Beatrice.

He clearly picked up on the tinge of regret in her voice. "You miss them."

"Of course I do. I can't help feeling that I'm a bad mother, leaving them with relatives like that. It should be me taking care of them."

He sat up. "You can't mean that. Think of how much worse their world would be if you weren't doing what you're doing."

"Anyone could take my place in Alliance, but no one can ever replace a child's mother." Her own words brought tears to her eyes.

"Hey." Léon turned her chin up so that she was looking directly at him. "Trust me when I say this—no one can ever fill your shoes, not as the leader of Alliance, nor as a mother to Beatrice and Christian. Your children will always love you unconditionally, but someday, when you tell them what you did during the war, they'll have a hell of a lot more respect for you."

She knew he was right. And as much as it pained her, she'd come too far to turn back now. "Thank you," she said simply.

After a few nights of Léon sneaking into Marie-Madeleine's room at the château, they abandoned all pretenses. Despite her reservations, she found herself falling for Léon, and she didn't care who knew. In fact, she had the overwhelming urge to confide in someone, and Monique seemed like the obvious choice.

The younger woman didn't seem at all surprised, and replied by saying, "There's something about the horrors of war that draws people together, forging bonds that are stronger than any they might have formed in times of peace."

That night, as the two were lying in bed, Léon touched Marie-Madeleine's diamond ring, reminiscent of the way he'd had the first time they met. "Are you always going to wear that?"

The thought had never occurred to her to take it off, even when Inspector Boubil returned it to her after retrieving it from the prison. "I guess I don't need it anymore." The last remnant of her old life, it slipped off easily due to the weight she'd lost since the rationing.

"I don't suppose you could ask for a divorce."

She sighed. She'd looked into it once, before the war, but under the Napoleonic Code, only the husband had the right to initiate the process, and even then it was only allowed on specific grounds, such as adultery. To make it even more difficult, the Vichy government had passed a law requiring couples to wait three years until they could file for divorce. Not to mention both spouses would have to be present in court, and she hadn't heard from Édouard in years. "I think it will be a long time before I can obtain a divorce."

Léon wrapped his arms around her. "Well in that case, I guess I'll just have to remain your *amoureux* until the war is over."

She gave him a sad smile, recalling that their time together was slipping away. "You can be my *amoureux* for now, but what happens when you go back to London?"

"What about it? Are you going to find someone else to take my place?" He said it jokingly, clearly not expecting her to say yes.

"Of course not."

"MI6 has not given up on the idea that at least one of the Alliance higher-ups would be paying them a visit, and we both know it won't be you going, so it'll have to be me. But…" He kissed her cheek. "I'll be back in no time, and we can pick up exactly where we leave off. If that's okay with you, naturally."

"It's okay by me," she said softly, nestling further into his embrace.

CHAPTER 40

JANUARY 1943

The January new moon appeared and Marie-Madeleine anxiously watched every night as its slender crescent expanded, knowing that once it was full, it would be time for Léon's departure.

Finally, the dreaded evening came.

They said their goodbyes in her bedroom. The blackout curtains were closed and the only light came from a dim lamp.

"I'll miss you, Léon." Her voice was barely above a whisper.

"I'll miss you too." He fastened the buckles on his suitcase. "But I'll be back before you know it."

She forced a small smile. "It won't be the same without you here."

Léon took a step closer and placed a hand on her shoulder. "You'll be fine," he said. "You're the strongest person I know, and you've got this network running like a well-oiled machine. You don't need me here."

"No." Marie-Madeleine shook her head, her eyes filling with unshed tears. "I still wish you didn't have to go."

"I know," he replied, his tone gentle. "But it's crucial that I go to England and make sure we have the necessary support to keep this fight going. Besides, MI6 is clueless about what life is like in France now that there is no such thing as an Unoccupied Zone."

She nodded again, and the two of them stood in silence for a few moments.

"I'll be in touch," Léon said finally. "As soon as I have any news, you'll be the first to know. Well, I guess Magpie will really be the first, but you know what I mean…" He walked over to her and enveloped her in a tight embrace.

"Be safe," Marie-Madeleine whispered into his ear.

"I will," he replied, his voice choking with emotion. "And you be careful, too." He reached into the bedside drawer and withdrew a tiny pistol.

"Have you been keeping that there this whole time?"

"Of course," he replied. "And now I want you to have it. Promise me you'll carry it with you."

"You know no Gestapo man travels alone. I can't possibly get into a shoot-out with that thing."

"I know, but I'll feel better if you promise me anyway."

"All right then, I promise."

Once again, he pulled her to him and their lips met in a deep, passionate kiss.

Someone knocked at the door. After Léon answered it, Magpie strolled into the room. "Mahout is here." Both Mahout and Magpie were going to escort Léon to the landing ground.

"Ready," Léon replied, picking up his suitcase. With one final glance, Léon left the room, the sound of the door clicking shut echoing like a gunshot. Overwhelmed with grief, Marie-Madeleine threw herself on the bed and wept.

After a few minutes, she checked to make sure the gun was loaded and then locked the door to her room. Sleep was not an option, so she busied herself going over the latest reports, but every once in a while, her mind would wander to Léon and all the possible things that could go wrong.

. . .

Just after dawn, her hands shook as she heard the sound of tires on the gravel outside her room. There was no way it could be Magpie back from the Lysander landing. She reached into the drawer and pulled out the pistol. She eased the catch off the way Léon had shown her and then crept closer to the door.

The banging on the door was familiar. "Boss?" It was Magpie, brandishing a suitcase.

She put the gun back in the drawer as he walked into the room.

"Relax, boss. The moon was as round and clear as you'd ever seen it, and the landing went off without a hitch."

"How did you get back so soon?"

He shrugged. "I knew you'd be anxious, so I got here as fast as I could."

She unpacked the suitcase which was, as usual, brimming with lovely gifts, encouraging letters, and coded dispatches demanding immediate information.

"Something tells me you didn't sleep well last night." Magpie picked up a tin of powdered coffee from the pile of goodies. "I'll be right back."

In a few minutes he returned with two fragrant, steaming cups.

Marie-Madeleine's first sip of real coffee was both strange and familiar. With each swallow, she could feel the warmth spread through her chest, as if it were a healing balm for her aching heart.

Magpie gulped his down even faster than her. Setting his empty cup down on the dresser, he asked, "Can you imagine Léon walking down Oxford street, ordering a hackney cab?"

She smiled. "Not as such, but I'm sure it would be an amusing scene."

"Oh, I almost forgot." Magpie dug into his trouser pocket and pulled out a small envelope. "He asked me to give you this."

She waited until Magpie had left before opening the envelope, which contained a slim gold ring. In the accompanying note, Léon had written,

I know it's not much. Once the war is over, I promise I'll buy you the biggest diamond the world has ever seen, but I need one more promise: for you to be mine forever.

Saying a quiet promise to herself, she slipped the ring on her left hand.

CHAPTER 41

FEBRUARY 1943

Without Léon's strong presence, the château seemed even more isolated and empty. During the day, Marie-Madeleine kept herself busy with work, but nights were when she felt his absence the most and she would often wander around the vacant halls feeling restless.

One afternoon she was working in the cavernous dining room, devising a research strategy based on the newest questionnaires, when Magpie shouted that someone was coming up to the château.

Her hands trembled with terror as she caught sight of the police car outside the window. Three burly policemen exited the car. *Oh no, here we go again.*

She gathered up all the questionnaires and tossed them into a cabinet. "Magpie," she hissed. "Your transmitter."

"It's okay, boss. I recognize one of them."

From outside, they could hear a man shout, "Open the door, it's Basset."

Marie-Madeleine was about to order Magpie to hide his transmitter again, but he opened the door and the three men strode in.

"I'm sorry, madame," the tallest man said. Marie-Madeleine recognized him as Superintendent Phillipe, whom she had hired in

Toulouse. "I wanted to pay my respects to you in full uniform." The skin around his eyes hung in loose folds, like the droopy, mournful eyes of a basset hound, hence his nickname. His eyes, however, once bright with intelligence, now seemed dull and despondent.

"You almost gave me a heart attack." Her hands still shaking, she led him into the kitchen, the most comfortable room in the house, leaving Magpie to deal with the other two men.

She sat down in one of the chairs before asking Basset what was happening.

"Nothing with the network specifically, but this morning, a circular arrived from Vichy, ordering the French police to round up hundreds of Jews and hand them over to the Nazis."

Marie-Madeleine put a hand to her chest. *Mon dieu.*"

Basset plopped down across from her. "Since 1940, I've been able to get by with not arresting a single Frenchman. And now they are demanding I persecute an innocent group of people who have just as much right to live as Laval himself." He hung his head. "It is my belief that any Frenchman complying with these orders is a traitor."

"I agree with you fully, but what are you going to do?"

"I handed in my resignation this morning and am offering you my full cooperation working with the Underground. The two men I brought with me are also policemen and can be trusted. They've set up a hideout in Toulouse from where I can command my sector."

"Excellent. I can provide you with money and equipment. Is there anything else?"

He cleared his throat. "I was hoping you could assign me a proven, trustworthy courier. I was thinking Zebra, the courageous young Pole I've had occasion to work with."

"He's yours," Marie-Madeleine agreed.

With that, she saw the three men out.

The next morning, Marie-Madeleine came down with a stomach ailment that made her throw up her breakfast. The same thing happened three days in a row.

"It's this stagnant air," she told Monique when she came into the bedroom to check on her. "I wrote to Basset to see if he could find us better housing in the Toulouse sector. Now that Léon is gone, we don't need all this extra space."

"Are you sure that is all it is?" Monique asked, her hands on her hips.

"Of course that's all."

"Did you, you know, use protection when you and Léon—"

"Sometimes." After that first night, when they both had not been expecting it, they were more careful.

"When was the last time you had your monthly cycle?"

Marie-Madeleine gave Monique a puzzled look. "I don't remember. With all this stress, not to mention my skimpy meals, it's been off and on since the Germans invaded." She opened her mouth as understanding dawned on her. "You don't think…"

"How do you feel other than that mess?" Monique gestured toward the chamber pot.

"Not like I'm carrying a baby in my womb." She tried to sound more confident than she felt.

There was no time to ruminate over whether or not she was pregnant. The next day, Zebra, Basset's new courier, announced that they had found a suitable house in Cahors belonging to a Spanish dentist. "It meets all your requirements: seven trains in both directions, a lookout window, and a double exit. You can move in as soon as you like."

"This dentist, is he still around?" Monique asked Zebra, glancing at Marie-Madeleine.

She knew what Monique was thinking, but a dentist was not the same thing as a doctor.

"No," Zebra replied. "He's Jewish and he fled back to Spain right after the Germans entered the Free Zone."

Monique left right away with Zebra to set up everything while Ernest Siegrist, the ever-reliable Elephant, volunteered to bring Marie-Madeleine and Magpie in his car the next day.

. . .

Marie-Madeleine had never been so excited to leave a headquarters before and threw all of her stuff into a bag. Once again, she struggled to fall asleep that night, and experience told her that this kind of insomnia signaled something possibly hazardous in her future. All these years of living so close to the noose had made her brain develop a sort of radar for danger.

Her unexplained distress deepened when, as Siegrist waited in the hall in the morning, his car running outside, Magpie insisted on sending one last transmission.

"Magpie, will you be long?" she demanded curtly. "We have to get going."

"QS-5, boss. I wanted to send all your latest messages."

The pounding in her head increased and she held up her hands. "Stop. I don't want you to send anything."

"But it's going so well." He tapped something on his Morse key, matching the pace of her throbbing temples.

Leave. We must leave at once. She turned to Siegrist. "Shut off the power."

"Boss?" Siegrist asked, clearly confused.

"Just do it."

Siegrist flipped the transmitter's 'off' switch.

"What a shame," Magpie said as he took off his headphones. "I've never had such good reception." It was clear from the pitying look he gave her that he believed she had lost her sanity.

CHAPTER 42

FEBRUARY 1943

The house in Cahors, which they nicknamed Castel Lolita, was ideally located on a spur in the hilly part of the city. A far cry from the chilly, austere château, the new headquarters was a charming and cozy space, made all the more welcoming by Monique's efforts to decorate it with homey touches.

Upon uncovering a hiding place for his radio in the molding of the dining room, Magpie asked if it were possible to retrieve his reserve transmitter, which was buried in the back garden of the château. "Just in case," he insisted.

Marie-Madeleine instructed Siegrist to get it the next day.

When Siegrist returned, he asked to see them in the dining room, where he paced up and down, full of nervous energy.

"Did you get the transmitter?" Magpie asked.

"No. A couple of peasants stopped my car on the way to the château. They said the Germans arrived hot on our tails yesterday, even before the dust had cleared. With their revolvers at the ready, they announced that they were after a dangerous spy named Mrs. Harrison."

"Wow." Magpie shot a glance at Marie-Madeleine, this one awed instead of cagey. "If you'd let me go on transmitting for even a minute longer, we'd have had it."

"Who is Mrs. Harrison?" Siegrist asked.

Marie-Madeleine burst into laughter. "They must mean *hérisson*," she said, emphasizing the French word for hedgehog. "They probably think I'm an Englishwoman!"

After a few more hours of thought, however, Marie-Madeleine concluded the situation wasn't so amusing after all. The Gestapo couldn't have possibly deduced she was in Sarlat through guesswork alone.

One of her agents had to have been followed to the château. Her inner radar began to go off again. Suddenly, the comfort and coziness at Castel Lolita felt out of place, like something a theatrical producer would have used as the backdrop for a classical tragedy.

Tragedy. Not on my watch.

She decided to impose strict regulations for anyone coming or going to the new headquarters. Each visitor arriving by one of the seven trains was subject to scrutiny.

When Zebra stopped by the house, she searched his person. She unearthed the lease agreement with the Spanish dentist among Zebra's business papers. "We've all dodged a bullet," she exclaimed. "If that paper had been found on you, it would have been a catastrophe. Now show me your wallet."

"Why all the precautions?" Zebra asked as he handed it over.

She ignored the question as she pulled out another address. "What's this?"

"Basset's cottage," he responded with a twinge of embarrassment. "I promise I'll destroy it after learning it by heart, but I haven't had time yet."

"It's not safe to keep this paper. I insist that you burn it, now."

"Hedgehog, I understand your orders, but please let me hold onto it for a couple more hours. It's quite intricate, but I can learn it on the train."

She called in Magpie, who was to accompany Zebra to Toulouse, and repeated her instructions.

"Got it, boss." Magpie gestured to Zebra that it was time to leave.

Following their departure, Marie-Madeleine kept watch through the night, listening to the serene melodies of nature outside the house, which were occasionally interrupted by the sharp whistle of passing trains.

Magpie arrived on the first train the next morning, clearly furious. "I reiterated your orders to Zebra, but he said, 'Hedgehog fusses too much.' We went to dinner, and then Zebra wanted to stroll along the Rue Clauzel, but I begged off and spent the night at the Toulouse headquarters. In the morning, I went by the Rue Clauzel, but it looked dubious with all the people wandering around and I left for the station."

Marie-Madeleine's head was once again throbbing, and she informed Magpie that she needed to lie down.

A few hours later, she was awakened by Magpie, who let her know that one of her Sarlat couriers had arrived.

Her head still ached, and she knew what the courier would say before the words came out of his mouth: Zebra had been arrested.

"There's more," the courier went on. "Bishop failed to show at the rendezvous we'd arranged. I felt it prudent not to wait around for him. I'm sorry, madame."

"Bishop?" He'd been with Alliance since almost the beginning, and it had been he who told her about Schaerrer's death. Marie-Madeleine instructed the courier to return to Sarlat to await fresh orders.

As soon as he left, the phone rang. It was Basset's adjutant calling to inform her of the arrest of several local operatives. Another phone call came in and the caller announced, 'Your little Basset hound has just been impounded. The rabies epidemic is so bad that the Colt will also have to leave the stable." The caller was Colt himself, informing her that he needed to flee the area in the wake of Basset's arrest.

An hour before midnight, Colonel Kauffman called to say that "Rabbit and Gavarni had been carried off by the fox."

She hung up the phone, pondering the fate of the hapless Gavarni, who hadn't worked for them for months. Her stomach twisted and she ran to the bathroom to throw up.

Afterward, feeling slightly better, she went into the dining room and sat down at the polished wood table. As Monique and Magpie looked over her shoulder, Marie-Madeleine coded a message to London.

"We can't stay in the house," she announced when she'd finished. "The address is known to some of the captured agents, and even our most competent men may be forced by the Gestapo's brutal interrogation methods to divulge information." She picked up her message and handed it to Magpie. "Send this out on your night frequency."

"You got it, boss."

As Marie-Madeleine packed, she heard Magpie furiously tapping on his Morse key, notifying the British of the latest catastrophe. In addition, she had asked them to pass on a memorandum to all the transmitters that were still functioning that she had 'arrived safely in London and conveyed her affectionate greetings,' hoping that would convince the Gestapo to give up their hunt.

Her last request to MI6 was to send Léon back in the next Lysander operation, which was scheduled for the February moon.

When he'd finished, Magpie threw his transmitter into a suitcase. Carrying her own double-bottomed case and a bag with the network's money, Marie-Madeleine nodded at him. With Monique in tow, and all of them laden down with luggage, they trudged off into the gloomy night to catch the next train out.

Their destination was Tulle, sixty miles north. The head of the region found them a hotel where they didn't have to register.

Feeling overheated, either from the day's trials or from a fever, Marie-Madeleine lay down, fully clothed, on the freshly-laundered sheets. She buried her head under a pillow, trying to drown out the terrifying memories of the newest disaster engulfing them.

. . .

The next morning, Magpie managed to establish communication with London from Tulle cathedral's bell tower while the Abbé stood guard.

Magpie's news was discouraging: the Nice, Toulouse, and Pau transmitters had fallen silent like the Marseille radio, from which nothing had been heard for weeks. And no one knew what was going on in Lyons. Worse yet, Léon was currently in Algiers and would not be able to return to France before the March moon.

Magpie handed her a personal note from Major Richards. *If you persist you will undoubtedly be arrested STOP Take the February Lysander STOP Awaiting you impatiently END*

She set the message down and told Magpie she was going back to bed.

She was awoken a few minutes later by shouting coming from the living room. "Colonel, calm yourself!" It took a moment to orient herself in the strange new room where her host's ancestors smiled down at her from their ostentatious frames. Another cry from the living room, this one even more heart-rending than before, compelled her to get out of bed.

She found Magpie, Monique, and a couple of other local agents gathered around Colonel Kauffman, who was slumped in a chair. When he saw Marie-Madeleine, he howled, "They've all been caught. Do you understand? My wife, my brother, my agents, my radio operator. All taken away by the Gestapo!"

Marie-Madeleine's knees felt wobbly, but she forced herself to stay standing. She sent everyone out of the room besides Magpie and Monique and then grasped Kauffman's hands, which he was wrenching in anguish. "What happened?"

He looked past her, his vision blurred by tears. 'You'll have to forgive me, madame. I'm exhausted." He shook his head. "My family, all of my friends. My wife won't be freed unless I turn myself in."

"No! You have no right to do that. We're not the only ones involved—if you go to the police, they will torture you to find out more information. I feel horrible about your family, Colonel Kauffman, but you have to remember that our duty is to the network."

Kauffman, who was one of Léon's old air force buddies, gave a mournful nod.

Magpie put a hand on her shoulder. "What now, boss? Should I let London know you are coming?"

"Of course not," she snapped. Then, in a softer voice, she acknowledged they couldn't stay in Tulle since it was evident that a major Gestapo operation was targeting Alliance. "We will all go to Lyons."

This seemed to revive Kauffman, who sat up. "Very good, madame. I shall accompany you."

CHAPTER 43

FEBRUARY 1943

Marie-Madeleine knew she wouldn't be out of danger in Lyons, but she had exhausted all of her hiding places. She had acquaintances in the city that would provide her with a safehouse while she figured out how to rescue the network, among overcoming other problems.

Her stomach was still not quite right. Her nausea wasn't just confined to the morning, but it had been like that with both Christian and Beatrice, and her normally diminutive breasts were tender and swollen. All the signs pointed to the fact that she was indeed pregnant, but she pushed it out of her mind, judging that she had at least another six months to figure out what to do.

They made a plan for Lyons on the train. Magpie wanted to immediately contact Madeleine Crozet, code named Mouse, who was Rivière's new adjutant, but Marie-Madeleine convinced him not to, since they were still not sure if the Lyons branch of the network was still functioning. "We will pay a visit to one of my oldest friends, who, as of now, has nothing to do with Alliance," she declared.

The Baroness de Mareuil, who had once been a writer for *Marie-Claire*, welcomed them in her usual elegant way. Her flat in the middle of the city consisted of only one bedroom and a tiny living room, so

Magpie made a bed of cushions on the floor while the Baroness, Marie-Madeleine, and Monique crowded into the bedroom.

Colonel Kauffman appeared the next day on the brink of yet another nervous breakdown. He'd spent the previous day checking up on Mouse, Rivière's adjutant, and found out she'd been arrested. "She and Hummingbird, another agent, are being tortured by the notorious Klaus Barbie. They call him 'The Butcher of Lyons.' He's burning their bare breasts with cigarettes in order to make them reveal information about Alliance."

Marie-Madeleine's own chest burned as if in commiseration. "How did you find out about this Klaus Barbie?"

"I met the prison chaplain. He knows everything that goes on. I thought maybe we could organize their escape, but nothing can be done against the Boche's prisons." He clenched his fists as he repeated, "Nothing can be done—the network is finished."

"Colonel Kauffman—"

They were interrupted by Magpie, who entered the room accompanied by another wireless operator named Petrel. The sight of the mathematics graduate, who had once been bursting with vigor and intelligence, caused Marie-Madeleine to flinch in shock. With his emaciated frame and bloodshot eyes, he now looked like a drugged-up vagabond.

Petrel hugged her and then murmured, almost as if to himself, "All the Marseille people have been arrested: Panda, Jaguar, Pony, Badger. And Rivière's wife, and Basset's two bodyguards, along with numerous others whose identities I couldn't uncover."

"How do you know about Marseille?" Marie-Madeleine asked.

"Since Hummingbird's arrest—not that I'm afraid she'll talk, poor girl—I only sleep on the train. The work must go on: I've been to Marseille and Nice three times." He looked at Marie-Madeleine, his eyes even redder. "They've all been caught in Nice too."

Her head spun as she pictured her agents in shackles, battered and covered in bruises, soon to be gone forever. She felt as though she were drowning, being pulled under the water by forces unseen. As

Kauffman had put it moments earlier, nothing more could be done. It was time to give up.

Her stomach gurgled, reminding her of the possibility that she might bring yet another child into this world of oppression. Didn't she owe it to this child, and Beatrice and Christian—and all the children of France, for that matter—to do what she could to fight the oppressors?

The always composed Magpie called her back to reality. "Should we inform London that we are still functional, boss?"

She glanced at him and then around the room, at Monique, Magpie, Petrel, Kauffman, and the baroness. The five of them stood before her, linked together like the fingers of her hand.

Nothing can be done. No, that was untrue. There was nothing they couldn't achieve with people like this—or like Schaerrer, Vallet, and Noble—an entire squadron of volunteer fighters willing to give up everything to see the Nazis defeated.

She fingered the ring Léon had given her, knowing she had no choice. The second iteration of the network had been obliterated, but they must carry on.

CHAPTER 44

MARCH 1943

Although not everything was destroyed, the Nazis had ravaged Alliance's southern region. Most of the sectors had been wiped out, with the exception of Vichy and central France, and there were only a handful of key survivors: herself, Rivière, Petrel, Kauffman, Siegrist, Magpie, and Monique. And Noble and Léon, though she hadn't heard from either of them in months.

Finally she received confirmation that Léon was returning, and going to land by the light of the March full moon. Marie-Madeleine asked Magpie to scout a suitable landing ground, but he returned with bad news: a courier from Tulle had told him that the Gestapo had pounced on their flat the afternoon after they'd left. The Abbé had somehow rallied the local residents who had surrounded the apartment, insisting that, since they were not the French police, they had no right to arrest lawful citizens. Outnumbered, the Nazis had actually withdrawn, giving the remaining Alliance agents in the area sufficient time to flee.

"And the Abbé?" Marie-Madeleine asked.

Magpie shook his head. "He was urged to leave as well, but just as a soldier does not abandon his post, a priest does not abandon his church. He was arrested when the Gestapo agents returned the next day with the proper papers."

She blew out a breath she hadn't realized she'd been holding. "What about the Ussel field? It's far enough away from Tulle that it should be safe."

"It looks that way... at least for now."

Marie-Madeleine moved them again for safety, this time to a much larger house, owned by a kindly old woman named Mademoiselle Berne-Churchill. As Monique put it, the name could only be a good omen.

The brash mademoiselle was quickly folded into the network and given the code name Ladybird. She was able to introduce them to two couriers and four lieutenants. One of them was a Jewish doctor, Robert Worms, whom Ladybird had been concealing in her house for months.

When Ladybird introduced her to the doctor, she brought each of them a cup of tea and asked him to give the frail Marie-Madeleine a quick exam.

"What seems to be troubling you, madame?" Dr. Worms asked when Ladybird had left the room.

"Nothing out of the ordinary, doctor, apart from the nightmares and stomach aches that accompany my meals. Oh, and I think I might be pregnant."

He nearly choked on his tea. "Oh?" He carefully set his cup down and gestured toward the bedroom. "Do you mind if we have a closer examination?"

As she lay on the bed, her shirt pulled up, the doctor took out his stethoscope. He searched around her belly, frowning. When he removed his earpieces, he stated that, if she was pregnant, it was too early to hear the baby's heartbeat. "Are you certain that you are with child?"

She nodded. There was no question at this point.

Dr. Worms put the stethoscope back in his bag. "Well then, you need to take better care of yourself. Get plenty of sleep and find ways to minimize stress."

Minimize stress? She practically laughed in his face. As soon as he left, she started making plans for the Lysander landing that would bring Léon back.

On the morning of Léon's expected arrival, Ladybird prepared a marvelous breakfast of grilled pâté and pork sausages.

Marie-Madeleine, as per usual, hadn't gotten much sleep the night before. "Thank you for doing this," she told Ladybird.

"Of course. I cannot wait to meet the famous Léon Faye. This shall be a nice change for him, after dining on toast and marmalade while he was in England."

Their ears perked at the sound of hasty footsteps on the porch. But instead of Léon, the man who entered was Mahout. Marie-Madeleine was sending him to England for instruction on how to land bombers and he was supposed to replace Léon on the plane. He should have been in London by now.

"What happened to the landing?" Marie-Madeleine asked Mahout.

He stared down at his feet. "We were on the lookout all night. It never came."

She felt the coffee she'd been drinking rise up in her throat. The weather last night had been perfectly fine, the moon as bright as daylight. *Had there been a mishap with the plane? What if it had been shot down?*

"Madame?" Mahout inquired. From his raised eyebrows, it was obvious he had been trying to get her attention.

She shook her head clear of her thoughts. "What is it?"

"I met up with Ram as I was returning from the field. He is desperate to talk to you."

"Show him in."

"Moufflon's been murdered," Ram announced as he walked into the kitchen. "The Gestapo surrounded him at the train station. Moufflon tried pulling out his gun, but the Boches fired and got him in the throat."

Marie-Madeleine, feeling herself start to gag, hurried to the sink. After a moment, when nothing came up, she turned back to Ram. "Where was Moufflon going?"

"I think Paris," Ram replied.

Calmer now, Marie-Madeleine asked when it had happened.

"March 8th."

That was the same day the Gestapo descended on Tulle. She could feel the net closing in on them again. "Ram, you must clear everyone associated with Moufflon out as soon as possible."

"Right, although it's not going to be easy. The Germans have set up roadblocks everywhere and they are checking everyone's papers." He touched the coffee pot and then turned to Ladybird. "Do you mind? I need something to rouse me. I've been up all night."

"You're not the only one," Ladybird replied. She gestured to both Ram and Mahout. "Sit down and eat."

As soon as Ladybird took the cover off the food, Marie-Madeleine felt the urge to vomit again. She headed toward the bathroom, ruminating over what Ram had said. It had to be someone in their network who was double-crossing them. Léon was about to land in a hornet's nest.

As she retched into the toilet, she thought, *What if something happens to Léon? How could I carry on alone?*

When Dr. Worms checked in on her later that day, Marie-Madeleine confessed that she was consumed with worry about Léon's arrival. "Ram told me the military police have set up inspection sites on all the major roads, but chances are London will try another landing tonight."

The doctor sat back and stared at her for a few moments. Finally he said, "Normally I would never do this, especially not for a woman in your condition. But I know of a colleague who has an *Ausweis* authorizing him to transport sick patients in his car at any hour, day or night. He can say that he's taking you into town for an operation and Magpie can act as your anxious husband. You can then take the night train out to the landing site."

She grasped his hands in hers. "Thank you."

She had no trouble pretending to be ill when they were stopped at the checkpoint. Her forehead was covered in beads of perspiration, and she could only assume they were obvious in the glare of the Boches' flashlights. Dr. Gilbert, Worms' completely unruffled colleague, produced his *Ausweis* and explained why he was traveling so late at night.

Magpie, sitting on his transmitter suitcase, dabbed at her face with a rag. "Quickly doctor, she's losing consciousness!"

They were finally allowed to go and Dr. Gilbert drove as fast as he dared. Although the moon was the reason Léon's Lysander was able to try another landing, to Marie-Madeleine, it seemed hostile that night, shining in the night like a knife blade.

They arrived at the station just as the train was pulling away.

"We can still catch it!" Dr. Gilbert put his foot down on the accelerator and raced to the next station.

They made it just in time. As the train pulled into the station by the landing zone, Marie-Madeleine and Magpie hurried into the lobby, hoping they would still be able to meet Léon's plane. The reception committee was waiting at a table along with several soldiers in the grayish-green uniforms.

"Back to Lyons," she muttered to Magpie under her breath.

"*Merde alors,*" was his hushed reply.

CHAPTER 45

MARCH 1943

"Minerva, I don't recognize you anymore."

Marie-Madeleine got up from Ladybird's kitchen table, smoothing the locks of her badly-dyed hair before succumbing to a fit of uncontrollable laughter. The voice was unmistakably Léon's, but the figure before her was a decrepit hunchback with a shock of white hair, his eyes obscured by steel-framed spectacles.

"I hardly recognize you either." She attempted to hug him, but instead of feeling his muscles through his clothes, she felt the padding of a bodysuit. "Who put you in this outfit?"

"The head of makeup at MI6."

"Léon, is it your habit to make two return trips on a Lysander rather than one just to frighten me?"

He sank into the kitchen chair while Ladybird bustled around him. "It's a long story," he sighed. "The first night the pilot got lost, nearly ending up in Switzerland, and was forced to circle back to England before running out of fuel. Of course, I made them try again the next night. There's nothing I wouldn't have done to come to your aid. I've heard the network is in grave danger. Again."

She took the chair next to him and put her hand over his. "The network is surviving, as always." She sat back as Mademoiselle Berne-

Churchill delivered his breakfast. "This is our new hostess. We call her Ladybird."

Léon shook her hand. "Pleased to meet you."

Trying to breathe through her mouth so as not to smell the food, Marie-Madeleine filled him in on the past weeks while Léon scarfed down his breakfast. Afterward, he asked if she would show him her room. "I've got to take this kit off as soon as possible."

Once in the bedroom, and, after having taken off his peculiar get-up, Léon reached for her. This time when she embraced him, she was careful to keep her growing belly away from his trim stomach. "There's more news I have to share with you."

"Me too. London has decided to militarize Alliance."

"What?" She forgot her own big announcement. "That's absurd. What do they expect us to do, leap out the trenches shouting 'charge,' only to get shot up by the Wehrmacht?"

"Take it easy. Someday we'll be a proper regiment, fighting with guns and ammunition dropped by parachute, but for now we'll remain where we've always been: underground." He tried putting his arms around her but she backed away. The concern was obvious in his voice as he asked what was wrong.

"I'm pregnant."

His mouth opened and closed but no words came out.

"It's yours."

He let out a soft snicker. "I figured as much." As the news sunk in, a wide grin spread across his face. "Are you telling me I'm going to be a father?"

"Yes." She'd been so wrapped up in the network, it hadn't really registered with her either. "Yes," she repeated, throwing her arms around him.

He finally broke the embrace to peer at her. "But Marie-Madeleine, you look thinner than ever. Are you sure the baby is all right?"

"It's still early, but look…" she grabbed his hand and placed it over her stomach. "I have a tiny bump now."

"We have to get you food—you have to remember that you are eating for two now!" He opened the door and called for Ladybird.

When she appeared, he asked her to rustle up whatever they could find for Marie-Madeleine. "I want to ensure my baby is well-fed, even in the womb."

Ladybird put a hand over her chest. "Oh my." She went to hug Marie-Madeleine. "I thought you might be, with all the nausea you've been having." Her eyes traveled to Léon, whom she'd just met that morning. "Oh my," she said again before retreating down the hall.

"Léon," Marie-Madeleine hissed after he'd shut the door. "Most people don't make it a habit of telling near-strangers about their pregnancy, especially when the mother is technically married to someone else."

Once again his mouth dropped open. "I'm sorry. I guess I don't know the protocol." He sat down on the bed, slightly deflated. "Speaking of which, what are we going to do? I don't really want my first-born child to be illegitimate."

She conceded his point, but what could she do? "I've told you before—I can't ask Édouard for a divorce when I don't know where he is. It will have to wait until after the war."

"Right." He shook his head vigorously as if to convince himself. "Our first priority is to get you healthy."

An alarm went off in Marie-Madeleine's head and she grasped Léon's hand, feeling faint. "Léon, what if something happened to me? I'm constantly in danger, and not just because of this…" she gestured at her belly. "What would be the point of carrying on if the fire we have ignited goes out in the event of my capture… or worse?"

"Nothing is going to happen."

"But if it does… we need a successor." She went to the desk and grabbed a piece of paper.

"Who are you writing to?"

"Swift." He had been with Crusade since 1940, and was one of the last men standing whom she trusted implicitly.

Léon waited on the bed until she'd finished. "Now that you have a new second-in-command, I want you to lay low for a while. You won't be able to go out amongst the people of Lyons in a few months anyway."

"That's not necessary. Ladybird's been perfectly hospitable and Dr. Worms…"

Léon snapped his fingers. "That's it. Just before I departed London, they provided a list of possible safehouses in Lyons, in case something happens. One of them was a private hospital up on the hill. I can't think of a better place for you to stay for the time being."

The firmness of his voice left no room for argument, and Marie-Madeleine agreed to be installed in the Clinique des Cedres. "Just promise me you'll keep me informed of everything that's going on in the network."

"As long as you promise me you'll try to sleep whenever you can. And eat." His hand on her stomach, he gave her a tender, lingering kiss.

CHAPTER 46

MAY 1943

Léon called on Marie-Madeleine at the Clinique des Cedres every day. She was under the protection of the chief nurse, a Mademoiselle Prodon-Guénard, who vowed to conceal Marie-Madeleine's real identity as well as monitor her pregnancy.

One morning, when Léon came to visit, the look on his face set warning bells off in Marie-Madeleine's head. "What is it?"

He pulled a chair out for her. "I promised myself I wouldn't cause you any undue stress, but there's something you should know. This is the latest from Noble." He handed her a decoded message. It seemed that her sister, Yvonne, had been arrested and Georges had been forced to flee to Spain.

"Believe it or not, that's not the worst of it." Léon began to pace the room. "The headmaster of your son's boarding school sent word that he had been visited by the Gestapo."

"No." She felt a fluttering in her stomach, like a wounded butterfly trying to take flight.

Léon held up his hand. "They wanted him to turn over Christian to the secret police, in order to get you to surrender." He put his arms around her. "The headmaster refused. Christian—and Beatrice too—are safe for now."

She looked up at him. "You have to bring them here."

"It's too dangerous."

"Please, Léon."

"This place is literally the Lyons' den." He started pacing again. "And their mother is the bait." He paused. "Do you have any family in one of the neutral countries?"

She closed her eyes, thinking of the safest place in the world for her children right now. "My uncle owns a chalet in Switzerland."

"That's it. We'll send them there. That way they cannot be used as pawns in whatever game the Gestapo is currently playing."

"But Léon, I have to see them before they leave. I need to kiss them one more time."

He sighed. "I can get them here, but you have to stay out of sight. What if they are followed and lead the Gestapo to the den itself?"

She longed to hold them in her arms again, but knew Léon was right. Navarre's love of his family had been his undoing, and she must not repeat the same mistake.

Monique was put in charge of the two little ones. She was still staying with Ladybird, and Marie-Madeleine had no doubt the two women spoiled her babies rotten while they were in Lyons.

The day before they were to leave for Switzerland, Léon arranged for Monique to take them on a walk outside the clinic. Tucked behind a curtain, Marie-Madeleine was at last able to lay her eyes on Beatrice and Christian.

They looked like fragile little birds, powerless against forces larger than them. Léon's plan called for them to cross the border alone, climbing over barbed wire in the wilderness of France, while avoiding the border guards who'd been instructed to shoot refugees like them on sight. After that, they had to make their way to her uncle's chalet with nothing but the clothes they were wearing. It was an exceedingly perilous undertaking, but she knew her children were even braver than their mother. Faced with no choice, she had to have confidence they would be able to complete their journey to safety.

Still, as Marie-Madeleine watched them walk away, she had the distinct feeling she was being suffocated.

CHAPTER 47

AUGUST 1943

As the August moon drew near, Marie-Madeleine knew it was time to organize a crucial intelligence report to London. They were looking for information to enable General Giraud to land, possibly in Corsica or somewhere on the Mediterranean Coast. Consequently, she had requested that her agents, specifically Colonel Kauffman and a few other couriers, bring their intel to Lyons to be flown out by Lysander. Having such a large gathering of essential people and sensitive information all in one place, however, left her feeling very uneasy.

She was therefore not surprised when Léon arrived at the clinic unexpectedly, a grim look on his handsome face.

"Has something happened to the reports?"

"No." He sat down wearily in the chair next to the bed. "There was a problem with last night's parachute operation."

"Were the boys arrested?"

"Not yet. They—Rivière, Mahout, and Cockerel, the new radio operator—got into a bad crash on their way to the field. They're all in the hospital right now."

Bile rose in her throat and she choked it down with a gulp of water. Mahout had returned to France from London only a month ago. "We have to get them out, now."

"It's too late—apparently Cockerel talked while under anesthesia. The Vichy police have swarmed the landing field…"

The impending doom ringing in her ears drowned out the rest of his words. As if she were underwater, she heard him say he was going to find the nurse.

He came back a few minutes later, accompanied by Mademoiselle Prodon-Guénard, whose name Marie-Madeleine had changed to Kitten.

"There, there," Kitten said, her Burgundian tongue rolling the r's as she tended to Marie-Madeleine.

"I'm fine," Marie-Madeleine told Léon. "I just got too hot for a second."

"We need to take all safety precautions possible," Léon said. "Including relocating you somewhere else."

"No," Kitten replied. "I can move her to another room on the ground floor, one that overlooks the garden, where she'll be able to make a quick getaway if necessary."

Léon looked at Marie-Madeleine. "You sure you'll be all right?"

"I'm fine," she said again.

She spent the evening sorting through her paperwork, burning copies of her radio communications, and retaining only the coded notes.

The couriers were due to meet with Léon the next morning. Monique was supposed to stop by the clinic, but the allotted time came and went. Kitten tried to get Marie-Madeleine to eat lunch, but she had lost her appetite.

Late in the afternoon, the phone rang. Kitten answered it and then informed Marie-Madeleine it was her friend, Ermine.

Marie-Madeleine lunged for the receiver. "You're late."

"Yes," Monique proclaimed quietly. "But you see, I've hurt my foot badly. I can't come today… nor tomorrow… nor the next day." Marie-

Madeleine's heart sank as Monique's hushed voice continued, "Nor will the others either." And then the line went dead.

"Léon," Marie-Madeleine's voice croaked as she lay back on her bed. *Léon arrested again, for the third time.*

And the rest of them? Poor, beautiful Monique and Colonel Kauffman... With them gone and Rivière wounded in the hospital, who was she supposed to turn to now?

Kitten laid her hand over Marie-Madeleine's. "Tell me what you want me to do."

"Ladybird and the Baroness must be informed immediately. They can warn the rest of the network. And tell them to send Ernest Siegrist to me."

For hours, Marie-Madeleine remained on high alert, listening intently for any sound that would indicate Kitten's return.

At last she heard footsteps approaching, but they were much too heavy to be Kitten's. As the door opened, Marie-Madeleine took hold of the crowbar she kept behind the nightstand.

The person entered the room, and, through the fading light, she could see Léon's features. He flopped down on the bed.

"I thought you had been captured."

"I was. I've just escaped and came here as fast as I could."

Her pulse slowed a bit as she got up to get him a glass of water. He drank it eagerly, as if he had been stranded in the desert for days.

"What happened?" she asked, returning the crowbar to its hiding spot.

"I met up with Kauffman and the others, Vitrolles and Armadillo, for lunch at a bistro. As we were leaving, the police burst in and took us to the station. There, I confused the officer in charge by telling him I had the support of the Deuxième Bureau. It must have worked because he tried calling them to get confirmation. In the meantime, Vitrolles noticed that the main door to the courtyard was unguarded."

"So you just left?"

"We did. We split up once we were on the street."

"What about Monique?"

KIT SERGEANT

Léon blinked. "Monique wasn't with us. As far as I knew, she was still at Ladybird's."

"Then how did she know?" Marie-Madeleine filled him in on the phone call.

"The police must have them stuck in the house, waiting for one of us to arrive," Léon deduced.

"We should rescue them."

He put his arm around Marie-Madeleine's shoulders. "We can't. If what I said is true, they're ready to spring on us the moment we go over there. We'll have to wait it out. Monique is a smart girl: I'm sure she'll think of something."

Indeed, a few days later, they heard that Monique had managed to slip away from the guards keeping watch. Ladybird, however, was now in police custody, and the Gestapo had caught wind of the arrests and subsequent escapes. They were conducting a thorough search of the area and had established roadblocks to prevent anyone from escaping.

Marie-Madeleine was starting to find Lyons unbearable, as though it was swarming with undercover agents. London seemed to agree with her, as Richards sent a message demanding to know why she persisted in staying in Lyons and advising her to move.

Easy for him to say. Marie-Madeleine crumpled up the message and threw it into the fire. But at least they'd stopped asking for her to come to London.

Léon sought refuge at his lawyer's office and had taken to donning his hunchback outfit whenever he had to go out. Somehow he convinced one of their inspector contacts to retrieve Ladybird from her prison cell on the pretense of needing her for questioning.

When the inspector delivered Ladybird to the clinic, he asked Marie-Madeleine to arrange his safe passage to Britain, to which she agreed.

Ladybird appeared stunned but unhurt. "We've got to get you, and us, out of Lyons," Marie-Madeleine told her.

The older woman was silent for a few moments before her eyes grew wide. "I've worked with the Red Cross. I bet I could get us a lorry. Even the Nazis usually wave the Red Cross vans through."

"Excellent. We can leave as soon as we spring Rivière and the rest out of jail." The plan for that was fairly simple: one of their agents, Pegasus, would dress as a male nurse and try to convince the nuns there that the three injured men needed some fresh air.

Pegasus returned with only Mahout and Rivière. The man named Cockerel had disappeared outside of the hospital.

"Why would he leave like that?" Marie-Madeleine wondered.

"This whole thing was his fault," Rivière replied. "While he was under the knife, he talked about Ermine, the pretty girl he was working with. It wasn't long before the police tracked her down."

Marie-Madeleine gasped. If they'd followed Monique on her morning errands, she would have led them straight to the clinic. She thanked her lucky stars it hadn't happened that way.

Léon, Rivière, Magpie, and most of the other agents left Lyons by way of Ladybird's Red Cross lorry. Only Monique and Ernest Siegrist remained. Siegrist was busy making new identity cards for dozens of Alliance agents, and Monique had graciously volunteered to stay with Marie-Madeleine until the baby was born.

Marie-Madeleine now had a protruding stomach, though the rest of her was still quite thin. Kitten said that everything was proceeding smoothly and it should be any day now.

Kitten had instructions to summon Léon when the time was imminent, but Siegrist ended those plans when he informed Marie-Madeleine of the current goings-on in Lyons. "The local police have had a rough summer—they made six arrests to no avail, and the would-be prisoners in the hospital also somehow managed to escape. They've come to the conclusion that their roadblocks are about as useful as a broken dam in a flood."

"Well, that's a good thing for us." Marie-Madeleine put a hand on her stomach to feel the baby's kick.

"It would be, except the Gestapo has deported the chief of police, and now they are calling for the arrests of anyone remotely connected with the network, which, apparently, they've nicknamed 'Noah's Ark.' For all the animal names," he added, unnecessarily.

"Who have they taken?"

He ticked off a few unfamiliar names, but then he mentioned the Baroness and Ladybird's daughter. He also said the Gestapo had paid a visit to the Guillots' apartment building. The husband was an associate of the network and went by Dromedary. In fact, the Gestapo had asked Guillot, who had been gardening in the back with his wife, if he were familiar with 'Mr. and Mrs. Dromedary.' Guillot had replied that they lived on the fourth floor. After their backs were turned, he grabbed his wife and left out the front door.

"All of Lyons is imploding," Siegrist told her. "I no longer feel safe. We've got to get you out of here as soon as possible." His oversized ears twitched, like the Elephant he was named for.

"*Merde alors*," Marie-Madeleine replied. She'd been in Lyons for nearly seven months, but now everything she'd built up was collapsing, like a building during a Luftwaffe bombing. Were the lives of those in the Resistance destined to be as fragile as soap bubbles?

"*Merde alors*." This time Marie-Madeleine cursed in pain. She grasped Siegrist's hand so hard the man cried out.

"It's coming!" she shouted. "Go fetch Monique and Kitten!"

CHAPTER 48

SEPTEMBER 1943

The baby, whom Marie-Madeleine named Jacques, had eyes like his father. Though they weren't quite the exact shade as Léon's yet, they were the same shape and she had no doubt that they would take on that familiar grayish-green hue someday.

She cradled Jacques in her arms, forgetting how small newborns were, how fragile. At the back of her mind loomed the thought of the danger both she and her child were in, threatening to shatter her delicate happiness. Somehow she must protect her baby at all costs. With the police closing in on the remaining members of Alliance, she knew she only had a week to nurse Jacques—and heal herself—before she had to get out of Lyons for good.

Kitten was afraid of keeping Marie-Madeleine at the clinic after the birth and was able to secure her a room in a house of ill-repute, where no one asked questions about a single mother and newborn baby.

Monique came over often to watch the baby while Marie-Madeleine tried to catch some sleep. One day the young woman arrived late and out of breath, stating she thought she'd been followed, necessitating a speedy change of plans, and a long detour.

Marie-Madeleine exhaled wearily, knowing that the time had

come. "Monique, you have to evacuate. We've stayed far too long in one place, and those men that you ran away from are looking for you everywhere. I'm surprised you've lasted this long."

"You know I can't leave you…" Monique gently touched Jacques's tiny nose. "Or him."

Marie-Madeleine's eyes filled with tears. "You love him, don't you?"

"Of course I do." She took the baby into her arms.

Marie-Madeleine gingerly sat up in bed. "I'm going to ask you a favor. Please hear me out before you give an answer."

Monique turned away, rocking the baby. "I know what you are going to say. I've been thinking about it for a long time, and the answer is yes."

Marie-Madeleine's eyes were wet with tears as she contemplated the impossible situation she was in. She couldn't bear to say the words "Take my baby" out loud, but thankfully, Monique had been her faithful companion for over a year, and they had an unspoken understanding. Marie-Madeleine had been grappling with the idea of raising the child while continuing to manage Alliance, but deep down, she knew it wasn't possible, and there was only one person she could trust to take care of Jacques the way a mother would.

Monique faced Marie-Madeleine. "I know your work is not finished yet. I wish I could go on to help you fight, but the Gestapo know me now."

Marie-Madeleine wiped her tears with a handkerchief. "There's an Alliance safehouse in the south of France where we send people who are too recognizable. You can take Jacques…" her voice broke at the mention of her son's name, "there."

"But what about Léon? Won't he want to see his son?"

She nodded. "He will, after the war, when it's safe."

Monique gave the now-sleeping baby back to Marie-Madeleine. "What about you?"

"I have to get out of Lyons as soon as possible."

"But you are in no shape to leave. You've just had a baby."

Marie-Madeleine stroked Jacques's thick, dark hair, another trait he'd inherited from his father. "I'll have to manage somehow. If I don't go soon, I'll end up in the back of a Gestapo van."

Monique put her arm around Marie-Madeleine's shoulders. "I'll give you two some privacy to say goodbye while I make the arrangements."

After she left, Marie-Madeleine began to sob uncontrollably. Most babies would cry at the sudden sound, but gentle Jacques merely opened his eyes, as if checking to make sure his mother was okay.

She couldn't believe she was doing this again. The pain of sending Beatrice and Christian away had been unbearable, and now she was reliving it all over again with her new baby.

I could be the one to go to the south of France. She could send for her older children to join her, and they could wait out the war together, as a family.

As quickly as the thoughts popped into her head, she discarded them. Despite her heartache, she knew where her place was: at the top of Alliance. Her children would be in safer hands than hers for the duration of the war, and France needed her more—she would never be able to raise a family in a country occupied by monsters. The best thing she could do for her children was to keep fighting to make the world free again.

She looked down at Jacques, who had fallen asleep. "I love you," she whispered. "Someday you will meet your father, and your brother and sister, and we will live as a family. But right now I have to leave you."

She gently placed him in the cradle before she once again burst into tears.

CHAPTER 49

SEPTEMBER 1943

Asore and exhausted Marie-Madeleine left Lyons for Paris, carrying papers in the name of Pamela Trotaing that Ernest Siegrist had made for her. Heartbroken at having to leave little Jacques with Monique, she gazed out of the train window, watching the landscape pass by through eyes blurred with tears.

She reached the Gare de Lyon just past dawn, and, in the gloomy light, the station resembled a dark fortress. She had sent word that she was coming and requested that Noble meet her, so she was surprised to see Magpie waiting. After greeting him with a kiss on the cheek, she asked where Noble was.

Sorrow washed over Magpie's normally cheerful demeanor. "He's in the hospital. Josette is with him."

"What is wrong with him?"

He gave her a strange look. "I think you know that—the illness he'd been ignoring for months finally got the better of him."

Her already heavy heart sunk even deeper at the thought of Noble laid low by his horrible cough.

. . .

The new headquarters was a luxury suite, complete with exquisite artwork and opulent furniture, on the rue Raynouard. Marie-Madeleine was anxious to see Léon, but he was not at the apartment when they arrived.

"Léon arranged a dinner for us," Magpie said, noticing how her eyes searched the empty room.

She gave him a tentative smile.

He set her bag down. "Where is Monique, anyway? Is she still in Lyons?"

"Actually," Marie-Madeleine cleared her throat. "She's relocated to the south. She was too well-known by the Gestapo to remain an agent."

"Oh," was Magpie's simple reply, his expression unreadable. She was sure Magpie knew about the baby, but his British reserve prevented him from commenting further.

Léon was waiting at a table in the back of the posh black-market restaurant. He stood up to hug Marie-Madeleine as soon as she and Magpie walked in.

"You look much better." He poured her a glass of red wine.

"Léon," Marie-Madeleine hissed, her eyes darting around the room, which was brimming with Germans in uniform. "Do you really think this is a good idea?"

"I knew you would be in need of a nutritious meal, and this is the best Paris has to offer."

Magpie gave a low whistle as he opened his menu. "It's been a while since I've had a good duck."

Léon put his hand on Marie-Madeleine's shoulder. "Just forget about everything and enjoy your caviar." He sensed her hesitation, so he added, "Please, for me."

She took a long gulp of wine, which did seem to revive her. She supposed she should be grateful to know that neither Magpie nor Léon had changed in the wake of all the trauma of the last few months.

Magpie was also clearly enjoying the wine. "Who would ever think that the three of us were being hunted by the Gestapo?" he whispered near the end of the meal, his British reserve now abandoned. He raised his glass at a group of Wehrmacht officers at the next table. "To your health, gentlemen!"

The words Noble had spoken to her after seeing the Germans dining at Maxim's suddenly popped into Marie-Madeleine's head. *It won't be carelessness or rashness that will be our undoing.* She rubbed her face, hoping that Noble's illness wouldn't be his final downfall.

"To your health, Marie-Madeleine." Léon clinked her glass with his and they exchanged a long look.

When Marie-Madeleine and Léon arrived back at the apartment, they found Bumpkin, the young courier from Colonel Kauffman's unit, waiting for them.

"Elephant has just been arrested!" he announced.

Marie-Madeleine slumped onto the couch. Elephant was Ernest Siegrist, whom she just left in Lyons. "But Bumpkin, it was your job to find him a safehouse." Knowing how concerned Siegrist had been, this had been her first command after Jacques was born.

"I know," Bumpkin conceded, his voice trembling. "It happened when he was on the move."

Léon put his head in his hands. "Elephant was our security chief, not to mention the head of our forgery department." He set his keen, airman's gaze on Bumpkin. "Where were you during the arrest?"

Bumpkin stared down at his feet, avoiding eye contact. "I was in Nice, sir."

"Nice? What were you doing in Nice?" Léon demanded.

"I did find Elephant a safehouse, and I designated Lanky to escort him to it. But when Lanky got to the rendezvous point, he noticed that it was surrounded by Germans, so he left for the tram stop."

"Tram stop," Marie-Madeleine repeated. "Did Lanky really think Elephant was going to arrive by streetcar, with his three radios, a bag of transmitting crystals, suitcase full of identity cards, and all of his weapons?"

Bumpkin raised his head. "I've known Lanky since before the war, when we were still University students. He's continuously proved himself to be both steadfast and brave."

"Then what was he doing at the streetcar stop?" Léon asked.

"He was looking out for Elephant."

"But yet Lanky couldn't shout out a warning from there, and, due to his blunder, Elephant is now in custody," Léon replied.

Bumpkin's composure, already precarious, finally crumbled and he choked back a sob.

Marie-Madeleine decided to take a gentle approach. "Bumpkin, you made a critical mistake by entrusting your job to someone else. You're the one who had our confidence, not Lanky."

He nodded. "Just the same, Lanky would like to apologize to your face, madame, and offer an explanation for his actions."

"No," Léon said firmly. "Your man is either a fool or a traitor." He stood up and walked over to Bumpkin. "Listen carefully: Lanky is forbidden to be anywhere near Alliance safehouses."

"Yes, sir."

After Bumpkin had let himself out, Marie-Madeleine sighed. "I suppose I'm to blame for this too. They're just students, they're lacking the experience and maturity necessary for handling anything important." She looked down at her hands, recalling that Siegrist had a wife and two daughters.

"Bumpkin made a serious error in judgment, but you can't blame yourself." Léon had started rubbing her shoulders but stopped suddenly as something occurred to him. "I gave Siegrist the duplicate of the code book."

She turned to look at him. "Weren't you the one who told me not to write all the agents' information in one place?"

"I know but there are so many now to keep track of." He sat next to her on the couch.

"I wouldn't worry about it. No one but you can read your terrible handwriting." She took his hand in hers. "Has it ever occurred to you that Alliance has grown too large?"

"Large? I thought that was the goal."

She dropped his hand. "It was, but now I'm starting to have second thoughts. We mustn't be blinded by all our achievements.

Alliance is becoming unmanageable. I'd rather we retreat and regroup."

"Retreat? You mean roll up into a ball, like a hedgehog?" Seeing how his words stung her, he softened his tone. "I know you've been through so much lately. Maybe you're in need of a longer rest. I can make arrangements for you to visit Monique and Jacques."

"Do you know how hard it was to leave him the first time?"

"No." She'd never seen him look so sad. "I can only imagine, based on the times I've had to part with you." He took her hand again. "And believe me, I don't want you to leave again, but the net in Paris is tightening. The Resistance has been suffering from mortal blows: Jean Moulin, the leader of the Free French, was just arrested, and the SOE's Prosper network is rapidly collapsing. Maybe you should go to London and lay low for a bit. And rest. I don't know how you are still standing, with all that you've been through in the past few months, on top of giving birth to our... son." His voice cracked on that last word.

"I'll think about it," she lied, wanting to cheer him up. "I know it's hard for us both, but considering we haven't seen each other for months, can we drop the business talk for now?"

"Of course." His lips curved into a broad smile as he drew her closer for a long kiss.

CHAPTER 50

OCTOBER 1943

The network continued as usual for the next few days, and Marie-Madeleine was able to effectively table the discussion about her going to England.

Until Jack Tar appeared at headquarters with yet another tale about a near-arrest. He had been on his way to Paris from Brest via Redon, where his parents lived. However, as soon as he arrived at his childhood home, he found it surrounded by Gestapo agents. He was carrying a stash of confidential papers—military plans, troop movements, and supply routes—all highly incriminating.

"I barely had time to hide in the neighbor's house across the road," Jack Tar said, jumping up to sit on the countertop. "Meanwhile I could hear them shouting both my real name and code name. Thankfully everyone in the area has known me since I was a child and no one betrayed me."

Marie-Madeleine offered him a cup of tea. "But someone must have provided the Gestapo with your name and address."

"For sure. It wasn't a random raid—they were singling me out."

She cast a sidelong look at Léon, who'd been listening attentively. "You need to keep a low profile for a couple of months. We're going to arrange for you to go to London," he told Jack.

"That sounds good." He hopped down from the counter. "And I swear I haven't invented the story in order to get out of town for a bit."

After Jack Tar had left, Léon raised his eyebrows at Marie-Madeleine. She knew what he was asking: are you convinced yet?

When she didn't reply, Léon leaned forward. "You know, when I was at MI6, the trainers made a point of telling us that agents don't usually last longer than six months in the field. They're either captured or have to return to London because they've been compromised. You've been working in the underground for more than three years."

"Léon—"

He held up his hand, cutting her off. "I don't want any more close calls. You've promised me that we'll be a family after the war." His voice broke. "How can that happen if you're arrested? Who is going to mother your children?"

Tears filled her eyes, but she had no answer for him.

He took her hands in his. "Please don't think this is indicative of how our marriage will be—I don't intend to ever be a controlling husband. But I'm asking you to go to London, if only for a few weeks. For the sake of my own sanity."

The tears were now falling freely. How could she say no to such a request? And she could hardly deny that the last several months had finally taken their toll: she was exhausted and frankly tired of fighting. "Fine, Léon. You win."

He kissed both of her wet cheeks and then gave her a peck on the lips. "I'll make the arrangements," he said before enveloping her in his arms.

The more she thought about it, the more sure she was that she had made the right decision. There were several reasons for agents getting captured: being too daring, like, as much as she hated to admit it, Schaerrer; being caught red-handed, like Siegrist; and having the radio-detection vans pick up your signal, like certain radio operators.

But it was quite another thing to be betrayed. Someone was

feeding the Gestapo information about Alliance, and until they found the leak, they would all remain in grave danger.

Though she had experienced anxiety and trepidation during some of the more dangerous operations, her confidence had always won out, fueled both by hope and her unwavering faith in Alliance. But now, despite her faith remaining steadfast, her hope was beginning to slip away. Her biggest fear had always been that she wouldn't be able to see her mission through to its conclusion, and it was becoming clear that, if she stayed, her fear would come true.

The night after she agreed to go to London, she awoke in the middle of a nightmare, covered in sweat. She shut her eyes again in an effort to recall the haunting scene that had disrupted her sleep, knowing deep down that it was important not to dismiss it. Slowly the images returned: a landscape in the country, fields of pink heather, a Lysander landing. Magpie and Léon exiting the plane. Germans waiting for them.

Where was I in all of this? She dug into her subconscious, trying to figure it out, but Léon stirred and asked what was wrong.

"Léon, do we have a landing field that's covered with heather in bloom?"

"Heather?" he repeated sleepily. "No, I don't think so. Why?"

"Are you positive?"

"Yes."

She grabbed his arm. "Léon, you must promise me to never schedule a landing where there is heather."

"What?"

She shook him. "Just promise me."

"Okay, okay, I promise. Now can we please go back to sleep?"

CHAPTER 51

SEPTEMBER 1943

Swift had eagerly accepted Marie-Madeleine's invitation for him to become her successor. He'd moved to Paris a few weeks prior, and Léon had instructed him in all the ins and outs of Alliance. Although he would be inheriting a complex machine with many moving parts, thus far, according to Léon, Swift had been able handle all his new and unfamiliar duties remarkably well.

Léon and Swift arrived at the headquarters two days before Marie-Madeleine was due to leave for London, engrossed in a conversation that struck Marie-Madeleine as very lively, though they were barely talking above a whisper.

The three of them went into the dining room for a meeting of what was left of Alliance. Rivière, Jack Tar, Colonel Kauffman, and several other members of what Marie-Madeleine considered the 'old guard' were seated at the table while Magpie and Bumpkin were standing near the doorway. Marie-Madeleine gave Swift her spot at the head of the table, seating herself at Swift's right hand, Léon across from her.

She started off by explaining what she would be doing in London: making certain that the lines of communication remained open, obtaining proper military status for the agents and their families, assuring financial help, and forging a formalized path for Alliance to secure its reputation beyond the war.

When she'd finished, she nodded at Léon, who cracked his knuckles before speaking. "I know that some of you have been worried with which general Alliance's official loyalties lie: de Gaulle or Giraud, but I propose we forget this, remain united as a network, and continue our intelligence activities for the benefit of the Allied troops until the end of the hostilities."

"Hear, hear!" Rivière cheered.

As they discussed more details, Marie-Madeleine looked around the table. Rivière and Léon were the only ones left from the first wave, when the network had been Crusade and Navarre had been its leader. The rest of the 'old guard' were really from the second wave, her wave. And here was Swift, volunteering to be in charge in her absence. Three distinct periods with three different leaders. How many more iterations of the network would be there before it was over? How many more rounds of arrests and murders would they have to endure? And who at this table would survive until the end of the war?

"Minerva?" Léon was staring at her. "Your proposal?"

She cleared her throat. "In light of my temporary absence, I have asked Swift..." she nodded at him, "to take over my role as leader."

"What about Faye... Eagle?" Rivière asked.

"My priorities are making sure we're ready to fight when the Allies land, not running the network on a day-to-day basis," Léon replied. "So I propose that the official leader be Swift, at least for the time being."

Magpie, from the corner of the room, stepped forward. "I second the motion."

She saw that a few others looked uncertain, especially Colonel Kauffman, but no one said anything.

"Then it's settled," Marie-Madeleine declared.

Everyone else gave their assent, and then the discussion turned to new security measures.

When the meeting was over, Colonel Kauffman pulled Marie-

Madeleine aside. "There's something I wanted to ask you," Kauffman said as he pulled on his gray overcoat.

"Yes?"

"Why were you so harsh with Lanky?"

"Because the way he acted during Siegrist's arrest is suspicious."

"I myself interrogated him thoroughly and concluded that he was genuinely sorry for his mistakes. He ought to be given a second chance."

"If that's the case, I think you should keep questioning him, Colonel. Léon agreed with me about Lanky's suspect behavior."

He sighed. "I haven't got a prison cell where I can put the bad apples, and I can't kill them on sight. What if I make a mistake and shoot an innocent person?"

"I understand," she replied, thinking of the trouble they went through with Bla. She placed a hand on the old man's shoulder. "I trust your wisdom and experience as a soldier to make the right decision."

"If you trust me so much, then why did you select Swift, a recent addition to the team, for the leadership role?"

Ah, so that was really why the colonel was looking so sour. "Because my successor shouldn't be someone who is already known to the Germans."

He buttoned his coat. "He's not known *yet*. That's the difference between Swift and me."

Marie-Madeleine felt a pang of remorse as Kauffman stormed off.

The following day was filled with a flurry of activity as Marie-Madeleine made preparations to leave and said her goodbyes.

As she exited the flat, she ran into Swift's wife, dressed in a neat blue pleated skirt and polka-dot scarf. The lady cleared her throat as she looked Marie-Madeleine up and down. "Madame, do you plan to arrive in London in that outfit?"

Marie-Madeleine gazed down at her dress, which now hung too loose on her thin frame, its color faded and dull. "I suppose so."

The other woman wrinkled her nose. "You're representing both

Alliance and France. We may be under Occupation, but we still have style. Come with me, I think we are about the same size."

And so Marie-Madeleine, with a bit of long-forgotten delight, accepted a tailored suit and a brown batik dress from Swift's wife.

On the night of her departure, an intimate farewell celebration was held at an upscale lounge owned by a friend of Léon's. There they sipped on fancy cocktails, obtained through special permits, amidst the company of pretentious German officers sporting monocles.

In the calm of the evening, Marie-Madeleine, dressed in her blue suit, walked hand in hand with Léon along the Champs-Élysées, basking in the warm glow of the setting sun. Unspoiled by the usual fumes of traffic, the air was clean and crisp, scented only by the plane trees that lined the wide boulevard. She was giddy both from the drinks and being in love in Paris at sunset, especially when they stopped at the Arc de Triomphe, where the beauty of the city was spread before them.

Léon didn't seem quite so enchanted as he watched the swastika flag on the Arc flap in the wind. He sat on a bench and pulled her down next to him. "I'll sleep better knowing you're off the streets of Paris and out of the Nazis' reach."

She squeezed his hand, wishing she could say the same. Last night she'd been plagued by another one of those nightmares with the Lysander touching down in the field of heather. "Promise me—"

"I know—never use a landing field with any hint of heather on it."

She gave him a shy smile. "You must think I'm crazy."

"No." His face was serious. "I think you are the most amazing woman I've ever met."

Moved to tears by his words, she didn't reply for a few moments. Finally she told him she was tired of goodbyes.

"Me too," he replied. "Let's not say goodbye this time. How about this instead? I love you and I look forward to being together permanently, when goodbyes are a thing of the past."

She nodded, afraid she'd start sobbing uncontrollably, right there on the street. "I love you too, and ditto to being together permanently."

He checked his watch. "It's just about time for you to meet Ant on the rue François." At her insistence, Léon would not be accompanying her to the landing field. She didn't want both of them in the same place in case something happened.

He kissed her one last time. "I've arranged everything down to the last detail—you'll be completely safe."

She nodded again as she picked up her suitcase. A part of her wanted her to toss it away and throw her arms around Léon, declaring that she would never leave him again.

But as usual, her sense of duty prevailed and she gave his hand one last squeeze before she strolled off.

Ant was waiting for her on a street corner, chatting with a bicycle-taxi driver. "Ah there you are," he said upon spotting Marie-Madeleine. He took her suitcase and then gestured toward the cab. "Get in."

As they darted through the streets of Paris, the cyclist straining against the pedals, Marie-Madeleine's mind was transported back to her youth in Shanghai. Before her father passed, her childhood had been unmarred by things like war or death. She longed for the day when her own children could bask in that same carefree joy, and the five of them could be a family.

As she arrived at the train station, she spotted Jack Tar in the queue for the booking office, a wide grin on his face.

Léon had purchased her ticket in advance. Without giving Jack Tar the slightest hint of acknowledgment, she and Ant went out to the platform, where the train was waiting, clouds of steam billowing from its engine. They went into the first-class compartment, and a few moments later, she saw Jack Tar walk by on his way to a back cabin.

When they got out at the station in Nanteuil-le-Haudouin, she waited with Ant for the other passengers to clear out so that Jack Tar could join them. Afterwards, they took refuge in a ditch at the roadside, where they bided their time until Dr. Gilbert arrived in his car.

Finally the faint sound of a motor chugging up the hill reached their ears. Jack Tar peeked out from the ditch as the car stalled near them. "It's him," he said before helping Marie-Madeleine swing her legs over.

Once they were all in, Dr. Gilbert drove off. No one talked, and the only noise to be heard was the sputtering of the engine. In a few minutes, he stopped in front of a newly-trimmed cornfield and turned off the car.

They joined the men of the reception committee, who were busy making out the landing strip with flashlights.

"It's amazing how calm and serene it feels here," Dr. Gilbert murmured.

In the light of the full moon, Marie-Madeleine finally got a good look at the face of the weary doctor who had given his life to healing the less fortunate. His unkempt gray hair and threadbare clothes belied the intelligence in his eyes.

"Why haven't you been assigned a code name, doctor?"

He chuckled. "I don't presume to compare myself to your magnificent birds and wild beasts. I'm more like a tiny fish."

Marie-Madeleine touched his arm. "I've been told you always refuse any form of compensation from us, even for the petrol you use driving our agents around. But there has to be something I can do for you."

He cleared his throat. "I must confess I could really use some toilet soap from London. You can't imagine how appalling it can be in my line of work, attending to the sick without clean hands."

Her promise to secure him some soap was drowned out by the approaching plane. The landing team signaled their location with flashing lights, and the pilot acknowledged them with its own torch. The signaling stopped and the Lysander taxied toward Ant. When it came to a stop, the rear cockpit opened and three men hopped out, their luggage in tow.

Marie-Madeleine greeted the three men, one of whom was Petrel, back from a training course. The other were two new radio operators.

She gave each of them a quick hug before Jack Tar helped her into the plane. Ant slammed the cockpit door shut, and the plane started its take-off.

Checking her watch, Marie-Madeleine noted with astonishment that the entire performance had lasted less than seven minutes from start to finish, an amazing feat considering they were only twenty-five miles from Paris, the epicenter of Nazi occupation.

The pilot couldn't turn on the plane's lights, so he asked her and Jack Tar to help out by looking for any birds that could pose a threat to the aircraft. As Marie-Madeleine gazed upon the dreary landscape below her, she realized the dark, lifeless cities mirrored her own despondency at leaving her adopted home. *And Léon.*

Soon the fields and houses gave way to the turbulent waters of the Channel. She touched the window, promising France she'd be back soon.

After they'd passed over the white cliffs of Dover, beacons of light guided them into the airfield. As soon as the pilot touched down, the door was thrown open and Marie-Madeleine was greeted by a sea of men in khaki uniforms inviting her to have something to eat or drink, though by her calculations, it was probably around 1 or 2 in the morning.

She immediately spotted Major Richards among her welcoming committee. "You've finally made it, Poz!" He shook her hand heartily. "We were awfully worried about you. Why didn't you come sooner?"

He showed her to a large room full of tables, which were filled with men in uniform, even at that late hour. They didn't break their lively conversations to even glance at the newcomers from France. British Intelligence allowed for no questions.

Upon catching sight of Jack Tar, who was lounging in an easy chair and savoring a Spam sandwich on white bread, Marie-Madeleine couldn't help but smile. His gaze, in turn, was fixed on his brothers-in-arms, the RAF officers, the admiration obvious on his freckled face.

Marie-Madeleine half-expected Richards to lead her to an army barracks for the night, but instead he showed her to an ivy-covered cottage that looked like it had been spawned from the pages of a children's storybook.

"This is Major Bertram's house," Richards stated before leading her inside.

A kindly woman with auburn hair greeted them.

Richards gestured toward Marie-Madeleine's muddy boots. "Go ahead and hand them over."

"I'm sorry." She began to wipe them off on the mat next to the door, but Mrs. Bertram told her to stop. She pulled out a dull knife and a bowl. "May I?"

As Marie-Madeleine sank gratefully in a chair, Mrs. Bertram went about scraping the dirt off her boots. The newcomer was about to ask if this was a form of British hospitality when Mrs. Bertram stood up. "I use the dirt in my garden. It helps the nervous lads about to leave for France to taste vegetables grown in French soil. Speaking of which, would you like something to eat?"

Richards said an enthusiastic yes, while Marie-Madeleine, who had no appetite, declined. "I've only just left France, so I'm not quite homesick yet." *That wasn't exactly true,* she thought as she joined Richards at the kitchen table. She could hear voices and the pounding of feet in the rooms above the kitchen.

"Are we not the only ones here?" she asked Richards.

"Of course not, Poz. Like your team, there are many others coming and going. Some of them are with MI6, some of them with the SOE. The most important thing is that you never cross paths—we don't want any agent to have more information to give up to the Gestapo than necessary. By the way," he asked through a gulp of tea, "I need to know your false identity so I can get your papers made out. What name are you planning to go by?"

Taken aback, she replied, "My real one, of course."

"That is not an option. Your identity must not be disclosed."

"But I thought I was coming to England to be away from the

Gestapo. Did I miss the message that they've infiltrated here as well?" She didn't mean to be so sarcastic, but she was exhausted.

He drained the rest of his tea. "Not Gestapo, not necessarily. But you never know, there could be double agents in our ranks."

"While I was in France, we passed a message to the BBC to make people think I was in England, and now I really *am* here, you want me to be someone else."

"That's just the way it is." He pulled out a pen and paper from his pocket and looked at her expectantly.

Another name. *What is this now, the twelfth? Thirteenth?* She was running out of ideas. "Villeneuve," she said eventually. That's where her father had been born. "Marie Villeneuve." She stood up from the table. "Now if you don't mind, I'd like to get some sleep."

Richards brushed his hands free of crumbs. "No problem, Poz."

PART IV
LONDON

CHAPTER 52

OCTOBER 1943

Late the next morning, Marie-Madeleine was awoken by a pounding on the door. *Gestapo!* She rushed out of the unfamiliar bed, still dressed in the suit from the night before.

"Poz, it's time to go to London!" The sound of a familiar voice calmed her nerves.

It's Richards. I'm in England.
But what about the network?

Despite the beauty of the autumnal English countryside, she once again sank into despondency as they drove to London. Although she was fully aware of how foolish she was being, she found herself unable to hold back the tears welling up inside of her.

Richards, sitting next to her and looking distinctly uneasy, patted her hand. "It's all right, Poz. Are you not happy to finally be here?"

"Happy? No. I never should have left France... my friends, Alliance..." *Léon and the baby.* With that she burst into a fresh round of tears.

They stopped at an elegant hotel near Buckingham Palace. "We've booked you a room here, for the time being anyway." Richards set her case on a desk. "I'll let you get situated and then, if you don't mind, we'd like a current list of all of your Alliance agents."

As soon as he left, Marie-Madeleine sat down at the desk and began mapping out the network for British Intelligence. It felt nice not having to hide anything every time she heard footsteps in the hallway.

When Richards returned mid-afternoon, he was accompanied by a doctor, who brought her vitamins and sedatives.

"Although, from the looks of it, what you really need is rest… and plenty of food," the doctor told her.

Richards nodded. "I'll go to the market right away." He turned to her. "And do what the doctor says, Poz. Make sure you get some sleep, as you'll have an early morning visitor. Sir Claude Dansey, the assistant chief of MI6, is very keen to meet you."

Sir Claude, sporting coke-bottle glasses and a receding hairline, arrived promptly at nine o'clock the next day. He greeted her by grasping both of her hands, exclaiming, "So this is the dreadful woman who gave all of us such a fright!" He dropped her hands. "I've always wondered what you looked like, Poz. It's a relief to finally have you here."

"Yes, but not for long." For some reason, the sight of this man, who controlled everything, intensified her fear of not being allowed to return to France.

"Ah, we'll see." He gestured for her to sit down. "According to our calculations, a Resistance leader can't last more than six months. It's nothing short of witchcraft that you've been able to last five times as long."

Léon had said something similar when he was trying to convince her to go to London in the first place. "When can I go back?" she asked Dansey.

"Soon," he said noncommittally. "Although we have many things to address, I wanted to take a moment to thank you sincerely for all that you have accomplished." He sat back in his chair. "Is there anything we can do for you in return?"

His words hit the mark, and she began to feel slightly better about the whole situation. "I'd like to be able to contact my children in Switzerland, as well as my agent Monique Bontinck, code-named Ermine."

She'd never told MI6 about the pregnancy, but if the request to get in touch with Monique surprised Sir Claude, he didn't show it. "Yes, that certainly can be arranged." He seemed eager to change the subject. "Now tell me, are those Occupiers as diabolical as they say?"

"Worse."

He nodded to himself. "The Hitler regime remains formidable. Our only feasible strategy is to relentlessly strike at it until it shatters." He smashed his hands together in emphasis. "In the meantime, Poz, get some rest." He stood up. "I shall be quite displeased if I hear you've been working."

In the afternoon, one of Richards' assistants escorted Marie-Madeleine around the London shops, Jack Tar in tow. She took great pleasure in purchasing little gifts for the people back in France: soap for Dr. Gilbert, coffee for Léon, souvenirs for her children, and various odds and ends for the other members of Alliance.

With the exception of the gifts for her children, she planned on having Jack Tar take the rest back with him when he left for France during the next full moon. She couldn't help extending her generosity to the young redhead who, she decided, was desperately in need of new clothes.

"You and I both know that I can't wear any English clothes in France," Jack Tar replied. After a moment he conceded, "But I wouldn't mind a dressing gown, chief. I've always wanted one."

After trying on seemingly endless options under the watchful but tactful gaze of the salesgirls, he finally chose the most expensive and quintessentially English-looking dressing gown in the store: a rich burgundy velvet one with a silk lining.

. . .

The next morning, Richards drove Marie-Madeleine to a nondescript building on Baker Street. "What are we doing here?" she asked as they exited the car.

"You'll see."

They took an elevator up to the third floor. The moment they stepped out, Marie-Madeleine's ears were assailed by a cacophony of noises: the clicking of dozens of Morse keys, the beeping of incoming transmissions, and the squeak of chalk.

"This is the transmission room," Richards told her, unnecessarily. "Ah, and here is our coding chief now." He shook the dark-haired man's hand before turning to her. "Marie-Madeleine, I'd like you to meet Leo Marks."

Clearly distracted, Marks merely nodded at her.

"Marie-Madeleine is the head of Alliance," Richards said.

That got the young man's attention. "Alliance? As in the largest network currently operating in France?"

"Indeed," she answered.

"I know you have a host of radio operators." Marks gestured around the room. "We've been working on ways to make communication more efficient."

Something Magpie once said to her popped into her head. "Have you ever thought about having the British call first instead of waiting for the field operator to start the transmission?"

"Absolutely out of the question," Marks replied tersely.

"But sometimes they wait several minutes for you to get back to them. And we are all mindful of the fact that every extra second gives the Germans' detecting vans more time to track the signal."

"You can avoid detection by changing frequency."

She gave Marks a condescending smile. "But you know radio operators. Once they've found a clear wavelength, security is the last thing on their mind and they won't stop until they've transmitted the entire message."

"But that's just it, isn't it? It's for *your* safety that we want you to call first. The detection vans hone into our central station, not your own frequency."

Marie-Madeleine refused to yield to this obstinate young man. He spent his days safely ensconced in this building on Baker Street, while her operators were practically on the front lines. "But the longer we struggle to establish communication, the greater the danger."

Marks waved his hand. "As you can see, I'm rather busy here." He strolled off.

"You'll have to forgive Marks," Richards said as he led her back into the elevator. "He's a bit high-strung, for sure, but keep in mind he's in charge of all the transmissions from every occupied country. He actually is quite dedicated to his job."

Marie-Madeleine recalled all the times her operators—Lucien, Magpie, even Tringa—threw their headphones down in despair, claiming that no one in London was answering. She grabbed Richards' arm as something occurred to her. "Do you think you could arrange for our chief of communications, Magpie, to be brought in? He might just convince this Marks character to change his tune."

"Magpie?" Richards looked confused. "Oh, you mean Ferdinand Rodriguez." It was the first time Marie-Madeleine had heard his real name. "I suppose it couldn't hurt—after all, it was Marks who trained Rodriguez in the first place. We can bring him in on the same Lysander that Jack Tar leaves on, during the next full moon."

* * *

After a week in London, Marie-Madeleine got used to the fact that there was no need for clandestine meetings or couriers having to conceal intelligence in false-bottomed cases. At the end of each day, Richards delivered a regular briefcase from the transmission room in London to Marie-Madeleine's hotel room and retrieved any outgoing messages. In this way, she was able to keep up with the goings-on in France and maintain daily communication with Léon, who continuously asked her for advice on field operations.

She was dismayed, however, to see references to 'Gibbet'—Léon's code name for the combined services of the Gestapo and the Abwehr—appear in the messages one evening.

"Anything wrong?" Richards asked, catching the look on her face.

"Ant has been arrested, along with several others."

"Let me see that," Richards reached out for the message she'd been reading. "Faye seems to think this was all a result of Elephant's arrest. Who is Elephant again?"

"Ernest Siegrist, our security chief. He also provided all of our agents with false papers." She sank her head into her hands when she recalled that he was carrying the copy of Léon's list of agents when he was captured. "They must have finally deciphered Léon's awful handwriting," she said aloud.

Richards looked suitably alarmed. "Is there anything we can do to help?"

"Yes." She fixed her steady gaze on him. "Can you arrange for Léon Faye to come to England with Magpie? We need to figure out how to tighten the network's security in the wake of this newest disaster."

"You got it, Poz."

CHAPTER 53

OCTOBER 1943

In addition to his dressing gown and all the gifts for the Alliance members, Jack Tar was going to be delivering the first decoration bestowed upon a member of the network: Noble had been awarded a Military Medal. Marie-Madeleine just hoped he would be well enough to appreciate it.

During the October full moon, Richards brought her back to the Bertrams' fairy-tale-like welcoming house next to the airfield to wait for Léon and Magpie.

Mrs. Bertram, with her homemade pies and nonstop chatter, did her best to cheer Marie-Madeleine up, but her mind was occupied by the thought that Ant would have been there to say farewell to his comrades, had he not been arrested. Not to mention she was always anxious whenever Léon went to or from a landing field.

As if reading her thoughts, Mrs. Bertram asked if she knew Léon Faye.

Despite herself, Marie-Madeleine felt a tiny smile form. "Yes, I'm familiar with the man."

"He's so kind—he brought me a bottle of French perfume the last time he came in."

Marie-Madeleine took a closer look at Mrs. Bertram. The first time she had met her, she assumed she was older, but she now saw that the woman was not that far from her own age, her well-worn face etched by years of tending gardens in the sun.

Marie-Madeleine had just finished agreeing with Mrs. Bertram when someone called from the airfield to 'put the kettle on for our new friends,' which was clearly code that Magpie and Léon had arrived.

Marie-Madeleine ran a hand through her hair and straightened her batik dress, courtesy of Swift's wife. She had never been overly concerned about her appearance—before the war, she had what Édouard, in his kinder days, referred to as 'an effortless beauty'—but now she was suddenly nervous. She hadn't been eating that much more than she had in France, and the dark circles under her eyes never seemed to disappear.

"Minerva!" Léon called, bursting into the kitchen. He wrapped his arms around her, whispering in her ear, "You are definitely a sight for sore eyes."

She beamed as he and Magpie greeted Mrs. Bertram. Having flown back and forth to England before, they knew the drill and handed over their boots, which were caked with French soil.

After she'd cleaned them, Mrs. Bertram poured the tea she'd made and produced a tray of biscuits, which she set in front of Marie-Madeleine. She then put her arm on the clearly exhausted Magpie. "Let me show you your room for tonight." She turned back to the two still seated at the kitchen table. "Your two rooms are next to each other. I hope you don't mind."

"I don't think we mind at all," Léon said, winking at Marie-Madeleine.

However, Marie-Madeleine resisted the overwhelming urge to fall into Léon's arms and the two of them ended up staying awake until nearly dawn, scrutinizing the intelligence Léon had brought with him on the plane.

"Look at this," Léon said, retrieving a piece of paper from the pile.

It was written on both sides and signed by Petrel, the mathematician turned wireless operator.

She scanned his neat handwriting, lingering on the phrases *50-100 bombs would suffice to destroy London* and *aimed at most of Britain's large cities during the winter* before putting the paper down in disbelief. "He's talking about the Germans developing a new type of bomb?"

"Looks that way." Léon put his hand over hers. "I can see it has the same effect on you as it did on me."

"Who was Petrel's source?"

"He won't say her real name, but they call her Amniarix, an outstanding young woman who apparently can speak five different languages. She has German 'friends,' whom she wines and dines."

Marie-Madeleine nodded knowingly. "Which is another way to say that she gets them drunk and then listens to them brag about their work."

"Precisely. As you can see, she has quite the memory, and can recall word for word what they say." Léon carefully folded the paper and put it in his coat pocket. "At any rate, I think it's essential that MI6 hears about this latest 'secret weapon' right away."

Sir Claude took Léon and Marie-Madeleine to lunch in London the next day. She was getting more accustomed to being able to talk openly about things in public, though she was dumbfounded when Sir Claude announced that she would be moving to a house, for 'better security.'

"Move?" she asked through a bite of fish. "I don't need to move around England, I need to go back to France."

"I understand, but your organization has grown so extensive—you are the only network covering the whole of France, and, as you French people say, 'You can't see the forest for the trees.' Here in London, Poz, you get a better viewpoint for organizing the network as a cohesive unit."

She stole a quick glance at Léon, who seemed to be more interested in his food than the conversation.

"Look Poz," Sir Claude set his fork down. "Our sources say that

KIT SERGEANT

your comrades are in for a difficult winter: Hitler is stepping up his drive against the Resistance. There will be a time when your return to France will be imperative, and, until that time comes, you must reserve yourself here."

Léon looked up suddenly. "When you say Marie-Madeleine's presence in France will be 'imperative,' I assume you are referring to the Allies finally landing in France. Will that be happening any time soon?"

Sir Claude's expression darkened. "Not overly soon. We're not ready yet."

"Speaking of Hitler stepping up his drive…" Léon cleared his throat before filling Sir Claude in on the Nazis' new secret weapon.

Sir Claude cursed softly. "We've heard about these weapons—we're calling them 'Doodlebugs' because of the buzzing sound they make. Despite the innocent-sounding nickname, they are said to carry one-ton warheads and they could very well change the course of the war. Until now, they've only been rumors, but your man appears to be confirming they are further along in their development than we've feared."

"Well," Marie-Madeleine brushed crumbs off her hands. "What's the use in assembling massive forces if Hitler plans to target London with these secret rockets?" Her hopes felt dashed—if it came to that, she would never be able to return to France.

"Have you finished?" Sir Claude gestured to her plate, and once she handed it to him, he said, "There's no need to concern yourself with this secret weapon stuff. All I ask is for your help until the end by following this old fox's guidance…"

That night Marie-Madeleine had another nightmare about Magpie and Léon landing in the field of heather. This time, as the plane took off, a German voice announced, "We finally have Faye in our hands now."

She woke up sweating, to find that Léon had already left. A knock on the door to her flat jolted her out of bed. "Just a minute," she called, throwing on some clothes.

It was Sir Claude. "Good morning, dear." He strolled into the room. "I'm here to tell you that Léon must not go back to France."

She'd been thinking the exact same thing, but for some reason, didn't want to give Sir Claude the upper hand. "It seems to be becoming an obsession with you. Are you planning to lock us all up one by one?"

He chuckled as he settled onto the couch. "I've seen many resistance fighters come and go over the past three years, Poz, and I can confidently say that our friend Léon is someone I hold in the highest regard and feel a personal fondness for."

"I can't say I disagree with you."

He lit his pipe. "Both of you have spoken highly of your successor—what's his name again?"

"Swift."

"Right." He took a puff of his pipe, exhaling a cloud of smoke. "I said to myself, if we let this Swift fly on his own for a bit, for a few months, let's say, it would be better than trying to replace you or Léon if you ran into trouble on the ground."

"That's true, although my people are expecting me back and deserve an explanation."

"Your job is to give orders, not explanations."

"The agents are under *my* employ. If I was arrested, they'd work voluntarily under my replacement, but I can't say whether they'll continue to blindly follow Swift if I'm in England for some undisclosed period of time."

He took another deep drag of his pipe. "Well, you French are certainly temperamental."

She decided to change the subject. "Why don't you want Léon to leave?"

"Because he'll be captured. I've been through his file again with my specialists: three arrests, two escapes, multiple return Lysander trips. We can pretty much assume the Nazis have a target on his back."

She nodded. "Your law of averages again." After a moment she added, "You are right, but there's something that might be even more powerful than statistics: premonition. I've been having nightmares that Léon is apprehended as soon as he lands in France."

Sir Claude placed his pipe down and involuntarily shuddered. "I suppose war sharpens one's intuition. We both sense the same thing, albeit in different ways."

"But Léon will never consent to staying here. He's a soldier through and through and he longs to be in the thick of things."

Sir Claude stood. "If you order him not to return, Poz, we won't provide him with a Lysander. His fate is now in your hands."

Marie-Madeleine paced up and down her flat as she waited for Léon, dreading what she had to tell him.

Finally he returned and she practically pounced on him, even before he had shut the door. "Sir Claude and I have agreed that you should not go back to France."

He looked predictably bewildered. "Did you have the nightmare again?"

"Yes, but, more than that, Sir Claude thinks you are no longer able to evade the Nazis."

"Damn him and his law of averages! Does he know that I've also got fifty bombing missions under my belt, that I was in the trenches when I was 17? According to his supposed logic, I ought to be long dead by now. And you can tell Dansey that this ghost will never fall down on his job. I'm going back to France by the light of the next moon."

"Only if I say so."

He opened his mouth and shut it again, anger etched over every feature on his face. After a moment, he took a deep breath and stated in a calm voice, "Listen, Minerva, I can't allow all the airmen working under me to be caught in my stead."

The injustice of it all overpowered her. Sir Claude had entrusted her to make the decision regarding Léon, while at the same time both of them were adamant that she herself couldn't return to France. The Nazi grip was tightening more each day, and Swift lacked the experience and expertise to keep Alliance going in the face of such danger. She sank onto the couch cushions. "I can't force you to stay in London, but that doesn't mean I'll stop worrying about you."

He reached out to touch a lock of her hair. "I know. And trust me when I say the same, though I have to admit I'll be a lot more focused on my work if I know you are safe here, at least for the time being."

She gazed up at him, her eyes moist with tears. "Promise me you'll slip away from the reception committee as soon as you land…"

"Minerva, they've used that same field for ages and are experts by now."

"Yes, but this will be the first landing that neither you nor I have organized." She grabbed his hand. "You have to promise me you'll go to Paris on your own and thoroughly investigate what has been happening with the network before you make the slightest move."

"Anything you say, chief." His voice turned serious as he asked, "And then?"

"You'll return by the next moon, on the same plane that I'll be flying back to France on. That way, we'll divide up the job while we wait for the Allies to land."

"Which means you and I won't be seeing each other much…"

"No." The tears were falling freely now. "But we all have to make sacrifices for the good of France."

"The good of France," Léon repeated before taking her into his arms.

After they'd made love, Marie-Madeleine phoned Sir Claude to let him know that she had agreed that Léon could return to France, under the terms she'd established.

"It's your decision, my dear," Sir Claude replied. "I just hope you haven't literally made a grave mistake."

"Me too."

CHAPTER 54

OCTOBER 1943

During the afternoon before Léon was scheduled to fly back to France, Richards arrived at Marie-Madeleine's hotel room to announce that the weather was indeed favorable and the car was waiting outside. Operation Ingres, the name for the landing, was on.

Léon put his suitcase in the trunk of the car. The remainder of the equipment and supplies had already been sent to the airfield. Marie-Madeleine accompanied him on the drive to the Bertrams' cottage, stopping to pick up Magpie on the way.

As they drew closer to the airfield, Marie-Madeleine was startled to see a field of heather extending as far as she could see across the English countryside, the rosy hues of the sunset serving as a stunning contrast to the faint purple of the bushes.

"Why is there heather blooming now?" she demanded, a shrill tone in her voice.

The driver, one of Sir Claude's many assistants, peered curiously at her through the rearview mirror. "It does bloom in the autumn around here, and, since it's been relatively mild, I suppose the wind hasn't scattered their flowers yet."

Léon, his eyes wide, patted her hand. "It's just a coincidence.

Besides, you said your dream is about heather in the landing field, not the takeoff."

Her mind was a chaotic jumble, her thoughts racing and colliding inside her head like the autumnal insects bashing against the windows of the car. Should she order the driver to turn back and blame her nightmares for preventing these men from carrying out their mission? She would surely be declared crazy, but if Magpie and Léon were being sent to their demise, how could she live with herself if she didn't intervene?

As if sensing her inner turmoil, Léon's grip on her hand tightened and he mouthed the words, "I'll be okay."

She turned around in her seat, watching the heather fade into the distance with a growing sense of dread.

Mrs. Bertram had prepared a mouth-watering sendoff dinner, complete with fresh butternut squash, but none of them ate any of it.

When it came time for him to depart, Léon embraced Marie-Madeleine. His voice was hoarse with emotion as he told her he loved her.

She wanted to tell him not to go, but she knew the words would be meaningless: she was powerless to stop him. She also knew without him uttering a word that he'd indulged her long enough, and, as a veteran of the air force and a dedicated leader of Alliance, he had no more use for her premonitions. "I love you too."

As she watched him walk away, her heart sank further. She suddenly experienced an unwavering conviction that this was the last time she would ever see him.

Marie-Madeleine spent the next few hours anxiously awaiting news of the landing, Mrs. Bertram's knitting needles clicking in tune with the second hands of the clock.

The ringing of the phone startled them both. "Tea for our new friends," Major Bertram's voice called.

Léon's plane had left for France, regardless of her own feelings.

KIT SERGEANT

Saluki, the Duke of Magenta, and Mandrill were due to arrive, and Marie-Madeleine jumped up as soon as they entered the cottage, grateful for the distraction.

"How did the landing go?" she asked the Duke.

"It could have been improved." Saluki's once elegant clothes were wrinkled and his fedora had clearly seen better days. "It was sheer chaos on the ground—since Ant's arrest, they've recruited new boys for the reception committee. And none of us could shake the feeling that we were under surveillance."

She gasped. "Were you able to warn Léon?"

"I think so. When he exited the plane, I tapped him on the shoulder and said, 'Scram, old boy, don't stay a second longer than you have to. Something around here stinks'."

Marie-Madeleine crossed her fingers, hoping the obstinate Léon would obey the warning.

The newcomers sat down to the ample leftovers as Mrs. Bertram made tea.

"It was cursed ground," Mandrill mumbled after a few minutes.

"What was that?" Marie-Madeleine asked.

Mandrill, who, with his disheveled clothes and his wild hair, was almost unrecognizable from the Little Lord Fauntleroy lookalike she'd first met. "My father fought on that same field during the Great War and told me the ground was cursed." He shook his head. "We should have chosen a different spot."

Saluki waved his hand. "Ignore him. He's exhausted. As Noble would say, it's just an airman's intuition, nothing more." He leaned in closer to Marie-Madeleine. "Once, one of my comrades caused us a hell of a lot of trouble when he dreamt he saw his best friend crash. We didn't sleep a wink in the squadron that night. In the end, this friend returned all in one piece, with a fine bag of victories." He took a sip of tea before adding, "Don't worry, Marie-Madeleine, I've known Léon for years: he always comes out on top."

Barely listening, she checked her watch. Magpie's first scheduled contact was in less than twelve hours. She was desperate to hear that Léon was okay and the thought of waiting that long seemed unbearable.

CHAPTER 55

NOVEMBER 1943

The time for Magpie's first transmission after he returned to France came and went with no contact. To make matters worse, none of the Paris operators were meeting their skeds either.

Saluki tried to console Marie-Madeleine by pointing out that it usually took some time for radio operators to set everything up before they could start working.

"But what about all the other operators—the ones who've had regular skeds for months? Why aren't they calling?" she demanded.

Saluki, who had no answer, merely shrugged.

After what seemed like an eternity, Richards burst into her room, carrying the black briefcase that they used to transmit messages back and forth from the radio room.

"We've finally heard from an Alliance member," Richards told her, setting the case on a table. "But I'm going to warn you—the news is not good." He pulled out a crumpled piece of paper and handed it to her.

It was from Swift in Le Mans: *Three passengers Operation Ingres plus Bumpkin, Lanky, Mahout arrested by the Gestapo Paris train STOP All radio operators arrested headquarters STOP Dragon and Jack Tar studying ways to repair damage END*

So the new arrivals had been arrested. But if that was true, why did Swift mention three passengers?

"I guess now we know why we haven't heard anything from Paris," Marie-Madeleine remarked drily. "All the operators have been captured." Suddenly overcome with fear, she buried her head in her hands.

Saluki walked over and retrieved the discarded message, reading it silently.

Richards, standing in the corner and visibly uneasy, shifted his weight from one leg to the other. "If Léon obeyed your order to abandon the reception team, he was nowhere near the rest of them when they were arrested."

Marie-Madeleine, unconvinced, nodded anyway. "Please send a message to Swift asking for the names of the captured passengers he was referring to."

"Right away."

After Richards left, Saluki put his hand on her shoulder. "What are you going to do?"

Marie-Madeleine's head was spinning. "Try to get more information from Swift. Try to get someone into France to help them. Try to go back to France by myself."

Saluki gave her shoulder one more squeeze before he let himself out. "And Marie-Madeleine," he said, poking his head through the door opening, "You should get some sleep."

She could have laughed at that last comment, but, peering at herself in the bathroom mirror, she realized it was no laughing matter —in fact, she was downright frightened by her own reflection. Touching the bags under her eyes, she said aloud, "I'm going mad. But I have no right to go mad." After all, she wasn't the one who was arrested.

Casting her eyes helplessly around the room, she saw the little bottle of sedatives the doctor had prescribed her first day in London. She picked up the bottle and, not paying attention to the recommended dose, took a giant swig.

. . .

Marie-Madeleine heard a buzzing sound in her head. It took her nearly a minute to recognize it was the phone ringing. With a hand as heavy as a brick, she finally picked up the receiver.

"Poz, what's the matter? We were about to break down your door." The panicked voice could only belong to Sir Claude.

"I'm sorry," she said before exhaustion overcame her again and she hung up.

It seemed like only seconds later that someone was banging on the door. *He must have called me from the lobby,* she thought as she heaved herself out of bed to answer the door.

"The London air really doesn't suit you, my dear child," Sir Claude remarked as he strolled in.

Suddenly awake, Marie-Madeleine agreed with him. "What I need is French air. I have to go back."

"Listen, Poz," he gestured for her to sit down. When she refused, he continued, "What has happened is terrible, but you must realize that I will never consent to you setting foot in such a hornet's nest."

"You mean an empty Eagle's nest."

He blew out his breath. "If Faye did what you told him, then he hasn't been arrested. Do you want us to send out a message over the BBC stating that he's back in London?"

"No. If he's indeed in the Gestapo's hands, it will only serve to make him look silly." She had to examine the possibility that Léon had disobeyed her command and was on the same train as the reception committee. She spoke her next thoughts aloud, "Mahout knew better than to have the whole team travel together. And why were Bumpkin and Lanky there, anyway? They weren't normally part of the committee, and besides, there was that snafu with them regarding the arrest of Ernest Siegrist."

Sir Claude focused his unwavering gaze on her. "You know how fond I was of Faye. I shall regard this as a personal loss, and trust me when I say, whatever it takes, we will avenge him."

As soon as he left her flat, Marie-Madeleine crawled back into bed.

. . .

The next morning, Richards confirmed that Swift had been confused about the third passenger and Léon, Magpie, Mahout, Lanky, and Bumpkin had been taken to the Paris Gestapo headquarters.

Marie-Madeleine quickly penned a message to Swift, ordering him and any other Alliance agent in France to lay low for a few weeks, adding that they would be given assistance as soon as possible.

Her intent was to stop the tide of arrests, to no avail. Day after day new messages came in, informing her of the capture of dozens more Alliance agents, including Rivière and Colonel Kauffman, two of her most trusted men. The Gestapo had broken Kauffman's arms and legs in an attempt to get him to reveal where the weapon stores were. He didn't, and luckily the Gestapo stopped their torture of the elderly man.

The next day they received word that Jack Tar had been arrested while walking down the Champs-Élysées. Marie-Madeleine closed her eyes, picturing Jack Tar's delighted face on their shopping trip when she'd bought him that dressing gown.

She turned to the list of network members she kept in a notebook. Though it served as a distraction from thinking about Léon, keeping track of all the arrests felt like a macabre chore. Every time she crossed off a name, she had the sense she was wielding an executioner's axe, cutting down lives with each stroke of her pen.

In less than a month, in addition to Léon and Magpie, over 150 Alliance members had been captured. How many in total were now in the Gestapo's torture chambers? 300? 400? Would they reach a thousand victims before the end of the war? Despite the unshakable devotion and unwavering determination of these men and women, the Nazis had won.

Marie-Madeleine's hands shook as she grabbed a pen and paper.

Implore seek cause of disaster STOP Undoubtedly due to treason STOP We are trying to send you messenger STOP Congratulations to all for admirable sangfroid thanks loyalty STOP

She paused, wondering if there was any way to raise what had to be very poor morale among the remaining network members. With the slightest resemblance of a smile, recalling the conversation she'd had with Léon the second time he returned from London, she finished off with *Forward the Alliance STOP Much love*

She folded the paper and handed it to Richards. "Please send this off to Swift as soon as possible."

Swift replied that he didn't suspect any treachery within Alliance and blamed the Léon/Magpie tragedy on an inexperienced pilot who'd drawn attention to his landing.

Marie-Madeleine didn't agree with his assessment, especially in the wake of all the other arrests, but there wasn't much she could do from her own perch in London.

CHAPTER 56

NOVEMBER 1943

Unlike that of Marie-Madeleine, Mandrill's outlook seemed to improve with his time in England, which he spent in Intelligence training. He came to visit her right before he was due back in France and Marie-Madeleine made him a cup of tea in the tiny kitchen of her hotel room as they chatted amicably.

"I know we're not supposed to tell each other our real names, but seeing as everyone in the network knows yours, I figure I might as well tell you mine too: it's Philippe Koenigswerther."

"Are you—"

"Jewish? Yes."

She set the tea tray down. "How did you avoid detection?"

"Ernest Siegrist provided false papers to my family and I. My parents managed to get out before the deportations started. They are currently in America, living under the last name King." He shot Marie-Madeleine a sad smile. "Ironic considering where I am now." He took a sip of tea. "Actually, my mother just wrote to me to let me know that one of our fabulously wealthy uncles has just passed and left all his money to my sister and me. Mitzi wants me to go to New York to figure out what to do with this windfall."

"Why Mandrill, er, Philippe, that's wonderful news. You should go to New York and live life as a rich man."

He scratched his nose, which she was beginning to realize was a habit of his. "I don't care about money. In fact, if I survive the war, I want to go to Tibet and become a monk."

"That's quite admirable of you."

"But right now I want to go back to France and resume command of the Bordeaux sector."

She nodded and, in view of his determination, decided to be frank with him about the chaos threatening the network. "Listen, given what happened to Léon, whatever you do, I want you to avoid the reception committee, especially if someone called Lanky is there."

"Lanky?" Mandrill spat the name out. "He better not be there: he's a traitor."

She nearly spilled the hot tea all over herself. "What makes you think that? He was just arrested with the others."

"No. Lanky's a traitor, I'm sure of it." He got up and walked around the room before pausing in front of the pile of messages. He picked one of them up and then nodded in confirmation. "Bordeaux and the south are still going strong, but all the places Lanky got a hold of with his grubby little hands have fallen."

She pursed her lips as she considered his logic. Lanky was at the reception committee for Operation Ingres: if Mandrill was correct, then Lanky was directly responsible for Léon's arrest.

"As I was waiting for the Lysander pick-up, Lanky kept asking me questions, which I answered with lies. Lots of lies." Mandrill made a gesture of wringing someone's neck. "Don't worry, Marie-Madeleine, I'll get to the bottom of it as soon as I land in France."

She put a hand on the young man's arm. "And while you're at it, see if you can dig up any news about Léon."

The day after Mandrill was supposed to leave, he returned to Marie-Madeleine's apartment, fuming. "The fools—they missed the landing place. I grew up in that area and knew exactly where it was, but the

RAF pilot wouldn't descend unless we saw the signals from the ground."

Richards entered after him. "We just got word from Nero that the failure of the reception committee was due to bad weather." Nero was the Alliance radio operator in Nantes, having earned the nickname for carrying on, his skeds mostly unimpeded, while the rest of the network burned.

"Can I leave tonight?" Mandrill asked.

"No," Marie-Madeleine answered. "It's a new moon now."

He sat heavily into a chair. "So I have to wait another month?"

Her heart sank and she felt as despondent as Mandrill sounded. She had to get someone into France, one way or another. She turned to address Richards. "Could Mandrill get in by boat?"

Richards nodded. "I'll see what I can do."

As Mandrill left, slightly more buoyed than when he came in, she asked Richards if he could also arrange for her return.

"Patience, Poz." He took Mandrill's vacated seat. "All the networks have suffered heavy losses and Dansey is still fearful of losing you as well, now that Léon…" Richards cleared his throat. "But it's not the time to stop. I have to tell you that MI6 is most pleased with Petrel's intelligence regarding the secret weapon. We've been putting it to great use."

Finally some good news. "Really? Since neither you nor Sir Claude mentioned it again, I didn't think it was worth anything."

He gave her a strange look. "Is that so?"

"All this talk about Hitler's secret weapons that never surface. They're like the Loch Ness Monster."

"No, I can assure you they are very real… and very dangerous."

The tone of his voice frightened her. "Will the Boches be using them anytime soon…" she swallowed hard. "On London?"

"We hope not. Otherwise… we'll just say it will be rather difficult for you to return to France." He stood to leave. "Impossible, in fact."

She felt even more worried after he'd left. How would an intelligence network like Alliance withstand the physical threat of German guided missiles?

. . .

British Intelligence commanded the few functioning Alliance transmitters to find any hint of the so-called secret weapons, which had been identified as V-1 rockets. Together with Petrel's source's intelligence and the aerial photographs provided by British reconnaissance planes, MI6 was able to pinpoint the source of the rockets to a missile testing center on the island of Usedom, in the Baltic Sea.

The RAF set its sights on the testing facilities, and, according to Richards, 'bombed the hell out of the island.' A significant quantity of the bombs hit the foreign workers' living quarters, and Marie-Madeleine wondered if she was the only one struck by the cruel irony of it all: many of these workers had likely aided MI6's intelligence-gathering efforts, unwittingly contributing to their own deaths.

In late November, Operation Duck II, the naval effort to deposit Mandrill on the coast of Brittany, was set to go. It was to be the first operation to return an Alliance agent to France in more than a month.

That very night, Nero sent a message to let them know that, although Mandrill had come ashore in an area infested with German patrols, he'd managed to dodge them and find the members of the reception committee, who had given up for the night and were resting at a local inn.

"Good old Philippe," Marie-Madeleine thought when she heard the news. He was carrying two million francs for Swift to deliver, along with new codes and the latest questionnaires. In addition, he would tell everyone personally about Lanky's betrayal, and maybe, just maybe, be able to locate Léon.

CHAPTER 57

DECEMBER 1943

In December, Nero sent a message stating he'd learned from a reliable source that the Nazis were about to launch their self-propelled rockets, which were 'intended for the bombardment of southern England.'

Her hands shaking, Marie-Madeleine put the message down. It seemed that, though the raid on the missile testing site had pushed the Germans' timeline back slightly, they had suitably recovered. She focused her gaze on Richards, whose expression was inscrutable. "I'm getting the impression that you've known the secret weapons have already been installed for a while. What are you going to do to spare us the 'Happy Christmas' Hitler appears to have in store for London?"

"We're doing everything we can. As soon as we receive the information from your network, the RAF goes and takes photographs. When they confirm where the rockets are, they start bombing."

"A pity the poor French have to be bombed to be liberated," Marie-Madeleine murmured.

"We're trying to do things as efficiently as possible," Richards replied.

She turned back to one of the other messages, which had been transmitted several days ago from Osprey, operating in Lille. Osprey went back as far as the Crusade network and was always reliable. He had ended his last message with *More follows...*

"Have you heard back from Osprey?" she asked Richards.

"No." He rubbed his face. "And we haven't received anything from Mandrill for quite some time either."

With a sigh, she dug through a pile of papers to find his last message, dated December 5th, sent a couple of days after he'd returned to France. He'd requested parachute drops providing radios, guns, and transmitting crystals. It ended with *View new situation due to intense radio detection campaign END*

"If Mandrill is requesting weapons, it means he's concerned about the possibility of being surrounded," she remarked. "Can we get them to him?"

Richards shrugged. "The weather is always questionable in December. Not to mention the RAF is rather busy at the moment, and, I might add, suffering quite a few losses themselves."

She tapped her fingers on the desk, hoping that there hadn't been yet another wave of network arrests. "Have you warned Nero about the silence from the other transmitters?"

"Yes, we've suggested he hide out in the forest with the maquis for a couple of days, and he replied, 'just as soon as we receive our December drop'." Richards stood. "Now I'm off to convince the RAF to help us out with the planes."

The weather did not, in fact, interfere with the drop. Fate's joke was on MI6, however, for the returning pilot stated he'd seen 'a lot of activity' in the dropping zone, which meant that the parachuted canisters full of guns and ammunition had landed right into the outstretched hands of the Boches. This time, even the invincible Nero had been unable to escape the flames that threatened to devour the entire network.

Marie-Madeleine knew that, like a phoenix, Alliance would rise again from the ashes, if only the British could provide them aid. But for once that aid didn't seem forthcoming.

The first clue was that Richards ended his daily visits to her hotel room. Sir Claude, too, seemed to be avoiding her. The only contact she had with MI6 was the messenger who delivered the black bag of transmissions from the Radio Room.

The bag had become much lighter as of late, as there weren't many transmitters still functioning, except those of Petrel and someone named Grand Duke, operating out of the southeast, whom the British called 'Post Office' because his transmissions were so regular. And, of course, Swift, who besieged Marie-Madeleine to send in more supplies. It was clear from Swift's messages that, like herself, he was paranoid that London's interest in the network was beginning to wane. She traced a finger over his latest one: *With the new and unprecedented dangers we are facing, we urgently need more aid to keep going END*

As she sat in her London hotel room reading days-old messages, Marie-Madeleine experienced a deep frustration at her inability to stop the bloodshed in France. She wished desperately that she could encourage Swift to carry on no matter what, but knew it was a lot to ask.

Her reply to Swift was succinct and devoid of the turmoil of emotions she felt as she wrote it: *If I do not succeed in normalizing the situation, I will restore freedom of action to everyone on Jan 1...*

As a Christmas present, MI6 presented her with a house on Carlyle Square, which was finally ready. Marie-Madeleine decided to name the modest two-story, 'Alliance House.' The sofa had been recovered with a flowery cretonne fabric and the walls of the living room had been painted a sage green. Overall, it was a pleasant place to live in, if not exactly in her taste, but Marie-Madeleine had misgivings about moving in since it seemed a more permanent accommodation than the hotel, and she was still chafing to return to France.

Though the bedroom was as tastefully decorated as the living room, she decided to set up a camp bed in the office, which had a direct telephone line to British Intelligence. Given the circumstances, that telephone was about as close as Marie-Madeleine could get to France.

* * *

Marie-Madeleine was invited to a New Year's Eve party at the stately home of Viscount Astor and his wife. As soon as she stepped into the dining room, with its oak tables set with exquisite silverware and crystal goblets, she regretted accepting the invitation. She couldn't help wondering if the guests, who were equally as exquisite in their clothes and jewelry, knew there was a war going on.

To avoid the partygoers who kept asking her about life in France, Marie-Madeleine slipped into a nearly empty room. She went to the window and opened the blackout drapes to peer out at the impenetrable fog surrounding the house. *Bad weather.*

Somewhere out there the Germans had their secret weapons aimed at London. The image of a Doodlebug rocket suddenly plunging into the dense, pea-soup fog that shrouded the city filled her with horror. Would 1944 be as devastating as 1943?

With a start, she realized where she'd been at this same time last year: in the château, surrounded by people she loved and respected: Noble, Rivière, Colonel Kauffman, Jack Tar, and of course, Léon. And here she was now, at a party filled with strangers, while her boys languished in prison. *1944 has to be better,* she promised herself. After all, she couldn't see how it could possibly get worse.

CHAPTER 58

JANUARY 1944

The fog prevented any landings for the month of January. With most of the Alliance operators in hiding or in jail, Marie-Madeleine felt cut off from the network and was desperate for news.

Thankfully, the return of Kenneth Cohen, the same man who'd met with Navarre in Lisbon all those months ago, proved to be the solution to many difficulties. As Navarre had told her, Cohen was a compassionate, fair-minded individual, and the severe losses that Alliance had suffered appeared to weigh heavily on him. "I'm not a naval officer for nothing," he declared to Marie-Madeleine after the moon passed without any drops. "We'll get a sea operation going to bring gear in, and we'll make arrangements so you can get your reports."

Grand Duke was put in charge of the mission and chose a rocky, 10-meter jetty as the rendezvous point. Mahout's successor, a short, slim man named Shepherd, ended up hugging the jetty for dear life in the pouring rain for three and half hours, clinging desperately to the mailbag, made extra heavy by the presence of photographic plates.

Thanks to Shepherd's desperate feat, Marie-Madeleine finally had access to letters too long to be sent by transmitter, some from months ago, penned by agents like Jack Tar who had subsequently been arrested. He'd written, "As a reward for our stubbornness, Alliance continues its steadfast forward march…"

She felt the sting of tears prickling behind her eyes. *If only Jack Tar were still around to lead that march.* The tears began their freefall as she picked up the next letter, which was a short missive informing her of Noble's death from whatever mysterious illness he'd been suffering. He'd been in the hospital for several months, but when, in their relentless pursuit of network members, the Gestapo raided the hospital, a helpful worker bundled Noble into an ambulance. He had passed away just as the Gestapo overtook the speeding ambulance.

Noble had once told her that the Boches would never get him alive, a prophecy that rang true, though at what a cost. Josette, the faithful Villa Etchebaster housekeeper, had been with him in the ambulance and was not so lucky. The writer of the missive lost track of what happened to Josette, but believed she had been deported to Germany.

Marie-Madeleine tried to reign in her emotions, remembering more words Noble had spoken: *little one, a soldier doesn't cry.*

Her efforts were in vain, however. The letters in her lap contained so much information she hadn't been aware of—the arrests of more agents, including Mandrill and other names of new recruits she'd never met, and the collapse of letter boxes only members of the network had known about. The families of some of her boys had also been arrested, innocent men and women who'd already suffered greatly due to the capture of their loved ones. The enormity of their sacrifices begged her to question who could ever repay such a debt?

At long last she came to a letter from Mandrill, written two days after he'd landed and probably hours before his arrest. After some digging, he had discovered that Léon was being kept at 84 Avenue Foch. Having lived on the street very briefly, Marie-Madeleine was familiar with the address, a stately home the Gestapo had commandeered near the Arc de Triomphe. They used the ground floors—where the wealthy owners had once slept and entertained—as their offices and sleeping quarters, and housed prisoners of the Reich on the upper floors. Somehow Mandrill had found out that Léon had tried to escape, along with two other prisoners, by sawing through the bars in their rooms that led to the roof.

Marie-Madeleine couldn't help smiling at this: Léon always managed to find a way out. He and the other two prisoners, which included an SOE wireless operator of Indian descent named 'Nora,' were able to get onto the roof, but then an air raid siren sounded. All three of them ended up getting captured. After this daring but failed attempt, it seemed Léon too had been deported.

A tear dropped onto the paper, smearing Mandrill's signature. With shaking hands, she refolded the letter, hoping against hope that someday Jacques's father would manage to find his way home to his son. *And his future wife.*

Marie-Madeleine, overwhelmed with a loneliness unlike any she had experienced before, curled into a ball and wept for all that she had lost.

CHAPTER 59

MARCH 1944

*I*t wasn't until the March moon that another Lysander carrying Alliance agents took off for France. However, the plane never returned to London and Marie-Madeleine fell into a deeper despair. Finally, word came that the pilot had been injured but was alive. The agents who had been passengers, also groaning with pain, somehow managed to conceal the six-foot tall, red-haired RAF pilot until another plane arrived to bring him home.

An unexpected returning passenger was also on the plane. Marie-Madeleine was startled when Jean Sainteny, code named 'Dragon,' appeared at Alliance house bearing a suitcase full of documents: thick files containing extensive information about Hitler's secret weapons, and the pièce de résistance: a meters-long, finely detailed map of the Boches' defenses lining the Normandy coast.

"*Merde,*" Marie-Madeleine said when Sainteny unfurled the map. "If the Allies have indeed targeted Normandy for their much-anticipated landing site, this will be indispensable to them."

"And now that I've delivered it to you in person, I'd like to go back as soon as possible," Sainteny nodded to the pile of personal messages and letters he'd brought with him from France. "Despite what those may say."

She gave him a curious look as she got up to sort through them. There was a small envelope, on which was printed 'For Hedgehog only.' The handwriting was undeniably Swift's. In the letter, he complained of problems within the network: he and Petrel, his second-in-command, had argued over the organization of Alliance. It also seemed that Swift and Sainteny did not see eye to eye.

"Swift needs a new deputy leader," Sainteny explained. "Like the rest of us, he's suffering from exhaustion and paranoia. The obvious choice would be myself, but..."

"He wants you to stay in London," Marie-Madeleine filled in.

"Right."

She sighed. The network had plenty of problems as it was—they didn't need infighting to add to it. She picked up the map. "We'll see what MI6 has to say about this—something tells me they're going to want you to return to the Normandy coastline by the next moon, with more of their questionnaires in tow."

Marie-Madeleine's prediction about Sainteny's return came true, though not necessarily because of her reasoning. It was more that Swift, along with many others, was arrested.

The day after she'd heard the news, she was invited to a dinner hosted by a high-ranking RAF officer to thank the network for rescuing the downed pilot. Remembering the disastrous New Year's Eve party, Marie-Madeleine wanted to beg off, but then she remembered what Bishop had told her so long ago: *In war, one must never talk about those who have disappeared.* Still, she kept Swift and all of the rest of them in her thoughts.

Contrary to her own feelings, the mood in London seemed to have shifted as of late, presumably in anticipation of the Allied landing in France, which had come to be known as 'D-Day.' Despite the dancing and revelry around her, Marie-Madeleine had lost all sense of her surroundings, and, as per usual, her focus was on Alliance.

Even if she could convince MI6 to send her back to France, what could she do with a broken network? She'd repaired it before, but clearly the Gestapo had tightened their grip on the Resistance. How could she succeed when so many had failed? Navarre, Swift, Léon, all had done their best for Alliance, and all had wound up captured. *Sir Claude was right: leaders don't last more than six months.*

Six months.

Once D-Day occurred, surely the war itself wouldn't last more than six months… provided D-Day proved to be successful.

The party went on all night, and Marie-Madeleine was dropped off at Alliance House early in the morning, just as air-raid sirens began to sound.

Despite the danger, Marie-Madeleine, refusing to go down to the basement, stared out the window in the living room. Above the deserted streets, the flickering glow of searchlights illuminated the clouds, casting an eerie pall over the city. As the sounds of bombs and gunfire echoed in the distance, filling the air with an ominous rumble, Marie-Madeleine was consumed with a fiery desire for vengeance against the perpetrators of the attack, who seemed hell-bent on destroying all of Europe.

When the all-clear sounded, she turned away from the window and headed toward her office to get back to work. The way to achieve that vengeance was to keep dealing blows to Hitler and his regime. And the best way to do that was to revive Alliance.

She laid a piece of paper on the desk and sketched a new map of France, divided into four equal parts. In order to prevent infighting and ensure everyone's safety, she decided to completely isolate the remaining Alliance leaders from one another. Unfortunately, she could count them on one hand: Sainteny, Petrel, Opossum, and Grand Duke, but that was enough to fill the spots.

Four men, who represented the last hopes of the network.

And me.

The next day, Major Richards finally paid Marie-Madeleine a visit. "I wanted to tell you personally that Alliance has officially become part of de Gaulle's Free French organization."

She opened her mouth to protest that she'd always strived to stay firmly out of politics, but Richards held up his hand. "Don't you see, Poz, this is a good thing for you. They've promised to preserve the network's autonomy and maintain open communication—including with MI6. Alliance's future has been secured."

"And my return to France?"

"They're saying June." Richards put on his hat. "Who knows—maybe you'll be part of the Allied invasion."

"Do you think the Allies will really land in Normandy?"

"No one can be sure until D-Day," he replied. "They are taking extraordinary measures to keep it all a secret."

She shut her eyes, picturing the British in their khaki uniforms and the Americans in their olive ones, marching up the beaches of Normandy in accordance with Sainteny's map. "But it will be in France, correct?"

"It can only be in France."

CHAPTER 60

JUNE 1944

At long last, MI6 finally agreed to deliver Marie-Madeleine to France. She was to assume yet another new identity: Germaine Pezet, the wife of Raymond Pezet, an Alliance agent with the dubious code name of Flying Fish.

As she prepared for her long-awaited homecoming by dying her hair black and getting fitted for false teeth, the Allies were also gearing up for D-Day. The date and location of the Allied landing still remained a mystery, but it was obviously drawing closer as the roads to and from London became clogged by transport trucks, the coasts crowded with warships.

Marie-Madeleine was in the midst of last-minute preparations on the evening of June 5th when she began to hear a faint, almost imperceptible buzzing noise. She went to the window and opened it wide, causing the noise to increase tenfold.

There were no searchlights illuminating the sky and the cloud cover blocked her view, but from the sound of it, somewhere above her was an unending stream of British aircraft heading for France, and then, eventually, Nazi Germany. In the east, the sun would rise soon, bringing with it a first glimpse of victory.

She gripped the windowsill and leaned out as far as she dared, trying to soak in the fact that D-Day was about to happen, something for which they'd been hoping and praying for four years. Léon, and the rest of her comrades, were somewhere out there over the Channel. Tears filled her eyes as she imagined the joy and relief on their faces. Hopefully they too could sight the Allied planes soaring overhead and know that their sacrifice and bravery had not been in vain.

That night, Marie-Madeleine had no trouble falling asleep, and, for the first time in a long time, her dreams weren't plagued by nightmares.

The next evening, Kenneth Cohen invited Marie-Madeleine to his house to celebrate the momentous occasion of the Allied landing. He had opened a bottle of claret and they both said a cheers to the long-awaited arrival of D-Day.

"The worst part is over," Cohen assured her. "As soon as we establish a foothold on the beaches, everything will progress as planned. And the enemy seems to have been taken completely by surprise."

"Thank God for that!" Marie-Madeleine said before taking a gulp of claret.

Cohen started to say something else, but his words were drowned out by an air-raid siren. This was quickly followed by the boom of anti-aircraft guns. The sirens stopped and Marie-Madeleine gave Cohen a confused look.

"That was quick," he said, also looking perplexed.

The sirens sounded again, this time accompanied by a burst of tracer shells. As the warnings turned off for the second time, she stood. "I should probably get back."

"I'm not so sure you should leave right now," Cohen's eyebrows furrowed. "I don't know what's happening with the sirens, but if there's gunfire, you could catch a piece of shrapnel."

As the sirens started wailing yet again, Cohen threw up the blackout shade to look out the window. Searchlights dotted the night sky in all directions, but there didn't seem to be any German planes in the vicinity. Every once in a while, they could hear an unfamiliar sound slice through the night, like the revving of a motorcycle, only to be cut short by a deafening explosion.

"Is it the secret weapon?" Marie-Madeleine asked Cohen.

"Pray God, I hope not," he replied.

CHAPTER 61

JUNE 1944

Due to the Allied invasion, the Lysander landing scheduled for June that was supposed to bring Marie-Madeleine back to France was, of course, cancelled.

Less than a week after D-Day, Marie-Madeleine was informed that one of Alliance's new leaders, Sainteny, aka Dragon, had been arrested. Surprisingly, this news seemed to invigorate Sir Claude Dansey. "You see my dear, child," he told Marie-Madeleine, "there's absolutely no point in you going to France now."

"Your law of averages is incorrect," she countered. "This is the third leader to fall in under a year, and Sainteny didn't last six weeks. It's my duty to take his place."

"Unless your security measures are air-tight, Poz, you won't last six days."

Still, Marie-Madeleine remained unwavering in her determination to return to the field. Sir Claude's warning echoed in her ears as she went to the British Intelligence office to obtain a French identity card made out in the name of Madame Germaine Pezet, which was the same name of Flying Fish's real wife.

For the photograph, she used a hairnet to make her forehead narrower, which in turn made her face look heavier. She then produced the masterpiece made by one of MI6's dentists: a plastic monstrosity that made her teeth appear yellow and crooked. Her final touches were a pair of broken glasses and clumsily-applied makeup.

The officer in charge of IDs burst out laughing when she turned around. After he'd taken her picture, he asked for the dates of her new identity's grandparents' births.

"You must be crazy," she replied. "I don't even know my own grandparents' birthdays."

"The French always know these things," the officer retorted.

Deciding not to argue, she gave him the dates of Christian's and Beatrice's birthdays and then added 1870 as the year of birth for both of Madame Pezet's grandparents.

She was so wrapped up in her preparations that she'd given little thought to her family. The realization that her children wouldn't know she had left England hit her hard and as soon as she returned to her hotel room, she summoned Richards to ask if he thought she should at least contact Monique to let her know she'd be back in France. Marie-Madeleine had never told him about Jacques, but something in his sympathetic expression revealed that he was aware of the baby.

"I don't think it's a good idea at all," Richards countered. "You wouldn't want to put anyone in more danger than strictly necessary. If the Gestapo caught wind—"

"Right," Marie-Madeleine interrupted. "I understand."

"In fact," Richards continued cautiously, "I don't think it's necessary to inform the entire network of your return either, only your supposed husband, Flying Fish, Grand Duke—who is our man in Aix—and Petrel. Any more than that could compromise you."

"Got it."

In the end, she was only informed it was time to leave two hours before her impending departure. She donned her gray wool suit along with her hairnet and false teeth and then tucked some money into the false bottom of her purse. She had no need for questionnaires as she knew the requested information by heart.

Sir Claude came to see her off. "I want you to know, Poz, that but for the Free French, I would never have allowed you to go back. It's absolute lunacy to be sending you into the wolf's den so near the end."

"I have to return," she replied. "I have to see this thing through, and, at any rate, I've been in London for far too long."

The lines on his forehead deepened as he furrowed his brow, clearly lost in thought. In the distance, the buzzing of V-1s could be heard, which was followed by a barrage of anti-aircraft fire. Since D-Day, Britain had been bombarded by low-flying and extremely fast Doodlebug rockets, causing widespread damage and casualties. Despite the triumphant success of the Allied landing, the mood in London had soured, the public shrouded in fear and uncertainty from the incessant attacks and the haunting sound of air-raid sirens piercing the night.

Sir Claude, clearly ignoring the latest Doodlebug threat, stepped forward and handed her a tiny pill. "This is cyanide. Take it if you are arrested and think there is no way out. Although, I should add to never identify yourself to the Gestapo as the head of the network, or that…" He gestured toward the pill. "Will be the only way. Instead, tell them that MI6, and I personally, dispatched you to France to gather intelligence on the Communist Party. They'll know my name, and be very intrigued, so much that, hopefully, they won't kill you."

Marie-Madeleine wasn't convinced. "And the network?"

"Just tell them the network is finished—there's nothing left and that your job is still to gather information, but about the Russians this time, not the Nazis. Believe me, they'll all comply with whatever you say when you mention my name, including all my titles, of course."

"No Gestapo agent, no matter how crass and dim-witted, would ever accept a tale like that at face value."

"If not, then get them to send me a message over the radio and I'll confirm it." He gazed squarely into her eyes. "Trust me, Poz, I've never made this offer to anyone before."

"Why me then? I'm not British."

"You're a woman." He grimaced, as if his next words pained him.

"And I'm ashamed of the years spent watching you doing things I couldn't do myself. I also deeply pity you. I know you place probably too much faith in your premonitions and superstitions, but I thought you'd like to have this, too." With that, he took her hand in his and placed something in her palm before closing her fingers over it.

After he left, Marie-Madeleine opened her hand to see that he'd given her a rabbit's foot.

PART V
THE BEGINNING OF THE END

CHAPTER 62

JULY 1944

The Hudson plane taking Marie-Madeleine back to France was part of a bombing convoy. She stared out the window as the aircraft gained speed, blurring the ground beneath them. Suddenly they were soaring upward, the plane straining to gain altitude as they followed the other bombers into the clouds.

The sergeant in charge of the flight reached over to close the curtains, casting the interior of the aircraft into a disquieting gloom.

"Why won't he let us look out the window?" Marie-Madeleine asked Flying Fish in a whisper. "I wanted to catch the first glimpse of France."

"They don't want us to see the course we're taking since we're going into the war zone." Flying Fish got up to approach the navigators, whose forms were nearly obscured by the labyrinth of colorful dials and gauges surrounding them.

"We're over the Channel" he announced when he returned to his spot beside his supposed wife.

"Then we're almost there?"

"No," Flying Fish replied. "In order to steer clear of the battlefront, we'll be using a longer route to Paris. We'll fly around Brittany, follow the Loire River, and approach the city from the southeast before landing in Maisons-Rouges."

Half an hour later, the aircraft began to tilt sharply to the left and right, throwing the passengers off-balance and causing the sergeant to stumble about. Marie-Madeleine gripped the armrests tightly, trying to steady herself.

As she peeked through the curtain, she saw the reception committee's dazzling array of red lights twinkling in the darkness. The Hudson descended gracefully, making full use of the lights to guide its landing.

The man who helped her down from the plane greeted her by saying, "Welcome to France, Marie-Madeleine."

So much for the network being unaware of my return.

She was brought to a farmhouse in the heart of Maisons-Rouges, about an hour south of Paris. There must have been thirty or forty people gathered in the house, eating, drinking, celebrating, yet Marie-Madeleine felt terribly alone. Except for Flying Fish and a few others, most of the people surrounding her were strangers. The days of festive dinners with Noble, Magpie, Rivière, and Léon were now a distant memory. Noble was now gone forever, but would she ever see the rest of her friends again? Only time would tell.

The thought of Léon and what happened to him sent a jolt through her, causing her to stand up and march over to Flying Fish. "We have to go, now."

"Now?" He eyed her curiously. "You must be exhausted from the trip."

"Not enough to stay here." She pulled his arm. "You've been around a long time and must have known about Eagle. If he'd left as soon as he landed, he wouldn't have been caught."

"Where are we going?"

"Toward Aix." One of the only solid sectors remaining was in Aix-en-Provence, run by a man with the fitting code name of Grand Duke.

Flying Fish shrugged off her arm. "Are you telling me we're going to walk?"

Aix was in the south of France, near Marseille, which meant they had to travel hundreds of kilometers. "Some of the time, yes."

They trudged through the ditch next to the road for a few kilometers in complete silence. Flying Fish carried his case and one of Marie-Madeleine's bags, while she had hoisted the rest onto her shoulders. To minimize the risk of bombings, the villagers had extinguished every source of light and it seemed that even the most ordinary nocturnal noises, such as owls hooting and tree branches scraping, sounded ominous in the enveloping blackness.

As the realization that she was at last back in France hit her, Marie-Madeleine bent down and picked up a small piece of soil, rolling it into a ball between her fingers as she walked along.

The faint creaking of wheels announced the approach of a cart that was nearly indistinguishable in the darkness. Flying Fish called out to the driver, who pulled up next to them, his eyes landing on the suitcases.

"Forgive us, monsieur, but we've just returned from a black-market trip," Marie-Madeleine told the driver. "Which means we have money to pay you for a ride."

He nodded and patted the seat beside him. "Where are you headed?"

"The nearest train station," she said as she climbed into the wagon.

"I'm sure you know this, you being involved in the... black market and all, but you can't count on the trains lately. The Allies are constantly bombing the railways. And the Germans are everywhere."

As the clearly exhausted horses started to plod along at a glacier's pace, Marie-Madeleine sighed to herself. It was going to take them forever to get to Aix.

. . .

After three days of hitching rides and encountering delayed trains, all the while surrounded by the explosions and gunshots of Germans on the move, they finally reached Aix.

Although Marie-Madeleine had been corresponding with Grand Duke for months, she had never met the man and was therefore unsure how to greet him when he approached them at the train station.

The tall, graceful Grand Duke apparently had no such qualms. He kissed her hand before stating, "I'm glad you're finally here, madame. We've been anticipating your arrival for so long." He leaned in toward her ear, and, in a lowered voice, continued, "I've got hundreds of letters and reports waiting for you. The letter box you gave me from London is a goner—the men who ran it were shot six days ago. Sainteny has escaped and needs to be evacuated, but we're having trouble making contact with London; they don't seem to be listening to us."

It must have been apparent that she was overwhelmed, as Grand Duke's face softened before he asked, "Shall I take you to your hideout?"

She said a quick goodbye to Flying Fish and then Grand Duke led her to a first-floor flat owned by a nurse whose father had been killed by Germans in 1914.

"Besides the owner, you and I are the only ones who know this place," Grand Duke said as he unlocked the door. "You'll be perfectly safe here."

Once Marie-Madeleine had set her bags down, she asked him to tell her about Sainteny's escape.

"They tortured him, of course, but somehow he managed to saw through an iron bar. At the moment, some of our network members are nursing him back to health. But the Gestapo is searching high and low for him. We must get him away as soon as we can."

"Who told you all of this?"

"Petrel—he left Aix just this morning, actually, disappointed that you still hadn't arrived yet." Grand Duke opened a cupboard and took out boxes upon boxes of mail.

Marie-Madeleine sighed again. "How did we get so much? We have to send the most recent messages to London by radio."

Grand Duke frowned. "I wish we could, but as I said, London is not answering our calls."

She sank into a chair at the kitchen table and began to sort through the mail, separating out the newest correspondence into one pile and everything else that was over a week old into another.

Grand Duke poured them both a glass of brandy. "Do you know when the Allies are planning to land here, in the south of France?" he asked as he sat down.

"Three to four weeks at the most."

He nodded. "Then we should take precautions—after the Normandy landing, the retribution was fierce. They emptied the prisons by deporting our agents to Germany, and some of the others were shot on the spot."

Marie-Madeleine's thoughts were on Léon. "Where in Germany did they go?"

"Nobody knows what happened beyond the Rhine."

She took a long drag of brandy as Grand Duke filled her in on other network news. She then told him about the reaction to Petrel's 'secret weapon' intelligence and of the true impact the V-1s had when they were unleashed on London. Their conversation continued in this vein until sunset, their shared misfortunes rapidly forging a close friendship between them.

When Grand Duke stood to leave, she once again marveled at his height. Oblivious to Sir Claude's statistics, Grand Duke had kept Alliance churning through some of the most treacherous waters—not to mention had stayed in the same place and used the same name—for over a year. It seemed fitting that this was the man whom fate had chosen to save her Ark from sinking.

CHAPTER 63

JULY 1944

Within less than a week of her arrival in Aix, Marie-Madeleine had succeeded in dealing with the enormous pile of mail and sent any recent item dealing with troop movements, the battles on the Normandy front, or railway traffic, to London. The transmitter was functioning once more, and it was evident that the issue hadn't been with Grand Duke since he managed his sector with the meticulous precision of a military veteran, as he undeniably was. Under his wing, the remaining members of Alliance—who streamed into Aix from Marseille, Paris, and even Verdun—were able to reestablish the network to a level reminiscent of its former strength.

Marie-Madeleine dined nearly every night with Grand Duke and his family at their cozy farm just outside of Aix. Although she found herself captivated by the enchanting Provençal way of life, with its sweet smell of plane trees and roses, she refused to spend her time relaxing.

Since Grand Duke had Aix running so smoothly, she decided to head to Marseille to meet up with Petrel, who would then accompany her to Paris. She had one last dinner with Grand Duke and his wife, a charming beauty who was at least a decade younger than her dignified husband and whom Marie-Madeleine had nicknamed Duchess.

After saying a heartfelt goodbye to Grand Duke and Duchess, Marie-Madeleine went home to her flat to finish packing. Exhausted, she then sat down on a chair in the living room, her feet propped up on a threadbare ottoman.

At dinner, Grand Duke had told her that the Germans had massacred all of the prisoners being held in Caen, including the men who had helped make the map of the Normandy coastline that Sainteny had provided MI6 and which had undoubtedly enhanced the efficiency of D-Day.

If Hitler was indeed intent on exterminating all his political prisoners, what hope did her friends have? And Léon? She was seized by a fearful shudder as she heard a scratching on the front door.

Knowing that it must be someone friendly—if it were the Gestapo, they'd be banging away or even bursting down the door—she opened it to see Grand Duke, his eyes wide.

After she shut the door behind him, he told her, "The Boches are preparing to make a sweep of the town tomorrow evening. They're hunting for men in the maquis. I've got to get you out of here."

Marie-Madeleine recovered from her earlier fear. "I'm not worried—they're out for bigger fish than a woman traveling by herself. Besides, they won't find much—the maquis have all fled for the forest."

"I'm afraid it's not bigger fish they're after, but a female Flying Fish, if you get my drift." Grand Duke moved into the kitchen. "What happened to the francs that came in by parachute the other day?"

"They are in a crate of potatoes under the sink."

"And the mail?"

She pointed to the ottoman she'd propped her feet on earlier. "I stuffed it in there with the cotton."

"At any rate, you'd better come with me. I brought my bicycle: you can ride it and I'll walk and bring whatever else we want to get rid of."

"But we've got plenty of time. You said yourself the raid is tomorrow. You can come in the morning by car and we'll load it up." She nodded when he didn't move. "You should get going if you want to make it home before curfew—I wouldn't want Duchess to be worrying too much about you."

He reluctantly headed toward the door.

The inexplicable pounding in her head began again. "Grand Duke, do you mind taking this back with you tonight?" She retrieved the false-bottomed bag she was planning on bringing to Paris, full of coded information meant for Petrel. "Not that I think there's anything to worry about, but just in case."

He took it from her. "I'll see you first thing in the morning then."

"First thing," she promised.

She still felt shaky, so she decided to make herself something to eat. Duchess had given her a bottle of fresh olive oil and she dunked a couple of tomatoes in it. After a minute, she heard footsteps in the hallway outside the flat and wondered if Grand Duke had returned to try to convince her to leave.

When she went into the living room, she realized she'd forgotten to lock the deadbolt after Grand Duke left. She sprinted forward, desperate to secure it, but the door was already opening. She shoved into it with all her strength. If she could get it to latch, that would buy her two minutes of time with which to escape through the courtyard and run the other way.

A loud knock just above her head reverberated through her skull. "German police," someone called in French. "Open up."

Marie-Madeleine felt her strength fail and suddenly the living room was filled with a dozen men in grayish-green uniforms and a few in civilian clothes.

"Where's the man?" one of the plain-clothed men demanded.

When she didn't reply, a soldier pointed his gun at her. "Where is he?"

"What man?" Marie-Madeleine inquired. "I live here by myself."

"He went that way." The first man gestured toward the courtyard.

Marie-Madeleine took on an indignant tone. "There are other flats in this building, you know. If you are trying to find someone, why do you think he'll be in the first place you look?"

"She's right," another plain-clothed man, this one exceedingly tall, almost as tall as Grand Duke, admitted. He seemed to be in charge, as he ordered the soldier with the gun trained on Marie-Madeleine to watch her.

The tall man departed, taking a few soldiers with him, and in a moment, she could hear doors opening and closing, followed by the protestations of the other tenants.

To her horror, she noticed the square coding cards she'd left on the kitchen table. "Can I finish the snack I was eating before you all came?" She nodded toward the counter, where the tomatoes and olive oil still sat out.

The one with the gun exchanged glances with another soldier, who shrugged. "Sure," the first one told her.

As she passed the table, she scooped up the messages, using a napkin to cover them. She stuffed a few tomatoes into her mouth before walking back into the living room. She pretended to sneeze and then turned around to blow her nose noisily with the napkin. She sneezed again, this time bending over to throw the messages underneath the couch.

"What are you doing?" the soldier with the gun barked.

"Blowing my nose," she said, standing up straight, hoping he couldn't hear her pounding heart.

"How could you possibly have a cold in this heat?" He lowered his gun and rubbed his arm.

"Whoever this man is, he must be quite dangerous, what with all these weapons you have," Marie-Madeleine said conversationally.

"Indeed." Now he stood the gun down next to the fireplace. "He's a terrorist, in fact."

She put her hands over her mouth, pretending to be frightened. "Is he from the maquis?"

The soldier nodded emphatically. "He came into the building about half an hour ago. We were sent to get him."

"What does he look like?"

"He's tall and balding." Marie-Madeleine's heart sank as the soldier continued, "The Gestapo chiefs call him Grand Duke."

The Gestapo. That would be the men in plain clothes, she decided, attempting to keep her face as neutral as possible. But how did they know about Grand Duke?

The main Gestapo man returned. "He's not upstairs," he informed the soldier. "This woman is lying to us to gain time." He then grabbed Marie-Madeleine by the shoulders. "Why did you push against the door when we were trying to get in?"

She opened her eyes wide. "What should I do? I'm a woman living by myself and you gave me quite the fright—I thought you were terrorists from the maquis. That's why I let you in when you said you were the police."

The Gestapo chief relaxed his grip. "What are you doing here by yourself?"

"Escaping the bombing in Toulon—all the air raids were driving me mad." She wrung her hands for good measure. "I came here to get some peace and quiet, but a lot of good that did me." She then crossed her arms over her chest. "Can't you go about things with more consideration? I've always heard that Germans were efficient and polite. If I'd known you were Gestapo, I would have opened the door straight away."

The chief nodded to the rest of the men, who had once again filed in. They started roaming the flat: flipping over chairs and rummaging through cabinets. Her former watchdog used the barrel of his gun to pick through the ashes in the fireplace. Marie-Madeleine forced herself to remain calm. "What are you looking for, anyway?"

"This man we're after is a leader of a big Resistance network. We call it Noah's Ark because a lot of the agents have animal names," one of the other soldiers replied.

The Gestapo man gave him a look that shut him up.

"Oh, the Resistance," she repeated. "How horrible. Is there something I can do to help?"

One by one, the soldiers returned to the living room. "We didn't find anything suspicious," one of them remarked.

The chief handed Marie-Madeleine a card. "Here's the address of our office. If the man we've described comes back, please let me know at once." He turned to one of the other plain-clothed men. "He may have dove under the porch while these idiots were raising the alarm instead of taking him down."

She felt a surge of relief as the soldiers gathered up their weapons and moved toward the door. Suddenly one of them, as he was leaving the kitchen, bent down on all fours. The pounding in her head started again. As if in slow motion, she watched his arm reach underneath the couch and pull out the messages.

And just like that, her hour of reckoning had arrived as multiple guns were trained on her. The visions of her captured comrades—Navarre, Léon, Schaerrer, Rivière—swam before her eyes, giving her some semblance of courage. It was inevitable that she would join them—it would be unfair to have it any other way.

The chief gave another order and his thugs began to berate her with insults as some of them wielded their rifle butts to destroy the furniture. One of them forcefully thrust her aside to get at a glass table, which he then obliterated, the glass shattering into tiny pieces on the carpet.

The fear that had been plaguing Marie-Madeleine for the last hour morphed into a seething fury. "Stop! This isn't my house: those are not my things. You can't just barge in here and smash up the furniture with no regard to anything."

The Gestapo chief grabbed her again, this time shaking her like one of the plane trees outside. "Whose house is this? And who are you?"

Fear turned to contempt as she glared back at him. "You're not important enough to know."

"You're British?"

"No. I'm French."

"When did you arrive?"

"A few weeks ago. I parachuted in during the night, not far away from here."

"Who is the man who came here? Who is the Grand Duke?"

She finally managed to wrangle out of his grasp. "I don't know him by that name. Tonight was the first time I'd seen him."

"What was he doing here?"

A part of her understood that providing misleading, yet

convincing statements could buy her time, but the responses had to be formulated faster than her thoughts could process. "He wanted me to meet someone in the Place de Marché tomorrow."

"Who are you meeting?"

"I don't know." She needed to do better than that. "I just do as I'm told."

"How will you identify this person if you don't know who it is?"

"He will identify *me* by the scarf I'm supposed to wear."

"What's your name?"

Her former watchdog dumped out her purse and then held up her identity card. "It's Germaine Pezet."

She gave a hearty laugh to hide her unease— Germaine Pezet was Flying Fish's actual wife. If she somehow did manage to escape, she didn't want the Gestapo to circulate wanted posters with that name. "That's a fake name of course. We've all got them. London comes up with them."

The chief plunged his knife into the ottoman in anger and ripped open the cover, causing her reports to burst out like a flurry of moths.

Marie-Madeleine shut her eyes. *They're going to lynch me now for sure.* Indeed, a few more soldiers leveled their rifles at her.

The leader nodded at one of the soldiers, who had found the bottle of brandy, and they were soon passing around both the liquor and the messages.

The chief pulled Marie-Madeleine into a corner of the room. "Somehow you don't seem to be all that frightened."

Inside she was terrified, but she replied, "I've nothing to be frightened of."

"At least tell me who you are."

Time. Even through the throbbing of her head, she recognized the need to stall for time. She narrowed her eyes contemptuously. "I can tell you're not high enough in the hierarchy to know my real identity. I can only tell your top boss."

For some reason, he accepted this. "Well then, if we escort you to this rendezvous at the Place du Marché, will you make contact with this agent and allow us to get a good look at him? If not, we have ways of making you talk… and beg for mercy," he sneered.

"Tomorrow?" Obviously there was no such agent to contact. "I won't do anything you say until I speak to your leader."

The plain-clothed men huddled up. After a brief discussion, the chief approached her again. "You're lucky. Our regional boss will be in Aix tomorrow night. I'm sure he will be willing to meet with you."

You bet he will. She smiled at the chief. "Considering how long he's been hunting me, he's going to have a very pleasant surprise."

"For now, you are coming with us. Go pack your bag." He nodded at a soldier, who followed her into the bedroom, his pistol aimed at her back.

They were going to throw her in jail. And Grand Duke would be returning first thing in the morning—he would walk directly into their trap. *I have to find a way to escape... tonight,* she decided as she threw a toothbrush and a change of clothes into a bag. She hadn't spent all that time trying to get back to France only to get caught. Not to mention place others like Grand Duke in danger. She had to save him, somehow.

The soldier shouted at her to get moving.

She gave him the sweetest smile she could muster. "I just have to use the toilet."

Once the bathroom door was closed, she reached into the medicine cabinet to grab the cyanide pill that Sir Claude had given her. If she hadn't discovered a solution by tomorrow morning, this might be what he referred to as her 'only way out.'

Lying next to the pill was the rabbit's foot. She took that too and stuffed it into her bag. "I'm ready," she announced as she returned to the living room.

CHAPTER 64

JULY 1944

Instead of a prison, Marie-Madeleine was taken to an army barracks and led to the back room, where they kept the 'punishment cells.' After the men who had been occupying the cell were removed, the Gestapo chief forcefully shoved her inside, the acrid odors of German cigarettes and urine overwhelming her senses.

He put her bag on the edge of the bed, which was covered with a threadbare gray blanket. "I'll be back tomorrow morning to fetch you to meet our leader." His voice took on a tone that was almost kind. "Do you want me to turn the light off?"

"Please. I need to get some sleep."

He hesitated at the door to the cell. "You're not going to commit suicide, are you?"

"Me?" She didn't have to fake her surprise. Did he know about the cyanide pill? "Why would I do that?"

"Because all British spies commit suicide as soon as they're left alone."

The validity of the statement sounded doubtful, but she decided not to question it. "As I told you, I'm not British, and there is no reason for me to take my own life."

"So I don't need to worry?"

"Of course not," she snapped back. The audacity of these people astounded her: they'd arrested her, presumably intending eventually to shoot her or slit her throat, but here they were asking for her assurance that she wouldn't off herself in the middle of the night.

The bare lightbulb hanging from the ceiling was extinguished and then she heard the sound of the chief bolting the door.

The only light now came from the half-moon outside the window. Marie-Madeleine started to make her way over there, but, as she passed the foul-smelling waste bucket, she was overtaken by a wave of nausea and vomited violently into the bucket.

If only the Gestapo thugs knew how terrified she was, how the courage she'd conjured up had been exhausted, leaving her gasping and drained. The pounding in her skull had finally receded, and she felt empty-headed, devoid of any thoughts whatsoever.

Despite the dirty blanket and the tiny lumps in the sheets which could only be bedbugs, she collapsed onto the bed, desperate to get sleep to face up to tomorrow's interrogation.

She sat up again, suddenly awake. *A Gestapo interrogation.* She'd always assumed they were mindless thugs, but would she be able to keep her wits about her enough to deny her knowledge of Grand Duke and all the others? Could she endure the humiliation and torture that was sure to be inflicted on her tomorrow? A wry smile crept onto her face as she thought that the true meaning of Resistance was to resist the Gestapo's cruel tactics.

But it didn't have to be that way. She groped near the end of the bed to find her bag. Should she take the pill now, or in the morning when they came in?

No. That wouldn't help Grand Duke, who was due to arrive at her flat in a few hours. She must try everything else first. Besides, there was the potential of the pill not working at all, like what happened when Léon tried to give it to Bla.

Escape. The idea that had been at the forefront of her mind earlier that evening seized her once more. She had to try to escape.

She checked her watch: midnight, which gave her only six hours before dawn. She crept closer to the door. Through the crack, she could see figures moving around and decided the soldiers must be changing guard.

As if on its own accord, her fist struck the door. She could hear the chatter outside the door come to an abrupt halt. She pounded again.

A tall soldier opened the door. *"Ja?"*

"I need to go to the bathroom. *Toilette.*"

He sighed before going to the table and picked up his gun.

He led her into the courtyard and pointed to the lavatory. As she walked toward it, she took in the layout: the courtyard was smack dab in the middle of the barracks, surrounded on every side by high walls. There was no way out.

As she made her way back, she tried to come up with another plan.

Once she was back in her cell, Marie-Madeleine flopped back onto the bed, chiding herself for even thinking of escaping. She would be better off getting some rest.

Yet she couldn't sleep. It felt as if a heavy weight was pressing down on her chest, making it hard to breathe. She needed some air and once again went toward the window. A thick plank had been screwed into the frame, blocking most of the light, probably to keep the punished soldiers from communicating with anyone outside. Behind the plank was a vertical row of bars covering the opening. She reached under the board and in between the bars, marveling that her arm went all the way through. There was no glass.

She pushed the bed underneath the window, making sure to make as little noise as possible. It wasn't quite high enough to reach, so she searched the cell for something to stand on. The only option was the waste bucket she had retched in earlier. Holding her breath, she dumped it out over the drain in the floor before putting it upside down on the bed, knowing that, if this attempt ended up failing, there was no way she would be able to sleep now.

She removed her shoes and climbed onto the bucket. She was now level with the opening above the wooden board. She took in a deep breath of clean, cool night air as she grasped one of the bars. It wasn't as sturdy as a prison bar; it was more like the bars found on the ground floors of Paris flats. Still, there was no way to remove them or the board without the proper tools. She recalled what Mahout had written about Léon's almost escape from Avenue Foch. How had he managed? She was suddenly overcome by sadness, as she always was when she thought about Léon.

She pushed him out of mind to focus on the here and now. But that didn't change the fact that she had no way of removing the bars from the window.

Frustrated, she climbed back down, her bare feet landing on the filthy floor. She glanced toward the door. Beyond it, the guards were chatting loudly. She figured there would be another guard change at three o'clock. Her stomach growled and she realized she hadn't had anything to eat since the tomatoes and the olive oil. It was too bad they hadn't let her bring it with her.

Suddenly a story popped into her head, one her father used to tell her when she was growing up in Shanghai. He'd said that there were burglars who would break into houses at night, their bodies covered with grease to slip right through the grasp of anyone trying to apprehend them.

She climbed back onto the bucket. She had no oil, but the bars were far enough apart that she might be able to fit through them, as long as she could get past the gap between the board and the bars. It might just be possible, but she'd have to take all her clothes off.

She got down again and took off her skirt and jacket. She'd packed the batik dress Swift's wife had given her in her overnight bag. She retrieved it and practiced moving around with the dress clenched in her teeth and several francs in her hand.

At three o'clock, as predicted, there was more noise as new guards came in.

After a few minutes, she cautiously peered through the crack in the door, but didn't see any movement. She put her dress back on and then lightly rapped on the door, intending to repeat the bathroom request if anyone answered. No one did. She pressed an ear to the door, but all she could hear was snoring. These guards clearly assumed she was asleep and were taking the opportunity to catch up on their own rest.

It was now or never. She took the dress off again before getting back up on the bucket. Holding the tops of the bars with either hand, she inserted her legs into the gap, losing the banknotes in the process.

With her whole body now behind the plank, she tested the spaces between the bars. Would any of them allow her head to go through? The ones in the middle were definitely not wide enough, but two of those closer to the side seemed to be, provided she was willing to apply ample force.

With some effort, she managed to get her heard through the bars. At that moment, however, a large truck ground to a halt directly outside the window.

She yanked her head back so abruptly that she feared she'd severed her ears. Tears pricked her eyes, both from the excruciating pain and the thought that the Gestapo thugs would find her stripped naked, her dress hanging from her mouth, and pinned to a board that was pricking her back with splinters.

A man exited the truck and called out. A voice answered from only a few meters away from Marie-Madeleine. There must have been a sentry posted near her cell in the same direction she had planned on fleeing once she was free.

Shutting her eyes—as though she were a child under the impression that if she couldn't see them, they couldn't see her— she waited while the truck driver asked the sentry for directions. Finally the man got back in the truck and drove away.

With renewed determination, Marie-Madeleine pushed her head back through the bars, gritting her teeth against the pain which was even worse the second time. With her body now slick with sweat, her chest and arms squeezed through easily, but getting her hips through was utter misery, as if her body was in a vice. She convinced herself that the torment she felt now would be nothing compared to what was in store for her tomorrow during the interrogation. With one last push, she'd wrenched free.

The audible thump as she dropped to the ground must have attracted the sentry's attention. *"Wer da?"*

Still naked, she pressed against the ground, holding her breath, as the soldier's flashlight sliced through the black night.

As the light finally retreated, Marie-Madeleine threw on her dress and got down on all fours to crawl in the other direction. When she was far enough away, she staggered upright and began to run, her bare feet stumbling in the darkness, the thorns from wild roses clawing her skin.

Ignoring the pain searing through her body, she focused on putting as much distance as possible between herself and the army barracks. She knew that if the sentry spotted her and sounded an alarm, they would send the dogs after her and she would be caught in no time.

Finally she came upon a church cemetery. Figuring it was as good a place as any to rest, she sank down in the grass beside a tombstone. After she caught her breath, she heard the trickling sound of water. Realizing it must be the stream that ran through Aix, she headed towards it to rinse off her raw, burning skin and cool off her blistered feet, which felt as though they'd been running through hot coals.

The first signs of morning were starting to appear. As a bird chirped nearby, Marie-Madeleine glanced around her, trying to determine the way to Grand Duke's farm. Finally getting her bearings, she realized she had to go back the way she came, straight through town and toward the army barracks. With a sigh, she started back.

The sentry stood vigilantly near the window with the wooden plank, seeming oblivious to her escape just a few hours before. Still, Marie-Madeleine's nerves overcame her and she ducked into a garden on the other side of the street. Nestled in among the hollyhocks and more roses, she tried to summon the courage to keep going.

Two words finally convinced her: *Grand Duke.* If she didn't stop him, he was sure to go to her flat in just a couple of hours and find himself under arrest.

She increased her pace as the sound of the morning bugle echoed off the barracks. It would only be a matter of minutes before the guards charged with delivering food to her cell would discover her absence.

As she entered the town square, there were a handful of people milling about, many who stared open-mouthed at her wild hair and bare feet. A woman in a black dress and veil covering her face approached Marie-Madeleine. "Are you hurt, madame?"

Her throat was parched. "I'm looking for the road to Vauvenargues."

"I can show you—I happen to be going that way." The woman took her arm as they crossed the square. Marie-Madeleine could hear dogs barking in the direction of the barracks and black cars were now on the prowl.

When they reached the Sainte-Marie-Madeleine church, the woman gave her hand a reassuring squeeze. "Keep heading straight and you'll find Vauvenargues."

"Thank you." Marie-Madeleine walked on, feeling the kindly woman's eyes following her, hoping the name of the church was a sign that everything would be okay. But a bit farther down the road, she saw that one of the black cars had stopped and soldiers were setting up a roadblock. To the left of the roadblock, there was a field of corn, the yellow cobs glinting in the morning light.

Marie-Madeleine strolled into the field to join the peasant women. Bending over, pretending to be picking corn, she made her way to a road beyond the field.

As she doubled back on the Vauvenargues road, she was stunned to see that, tucked in among the olive and cypress trees, all the farms looked the same to her exhausted eyes. Finally she spotted a familiar house surrounded by the Duchess's prized geraniums.

The front door was unlocked. *I must remind Grand Duke to lock the door.*

She went into the hall and called out. Grand Duke came running down the stairs, tying his robe over his pajamas.

Marie-Madeleine choked out the words, "I've just escaped. I've saved your lives," before the room began spinning and she fell to the floor.

CHAPTER 65

JULY 1944

Grand Duke brought Marie-Madeleine to his hideout located further along the road to Vauvenargues. The grounds consisted of an old barn, in which Grand Duke stored the arms and ammunition secured through parachute drops, and a one-room cabin, where he had made up a bed for Marie-Madeleine. He told her to rest while he busied himself in the kitchen area, which was really just a counter and a sink.

As she laid down on the rough but clean sheets, she heard the rustle of leaves outside the cabin. She sat up, wondering if the Gestapo had discovered the hideout.

But it was only Petrel. It was just like the math expert to arrive right on time, despite the sudden change in meeting place. "Finally, Marie-Madeleine!" His heavy eyebrows knitted together. "I don't suppose there was much point in having a relaxing break in England if you're going to do that to us directly upon your return."

She hung her head. "I'm so ashamed."

"Hey." He placed a hand on her shoulder. "It's not your fault—the Gestapo have been after us constantly, even more so since D-Day. Anyway, I've come to escort you to Paris. Our people are getting anxious for your arrival."

"She's not fit to travel to Paris at this moment," Grand Duke informed him, setting down the knife he'd been using to cut carrots. "Look at her feet—she can't even get into a pair of shoes. You'll have to wait for her to heal."

As much as Marie-Madeleine wanted to get back to work, she had to admit that Grand Duke was right. "Go on to Marseille," she told Petrel. "I'll meet you there in a few days."

After Petrel left, Grand Duke asked if she was going to try to sleep.

She sighed. "I'm not sure I'll ever feel comfortable sleeping inside again. I'd rather listen for unfamiliar sounds out in the open. That way, if anyone comes upon me, I'll be ready."

And so, with some of Alliance's men acting as guards, she drifted off into a pleasant, dreamless sleep in the garden outside the farmhouse.

She was awakened at dawn by a loud rumbling noise. Through the rosy glow of sunrise, she spotted Grand Duke, brandishing a Sten gun as he stared out at the Vauvenargues road.

"What is it?" she asked sleepily.

"Nothing much. Just some planes out on patrol from the nearby base." He turned back to her. "Did you get a good rest?"

"Yes," she replied, stretching out on the ground before folding up the blanket someone had brought her in the middle of the night.

"Good because I don't think we should stay here. I want to go with the maquis."

She nodded. She knew that most of the maquis were young men who had fled to the forest to avoid being sent to German work camps due to the *Service du Travail Obligatoire,* Vichy's forced labor service. Many of them had become part of the Resistance as well.

"We may have to run through the forest if we see any hint of German troops." Grand Duke took a small container from his pocket. "So I have to try to do something about your feet." Tenderly, he spread the cream on her blisters. "Pretend I'm the Gestapo," he said, taking on a stern tone. "Hedgehog, where is Grand Duke? Where are the rest of your so-called Noah's Ark?"

"They've set sail," she replied, laughter in her voice. She stopped short when a burly, bearded man emerged from the woods.

"My contact," he moaned. "I'm going to miss my contact."

She cast a frightened look at Grand Duke, who told her not to worry. "That's Weevil, our wireless transmitter."

"Ah." She watched as he strung his aerial around a cypress tree. It had been a while since she'd seen a transmission from the field; for several long months, Alliance's intelligence had been delivered right to her doorstep in London, and here was an operator now, calling from the battlefield.

She quickly coded a message to London, letting them know she had been arrested but had escaped. She decided to leave out the more salacious details, including her nude descent through the window.

Weevil was able to make contact with London easily, and, as he was tapping away on his Morse key, Marie-Madeleine and Grand Duke went into the house to scrounge up some breakfast. One of the female agents, Turtle Dove, delivered a basket of fresh fruit along with her latest reports. She was followed by half a dozen other agents, all bringing news of the Gestapo's thus far unsuccessful search for Germaine Pezet.

"What about Flying Fish?" she asked an agent with the rather unfortunate code name of Roach.

"He was warned off and fled to Marseille."

She nodded as Roach went on, "And the owner of your building, Mademoiselle de Weerdt, had the audacity to lodge a complaint with the Gestapo on how one of her apartments was being used as a trap for Resistance agents. They agreed to move their sentries out as long as she signed a document guaranteeing she'd report you if you dared show your face at the flat again."

This made her smile. Mademoiselle de Weerdt must have known there was no way Marie-Madeleine would go back to the flat, yet she managed to make sure no one else would get caught by the Gestapo. If there was one thing she'd learned from this infernal war, it was that bravery could come in the most unexpected ways, and from the most unexpected people.

The next agent, Boar, informed them that the police chief had ordered the officer in charge of the guard at the Miollis Barracks to be hanged. Clearly the unfortunate man was the one to take the blame for Marie-Madeleine's escape.

"Forget him," Grand Duke checked his watch and then stood up. "It's time we joined up with the maquis."

As night fell again, Grand Duke, Roach, and Marie-Madeleine set out on the Vauvenargues road. Weighed down by her bag and a Sten gun, it was a strenuous climb uphill, made even more challenging by the blisters that had reopened in her too-tight shoes.

Any time headlights appeared, the three of them would dive into the ditch by the side of the road. Luckily, none of the cars stopped, though they were clearly Wehrmacht lorries.

As the night dragged on, it became increasingly difficult for Marie-Madeleine to walk and she had to lean on both men for support. Embarrassed, she suggested they go on, and leave her to spend the night in a ditch. "There's no sense in all three of us being picked up by a patrol."

"No," Grand Duke replied resolutely. "We must first get within sight of the maquis and they'll come out to help."

When the soft light of dawn started to illuminate the turrets of the Vauvenargues's castle, Marie-Madeleine's legs gave out. Roach soon disappeared.

She and Grand Duke sat down to rest and eat in silence, in case there were any patrols in the area. A part of her hoped Roach had taken her advice and gone out on his own. But he returned in less than half an hour, wheeling a cart down the steep road.

Both men lifted her into the cart and they continued on their way. At long last they stopped in front of a tiny house set in among the ruins of the medieval town. Grand Duke knocked on the door and whispered a password. A few minutes later, a haggard-looking couple was peering over the sides of the cart. "She needs some tea and a long rest," the woman said.

Marie-Madeleine blinked, remembering how Boutron had insisted all she needed was a brandy after spending nine hours in a mailbag.

Grand Duke and Roach whisked her into the couple's house and deposited her in a warm bed, promising to be back in the morning.

CHAPTER 66

JULY 1944

Although the maquis had a reputation of being a rag-tag group akin to Robin Hood's Merry Men, the Vauvenargues branch was quite organized. The parachute drop Marie-Madeleine had arranged from London gave them plenty of supplies: weapons, ammunition, food, even Spam and coffee. She quickly ascertained that most of the maquis members were Spaniards who had fled to France during the Spanish Civil War and then built new lives. After Vichy issued the STO, they'd left their homes and their loved ones once again and fled to the forest.

As dusk fell, Marie-Madeleine joined the men huddled around the smoldering embers of a fire, which had been set up by one of the maquis in a way that would never be detectable from a distance.

Boar took a sip of wine and then nodded at the castle, which was quickly disappearing in the fading light. "I much prefer your château to theirs." He had arrived earlier in the evening after a close call: the Gestapo had gotten his address through a courier they'd picked up, and, unlike Marie-Madeleine, had managed to escape through the back door when he saw them coming.

"What about your cell bars, chief?" Roach leaned forward. "You have to tell us how you came up with the inspiration for your escape plan."

She told them about her father's tale of the burglars covered in grease. "But, what was most surprising to me, was that the gaps between the bars were so uneven, leaving two of them wide enough to fit through."

The maquis man stirring the fire gave a chuckle. "Señora, you should know I was a mason, whose job it was to put the bars up in prisons." The group shifted closer to hear his next words. "I can tell you how it happens: after the officials have come in with their tape measures to inspect the gaps, and while the cement is still wet, we shift one of the bars a bit further away. We call it 'the bar of freedom.' It is because of men like me that you were able to get through."

She didn't know what else to say besides, "Thank you."

The maquis man went back to stirring his remarkable fire, which filled them all with warmth, yet produced almost no smoke or flames. *How long do you have to live in the maquis before you can make a fire like that?* She could have watched him keep it going all night, but, one by one, the men started to slip away to their makeshift beds in the woods.

She stayed to see the embers burn out and then found a suitable spot next to a bush. She slept huddled under her blankets while a maquis man stood vigil, a dark figure outlined against the star-dotted sky.

* * *

After a couple of days with the maquis, Marie-Madeleine decided she was well enough to travel and said a hasty goodbye to Grand Duke and the rest.

Carrying new identity papers made out in yet another alias, she climbed onto a maquis man's motorcycle, her arms firmly hugging his waist. As he sped off, she took a cautious peek behind her and was just able to spot Grand Duke, Roach and Boar before the winding road obscured them from view.

. . .

The last time she'd been in Marseille was in 1942, just before the Germans broke the armistice and marched into the Free Zone. It looked very different in 1944, especially the area of the Old Port, which had once held a large Jewish population. After the Germans and the French Police had deported the majority of the residents, they had blown up the vacated homes with dynamite.

Petrel was waiting for her in the lobby of an inn, brandishing her newest disguise: a mourning ensemble complete with a wool coat and a crepe veil that extended to her waist. Her still sore feet were stuffed into stockings and black patent leather shoes. It wasn't the most comfortable clothing to be donning in the hot and humid Mediterranean climate, but it would have to do for her journey to Paris.

She and Petrel split up on the train, but as soon as Marie-Madeleine sat down, she saw a familiar face a few seats down. The man, who was holding a bouquet of flowers, got up to take the seat across from hers, thrusting the bouquet at her without saying a word.

"Beaver!" Marie-Madeleine exclaimed as she removed her veil. "How wonderful to see you again." Beaver, whose once robust policeman's build had been reduced to a mere shadow of its former self, had been with the network since the days of Crusade and had owned the bar in Marseille. She lowered her voice to a whisper. "And what of our friends?"

"It was enough to drive a person crazy." He cracked the knuckles on his oversized hands as he talked quietly. "After the capture of Magpie and Léon, I thought the network was done for, that we had no chance of recovering. Then Swift came along, and had me run all over France, but then he was captured. And then Sainteny, and he was captured too." Beaver reached out to take her hands in his large ones. "But they mustn't get you."

She nodded in agreement as she pulled the veil back over her face.

As they were approaching Avignon, the air raid sirens started up, and they spent an uncomfortable night with the train taking cover in a tunnel. They began moving again at dawn, but then the train halted again.

Glancing out the window, Marie-Madeleine couldn't help but smile to see Petrel enjoying a makeshift shower on the platform. With all his traveling, he'd clearly gotten familiar with the railway men, who had provided him with buckets of water with which to wash up.

As another day came to a close, they again had to take shelter in a tunnel for the rest of the evening.

The uneven tracks, which had been hurriedly repaired after each bombing, made the ride become increasingly jerky as they approached Paris. The train finally stopped upon reaching a pile of debris a meter high.

"I guess we're walking." Beaver reached out to help Marie-Madeleine out of her seat.

She grimaced as she left the train, her feet once again burning.

Petrel stood waiting for them between two mounds of blackened rubble. "Everything okay?"

"Fine," she replied through gritted teeth.

Paris seemed as black and bleak as Marie-Madeleine's outfit, as if were a city mourning the loss of its former spirited self. She managed to make it to Petrel's headquarters near the Eiffel Tower without giving out this time, though each step she took sent shooting pains through her feet.

She had never been so grateful to shed her clothes and dive into a hot bath.

CHAPTER 67

AUGUST 1944

Petrel had secured Marie-Madeleine a tiny flat on the top floor of a building in the 16th arrondissement. The morning after she'd returned to Paris, one of Petrel's female couriers, Parakeet, insisted that Marie-Madeleine should dress the part of a true Parisienne and provided her with a tailored jacket and skirt and a fashionable over-the-shoulder purse. After Parakeet helped her cut her hair in the latest style, Marie-Madeleine felt remnants of her old self come surging back. In the last day or so, word had spread that the Allies were advancing toward Paris, and, mirroring her sentiments once again, the city was reinvigorated, with people milling about freely in the streets below them.

"What should I do with this?" Parakeet wrinkled her nose as she picked up Marie-Madeleine's brown dress.

"Burn it."

Jean Sainteny, otherwise known as Dragon, stopped by the apartment later that day. After greeting Marie-Madeleine with a heartfelt hug, he said, "I've heard that you also had the dubious pleasure of encountering prison bars." He held up a piece of iron. "I sawed through mine and kept this as a souvenir."

Her smile faded as quickly as it had appeared. "They told me you were tortured."

"Indeed. The Boches are despicable," he spat out. "They'll pummel you until you are almost unconscious, and then they'll fill your head with lies to confuse your already rattled mind."

"That's why I made sure I didn't stay." After a moment, she asked in a softer voice, "Have you heard any news of Léon?"

"No." He touched her shoulder. "I'm sorry."

She plastered on another smile, this one fake. "We'll find him. In the meantime, we have to ensure you are not recaptured. I will ask London to arrange your evacuation either by air or sea, whichever you prefer."

"Actually, I'd rather not leave France." He sat down in one of the apartment's only seats, a modest armchair. "I'll be safe once I cross the Allied lines, and I can take any intelligence reports you have with me."

"How do you plan to get across?"

"One of our agents who runs a café near the Arc de Triomphe has a motorcycle. He can take me."

"Right. Let me get those reports organized." Petrel had delivered a mail sack earlier that morning—in the confusion surrounding the approach of the Allies and the Germans retreating, the mail had gotten backed up again.

After Sainteny left to make his arrangements, Marie-Madeleine sat down in his vacated chair to repeat the arduous task of sifting through messages and identifying the most recent, much like she'd done in Aix. Mixed in with the reports were a few requests from Kenneth Cohen in London that Poz return to England by the next moon. Those ones she crumpled up and threw to the side.

She'd just about finished putting together a packet for Sainteny when someone knocked on the door of the flat. Her heart jumping in her chest, she opened it to find a man whose bright eyes and unlined face seemed to belie his age. As he was clearly not a threat, she invited him in.

He extended a pudgy hand. "Hedgehog, I'm Dr. Pierre Noal, code name Grouse."

As she shut the door, she searched her memory for a Grouse, but came up short.

He must have sensed her confusion. "You don't know me yet. I'm new. Petrel put me in charge of the agents in the northern zone. I'd heard that the leader of Alliance was in town and I, of course, wanted to meet you myself. And also to ask if there is anything you might need from me."

"Actually, yes." She gave him the stack of questionnaires that had yet to be answered regarding the positioning of the German troops left in Paris. "I think the Allies are fearful that the Germans are planning to defend Paris against them."

Grouse flipped through the paperwork. "My gut tells me the Boches are about to retreat. They've been requisitioning any wheeled vehicle they can get a hand on, including carts."

"Let's just pray they go quietly and leave the priceless monuments and landmarks alone."

Grouse sighed. "You and I both know that's not how they operate. They've already looted the museums. I'm afraid the Nazis are immune to the allure of even a city as beautiful as Paris."

Marie-Madeleine glanced out the window, where the Eiffel Tower stood tall and proud amongst the bright green grass and trees of August. "Let's hope not."

Magpie believed he'd been unsuccessful in his conversation with British Intelligence's arrogant chief of coding, but in the past few days, London had started 'broadcasting into the void,' which meant MI6 sent their instructions twice a day to all intact Alliance radios. The operators were to transmit the information back to London only if they were unable to deliver it directly to the generals in the field—clearly a more efficient method, as it eliminated the need for intermediaries.

Hence, on August 16th, Sainteny left to cross over to the Allied line according to plan. He and the bar owner/ motorcycle operator, Bernard de Billy, disguised themselves as telephone operators.

However, that evening, Sainteny returned to Marie-Madeleine's flat.

"What are you doing here?" she asked as he strolled in.

"The Americans, including General Patton, were incredibly impressed with all of our intelligence." He sat down in the same chair as before. "They were under the impression that the Germans had fled the city, but I was able to pinpoint some still-standing defense lines that I saw from the back of the motorcycle."

"Let me guess—the Americans want you to gather more information."

"You got it."

She walked over to peer out at the street. "I think it's highly dangerous to be crossing the lines like that. Yesterday the Germans started shooting people randomly in the streets. There are horror stories of women standing in front of the windows being hit by bullets." She took a few steps backward, though her window was several meters above the street. "And the French Communists are trying to consolidate their power before de Gaulle returns. The war isn't over yet."

"Exactly—that's why the Americans need us. The Boches really only have one goal: to retreat across the Rhine as quickly as they can. They know the Allies will be moving to Germany this winter. They won't be blowing up any more bridges—they require them to get out."

"Well, if that's the case, the Allies better enter Paris immediately, if only to save the city from imploding on itself from infighting and starvation."

Sainteny acknowledged the statement with a nod. "The good news is that Hitler agreed to spare Paris from any further significant damage. Besides, they haven't gotten enough fuel to set it on fire: the Wehrmacht needs every drop for their retreating tanks and jeeps." He stood. "What can I bring to the Americans? I have to get through the lines before dark."

She handed Sainteny several messages, which he then stuck in the hollow of his boot. He shifted his weight from one foot to the other to test out his hiding place as he stated, "I guess the only thing left is to see if the Americans let the Free French troops enter Paris first."

A few days later, Grouse brought the news that Sainteny and de Billy had been stopped by German patrols and were being held hostage in an abandoned house until the retreating army could figure out what to do with them.

"What now?" Marie-Madeleine asked Grouse. "The Allies need to know that the bridges into Paris are both intact and free of mines so they can enter the city as soon as possible. And then there's this..." she passed him the latest request from London.

Grouse quickly scanned it. "They want agents to scout out the Alsace region. Who do you plan on sending?"

"Myself." Now that the goal the local Alliance members had worked toward for many years—the liberation of Paris—was imminent, Marie-Madeleine couldn't in good conscience burden them with more tasks, especially given the dangers that were waiting just outside the city. Not to mention the sooner the Allies got to Germany, the earlier she would hear news of all of the captured agents... including Léon. "Petrel has left for Nancy to set up a headquarters. Once I've gotten to Strasbourg, I'll establish contact with both him and London."

"I'm going with you," Grouse declared. "The war isn't over until we get to Berlin."

She was hoping he'd volunteer. She hadn't known Grouse very long, but she had picked up on his dogged, fearless manner almost instantly. "How do you propose we get across the lines?"

He thought for a moment before his blue eyes grew even brighter. "I'm a doctor—I can get us an ambulance."

CHAPTER 68

SEPTEMBER 1944

Once again, Marie-Madeleine found herself in need of a new identity. This time she had to travel to a sympathetic policeman in the suburbs. To get to his station, she had to hire a bicycle-taxi, at the astronomical price of four thousand francs, and do all the uphill pedaling on her own. The outcome of achieving a credible identity card—in the name of Jeanne Imbert—made it well worth the effort.

In accordance with Grouse's plan, Jeanne Imbert's occupation was a nurse. The ambulance he'd procured had a giant red cross painted on the side, practically guaranteeing they would pass through the German roadblocks with ease.

Before she got in the ambulance, however, Marie-Madeleine was struck with another one of her headaches. She paused with one foot still on the ground, eyeing the large cases Grouse had placed in the back. "There isn't anything compromising in here, is there?" They intended to identify themselves as collaborators if anyone questioned them, and any intelligence or radio equipment they carried would give them away.

"Of course not. Those cases contain medicine and bandages."

. . .

Indeed, they were stopped multiple times, and as planned, Grouse informed the Germans that they were following the retreating army to provide aid to any wounded soldiers.

This was usually met with approval, and they were waved on without the need to inspect the inside of the truck.

They arrived at a safehouse in Verdun at dusk, but to Marie-Madeleine's consternation, there were no wireless operators in the vicinity.

"Are there any radios here?" she asked one of the agents.

He shrugged in return.

"We have radios," Grouse offered.

Marie-Madeleine turned to him, her mouth dropping open. "What do you mean, 'we have radios?'"

"In the cases in the ambulance. I put the crystals and codes in the medicine chest."

"Grouse, you promised me there was nothing compromising in the ambulance."

"A bird in the hand is worth two in the bush," he replied cryptically.

And she had been so at ease during all the German roadblocks! She sighed. "But it doesn't matter about the radios if we don't have a wireless operator."

"Well," the agent scratched his head. "We do have an American here. He was rescued after parachuting from a damaged Flying Fortress. I think he was their operator."

That was the last straw—clearly these men had been so caught up in the excitement of liberation that they had become reckless with their own security. "A downed American parachutist?" Marie-Madeleine repeated. "The entire Feldgendarmerie will be searching for him."

"He might be our only chance to communicate with London tonight," Grouse told her.

She thought briefly of Léon. He would surely go forward if he were here. "Please take us to the American."

The agent led Marie-Madeleine and Grouse to the garden, where a young man was lying on a chaise lounge, twiddling his thumbs.

"Welcome, first liberator," Grouse called in English.

The American sat up. "At last, someone who speaks American! When can I leave here?"

Marie-Madeleine's eyes traveled from his disheveled clothing to the floppy hair hanging over his eyes. She also spoke his language. "These heroic men saved your life. I presume you don't want to get them shot by demanding they take you to your countrymen."

"So I have to finish out the war here?"

"We might be able to take you back if you help us," Grouse offered.

The young man took a step backward. "I can't participate in the underground: the Germans would shoot me like a rebel. I'm a soldier—if I'm caught, I'm entitled to protection as a prisoner-of-war."

Marie-Madeleine fervently hoped all Americans were not like this insolent young man. "Are you saying we're not soldiers?"

"Such is war."

"Fine." She rolled her eyes. "Then stay here and rot."

His voice took on a whiny tone. "What is it you want me to do?"

"You're a radio operator. He'll get you set up with a radio." She nodded at Grouse. "We need you to make contact with London."

Over the next few days, they tried several times, but London was not answering their calls. Information was pouring in from couriers arriving from all around the region, but it piled up once again, to Marie-Madeleine's intense frustration. At this point, the Nazis had only minimal defenses surrounding Verdun, and the Allies could recapture it quite easily if only they were made aware.

Finally they heard that General Patton's army was approaching and Marie-Madeleine convinced one of the agents at the safehouse to bring him the intelligence they'd gathered.

The next day, Petrel and the Nancy wireless operator, Starling, came to Verdun, riding a tandem bicycle.

"Why did you come all the way here?" Marie-Madeleine asked them as they dismounted. "With everything going on around here, it's dangerous to move about."

"London's worried about you." Petrel leaned the bicycle against a tree. "They asked me to find you personally."

"I'm fine. They're the ones who haven't been listening."

Starling scratched his head. "I've been getting through without any problems."

"Maybe you can teach our American operator a thing or two." Marie-Madeleine told Starling where the radio was, and then she and Petrel walked down to the edge of the garden.

"The Allies finally landed in the south and are now advancing in both directions," Petrel informed her.

"It's what we've worked so hard for."

"But we're not done yet. I've a mind to cross the Rhine myself, before the Wehrmacht."

Her eyes widened. "Why, Petrel?"

"It's my duty…" he gave a heavy sigh as he sat down on the grass. "I feel as though it was my fault that Amniarix was caught. If it wasn't for her, the Nazis' secret weapons could have wreaked even more havoc upon London. And now she's rotting away in some German prison… or worse." He shuddered. "I have to see if there's anything I can do."

Marie-Madeleine had been contemplating something similar, but she knew it would be impossible to get into Germany and try to rescue anyone at this point. "I'm afraid we'll have to wait another winter."

"I can't." Petrel tore out a clump of grass. "If we want to have any chance of finding our friends alive, we have to get there now."

The fear that it would be too late to save Léon had been keeping her up at night. "The Nazis must not be allowed time to turn round again, otherwise it will be a bloodbath. You know what they're like—they don't compromise… or show mercy."

"I know. And that's why I need to push on."

"But you can't do it on your own. And neither can I. The only thing we can do is keep on with what we've always done: providing intelligence for the Allies. I'll wait here for Patton's army and you'll go back to Nancy for the arrival of General Patch. We'll get them to drive the Boches out."

"You're right." Petrel stood up. "You can count on me, Marie-Madeleine." He whistled to Starling, who'd fallen asleep on a garden bench. "We've got twelve miles back, but it should go quickly with two pairs of legs."

"I'll make sure London sends up plenty of supplies. It'll go easier now, I promise." She herself didn't believe the words, but they sounded good.

"I'll see you soon," Petrel called as they started pedaling off.

Marie-Madeleine was still roaming the garden, deep in thought, when Grouse found her. "The Germans are doubling back."

"Merde alors." It was just as she and Petrel had feared.

"My guess is that they're merely trying to regroup and count numbers before crossing the Rhine."

"But we can't stay here with our transmitters. And let's not forget the American."

"I agree. There's a maquis hideout in the Hesse forest. We should go there."

"Right."

They decided to spend the night in an abandoned barn, the ambulance parked outside the entrance. Marie-Madeleine spent a restless night tousling in the hay and worrying about Léon while Grouse slept soundly, even through the American's snoring.

A gunshot accompanied the first light of day. Grouse peered out the tiny window in the loft of the barn. "German soldiers. They must be taking the town."

As soon as the words left his mouth, there was a loud pounding on the door to the barn.

"Stay where you are," she hissed. "Maybe they'll go away if they see I'm only a woman on my own."

"If not," Grouse reached for his revolver. "I'll be ready."

She was just about to unlock the door when it banged open. Three large brutes in the black uniforms of the SS were standing there. "Car, garage, petrol."

"*Nein,*" Marie-Madeleine replied. She stepped past them to point to the ambulance. "Red Cross. I nurse. You sick?"

The man closest to her grimaced. "Sick? No. *Kaput.*"

Another one pointed to the ambulance. "Petroleum?"

"*Nein,*" she repeated. "Only castor oil." To her relief, the SS men walked off, shaking their heads with laughter.

"Well, I guess that means we can't use the ambulance," Grouse said with a sigh. He'd planned on bringing the transmission set with him while Marie-Madeleine and the American went with a local Resistance member, Musk Deer, in his hay cart. "I'll walk."

"With the radio case?"

"You'll have your hands full enough with the Yank. I'll figure it out."

Musk Deer arrived with the cart and some disguises. He gave Marie-Madeleine a peasant kerchief and shawl and then handed the American, who had slept through the Germans' visit, a hay rake before telling him to sit in the back of the cart.

Marie-Madeleine sat up front with Musk Deer. The roads were crammed again, reminding her of when she had fled Paris in 1940. It was as if they had come full circle, only this time the people clogging the roads were not civilians but German troops.

As Musk Deer stopped at a crossroads, she glanced back at the American, who sat with his legs swinging over the side of the cart, the rake pressed hard to his chest. Something glinted in the sunlight. She flinched, thinking it was a gun. She wasn't very relieved when she realized the glint was from the American's identity tags, which he had clearly neglected to remove. *If anyone sees those tags, we're done for.*

Musk Deer raised his hat to the German in charge of directing traffic, another SS in a black uniform. "We need to cross this here road."

"*Raus,* no time," the SS man replied.

"I peasant," Musk Deer insisted. "Have to deliver hay."

The SS man cursed before putting a whistle to his mouth. He blew it several times and then held up his hand. To Marie-Madeleine's surprise, the stream of infantry and convoys halted. She shut her eyes as she realized they'd have to cross in front of hundreds of troops, knowing they'd spot the American's gleaming tags straight away.

A horn blared and she glanced behind them to see Grouse's ambulance driving at breakneck speed. He leaned out the window to shout, "Doctor here, clear out. Emergency!"

The SS officer dove for the ditch as the ambulance raced past him.

"I guess that's our cue." Musk Deer shook the reins and they proceeded to follow the ambulance, the view of the Germans obscured by the clouds of dust the ambulance had stirred up.

The Hesse forest, where the maquis had taken refuge, was filled with dense, towering trees, a place where one could easily lose track of time and place. Remnants of the 1914 war could be seen here and there, and certain spots still reverberated with the echoes of battles fought long ago. An assortment of Sten guns, rifles, and shotguns were shoved into the bushes around the camp, their butts and stocks sticking up and forming a jumbled sort of armory.

Grouse had parked the ambulance in a copse of trees, camouflaging it the best he could with newly-trimmed branches. He'd already strung the aerial, and greeted the American before saying, "Let's make contact."

The American, obviously skeptical, tapped reluctantly on the Morse key.

Meanwhile, the men of the maquis scurried about, preparing dinner over a fire while their wine cooled in the nearby stream.

As darkness enveloped the forest, the noise from the adjacent road dwindled and soon Marie-Madeleine could hear the distinct sound of boots shuffling along the edge of the treeline. She reached for a gun just in case, but it was an Alliance courier.

"You aren't exactly easy to find," he panted as he headed toward Marie-Madeleine. "We've made contact with the Americans and handed off the messages. They've altered their course to avoid all of the roadblocks and pitfalls we pointed out."

"Excellent," Grouse stated.

"And they're requesting more intelligence on German positions before they advance through the Argonne forest."

"They're that close?" Marie-Madeleine asked.

"Yes. They could be here as soon as tomorrow. The Boches are still withdrawing, but beware: they are leaving the main roads to travel along the edge of the forest." Even in the darkness, she could see the courier sneer. "They're worried about being ambushed from behind."

The maquis crowded around the courier, asking questions about the American Army. Grouse and Marie-Madeleine coded more messages for a new courier, who then left the woods to move westward, intent on bringing the intel to Patton's army.

As the flames from the fire died down, the forest took on a life of its own. The trees that had stood tall and proud in the company of the maquis now seemed to loom over Marie-Madeleine with a menacing shadow and she jumped every time she heard a branch snap or caught a glimpse of movement. *Please don't let them get me now. Not with the end so close.*

Near dawn, a low rumbling began in the distance, gradually increasing until it sounded like thunder.

As the sun started to rise, Grouse whispered that he was going off to reconnoiter. He returned an hour later, his face ashen.

"What is it?" Marie-Madeleine asked, jumping up from the ground.

"We're liberated," he replied breathlessly. "Patton's at Verdun." He wrapped her in an embrace and then, as he let go, asked, "Why are you crying?"

"I don't know," she sobbed. "I think because the war is over."

"Yes. It's victory for the Allies. Finally."

She'd pictured Léon saying those words so many times, but now they fell on deaf ears. "What good is victory when those who worked so hard for it don't get to celebrate?"

Grouse took her hand. "Well, maybe it's not victory quite yet. For you and me, Patton's advance is a small step in a longer journey. But we should at least take a moment to rejoice in it."

Grouse and Marie-Madeleine drove to nearby Récicourt. In only a few hours, the now-liberated citizens had strung up banners and flags along the road and had gathered in the town square. When they spotted the ambulance, they surrounded it, shouting and laughing. They offered the newcomers copious amounts of the wine they'd been hiding away, waiting for this very occasion. As Grouse had said, this was only a momentary triumph for Alliance, but for the townspeople, it was a momentous occasion, one they'd been eagerly anticipating for four long, tumultuous years.

Grouse accepted an overflowing chalice of wine and gulped it down. Noticing Marie-Madeleine's face, his expression turned somber once again. "We'll get to Berlin soon. We'll find them."

Grouse and Marie-Madeleine returned to the safehouse in Verdun the next morning where she was informed that her presence was requested at the town hall. At first she panicked, but then she had to remind herself that it wasn't the Gestapo summoning her this time—the Free French had taken over the town.

As she made her way into the room, she was met with a cacophony of shouting men, all bearing the emblem of the Free French on their arm bands. Expecting to be praised for all her hard work, she was instead forced into a seat by one of the men.

He stepped in front of her, his arms crossed, demanding, "Who are you?" His eyes narrowed even more as she blinked rapidly, the myriad of names she'd had for the last few years racing through her head.

"Oh, I see—you're not going to tell us your name. Well then, maybe you can explain what this is." He pulled a case out from under the table, which she recognized as the radio set the American had been using.

She jumped up. "That's mine. Where do you get that?"

He held up his hand and she reluctantly sat back down. "Aha, you admit that it's yours. And tell us, who does madame contact with this thing?"

"London, of course."

The other men exchanged glances before bursting into laughter.

"London?" her interrogator repeated incredulously. "As if anyone could get in touch with London." He stuck a fat finger in her face. "You're a filthy Nazi spy. It was you who got us bombed, and trust me when I say you'll pay the price for that."

The unsettling sound of a gun being cocked reached Marie-Madeleine's ears. She nearly jumped out of her seat again as someone pounded on the door to the room. The leader left momentarily, leaving her to face the scowls of his accomplices. One of them still had his finger on the trigger of his pistol.

These fools are going to shoot me. Her temper flared. "Don't you realize we are on the same side?"

The leader finally returned, followed by Grouse, who mopped his sweaty brow before reaching out to Marie-Madeleine. "Sorry about that. It was quite a job to convince them of your real identity…"

The leader whispered something to the rest of the men. The one brandishing the gun tucked it back into his belt and then extended his hand to her. "Madame Hedgehog, we thank you for your service."

As they left the room, Grouse asked, "Can we go back to Paris now?"

CHAPTER 69

SEPTEMBER 1944

Paris was finally free. As she walked down the Champs-Élysées, Marie-Madeleine could sense the hope that permeated from the people who were set on rebuilding their bombed-out, bullet-scarred homes. In the distance, the Eiffel Tower stood tall, proud, and unscathed.

It took some time for Marie-Madeleine to adjust to the new reality: to be able to use her real name after suppressing it for so many years and to quell the paranoia that seized her with every unexpected knock on the door. She couldn't help wondering how long it would take to completely heal the stinging wounds the Occupation had left.

Still, she relished in putting a giant sign reading 'Alliance Intelligence Service' on the door of the sumptuous Champs-Élysées flat they'd requisitioned. The animals of the Ark became people again as the apartment flooded with agents pouring in from all corners of the country.

Kenneth Cohen arrived from London to present Marie-Madeleine with the Order of the British Empire. At first she tried to refuse it, as the war was not over and therefore her work was still unfinished. But Cohen wouldn't accept her refusal and she found herself at a posh restaurant, surrounded by members of the British Embassy in all their glorious finery: their garb an eclectic mix of the Royal Navy and Air Force's dark blue and the Army's khaki.

After Cohen had read a citation and pinned the cross on her dress, he inquired if there was anything else he could do for her.

"Indeed." She had anticipated his offer, and began reciting the list. "We'll have to supply our patrols in the east since it looks like they'll be traveling across the lines all winter long. We'll need a parachute drop for my agents in Verdun and also for Petrel in Luz, as the area is still occupied."

"I expected you to request your children be returned from Switzerland," Cohen replied.

His words felt like a stab in the chest. "Not yet. It's still not safe for them."

Cohen scratched at the stubble of beard that was beginning to form on his chin. "Sure, we can arrange for the parachutes. Besides, I've always wanted to see what a supply drop looked like from the ground."

"Great. Then I'll meet you in Verdun."

When Marie-Madeleine returned to Verdun, this time staying in an inn instead of the forest, couriers coming in from the east told her that the Germans were still in the area.

As soon as Kenneth Cohen arrived in Verdun for the parachute drop, Marie-Madeleine wasted no time in expressing her mounting concern about the Germans' presence in Luxembourg. "Why aren't the Allies pushing them further east?"

He grimaced. "If you must know, they are short on fuel."

"Fuel?" she repeated, struggling to comprehend. "After all this time and effort, they can't continue on?"

"The Allied supply chains are stretched thin and struggling to keep pace with their rapid advance."

"But what if the Germans regroup and return?"

"They won't," he said resolutely. "They're too scared."

She hoped he was right.

. . .

The parachute drop occurred in the afternoon, the sky filling with a kaleidoscope of colors as the planes released their cargo. Marie-Madeleine spent the remainder of the day distributing the loot: radios, boots, Sten guns, grenades, and other various provisions that promised to sustain the Resistance through what might prove to be a long winter.

As she worked, she couldn't stop picturing Petrel's excitement when he received similar spoils, although, since the Germans were still lurking in his region, his drop was to take place under the cover of night.

However, the next morning she received a transmission from London reporting that the planes circling above Petrel's drop zone could not release any parachutes because the entire village seemed to be on fire. The message ended by stating that Petrel's transmitter had gone silent.

A few days later, a courier arrived with the grim news that Petrel had been seen being taken into the woods by armed men, and that the unmistakable sound of gunshots had followed shortly after.

By now of course, Marie-Madeleine was no stranger to hearing of her friends' deaths, but this one, so close to the end, was a particularly hard blow. Petrel had been the first to raise the alarm regarding Hitler's secret weapons program, and he'd been instrumental at keeping Alliance alive while she was in London. And now he was gone.

A sense of hopelessness overcame her as she thought about Léon and the others who had been captured. If she could be absolutely certain of anything about the Nazis, it was their insatiable thirst for vengeance. As the Allies advanced, as slow as their progress may seem, would the Germans release their anger on her comrades on the other side of the Rhine? Would Léon ever make it home to see his son?

CHAPTER 70

APRIL 1945

Unfortunately, Marie-Madeleine had been correct in her prediction: while the Allies hesitated, the Germans saw their chance to defend the Moselle region. The members of Alliance, particularly Grand Duke, Grouse, and Sainteny, who'd escaped from the clutches of the retreating Nazis, continued to provide intelligence on the enemy's positions throughout the winter of 1945.

In the spring, Marie-Madeleine's main focus became tracking down the Alliance agents who had been captured. In the final stretches of the war, news regarding some of them who had been presumed lost in the depths of Hitler's prisons and concentration camps began to surface. Some of the lucky ones who'd been liberated returned to Paris, including Rivière's former adjutant, Mouse, and Hummingbird. They, along with Amniarix, Petrel's magnanimous source concerning Hitler's secret weapons, had been held at a women's concentration camp called Ravensbrück. All three women's heads were shaved, their figures skeletal. Bishop was not in much better shape after spending the last 22 months in prison, though traces of his previous wit surfaced every now and then.

Food in Paris was still scarce, but Cohen was able to provide them with supplies that he flew in from London. Marie-Madeleine traveled the same streets she'd once used to collect information to distribute the provisions to her former agents.

One morning when Cohen was dropping off some canned goods at the apartment, he paused and then placed his hand on Marie-Madeleine's shoulder. "Magpie's been found."

"Magpie?" she repeated, her heart filling with renewed hope. "Is Léon with—"

"No," Cohen said quickly. "Just Magpie, for now. But Poz, we have to warn you: he was in need of serious medical attention."

Indeed, the sight of the emaciated, frail Magpie left Marie-Madeleine reeling in shock. His eyes, which had once sparkled with life, now appeared dim and glazed over and his wrists were covered in yellowing bruises, scars of the manacles he had been forced to wear for fifteen grueling months.

To replenish his body, he'd been ordered to drink a concoction of chocolate, glucose, and eggs and spent the first few days in the Champs-Élysées apartment sleeping. Marie-Madeleine knew he'd been without any other human interaction for months on end and she wanted to give him suitable time to recover.

Eventually, however, he seemed willing to talk and she sat him down on the couch to ask what had happened after he and Léon landed back in France.

"They got us on the train to Paris," Magpie replied dully. "Lanky and Bumpkin instructed us to ride in the same car so they could protect us easier." He shook his head. "I knew it was a bad idea…"

"Were Lanky and Bumpkin taken too?"

"Yes. They brought us to a building on the rue des Saussaies, where they interrogated us for hours. But not Léon. He told me later that he ended up at Avenue Foch." Magpie's lips turned up in a wry smile as he recalled the story of Léon's almost-escape with the girl named Nora. "She was SOE and they communicated by tapping Morse through the wall. If it hadn't been for those air raid sirens, Léon would have..." The smile disappeared. "They beat him first and then sent him to Bruchsal prison in Germany, placing him in solitary confinement with barely any food or water."

Marie-Madeleine's mind was a whir of thoughts. Magpie had seen Léon after their arrest. If he knew Léon was alive, surely he would say so? Was he waiting to break tragic news to her? Finally she could stand it no longer. "Where is Léon now?"

"I left him at Sonnenburg fortress. They put us in adjacent cells. The walls were stone, but they were old and had gaps, so we could talk to each other. We'd been at Schwäbisch Hall together and then they transferred us to Sonnenburg. Léon always said he knew I'd get out alive." Magpie closed his skeletal fingers over Marie-Madeleine's. "He told me he'd left a will and papers for you behind the radiator in his cell in Bruchsal."

"Bruchsal?" Her mind was whirring.

"We'd been condemned to death. It was my countrymen, the British, who arranged a prisoner exchange. When they informed me I was leaving, I wanted to tell Léon, but I was at a loss for words." Magpie sat up, a hint of his old spark returning. "Perhaps the French can do a similar prisoner exchange for Léon—it may not be too late to save him, if we act quickly."

Marie-Madeleine immediately called Kenneth Cohen, who explained that an exchange was in the works: the Germans had agreed to release Léon Faye for Angelo Chiappe, a captured Nazi who'd been given a death sentence by the French.

After she'd pressed Cohen, he promised he'd get back to her with more information. "It's the least I can do for you," Cohen told her. "And, of course, for Faye."

But a few minutes later, Cohen called back, his tone grim. "Chiappe's been executed."

She nearly dropped the receiver. "When? Why?"

"I don't know. It was de Gaulle who ordered it. The Free French strike again."

Marie-Madeleine hung up the phone and turned to Magpie, who obviously knew something was wrong. "There will be no exchange," she said simply.

"Is Léon... dead?"

"I don't know."

Magpie got up unsteadily, his voice laced with anger. "Well, one thing is for sure—I'm not going to just sit here while they kill off all of our friends."

CHAPTER 71

JUNE 1945

*H*itler died by his own hand in a final act of cowardice at the end of April. As soon as the armistice was signed in June, Marie-Madeleine, along with Magpie and Beaver, set off for Germany in search of the hundreds of Alliance agents who'd never returned, including Léon.

The trio was armed both with Allied safe conduct passes and pistols, but found them to be unnecessary. The roads were empty and the destroyed towns were mostly silent.

They had barely crossed the Rhine when they made their first shocking discovery at a prison in the Black Forest. A warden provided them with a register and Marie-Madeleine felt her stomach churn as she recognized dozens of names. Some had been transferred to Berlin, while others—such as Philippe Koenigswerther, otherwise known as Mandrill, and Zebra—simply had the cryptic label 'left' printed next to their name.

"What does this mean?" she tapped her finger on the word.

The warden shuffled his feet, pretending he didn't understand the question.

"It means they killed them," Beaver stated. His large hands grabbed the warden's chin, forcing the older man to look him in the eyes. "Right?"

"Executed," the warden stammered.

The words seemed to suck the air out of Marie-Madeleine's lungs. "Where are their bodies?" she managed to choke out.

He pointed out the window, where, in the distance, they could see the river.

"In the Rhine?" she clarified, her voice stronger this time.

"Yes."

Magpie thrust his hands in his pockets but said nothing while Beaver shouted obscenities at the warden, who backed away with his arms up, insisting, "I didn't do anything. It was Gehrum."

"Who is Gehrum?" Marie-Madeleine asked.

Magpie finally tore his gaze away from the window. "The Gestapo leader in Strasbourg."

"When the Allies crossed the Moselle, Gehrum decided to execute the people who'd been caught as spies." The warden hung his head before whispering, *"Nacht und Nebel."*

"What does that mean?" Marie-Madeleine demanded.

"Night and fog," Magpie replied. "Hitler's decree that anyone captured for taking actions against the Reich, including spies, should disappear without a trace, so their relatives will never be able to learn of their fate." He pointed at the register. "That's what 'left' means. Unlike Léon and I, none of them actually went through a trial and received a death sentence. They were murdered to guarantee they wouldn't be liberated when the Allies got here." Magpie's voice broke, and he let out a deep, heaving sob.

Marie-Madeleine's anger quickly dissolved into sorrow. Some of the dead were women, including Tomboy, Colonel Kauffman's secretary. Every last one of them had fought tirelessly to break France free from the chains of tyranny, but the price they paid was the ultimate one. And now their memory had been condemned to obscurity. The Nazis had only one way to communicate: through the barrel of a gun.

. . .

The story was the same in the other prisons in the Black Forest. At Pforzheim, they learned that Ant—the fearless man who'd been part of the landing committee when Marie-Madeleine had flown to London—had been among the victims. The register showed that he and a dozen other men had been given eighteen marks, seemingly to make them believe they were being freed, before being shot in the back of the neck and dumped into a watery hole in the middle of the forest.

All in all, Gehrum and his thugs had murdered almost seventy Alliance agents. As the network's only remaining leader, Marie-Madeleine couldn't help feeling responsible for their deaths. Whether directly or indirectly, it was because of her that they had gotten involved in the first place. They were what Kenneth Cohen had referred to as 'enthusiastic volunteers,' not trained MI6 operatives, and were therefore unprepared to confront the cunning and formidable alliance of the Gestapo and Abwehr, whose sole purpose was to eradicate them.

She resolved to do her best to stand against *Nacht und Nebel*—it was imperative that she provide the fallen agents' families with as much information as she could about their loved ones' last days, however tragic they were. Which included locating Léon, though Marie-Madeleine now had little hope of finding him alive.

Their next stop was Freiburg, where Léon and Magpie's trial had taken place. After a few false leads and half a day spent wandering the devastated town, Magpie was able to locate the lawyer who had been assigned to defend them.

Over weak tea in a coffee shop whose front door had been blown off by a bomb, the lawyer, Doktor Hermann explained what had happened.

"I have to say that in all my years of practicing law, I'd never seen anything as moving as these trials," Hermann told them. He nodded at Magpie. "We could see the depths of your patriotism, but you still managed to maintain your composure at all times. And I must pay homage to Commandant Faye as well. He insisted that he alone bore responsibility for the network, and that everyone else should be allowed to go free."

Marie-Madeleine closed her eyes, trying to hold back the myriad memories of Léon that threatened to overwhelm her. "What were the main charges?"

Hermann took a sip of tea as he thought. "The flight of General Giraud, to be sure. And your considerable radio network. Actually, it was really all the actions by what the tribunal had called 'Noah's Ark'." He set his coffee cup down. "Of course the court expressed regret over their inability to bring charges against the distinguished Hedgehog."

"Thank God for that," Beaver cut in.

"By law, the execution of officers could only be authorized by the Führer himself. Since Faye had claimed all his agents were officers, I insisted that Hitler had to give direct permission in order for their death sentences to be carried out." He shook his head. "But my request for a stay was always refused."

Hermann accompanied them into the hulking fortress of Freiburg-im-Breisgau. The messages and drawings on the walls of the prison cells were a somber reminder of the pain and sacrifice endured by her friends. Each signature was like a fresh stab to Marie-Madeleine's already severed heart: Jack Tar, Mahout, Colonel Kauffman. She gasped when she saw Rivière's sprawling autograph, next to the words, 'Long live Alliance.'

When they entered the cell where Magpie had been kept, the young man visibly paled and he dropped to his knees. "Where are the manacles? What about the chains for my feet?"

Their jailor escort stared at Magpie, his jaw agape. "You? You're not dead?"

"Not yet."

"That's enough from you, you bastard." Beaver clocked the jailer right in the face. The man fell onto the bed, and the rest of them exited the cell. Beaver bolted the door behind them, leaving the jailer alone in the room to grapple with the ghosts of the men who had fallen under his custody.

. . .

Magpie seemed to recover a bit of his composure as he bent over the register in the warden's office. "They all went to several different prisons: Schwäbisch-Hall, Ludwigsburg, Bruschal—that's where Léon went after Avenue Foch. Some went to concentration camps. For three, there's no destination."

Marie-Madeleine's voice wobbled as she asked, "Who were they?"

His eyes clouded over. "Colonel Kauffman and two of his agents."

Beaver gripped the warden's shirt. "Where are they? Where is *Oberst* Kauffman? Where is *Hauptmann* Pradelle?"

Tremors shook the warden's body.

"Tell them," Doktor Hermann said gently. "They won't hurt you."

"They are here," the warden said when Beaver released his grip.

Marie-Madeleine glanced around her, as if her comrades were hiding in the room. "Where?"

The warden lifted a shaking finger and pointed out the window, past the drawbridge and moat. "In that bomb crater."

"Let me guess," Beaver folded his arms across his chest. "Gehrum came to deliver a bullet in the back of the head to each of them."

"Yes," the warden whispered.

Two dozen of the men from Freiburg had been transferred to a military camp at Heilbronn. They too had been shot, but they had been given an actual burial in an apple orchard. Marie-Madeleine requested that the bodies be exhumed for identification purposes.

Though it had been over a year since their execution, many of them were still recognizable. Tears ran down her face as she walked past Rivière, Ernest Siegrist, Mahout, and, the most pitiful sight of all, the freckle-faced Jack Tar shrouded in the dressing gown she'd bought for him in London. They all had a piece of crimson cloth sewn onto their clothes: a target, to show the Nazis where their heart was. Only one of them had accepted the offer to wear a bandage over their eyes before they were shot. All of these people, her friends, their lives extinguished in an instant, leaving only the bitter taste of injustice in their wake.

She put her head on Beaver's chest as she sobbed. After what seemed like an eternity, she told him, "We must return their bodies to the families so they can be buried in French soil."

She felt him take a deep breath. "I will claim the honor, Marie-Madeleine. I will bring them all back to France. But first we have to find Léon."

To Marie-Madeleine, Bruschal was the worst of all the fortresses. The warden there, a squat, hunched-over man with beady black eyes, led her, Beaver, and Magpie to the underground dungeon Léon had been held in.

Magpie headed straight for the radiator and peered behind it. "Where are the messages?"

The warden shrugged. "Someone from London told me to send them to Paris." He focused his black eyes on Marie-Madeleine. "I believe they were addressed to you."

She nodded before bending down to touch the chains at the foot of the bed.

"He was a terrorist," the warden stated. "And an escape artist. We had to chain him, you see. And they instructed me to give him half rations."

Once again, Beaver had a hard time controlling his anger and lunged toward the warden, knocking him to the ground. "You chained him like some animal and left him to starve!"

Marie-Madeleine stepped between the two of them. "Let him be, Beaver. He's just another former Nazi without any sense of responsibility."

The man struggled to his feet, weeping incessantly and repeating the words, "Forgive me, *Oberst* Faye. Forgive me, *Oberst* Faye."

Magpie, who had been kneeling next to the bed, his head bowed, stood up. "We have to get to Sonnenburg."

"Sonnenburg?" The warden's ears perked.

"Yes. I was transferred there. It's the last place Léon, *Oberst* Faye, was known to be."

"Sonnenburg is in the Russian zone," the warden said softly. "You won't be able to go there, but there's a man in town who left Sonnenburg in February with a column of prisoners."

The man was immediately fetched and told his story to the three Alliance members in the warden's stuffy office. According to him, at the end of January, the SS had received orders to execute all the prisoners before the imminent arrival of the Red Army. "But I and a few of my comrades managed to save around 500 prisoners, mostly Germans."

"And the others?" Marie-Madeleine asked, fearing the answer.

The man averted his gaze. "Massacred."

"How many?" Beaver asked.

"About 800… they were ordered to line up, then were shot and the bodies were burned with flame-throwers."

"Stop." Magpie put his hands over his ears. "I don't want to hear anymore."

The gruesome details of Léon's death had left them all in a state of shock and disbelief. Marie-Madeleine was finding it difficult to breathe, and the walls of the warden's office felt like they were closing in. *Be brave,* she told herself. She wouldn't collapse here, not after everything she'd been through. She could get through this, for Léon's sake.

After a few moments, Beaver offered, "I don't believe it. Not Léon. Maybe he was with the column of prisoners."

"Or perhaps he escaped to Russia," Magpie said.

"No." Marie-Madeleine took a deep breath as the air returned to her lungs. The same intuition that had helped her navigate the war was telling her that Léon's remarkable spirit had passed from this earth. And if the Nazis had indeed burned the prisoner's corpses, there would be no way to identify Léon's body and therefore they couldn't bring him back to France. Forever a military man, he would maintain his airman's gaze on the vast and distant horizon of the eastern front. "Léon's gone. And it's time we go back home."

CHAPTER 72

JUNE 1945

When Marie-Madeleine entered her apartment on the Champs-Élysées, all she wanted to do was lie in bed and grieve. Instead, she found two gaunt, balding men seated at the kitchen table, waiting for her. Navarre, after four and a half years languishing in various prisons and concentration camps, had at last returned. And with him was Swift, who had been at Kehl prison in the Black Forest. For some reason, the Nazis had spared him the fate of the other Alliance agents who'd been held there.

She poured both of them a glass of brandy. Like most concentration camp survivors, Swift found it an effort to talk, and even Navarre was noticeably quiet. A few sips of brandy, however, helped her former boss warm up. She told them an abbreviated version of what had happened after they were arrested and the fates of their Alliance friends. Her voice broke when she mentioned Léon, but she felt she owed it to him to disclose what she knew.

Afterward, both men were silent. After several minutes, Marie-Madeleine decided to change the subject. "What are your future plans now that the war is officially over?"

Navarre answered first, his sunken face turning up into a wry smile. "Well, I think the next logical step would be for me to go into politics."

Swift acknowledged this with a nod. He stared off into space for a moment before answering, "Every night in prison, I wished I could fly away, like a true bird." He waved his gnarled, heavily veined hand in the air to demonstrate. "So I shall create an air navigation company."

"And you, Marie-Madeleine?" Navarre asked.

She thought of the last few months, which had been some of the most challenging she'd ever faced, even despite all the hardships the war had thrown her way. "I need to make sure the families of those we lost are provided for."

They fell into silence again, three of the main leaders of Alliance, united for the first time since the early days of the war. But where was the fourth? Gone, in a horrid twist of fate.

As if sensing her thoughts, Navarre slid a thick envelope in front of her. "I almost forgot—this came for you."

It was postmarked from Bruchsal. She hesitated, tracing her fingers over her name on the address, knowing the words inside would be the final contact she'd have with Léon. If she put off reading it, could she pretend he was still alive?

But she would only be postponing the inevitable. Her grief was not isolated—the Nazis' bullets had claimed the lives of nearly 500 members of Alliance, some of whose fates would never be known. She was fortunate enough to know a little about Léon's last hours. And now she had the chance to read his last words to her.

With shaking hands, she opened the envelope. He'd written on a scrap of paper, his handwriting skewed by his manacled wrist.

Minerva,

I ask you to serve our unhappy country so that it may enjoy peace again and happiness, song, flowers, and flower-covered inns... like many other countries, France will have to tend, cleanse, and heal cruel wounds and rebuild vast numbers of ruined places. But she is the only one whose moral unity was broken, pulled and torn in all directions. Everything must be done to get out of this impasse. Act to this end, my dear Minerva, that is my last wish... that and for you to always go forward knowing that I loved you to the depths of my soul.

Love Always,
Léon

Wiping tears from her eyes, Marie-Madeleine folded the paper and put it back in the envelope.

It was Swift who broke the silence this time. "Léon met his end after enduring unspeakable torture, as did many of our friends, but I know he would never regret a moment of what he did for the Resistance. Meanwhile, we are the ones who will have to grapple with the harsh realities of post-war life."

"You're right," Navarre confirmed. "A watchdog never sleeps."

She sensed that these once vigorous men—now so pale and haggard—were restless to start on the plans they had formulated during their time in captivity. They, like their fallen comrades, had given everything they could to the Resistance, but now it was time to move on. "Go. Take up your men's responsibilities," Marie-Madeleine told them. "I, who have had the extraordinary luck to have come through the war relatively unscathed—"

Navarre grinned, the light returning to his blue eyes. "You will carry on."

CHAPTER 73

JUNE 1945

The first thing Marie-Madeleine did after Navarre and Swift left was to contact Kenneth Cohen and ask him to accompany Beatrice and Christian back to France.

The next morning, Monique Bontinck arrived at the apartment, a small child in tow.

"Could this really be..." Marie-Madeleine found herself unable to contain her tears as she picked up the child.

"It's Jacques," Monique said with a smile. "Hasn't he gotten so big?"

He nestled into Marie-Madeleine's arms and grabbed a piece of her hair. When he chirped, "Mama," she felt as though she might keel over.

"Good boy!" Monique patted Jacques's shoulder before she turned to Marie-Madeleine. "I've been trying to teach him using your picture." She pulled an identification card out of her purse. "Who's this?" she asked Jacques in a lilting tone.

"Dada."

"That's right!"

Now Marie-Madeleine's knees were genuinely weak and she set Jacques down. The card was an old one of Léon's. "Where did you get that?"

"I found it in the safehouse in Lyons before I left." Monique frowned. "Is something wrong?"

"Léon's dead."

"Oh, Marie-Madeleine," Monique's voice was choked with sorrow. "I'm so sorry."

The two women embraced, both of them weeping. After a few minutes they broke to watch Jacques as he played with a ball. "He looks just like his father, doesn't he?" Marie-Madeleine asked, wiping the tears from her eyes.

"Yes," Monique replied softly.

Someone knocked on the door and Marie-Madeleine answered it to find Magpie standing there. "Lanky's been arrested," he announced as he strolled into the apartment, pausing next to Monique.

"Finally." A couple of days after they'd returned from their quest, Magpie had come upon the traitor walking the streets of Paris in a Free French uniform. As the only survivor of the disastrous Operation Ingres, Magpie had made it his new mission to ensure Lanky paid the price for what had happened to his friends. "I don't know how I'll ever thank you," Marie-Madeleine told him.

"Actually," his gaze had been focused on Monique, but now he gave Marie-Madeleine a salute. "There is something you could do, chief. I would like to ask you for the honor of Monique's hand in marriage."

Marie-Madeleine gasped in surprise. "I had no idea…"

Monique took Magpie's hand. "I didn't either, not really, but when I saw him again, after all this time, I just knew."

Marie-Madeleine hugged Monique once again and then Magpie. "I know you two will be so happy together."

"We will," Monique affirmed. She picked up Jacques and covered his face with kisses. "And someday we'll have babies as wonderful as this one." Sobbing, she touched his nose one final time before handing him to Marie-Madeleine.

The little boy looked back and forth between the two women.

"You be good for your mama," Monique said, her voice choked with tears.

Jacques threw his arms around Marie-Madeleine's neck, squeezing tight. She breathed in the scent of his hair before saying her final goodbyes to the couple. As she watched them walk out the door, she hoped Monique was right and that they would have many babies and find the eternal bliss she and Léon had been denied.

Hope. With a start, Marie-Madeleine realized she hadn't allowed herself to hope for anything in a long while.

But now it is time to hope again. Hope lay in the future, in Magpie and Monique's happiness, in the innocence of children like Christian and Beatrice. And, of course, Jacques, a little boy who might never know how brave his father was or understand the sacrifices he made so that all children like Jacques could grow up free.

Hugging her little boy tightly, Marie-Madeleine promised to carry out his father's final wish: to help heal France's deep wounds. "But my first priority is to be a good mother."

With that, she set him on the ground and took his tiny hand in hers. "C'mon, Jacques. Let's go find your brother and sister."

EPILOGUE

Marie-Madeleine and Édouard Méric were divorced in 1946. Soon after, she married Hubert Fourcade, the man she had met in Avignon in September 1942, and whom she'd had a feeling she'd meet again. They had another child, a girl named Penélopé, in 1949.

Despite Marie-Madeleine's resolve to have Alliance stay politically neutral, her new husband had always been an advocate of Navarre's old nemesis, Charles de Gaulle, and the couple were integral in helping de Gaulle return to power in France in 1958. Marie-Madeleine's involvement in politics also included a stint in the European Parliament.

Throughout her life, Marie-Madeleine also worked tirelessly to ensure that the former members of Alliance and the families of those who had lost their lives received financial support. She remained lifelong friends with many of the network's survivors, including Kenneth Cohen and Helen des Isnards (Grand Duke) and their wives and was the godmother of the oldest of Magpie (Ferdinand Rodriguez) and Monique Bontinck's three children.

When Marie-Madeleine passed away in July 1989 at the age of 79, she became the first woman to be honored with a funeral at Les

Invalides, where Napoleon and other notable figures in French history were laid to rest.

For more information on the fates of the characters in this book, be sure to visit https://www.kitsergeant.com/?page_id=951

A note to the reader: Thanks so much for reading this book! If you have time to spare, please consider leaving a short review on Amazon. Reviews are very important to authors such as myself and I would greatly appreciate it!

Be sure to check out my other books, including *The Women Spies of WWII Series*, starting with *The Spark of Resistance* and/or join my mailing list at www.kitsergeant.com to be the first to know when my newest Women Spies book is available!

Read on for a sample of *L'Agent Double: Spies and Martyrs in the Great War!*

L'AGENT DOUBLE PROLOGUE

OCTOBER 1917

The nun on duty woke her just before dawn. She blinked the sleep out of her eyes to see a crowd of men, including her accusers and her lawyer, standing just outside the iron bars of her cell. The only one who spoke was the chief of the Military Police, to inform her the time of her execution had come. The men then turned and walked away, leaving only the nun and the prison doctor, who kept his eyes on the dirty, straw-strewn floor as she dressed.

She chose the best outfit she had left, a bulky dove-gray skirt and jacket and scuffed ankle boots. She wound her unwashed hair in a bun and then tied the worn silk ribbons of her hat under her chin before asking the doctor, "Do I have time to write good-byes to my loved ones?"

He nodded and she hastily penned three farewell letters. She handed them to the doctor with shaking hands before lifting a dust-covered velvet cloak from a nail on the wall. "I am ready."

Seemingly out of nowhere, her lawyer reappeared. "This way," he told her as he grasped her arm.

Prison rats scurried out their way as he led her down the hall. She breathed in a heavy breath when they were outside. It had been months since she'd seen the light of day, however faint it was now.

Four black cars were waiting in the prison courtyard. A few men scattered about the lawn lifted their freezing hands to bring their cameras to life, the bulbs brightening the dim morning as her lawyer bundled her into the first car.

They drove in silence. It was unseasonably cold and the chill sent icy fingers down her spine. She stopped herself from shivering, wishing that she could experience one more warm summer day. But there would be no more warmth, no more appeals, nothing left after these last few hours.

She knew that her fate awaited her at Caponniére, the old fort just outside of Vincennes where the cavalry trained. Upon arrival, her lawyer helped her out of the car, his gnarled hands digging into her arm.

It's harder for him than it is for me. She brushed the thought away, wanting to focus on nothing but the fresh air and the way the autumn leaves of the trees next to the parade ground changed color as the sun rose. Her lawyer removed his arm from her shoulders as two Zouave escorts appeared on either side of her. Her self-imposed blinders finally dropped as she took in the twelve soldiers with guns and, several meters away, the wooden stake placed in front of a brick wall. *So that the mis-aimed bullets don't hit anything else.*

A priest approached and offered her a blindfold.

"No thank you." Her voice, which had not been used on a daily basis for months, was barely a whisper.

The priest glanced over at her lawyer, who nodded. The blindfold disappeared under his robes.

She spoke the same words to one of the escorts as he held up a rope, this time also shaking her head. She refused to be bound to the stake. He acquiesced, and walked away.

She stood as straight as she could, free of any ties, while the military chief read the following words aloud:

By decree of the Third Council of War, the woman who appears before us now has been condemned to death for espionage.

He then gave an order, and the soldiers came to attention. At the command, *"En joue!"* they hoisted their guns to rest on their shoulders. The chief raised his sword.

She took a deep breath and then lifted her chin, willing herself to die just like that: head held high, showing no fear. She watched as the chief lowered his sword and shouted *"Feu!"*

And then everything went black.

* * *

A Zouave private approached the body. He'd only been enlisted for a few weeks and had been invited to the firing squad by his commander, who told him that men of all ranks should know the pleasure of shooting a German spy.

"By blue, that lady knew how to die," another Zouave commented.

"Who was she?" the private asked. He'd been taught that everything in war was black and white: the Germans were evil, the Allies pure. But he was surprised at how gray everything was that morning: from the misty fog, to the woman's cloak and dress, and even the ashen shade of her lifeless face.

The other Zouave shrugged. "All I know is what they told me. They say she acted as a double agent and provided Germany with intelligence about our troops." He drew his revolver and bent down to place the muzzle against the woman's left temple.

"But is it necessary to kill her—a helpless woman?" the private asked.

The Zouave cocked his gun for the *coup de grâce*. "If women act as men would in war and commit heinous crimes, they should be prepared to be punished as men." And he pulled the trigger, sending a final bullet into the woman's brain

L'AGENT DOUBLE CHAPTER 1

M'GREET

JULY 1914

"Have you heard the latest?" M'greet's maid, Anna, asked as she secured a custom-made headpiece to her mistress's temple.

"What now?" M'greet readjusted the gold headdress to better reflect her olive skin tone.

"They are saying that your mysterious Mr. K from the newspaper article is none other than the Crown Prince himself."

M'greet smiled at herself in the mirror. "Is that so? I rather think they're referring to Lieutenant Kiepert. Just the other day he and I ran into the editor of the *Berliner Tageblatt* during our walk in the Tiergarten." Her smile faded. "But let them wonder." For the last few weeks, the papers had been filled with speculation about why the famed Mata Hari had returned to Germany, sometimes bordering on derision about her running out of money.

She leaned forward and ran her fingers over the dark circles under her eyes. "Astruc says that he might be able to negotiate a longer engagement in the fall if tonight's performance goes well."

"It will," Anna assured her as she fastened the heavy gold necklace around M'greet's neck.

The metal felt cold against her sweaty skin. She hadn't performed in months, and guessed the perspiration derived from her nervousness. Tonight was to be the largest performance she'd booked in years: Berlin's Metropol could seat 1108 people, and the tickets had sold out days ago. The building was less than a decade old, and even the dressing room's geometric wallpaper and curved furniture reflected the Art Nouveau style the theater was famous for.

"I had to have this costume refitted." M'greet pulled at the sheer yellow fabric covering her midsection. When she first began dancing, she had worn jeweled bralettes and long, sheer skirts that sat low on the hips. But her body had become much more matronly in middle age and even M'greet knew that she could no longer get away with the scandalous outfits of her youth. She added a cumbersome earring to each ear and an arm band before someone knocked on the door.

A man's voice called urgently in German, "Fräulein Mata Hari, are you ready?"

Anna shot her mistress an encouraging smile. "Your devoted admirers are waiting."

M'greet stretched out her arms and rotated her wrists, glancing with appreciation in the mirror. She still had it. She grabbed a handful of translucent scarves and draped them over her arms and head before opening the door. "All set," she said to the awaiting attendant.

M'greet waited behind a filmy curtain while the music began: low, mournful drumming accompanied by a woman's shrill tone singing in a foreign language. As the curtain rose, she hoisted her arms above her head and stuck her hips out in the manner she had seen the women do when she lived in Java.

She had no formal dance training, but it didn't matter. People came to see Mata Hari for the spectacle, not because she was an exceptionally wonderful dancer. M'greet pulled the scarf off her head and undulated her hips in time with the music. She pinched her fingers together and moved her arms as if she were a graceful bird about to take flight.

KIT SERGEANT

The drums heightened in intensity and her gyrations became even more exaggerated. As the music came to a dramatic stop, she released the scarves covering her body to reveal her yellow dress in full.

She was accustomed to hearing astonished murmurs from the audience following her final act—she'd once proclaimed that her success rose with every veil she threw off. Tonight, however, the Berlin audience seemed to be buzzing with protest.

As the curtain fell and M'greet began to pick up the pieces of her discarded costume, she assured herself that the Berliners' vocalizations were in response to being disappointed at seeing her more covered. Or maybe she was just being paranoid and had imagined all the ruckus.

"Fabulous!" her agent, Gabriel Astruc, exclaimed when he burst into her dressing room a few minutes later.

M'greet held a powder puff to her cheek. "Did you finalize a contract for the fall?"

"I did," Astruc sat in the only other chair, which appeared too tiny to support his large frame. "They are giving us 48,000 marks."

She nodded approvingly.

"That should tide you over for a while, no?" he asked.

She placed the puff in the gold-lined powder case. "For now. But the creditors are relentless. Thankfully Lieutenant Kieper has gifted me a few hundred francs."

"As a loan?" Astruc winked. "It is said you have become mistress to the *Kronprinz*."

She rolled her eyes. "You of all people must know to never mind such rumors. I may be well familiar with men in high positions, but have not yet made the acquaintance of the Kaiser's son."

Astruc rose. "Someday you two will meet, and even the heir of the German Empire will be unable to resist the charms of the exotic Mata Hari."

M'greet unsnapped the cap of her lipstick. "We shall see, won't we?"

. . .

Now that the fall performances had been secured, M'greet decided to upgrade her lodgings to the lavish Hotel Adlon. As she entered the lobby, with its sparkling chandeliers dangling from intricately carved ceilings and exotic potted palms scattered among velvet-cushioned chairs, she nodded to herself. *This was the type of hotel a world-renowned dancer should be found in.* She booked an apartment complete with electric Tiffany lamps and a private bathroom featuring running water.

The Adlon was known not only for its famous patrons, but for the privacy it provided them. M'greet was therefore startled the next morning when someone banged on the door to her suite.

"Yes?" Anna asked as she opened it.

"Are you Mata Hari?" a gruff voice inquired.

M'greet threw on a silky robe over her nightgown before she went to the door. "You must be looking for me."

The man in the doorway appeared to be about forty, with a receding hairline and a bushy mustache that curled upward from both sides of his mouth. "I am Herr Griebel of the Berlin police."

M'greet ignored Anna's stricken expression as she motioned for her to move aside. "Please come in." She gestured toward a chair at the little serving table. "Shall I order up some tea?"

"That won't be necessary," Griebel replied as he sat. "I am here to inform you that a spectator of your performance last night has lodged a complaint."

"A complaint? Against me?" M'greet repeated as she took a seat in the chair across from him. She mouthed, "tea," at Anna, who was still standing near the door. Anna nodded and then left the room.

"Indeed," Griebel touched his mustache. "A complaint of indecency."

"I see." She leaned forward. "You are part of the *Sittenpolizei*, then." They were a department charged with enforcing the Kaiser's so-called laws of morality. M'greet had been visited a few times in the past by such men, but nothing had ever come of it. She flashed Griebel a seductive smile. "Surely your department has no issue with sacred dances?"

"Ah," Griebel fidgeted with the collar of his uniform, clearly uncomfortable.

Mirroring his movements, M'greet fingered the neckline of her low-cut gown. "After all, there are more important issues going on in the world than my little dance."

"Such as?" Griebel asked.

The door opened and Anna discreetly placed a tea set on the crisp white tablecloth. She gave her mistress a worried look but M'greet waved her off before pouring Griebel a cup of tea. "Well, I'm sure you heard about that poor man that was shot in the Balkans in June."

"Of course—it's been in all of the papers. The 'poor man,' as you call him, was Archduke Franz Ferdinand. Austria should not stand down when the heir to their throne was shot by militant Serbs."

M'greet took a sip of tea. "Are you saying they should go to war?"

"They should. And Germany, as Austria's ally, ought to accompany them."

"Over one man? You cannot be serious."

"Those Serbs need to be taught a lesson, once and for all." Upon seeing the pout on M'greet's face, Griebel waved his hand. "But you shouldn't worry your pretty little head over talk of politics."

She pursed her lips. "You're right. It's not something that a woman like me should be discussing."

"No." He set down his tea cup and pulled something out of his pocket. "As I was saying when I first came in, about the complaint—"

"As *I* was saying..." she faked a yawn, stretching her arms out while sticking out her bosom. The stocky, balding Griebel was not nearly as handsome as some of the men she'd met over the years, but M'greet knew that she needed to become better acquainted with him in order to get the charges dropped. Besides, she'd always had a weakness for men in uniform. "My routine is adopted from Hindu religious dances and should not be misconstrued as immoral." She placed a hand over Griebel's thick fingers, causing the paper to fall to the floor. "I think, if the two of us put our heads together, we can definitely find a mutual agreement."

He pulled his hand away to wipe his forehead with a handkerchief. "I don't know if that's possible."

M'greet got up from her chair to spread herself on the bed,

displaying her body to its advantage as a chef would his best dish.

"Perhaps we could work out an arrangement that would benefit us both," Griebel agreed as he walked over to her.

Griebel's mustache tickled her face, but she forced herself to think about other things as he kissed her. Her thoughts at such moments often traveled to her daughter, Non, but today she focused on the other night's performance. M'greet always did what it took to survive, and right now she needed the money that her contract with the Berlin Metropol would provide, and nothing could get in the way of that.

M'greet was glad to count Herr Griebel as her new lover as the tensions between the advocates of the Kaiser—who wanted to "finish with the Serbs quickly"—and the pacifists determined to keep Germany out of war heightened throughout Berlin at the end of July. Although Griebel was on the side of the war-mongers, M'greet felt secure traveling on his arm every night on their way to Berlin's most popular venues.

It was in the back room at one such establishment, the Borchardt, that she met some of Griebel's cronies. They had gathered to talk about the recent developments—Austria-Hungary had officially declared war on Serbia. M'greet knew her place was to look pretty and say nothing, but at the same time she couldn't help but listen to what they were discussing.

"I've heard that Russia has mobilized her troops," a heavyset, balding man stated. M'greet recalled that his name was Müller.

"Ah," Griebel sat back in the plush leather booth. "That's the rub, now isn't it?"

Herr Vogel, Griebel's closest compatriot, shook his head. "I'd hoped Russia would stay out of it." He flicked ash from his cigar into a nearby tray. "After all, the Kaiser and the Tsar are cousins."

"No," Müller replied. "Those Serbs went crying to Mother Russia, and she responded." He nodded to himself. "Now it's only a matter of time before we jump in to protect Austria."

As if on cue, the sound of breaking glass was heard.

M'greet ended her silence. "What was that?"

Griebel put a protective hand on her arm. "I'm not sure." He used his other arm to flag down a passing waiter. "What is going on?"

The young man looked panic-stricken. "There is a demonstration on the streets. Someone threw a brick through the front window and our owner is asking all of the patrons to leave."

"Has war broken out?" M'greet inquired of Griebel as she pulled her arm away. His grip had left white marks.

"I'm not sure." He picked up her fur shawl and headed to the main room of the restaurant. Pandemonium reigned as Berlin's elite rushed toward the doors. Discarded feathers from fashionable ladies' hats and boas floated through the air and littered the ground before stamping feet stirred them up again. M'greet wished she hadn't shaken off Griebel's arm as now she was being shoved this way and that. Someone trampled over her dress and she heard the sound of ripping lace.

She nearly tripped before a strong hand landed on her elbow. "This way," the young waiter told her. He led her through the kitchen and out the back door, where Griebel's Benz was waiting. Griebel appeared a few minutes later and the driver told him there was a massive protest outside the Kaiser's palace.

"Let's go there," Griebel instructed.

"No." M'greet wrapped the fur shawl around her shoulders. "Take me home first."

"Don't you want to find out what's happening?" Griebel demanded, waving his hand as a crowd of people thronged the streets. "This could be the beginning of a war the likes of which no one has ever seen."

"No," she repeated. It seemed to her that the Great Powers of Europe: Germany, Russia, France, and possibly England, were entering into a scrap they had no business getting involved with. "I don't care about any war and I've had enough tonight. I want to go home."

Griebel gave her a strange look but motioned for the driver to do as she said.

They were forced to drive slowly, as the streets had become

jammed with motor cars, horse carts, and people rushing about on foot. M'greet caught what they were chanting as the crowd marched past. She repeated the words aloud: "*Deutschland über alles.*"

"Germany over all," Griebel supplied.

The war came quickly. Germany first officially declared war on Russia to the east and two days later did the same to France in the west. In Berlin, so-called bank riots occurred as people rushed to their financial institutions and emptied their savings accounts, trading paper money for gold and silver coins. Prices for food and other necessities soared as people stocked up on goods while they could still afford them.

Worried about her own fate, M'greet placed several calls to her agent, Astruc, wanting to know if the war meant her fall performances would be canceled. After leaving many messages, she eventually got word that Astruc had fled town, presumably with the money the Metropol had paid her in advance.

She decided to brave the confusion at the bank in order to withdraw what little funds she had left.

"I'm sorry," the teller informed M'greet when she finally made it to the counter. "It looks as though your account has been blocked."

"How can you say that?" she demanded. "There should be plenty of money in my account." The plenty part might not have been strictly true, but there was no way it was empty.

"The address you gave when you opened the account was in Paris. We cannot give funds to any foreigner at this time."

M'greet put both fists on the counter. "I wish to speak with your manager."

The teller gestured behind her. M'greet glanced back to see a long line of people, their exhausted, bewildered faces beginning to glower. "I'm sorry, fräulein, I can do nothing more."

She opened her mouth to let him have the worst of her fury, but a man in a police uniform appeared beside her. "A foreigner you say?" He pulled M'greet out of the bank line, and roughly turned her to face him. "What are you, a Russian?"

M'greet knew her dark hair and coloring was not typical of someone with Dutch heritage, but this was a new accusation. "I am no such thing."

"Russian, for sure," a man standing in line agreed.

"Her address was in France," the teller called before accepting a bank card from the next person.

"Well, Miss Russian Francophile, you are coming with me." For the second time in a week, a strange man put his hand on M'greet's elbow and led her away.

M'greet fumed all the way to the police station. She'd had enough of Berlin: due to this infernal war, she was now void of funds and it looked as though her engagements were to be canceled. She figured her best course of action would be to return to Paris and use her connections to try to get some work there.

When they arrived at the police station, M'greet immediately asked for Herr Griebel. He appeared a few minutes later, a wry smile on his face. "You've been arrested under suspicion of being a troublesome alien."

M'greet waved off that comment with a brush of her hand. "We both know that's ridiculous. Can you secure my release as soon as possible? I must get back to Paris before my possessions there are seized."

Griebel's amused smile faded as his lip curled into a sneer. "You cannot travel to an enemy country in the middle of a war."

"Why not?"

The sneer deepened. "Because…" His narrowed eyes suddenly softened. "Come with me. There is someone I want you to meet." He led her to an office that occupied the end of a narrow hallway and knocked on the closed door labeled, *Traugott von Jagow, Berliner Polizei.*

"Come in," a voice growled.

Griebel entered and then saluted.

The man behind the desk had a thin face and heavy mustache which drooped downward. "What is it, Herr Griebel? You must know I am extremely busy." He dipped a pen in ink and began writing.

Griebel lowered his arm. "Indeed, sir, but I wanted you to meet the acclaimed Mata Hari."

Von Jagow paused his scribbling and looked up. His eyes traveled down from the feather atop M'greet's hat and stopped at her chest. "Wasn't there a morality complaint filed against you?"

M'greet stepped forward, but before she could protest, Griebel cleared his throat. "We are here because she wants to return to Paris."

Von Jagow gave a loud "harrumph," and then continued his writing. "You are not the first person to ask such a question, but we can't let anyone cross the border into enemy territory at this time. People would think you were a spy." He abruptly stopped writing and set his pen down. "A courtesan with a flair for seducing powerful men..." He shot a meaningful look at Griebel, who stared at the floor. "And a long-term resident of Paris with admittedly low morals." He finally met M'greet's eyes. "We could use a woman like you. I'm forming a network of agents who can provide us information about the goings-on in France."

M'greet tried to keep the horror from showing on her face. Was this man asking her to be a spy for Germany? "No thank you," she replied. "As I told Herr Griebel, I have no interest in the war. I just want to get back to Paris."

Von Jagow crossed his arms and sat back. "And I can help you with that, provided that you agree to work for me."

She shook her head and spoke in a soft voice. "Thank you, sir, but it seems I'll have to find a way back on my own."

"Very well, then." Von Jagow picked up his pen again. "Good luck." His voice implied that he wished her just the opposite.

L'AGENT DOUBLE CHAPTER 2

MARTHE

AUGUST 1914

Marthe Cnockaert didn't think anything could spoil this year's Kermis. People had been arriving in Westrozebeke for days from all over Belgium. She herself had just returned home from her medical studies at Ghent University on holiday and had nearly been overcome by the tediousness of living in her small village again. She gazed around the garland-bedecked Grand Place lined with colorful vendor booths in satisfaction. The rest of Europe may have plunged into war, but Belgium had vowed to remain neutral, and the mayor declared that the annual Kermis would be celebrated just as it had been since the middle ages.

The smell of pie wafted from a booth as Marthe passed by and the bright notes of a hurdy-gurdy were audible over the noise of the crowd. She had just entered the queue for the carousel when she heard someone call, "Marthe!"

She turned at the sound of her name to see Valerie, a girl she had known since primary school. "Marthe, how are you? How is Max?" As usual, Valerie was breathless, as though she had recently run a marathon, but it appeared she'd only just gotten off the carousel.

Marthe refrained from rolling her eyes. "Max is still in Ghent, finishing up his studies." Valerie had never hidden the fact she'd always had a crush on Marthe's older brother, even after she'd become betrothed to Nicholas Hoot.

Valerie sighed as she looked around. "There's nobody here but women, children, and old men. All the boys our age have gone off to war and now there's no one left to flirt with."

"Where is Nicholas?"

"He was called to Liége. I suppose you've heard that Germany is demanding safe passage through Belgium in order to get to Paris."

"No."

Valerie shrugged. "They are saying we might have to join the war if Germany decides to invade. But the good news is some treaty states that England would have to enter on our side if that happened."

"Join the war?" Marthe was shocked at both the information and the fact that Valerie seemed so nonchalant about it. There were a few beats of silence, broken only by the endless tune from the carousel's music box, as Marthe pondered this.

"Ah, Marthe, I see you have returned from university." Meneer Hoot, an old friend of her father's, and Valerie's future father-in-law, was nearly shouting, both because he was hard of hearing and because the carousel had started spinning.

"Yes, indeed. I am home for a few weeks before I finish my last year of nursing school," Marthe answered loudly. "Glad to see you are doing well. How is your wife?"

"Oh, you know. Terrified at the prospect of a German invasion, but aren't we all?"

Marthe gave him and Valerie a tentative smile as the church bell rang the hour. "I must be getting home to help Mother with dinner."

Marthe knew something was wrong as soon as she entered the kitchen. "What is it?" she asked, glancing at her father's somber face.

"It's the Germans. They have invaded Belgium."

Marthe fell into her chair. Mother stood in the corner of the room, ironing a cap.

"Belgium has ordered our troops to Liége." Father sank his head into his hands. "But we could never defend ourselves against those bloody Boches."

Mother set her iron down and then took a seat at the kitchen table. "What about Max? Will he come home from Ghent?"

Father took his hands away from his face. "I don't know. I don't know anything now."

"I suppose we should send for him," Marthe said.

Mother cast a worried glance at Father before nodding at her daughter.

For the first time Marthe could remember, Kermis ended before the typical eight days. That didn't stop the endless train of people coming into Westrozebeke, however. The newcomers were refugees from villages near Liége and were headed to Ypres, 15 kilometers southwest, where they had been told they could find food and shelter.

Max sent word that he would be traveling in the opposite direction. He was going to Liége, a town on the Belgian/German border that was protected by a series of concrete fortifications. The Germans were supposedly en route there as well. Both Father and Mother were saddened by Max's decision to enlist in the army, but Marthe understood the circumstances: Belgium must be defended at all costs. She wrote her brother a letter stating the same and urged him to be careful.

As Westrozebeke became a temporary camp, Marthe's family's house and barn, like many of the other houses in the village, were quickly packed with the unfortunate evacuees. Soon the news that Liége had fallen came, and not long after, the first of the soldiers who had been cut off from the main Belgian army arrived.

Marthe stood on the porch and watched a few of them straggle through town. Their frayed uniforms were covered in dark splotches, some of it dirt, some of it blood. Their faces were unshaven, their skin filthy, but the worst part was that none of them were Max.

Upon spotting Nicholas Hoot's downtrodden form, Marthe rushed into the street. "Have you heard from Max?" she asked.

Nicholas met her eyes. His were wide and terrified, holding a record of past horrors, as though he had seen the devil himself. "No."

"C'mon," Marthe put his heavy arm over her shoulders. "Let's get you home."

Mevrouw Hoot greeted them at the door. "Nicholas, my son." She hugged his gaunt body before leading him inside.

After his second cup of tea, Nicholas could croak out a few sentences. After a third cup and some biscuits, he was able to relay the horrific conditions the Belgian soldiers had experienced at Liége, especially the burning inferno of Fort de Loncin, which had been hit by a shell from one of the German's enormous guns, known as Big Bertha. De Loncin had been the last of the twelve forts around Liége to yield to the Boches.

"Do you know what happened to Max?" Marthe asked.

Nicholas shook his head. "I never saw him. But it was a very confusing time." His cracked lips formed into something that resembled his old smile. "The Germans are terrified of *francs-tireurs* and think every Belgian civilian is a secret sniper out to get them." The smile quickly faded. "The Fritzes dragged old men and teenagers into the square, accusing them of shooting at their troops. It was mostly their own men mistakenly firing upon each other, but no matter. They killed the innocent villagers anyway." He set his tea cup down. "The Huns are blood-thirsty and vicious, and they are headed this way. We should flee further west as soon as possible."

Mevrouw Hoot met Marthe's eyes. "I'll tell Father," Marthe stated before taking her leave.

Mother was ready to depart, but Father was reluctant, stating that if Max did come home, he would find his family gone. Marthe agreed and disagreed with both sides. On the one hand, she wanted to wait for her brother, and judge for herself if the Germans were as terrible as Nicholas had said. On the other hand, if he was indeed correct, they should go as far west as possible.

The argument became moot when Marthe was awakened the next morning by an unearthly piercing noise overhead. The shrieks grew louder until the entire house shook with the crescendo, and then there was an even more disturbing silence.

Marthe tossed on her robe and then rushed downstairs. No one was in the kitchen, so she pulled Max's old boots over her bare feet and ran the few blocks to the Grand Place. She could see the mushroom cloud of black smoke was just beginning to clear.

She nearly tripped in her oversized boots when she saw someone lying in the roadway. It was Mevrouw Visser, one of her elderly neighbors. She bent over the bloodied body, but the woman had already passed.

The sound of horse hooves caused Marthe to look up. She froze as she saw the men atop were soldiers in unfamiliar khaki uniforms.

"Hallo," called a man with a thin mustache and a flat red cap. He stopped his horse short of Mevrouw Visser. "Met her maker, has she?" The way he ended the sentence with a question that didn't expect an answer made Marthe realize the British had arrived. The men paused at similarly lying bodies, giving food and water to those who still clung to life, but after an hour or so, they rode off.

Marthe went home, her robe now tattered and soiled, her feet sweaty in her boots. "What now?" she asked her father, who was seated at the kitchen table, also covered in perspiration, dirt, and blood.

"Now we wait for Max."

A knock sounded on the front door and Marthe went to answer it, fearing that she would greet a Hun in a spiked helmet. But the soldier outside was in a blue uniform. "The bloody Boches are on their way," he stated in a French accent. "You must flee the village, mademoiselle."

She glanced at Father, who was still sitting at the kitchen table. "I cannot."

The French soldier took a few steps backward to peer at the

second floor before returning his gaze back to her. "Our guns will arrive soon, but we are only a small portion of our squadron, and cannot possibly hope to hold them for long. We are asking the villagers to allow us access to their homes in order to take aim."

She nodded and opened the door. He marched into the kitchen and spoke to her father.

Marthe went outside, and looked up and down the street, which was now dotted with soldiers in the blue uniforms of the French. The sound of hammering permeated the air. The soldier she had spoken to went upstairs to pound small viewing holes into the wood of the rooms facing the street. She helped Father barricade the windows and front door with furniture.

Marthe and her parents sequestered themselves in her bedroom, which faced the back of the house. Although half of her was frightened, the other was intensely curious as to what would happen. She used her father's telescope to peer through a loophole in the wood-barricaded window.

"I see them!" she shouted as a gray mass came into view.

"Marthe, get down!" her father returned.

She reluctantly retired the telescope, but not before she peered outside again. The masses had become individual men topped by repulsive-looking spiked helmets. There were hundreds of them and they were headed straight for the Grand Place.

The windows rattled as the hooves of an army of horses came closer. Marthe knew that many of those carts were filled with the Boches' giant guns.

The French machine guns, known as *mitrailleuse,* began an incessant rattling. *Rat-a-tat-tat:* ad infinitum. Marthe couldn't help herself and peeped through the hole again, watching as the gray mob started running, men falling from the fire of the *mitrailleuse.*

Mother's face was stricken as a bullet tore through the wood inches above her daughter's head. Wordlessly Father grabbed both of their hands to bring them downstairs. At the foot of the stairs was a French soldier rocking back and forth, clutching his stomach. Father tried to pull Marthe toward the cellar, but she paused when she saw the blood spurting from the soldier's stomach. All of her university training thus far had not prepared her for this horrific sight, his entrails beginning to spill out of the wound, but she reached out with trembling fingers to prop him against the wall. "You must keep still."

His distraught eyes met hers as he managed to croak out one word. "Water."

Marthe knew that water would only add to his suffering. The sound of gunfire grew closer, and Father yanked her away.

They had just reached the cellar when a shell sounded and a piece of plaster from the wall landed near Father. He struck a match and lit his pipe. "Courage," he said. "The French will beat them back," but the defeated tone of his voice told Marthe that he did not believe it to be so. Nothing could stay that rushing deluge of gray regiments she had spotted from the window.

When the *mitrailleuse* finally ceased its firing, Marthe crept upstairs to retrieve water. The man at the stairs had succumbed to death, and there seemed no sign of any live blue-clad soldiers anywhere in the house. The hallway glistened with blood and there were a few spots where bullets had broken through the exterior wall. An occasional shot could still be heard outside, but it sounded much more distant now. Marthe glanced at her watch. It was only two o'clock in the afternoon.

The front door burst open and she turned to see a bedraggled young man standing in the doorway with his eyes narrowed. Something in the distance caught the sunlight and she glimpsed many men on the lawn, their bayonets gleaming. Marthe marveled that the sun had the audacity to shine on such a day.

The soldier before her holstered his revolver and spoke in broken French. *"Qui d'autre est dans cette maison avec vous?"* He marched into the room, a band of his comrades behind him. Marthe assumed he was the captain, or *hauptmann*. The men outside sat down and lit cigarettes.

She felt no fear at the arrival of the disheveled German and his troops, only an unfamiliar numbness. She replied in German that her parents were downstairs.

"There are loopholes in the walls of this house," the captain stated. "Your father is a *franc-tireur*."

Marthe recalled what Nicholas had said about the Hun's irrational fear of civilian sharpshooters. "My father is an old man and has never fired a shot at anyone, and especially not today. The French soldiers who were here were the ones shooting but they have gone."

"I have heard that story many times before. Yours is not the first village we have entered."

You mean demolished, Marthe corrected him silently.

"Fourteen of my men were shot, and the gunfire from this house was responsible. If those men who were with him have run, then your father alone will suffer."

"No, please, Hauptmann." But the captain was already on his way to the cellar. Two other burly men stalked after him. Marthe was about to pursue them when the first man appeared on the steps, dragging her mother. The other soldier, a sergeant judging by the gold braid on his uniform, followed with her father, who held his still smoldering pipe.

The soldiers shoved her parents against the wall of the hallway. Marthe bit her lip to keep herself from crying out in indignation, knowing that it couldn't possibly help the situation they were in. She cursed herself for her earlier curiosity and then cursed fate for the circumstances of having these enemy men standing in her kitchen, wishing to do harm to her family. If only they had left when Nicholas gave her that warning!

"Take that damned pipe out of your mouth," the sergeant commanded Father.

The soldier who had manhandled Mother grabbed it from him, knocking the ash out on Father's boot before he pocketed the pipe with a chuckle.

"Old man, you are a *franc-tireur*," the captain declared.

Father shook his head while Mother sobbed quietly.

"Be merciful," Marthe begged the captain. "You have no proof."

"You dare to argue with me, fräulein? This place has been a hornet's nest of sharpshooters." He turned to one of the men. "Feldwebel, see that this house is burned down immediately."

The sergeant left out the door, motioning to some of the smoking

KIT SERGEANT

men to follow him to the storage shelter in the back of the house, where the household oil was kept.

"Hauptmann—" Father began, but the captain silenced him by holding up his hand. "As for you, old man, you can bake in your own oven!" He dropped his arm. "Gefreiter, lock him in the cellar."

The corporal seized Father and kicked him down the steps, sending a load of spit after him.

"Filthy *franc-tireur*, he will get what he deserves," the corporal stated as he slammed the door to the cellar.

Mother collapsed and Marthe rushed to her. "You infernal butchers," she hissed at the men.

"Quiet, fräulein," the captain responded, taking out a packet of cigarettes. "Our job is to end this war quickly, and rid the countryside of any threats to our army, especially from civilians who take it upon themselves to shoot our soldiers."

The feldwebel and two other men entered the house carrying drums of oil. Mother gave a strangled cry as they marched into the living room and began to pour oil over the fine furniture.

The captain nodded approvingly before casting his eyes back to Marthe and her mother. "You women are free to go. I will grant you five minutes to collect any personal belongings, but you are not permitted to enter the cellar. Do not leave the village or there will be trouble." He lit his cigarette before dropping the match on the dry kitchen floor. It went out, but Marthe knew it was only a matter of time before he did the same in the living room where the oil had been spilled.

Marthe ran upstairs, casting her eyes helplessly around when she reached the landing. *What should she take?* She threw together a bundle of clothes for her and Mother, and, at the last second, took her father's best suit off the hanger. She shouldered the bundle and then went back downstairs, grabbing Mother's hand. They went outside to the street to gaze dazedly at their home where Father lay prisoner in the cellar.

The German soldiers walked quickly out of the house, carrying some of the Cnockaert's food. Gray smoke started coming from the living room. Soon reddish-orange flames rose up, the tongues easily destroying the barricaded windows. Marthe put her hands on the collar of her jacket and began to shed it.

"What are you doing?" Mother asked, her voice unnaturally shrill.

"Father's in there. I have to try to save him."

Mother tugged Marthe's jacket back over her shoulders. "No," was all she said. Marthe lowered her shoulders in defeat. As she stared at the conflagration, trying not to picture her poor father's body burning alive, she made a vow to herself that she wouldn't let the Germans get the best of her, no matter what other horrors they tried to commit.

Eventually Mother led Marthe away from the sight of their burning home and down the street to the Grand Place. The café adjacent to the square was filled with gray-uniformed men who sang obscene songs in coarse voices. A hiccupping private staggered in the direction of Marthe and Mother as the men in the café jeered at him. Marthe pulled her mother into the square to avoid the drunken soldier.

The abandoned Kermis booths had now become makeshift hospital beds for wounded Germans. The paving stones were soaked in blood and perspiring doctors rushed around, pausing to bend over men writhing in pain. In the corner was a crowd of soldiers in bloodied French uniforms. Marthe headed over, noticing another, smaller group of women and children she recognized as fellow villagers. She had just put her hand on a girl's forehead when a German barked at her to move on.

"Where should we go?" Mother asked in a small voice.

Marthe shook her head helplessly, catching her eye on Meneer Hoot's large home on the other side of the square. They walked quickly toward it, noting the absence of smoke in the vicinity. Marthe reached her fist out to knock when the door was swung open.

Marthe's heart rose at seeing the man behind the door. "Father!"

"Shh," he said, ushering them into the house.

"How on earth—" Marthe began when they were safely ensconced in the entryway of the Hoot home.

"I took apart the bricks from the air vent. Luckily the hauptmann and his men were watching the inferno on the other side of the house."

Mother hugged him tightly, looking for all the world like she would never let him go. Father brought them into the kitchen, where Meneer and Mevrouw Hoot greeted them. Several other neighbors, including Valerie, were also gathered in the kitchen, and they waited in a bewildered silence until darkness fell.

Meneer Hoot finally rose out of his chair. Taking the pipe from his mouth, he stated, "We have had no food this morning, and I'm sure it is the same for you all. Unfortunately," he swung his arms around, "the bloody Boches ransacked our house and there is nothing to eat here." He put the pipe in his mouth and gave it a puff before continuing, "I am going to get food somehow."

Mevrouw Hoot clutched his arm. "No, David, you cannot go out there."

Father also rose. "I will join you."

Meneer Hoot shook his head. "No, it is safer for me to go alone."

Mother gave a sigh of relief while Mevrouw Hoot appeared as though she would burst into tears. Meneer Hoot slipped a dark overcoat on and left through the back door.

An eternity seemed to pass as they sat in the dark kitchen, illuminated only by the sliver of moon that had replaced the sun. The silence was occasionally broken by Mevrouw Hoot's sobbing.

Marthe was nodding off when she heard the back door slam. Someone lit a candle, and Marthe saw the normally composed Meneer Hoot hold up a bulky object wrapped in blood-stained newspaper. His rumpled trousers were covered in burrs and his eyes were wild-eyed. He tossed the bulk and it landed on the kitchen table with a thud.

Mevrouw Hoot unwrapped the package to reveal a grayish sort of meat from an unfamiliar animal.

"I cut it from one of the Boches' dead horses," Meneer Hoot told them in a triumphant whisper. He lit a fire and put the horsemeat on a spit. Marthe wasn't sure if she could eat a dead horse but soon changed her mind as the room filled with the smell of cooking meat. Her stomach grumbled in anticipation.

Just then the kitchen window shattered. Marthe looked up to see a rifle butt nudging the curtain aside. The spikes of German helmets shone in the moonlight beyond the window. The Hoots' entire backyard teemed with them.

"We must get downstairs, now!" Meneer Hoot shouted. He grabbed his wife and rushed her into the hallway. Father did the same with Mother, and Marthe followed, stumbling down the steps to the Hoots' cellar.

To Marthe's amazement, she saw the large room was already nearly filled with other refugees—men, women, and children of all ages—with dirty, tear-stained faces.

The sound of many boots thundered overhead and it wasn't long before the Germans once again stood among them. One of them pointed his rifle at the opposite wall and shot off a clip, the bullets ricocheting around the room, followed by wild screaming. Somebody had been hit, a child Marthe guessed sorrowfully by the tone of its wail.

She wanted to go aid the poor creature, but she felt the sharp point of a bayonet at her chest. "Get upstairs," the bayonet wielder sneered.

The soldiers lined up the cellar's occupants outside, and separated out the men. Without allowing a word of parting, the Germans led the men of the village down the hill, and Marthe watched Father's lank form until she could no longer see him. The remaining soldiers shepherded the women and children back down into the Hoot's now blood-covered cellar.

L'AGENT DOUBLE CHAPTER 3

ALOUETTE

AUGUST 1914

The smell of gasoline and the wind in Alouette's hair was as intoxicating as ever. She eased back on the stick of her Caudron, enjoying the adrenaline rush that always ensued when the plane rose higher. The French countryside below appeared just like the maps in her husband's office: the rivers, railroads, even the villages seemingly unchanged from her vantage point. The world beneath her might soon be engaged in combat, but, a few thousand meters above the ground, she was alone in the sky, the universe at her beck and call. She flew along the Somme Bay at the edge of the English Channel, marveling at the beautiful beaches and marshes that must be thronging with wildlife.

After half an hour, she began heading back to the Le Crotoy aerodrome to land, using the coastline as a navigation guide. She held the tail of the Caudron low and glided downward.

. . .

Alouette found the aerodrome in a state of commotion, with men running all about on the ground. As she turned the engine off, Gaston Caudron, the inventor of the plane, climbed up the ladder to stare into the cockpit.

"What's going on?" Alouette shouted over the noise. It sounded as though every plane in the aerodrome was running.

"We're taking the planes to the war zone."

"Okay." Alouette refastened her seatbelt and tilted her head, indicating she was ready for Caudron to spin the prop to start the plane up again.

His eyes, already jaundiced, bugged out even more. "You can't possibly think you can go to war."

"This is my plane."

He held up a hand to his mouth and coughed. "As I recall, I designed it for your husband."

"You know that Henri lets me fly it any time I want to." She tapped the ignition switch with impatience.

"Still, civilians can't fly planes during wartime." His voice softened. "You wouldn't want to hurt the war effort, would you Madame Richer?"

Alouette's hand dropped to her side. "No. No I would not."

Caudron stepped as close as he could to the edge of the ladder as she climbed out of the plane. "I guess I'll see about my motor-car in the garage at Rue," she said, navigating down the ladder as Caudron arranged himself in the cockpit.

"You'll find it a challenge to get back to Paris—all the petrol supplies have been requisitioned for the army."

"I'll be able to get as far as Amiens," she said, jumping down to the ground. "After that I shall find a way to manage, somehow."

"Good luck," Caudron replied ominously as he started the engine.

She saluted as he pulled her plane out of the aerodrome.

Alouette estimated that her car had enough petrol to carry her 30 miles, figuring she could stop at the aerodrome in Amiens, or at least a garage somewhere along the route to Paris. But near Picquigny, the car began to sputter and soon stopped completely. Alouette walked a few miles and was relieved to find a garage, albeit looking abandoned. She knocked on the closed shutters of the attached house.

A woman's hand opened the window a sliver. "Yes?"

"Can you please tell me, madame, where the mechanic is?"

The woman opened the window enough to eye Alouette up and down, from the lace neckline of her fashionable dress to the flower-trimmed hat she had donned after changing out of her flight gear. "He's gone to war," the woman finally replied.

Alouette got a similar response from the next garage she tried. One elderly woman seated on her porch did not appear as hostile and Alouette called out to her. "Do you have any vehicle I could use to take me to Amiens? My car has stalled and I need to find a mechanic."

The woman appeared likely to flee back into the house, so Alouette pulled her wallet out of her purse. "I can pay you."

Alouette soon found herself in the back of a hay cart pulled by reluctant horses, and being jolted from side to side at every rut in the road. They had to pull into the ditch almost every mile, at least it seemed to Alouette, as regiment after regiment of soldiers passed them, heading north. They drove by several villages in turmoil, the residents packing every belonging they owned onto motor-cars, rickety carts similar to the one Alouette found herself in, or even on the backs of donkeys.

"Why are you leaving?" Alouette called to one man as he balanced his rocking chair on a small wagon.

"The Germans are advancing toward the Marne," the man replied, the terror obvious in his voice.

Alouette tipped her flowered hat and focused her eyes on the road ahead of them. She had to get back to Paris as soon as possible.

The farm woman pulled back on the reins when they reached the aerodrome, about half a mile outside of Amiens. "You sure this is where you want to be?" she asked, eyeing the aerodrome. The doors had been left open, revealing its nearly empty chambers inside.

"Yes, madame." Alouette placed a few extra bills into the farm woman's hand. "If you could just wait a minute."

The farm woman gave a deep sigh before nodding her acquiescence.

When Alouette entered the practically deserted cavern, she heard someone call, "Madame Richer! Whatever are you doing here?"

As she turned, she caught sight of the well-built Captain Jeanneros. "Oh, Captain, is it possible for you to send a mechanic to help me with my car? It has stalled on the road."

The captain threw his head back and laughed. "Only such things could happen to you, Madame Richer. The Germans are pushing toward here and I only have a few litres of petrol left. Of course, you can have some if you need it. But as for the mechanic, I cannot spare one. I'm very sorry, but I'm the last of the squadron now. All the others have gone."

Alouette sighed. "I'm not sure the petrol will do me much good if I cannot get my motor-car fixed."

Captain Jeanneros scratched his head. "I can give you one tip, madame. Do not stay long in this district, or soon you may find it impossible to leave at all."

They had passed the first houses in Picquigny on the return journey when Alouette heard the farm woman suck in her breath. Alouette sat straighter in the cart, catching sight of a crowd assembled in the spot where she'd left the car. To her horror, she noted two armed gendarmes approaching.

"Now you've really done it," the farm woman muttered.

The gendarmes paused near the back of the cart. "Hand over your papers," the shorter one commanded.

Alouette did as she was bid, her heart racing. She garnered that her presence in the back of the farm cart, combined with her Parisian attire, not to mention her presence in the war zone, must have looked suspicious to the rural population of Picquigny.

The short gendarme folded Alouette's papers and tucked them into the pocket of his uniform.

"Sir," the farm woman spoke up. She hesitated for a brief second before resignedly pointing a gnarled finger to the cans of fuel in the rear of the cart.

Alouette's heart sank at her escort's sudden betrayal.

"Where did you get that petrol?" the other officer demanded. "Why are you harboring fuel when the Allies are in desperate need of it?"

"Monsieur—" Alouette attempted an explanation, but the short gendarme cut her off. "You must come with us." He gave a sharp whistle and the farm woman set the horse in motion, both officers keeping pace on either side of the cart.

"Death to the spy!" an old man shouted as the crowd of villagers also started moving forward.

Alouette felt terror rise in her chest. The mob swirled around the cart like an ocean tide. The villagers had already deemed her a traitor and any attempt she made to contradict them would be futile.

She was under arrest.

The mob of villagers followed the gendarme-escorted farm cart to the police station.

One of the gendarmes pulled Alouette out of the cart. "Lynch the spy!" someone shouted as a spray of gravel landed at her feet. She looked up to meet the angry glare of a white-haired man. The tears that gathered in her eyes did not soften him—if anything, they seemed to be an admission of guilt—and he drew back his arm to launch the next cluster of rocks. "Die, double-crosser!" This time a sharp stone connected with Alouette's jaw and the tears coursed their way down her face.

Although the villagers were not permitted into the police station, the window in the room where Alouette was taken for questioning stood open and the crowd gathered outside of it.

The evidence of Alouette's supposed damnation was spread out on the table. Her revolver was placed prominently in the center, surrounded by the cans of petrol and the documentation she had presented to the gendarme.

An older officer sat himself at the table across from the still-standing Alouette. "Name?" he demanded.

"Alouette Richer," she replied, a hint of pride in her voice. She briefly crossed her fingers behind her back, hoping he would recognize her name from the newspapers.

The village gendarme gave no sign of appreciation as he copied it down. "Sit."

She fell into a chair with a sigh. She had recently flown from Crotoy to Zürich, to great fanfare, and the Parisian papers followed her triumphs, publishing several articles and photographs of her in aviator gear standing beside her plane. But now that war had come, a curtain had dropped over everything that had occurred before its outbreak.

"You have no right to a revolver," the officer commented, a growl in his voice. "How did you come by it?"

"My husband, Henri Richer, gave it to me. He knew I'd be traveling alone and wanted to ensure my safety."

Once again, the gendarme showed no recognition of the name. "Let me see your handbag."

Reluctantly, she passed it across the table.

He dug out her wallet and pulled out a wad of bills. "Who gave you all this money?"

Alouette bit back another sigh. She supposed the 300 francs in her wallet was a small fortune to the country inspector, who probably earned less than half that in a month.

"I am not a spy," she insisted. "My husband is a wealthy man…"

"I know, I know," the gendarme held up his hand. "He must have given you all that money to ensure your safety." He rose heavily to his feet. "What he didn't understand was how incriminating carrying that amount of cash would be in a warzone. I have no choice but to detain you."

"But monsieur—"

"Pending further inquiries, of course," the inspector remarked as he shut the door behind him.

. . .

Alouette was left in the room for over half an hour. She used that time to compose herself. The last thing she wanted was to show fear to the men at the station. Indeed, when a younger officer at last unlocked the door, she kept the expression on her face neutral. He escorted her to an empty cell.

Alouette patted the pillow and then spread her skirts prettily before she sat on the bed.

The young gendarme watched, an amused expression on his face. "This is not the first time you've spent the night in jail," he stated.

"Oh, it is, monsieur," Alouette said, taking her hat off and running a hand through her golden hair. "But it's better than sleeping in my broken-down motor-car by the side of the road."

"Indeed, it probably is." He returned shortly with a packet of biscuits and stale coffee. Alouette could sense that she'd at least made a friend of one of the aloof gendarmes.

That same young man came in early the next morning to announce that Alouette had been released. He waved a telegram with the word PARIS stamped on the front. "It seems you have friends in high places."

Alouette picked her hat off of the chipped nightstand and tucked her hair beneath it. "It would seem so, wouldn't it?"

"Where will you go now?"

She pursed her lips. "My petrol?"

He shook his head. "Seized for the army."

"Then I shall walk to Amiens."

The young man's face spread into a smile. "Good luck, Madame Richer."

"And to you, monsieur."

Alouette passed many villagers going the opposite way as she. They were obviously refugees, judging from their weary, and in some cases, panic-stricken expressions. The pronounced silence was only broken by the occasional droning of an airplane. As soon as one became audible, the bewildered townspeople would duck their heads, as if heeding an unheard call, the call of terror that an enemy warcraft was about to drop a bomb upon them.

Alouette found Amiens in utter chaos. Every door stood open as the townspeople rushed to and from their houses, packing up all of their belongings. Children, dogs, and a few roosters ran wildly through the streets. All roads that led to the town seemed to be filled with refugees repeating the same desperate phrases: "The Germans are coming. What shall we do?"

She headed through the hordes of anxious people gathered outside the railway station. She found a man in a conductor's uniform to ask about the next train to Paris.

"Trains?" he asked in an incredulous voice. "My lady, this station is closed, and the rest of the staff has been cleared out. Gone to war," he continued proudly, but Alouette was only half-listening.

For a moment, she thought she would give in to the same useless panic that had overcome the people surrounding her. She allowed herself a few seconds of despair before returning to reality. She needed to find some other way to get to Paris if she desired to not be in a region that was about to be infested with the enemy.

She spotted an open garage across the street and walked over to it. A young woman in a tattered dress sat on the steps leading toward the door. She glanced up as Alouette approached. "They say that the Germans murder any children they see." She sniffed. "And I have two little boys." She buried her head in her handkerchief.

Alouette climbed up the steps and put a tentative hand on the woman's shoulder. "Nobody can be so cruel as to hurt young innocents," she stated. "Not even the Germans."

She handed the woman a soiled but dry handkerchief. The woman blew into it noisily before stating, "If you are looking for a vehicle, I have nothing left."

"Not even a cart?" Alouette asked, the hopelessness threatening to surface again.

The young woman looked doubtfully at Alouette's dress. "I do have a man's bicycle. Do you know how to ride?"

Alouette took a deep breath. Her brother had had one when they were growing up, but she was never allowed to ride since it couldn't be ridden sidesaddle. "Not exactly, but if I can fly planes, surely I can ride a bicycle." She dug into her purse to find the gendarme had left her a few francs, which she extended to the young woman. The woman pulled herself up, using the banister to steady herself, and led Alouette into the garage.

Alouette walked the bicycle along the road until she was well out of the way of the crowds. The threat of falling on her face paled in comparison to the possibility of being taken as a German prisoner if she stayed here. Mounting the bicycle proved a difficult feat given her dress and handbag. As she pushed down on a pedal, the bicycle wobbled sideways instead of going forward and she hopped off, the bicycle plunging into the dust of the roadway.

She heard a low noise and turned her head with her eyes closed, hoping that it was not the stomping of German boots. A young soldier in a blue coat and bright red trousers was sitting on a nearby bench, laughing.

Alouette put her hands on her hips. "Well, don't just sit there. Give me a lesson, would you?"

He pointed at the bandage covering one of his eyes. "Even I can see that is a man's bicycle."

"Oh, do you have a woman's available?"

The soldier shook his head.

"Then do you know of another reason why I should not ride this bike straight to Paris?"

"Yes," he said, recovering from his earlier mirth. "The road to Paris has been captured by the Germans."

Alouette wiped her sweaty palms on her skirts and gazed at the dust blowing across the road. A German invasion in the carefree French capital seemed as far-flung a threat as someone predicting a thunderstorm on a sunny day. "My husband is in Paris."

"Oh?" The soldier's voice dropped an octave. Alouette smiled to herself. There was something so naively amusing about young men thinking that every woman was ready to fawn over them.

"At least I think so," Alouette replied. "He enlisted as an ambulance driver, but hasn't gotten orders yet. I had to detour to Crotoy to check on our plane."

The young man raised his eyebrows.

"Confiscated," Alouette said in answer to his unasked question.

"Yes, the military will do that. When I was at Charleroi—"

"You were in the Battle of the Sambre?"

"Yes, why?"

Alouette looked down. "No reason." They said that war had a way of turning boys into men, but the young man's affable manner hadn't struck her as though he'd seen many hard battles. Even despite that bandaged eye.

"Anyway, both sides are using airplanes for reconnaissance now." He shrugged his shoulders. "What war innovations will they think of next?"

Alouette was lost for a second, dreaming of being in the sky, finding the enemy among the trees. When she returned to reality, all she could focus on were the man's bright red pants. "Those uniforms… are they new?"

"They are, but the style dates back to Napoleon."

"Perhaps General Joffre might want to reconsider the color of your trousers. A line of soldiers all wearing those would be quite easy to spot from the air."

"Perhaps," he agreed with a smile. "I think that trains are still running to Paris from Abbeville."

Alouette picked up the bicycle. "Well, what are you waiting for, then?"

The soldier taught her how to keep her balance. In only half an hour's time, Alouette was able to ride steadily, although she was only able to mount the bicycle from the curb and could not stop except by jumping off. "I think I'll be able to manage myself, now. Thank you for your kindness."

The young soldier tipped his hat toward her, revealing a bruised and bloody forehead. "Good luck, mademoiselle."

. . .

Alouette had no idea riding a bicycle could be such taxing work. She passed numerous refugees on her way to Abbeville. So preoccupied were they in their own misery that they did not pay much heed to the girl wobbling along, trying both to balance and keep her dress out of the bicycle's chain at the same time. She kept her berth wide, lest she fell again, and called out to a man pushing a wheelbarrow, who heeded her by moving closer toward the side of the road. As Alouette overtook them, she realized the wheelbarrow was not filled with food or worldly possessions, but an invalid woman.

Alouette saw she was approaching a hill and leapt off the bicycle. She tossed her hat into a ditch before picking the two-wheeler back up and walking up the summit. She could feel her stamina fading fast, but would not allow herself to rest, fearful that if she sat down, she might not be able to get back up again.

Catching a train proved just as difficult in Abbeville as Amiens. The watchman there told Alouette that there was no way to know when the next train to Paris would leave.

Alouette was about to turn around in anguish when the man told her there was a branch line in Sergueux. Knowing that was her last chance, Alouette managed to get her aching limbs mounted once again on the bicycle and pedaled off.

She was relieved to see a train sitting in the station, although it seemed to consist mostly of open cattle wagons. "Will that be leaving shortly?" Alouette inquired of an official standing near a car.

The man shrugged. "We are waiting for information on the movement of the troops."

Still, Alouette bought a ticket and boarded a cattle wagon.

Enjoyed the sample? Pick up your copy of *L'Agent Double: Spies and Martyrs in the Great War* today or read for free with Kindle Unlimited! Thanks for reading!

. . .

Be sure to join my mailing list at www.kitsergeant.com to be the first to know when my newest Women Spies book is available!

SELECTED BIBLIOGRAPHY

Fourcade, Marie Madeleine. Noah's Ark: The Secret Underground. Zebra Books, 1981.

Olson, Lynn. Madame Fourcade's Secret War. Random House, 2019.

ACKNOWLEDGMENTS

Thank you to my Advanced Review team as well as Matthew Baylis for his excellent editing skills and Hannah Linder for yet another beautiful cover.

And as always, thanks to my loving family, especially Tommy, Belle, and Thompson, for their unconditional love and support.

Printed in Great Britain
by Amazon